MIKE E...

THE
FOUR HORSEMEN

A NOVEL

TimeWorthy
·BOOKS·

P.O. Box 30000, Phoenix, AZ 85046

GameChanger: The Four Horsemen

Copyright 2013 by Time Worthy Books
P. O. Box 30000
Phoenix, AZ 85046

Design: Lookout Design, Inc.

Hardcover: 978-0-935199-72-7
Paperback: 978-0-935199-73-4
  Canada: 978-0-935199-74-1

MAJOR CHARACTERS

THE AMERICANS

David Hoag—deputy director for Middle East Analysis

Jenny Freed—CIA analyst, marries Hoag early in the story

Jack Hedges—president of the United States

Braxton Kittrell—president's chief of staff

Hoyt Moore—CIA director

Lauren Lehman—secretary of state

Carl Coulliette—secretary of defense

Russ Williams—President Hedges' national security adviser

Admiral Scott Marshall—chairman of the Joint Chiefs of Staff

Harry Giles—director of national intelligence

THE IRANIANS

Adnan Karroubi— member of the Assembly of Experts, Islamic scholar

Hasan Dirbaz—Karroubi's assistant

Kermani—president of Iran

Abadeh Ardakan—Iranian foreign minister

Maziyar Shokof—Iranian minister of intelligence and national security (VEVAK)

Ruhollah Tabrizi—VEVAK operative

General Mehran Bizhani—commander of the Iranian air force

General Reza Modiri—commander of the Iranian army

Admiral Emud Kianian—commander of the Iranian navy

THE AZERBAIJANIS

Tahir Shahat—president of Azerbaijan

Jalil Qurbani—foreign minister

THE ISRAELIS

David Oren—prime minister

Efraim Hofi—director of Mossad

General Grossman—chief of general staff, Israel Defense Forces

Simon Epstein—foreign minister

Yorman Herzliya—minister of defense

THE GERMANS

Josef Mueller—president and chancellor of Germany

Gregor von Bettinger—pagan priest and Mueller's confidante

Georg Scheel—foreign office minister

General Erhard—commander of the German air force

Jürgen Stabreit—German ambassador to the United States

Konrad Hölderlin—head of German Foreign Intelligence

THE CHINESE

Ming Shao—president and chairman of the Communist Party

Yong Shu—the president's assistant

Hu Chang—commander of the People's Liberation Army

Quan Ji—chief of Foreign Intelligence

Geng Yun—minister of State Security

Li Chengfei—commander of the Second Artillery, China's strategic missile arsenal

Admiral Xian Linyao—commander of the Chinese navy

THE RUSSIANS

Vladimir Vostok—president of Russia

Anatolyn Luzhkov—Vostok's chief of staff

Vasily Kerensky—chief of Foreign Intelligence Service

Mikhail Mirsky—the foreign minister

General Garasimov—the secretary of defense,

Gennady Panova—Russian ambassador to Germany

Alexander Nevsky—a Russian soldier

PREVIOUSLY IN THE
GAMECHANGER SERIES. . .

David Hoag, the son of a wealthy Ohio banker, attended Yale University where he earned a degree in Near Eastern History. Along with the degree, he obtained a proficiency in Arabic and ancient Hebrew. Following graduation he and his friend Dennis Kinlaw enrolled at Harvard Law School. A CIA recruiter found them during their first year. After completing law school they worked for the agency as field officers assigned to the US consulate in Istanbul. Later, they were posted to service in London, Paris, and other key locations around the globe. Finally, at the ripe old age of thirty-five, they were relegated to part-time positions with the CIA and placed on the faculty at Georgetown University.

Then terrorists aboard the Panama Clipper, a container ship loitering off the coast of New York, launched a missile toward the United States. When the nuclear warhead it was carrying detonated high above Washington, D.C., the electrical grid for the eastern half of the country was destroyed, plunging millions into sudden darkness.

With the country struggling to survive, US President Jack Hedges ordered the executive offices of the government relocated from Washington to Offutt Air Force Base in Nebraska. The rest of the government followed suit, transferring the core of operations to the base. Air force personnel cobbled together offices from unused military facilities and newly constructed additions hastily thrown together to accommodate the sudden influx of bureaucrats.

At first, members of the US intelligence community thought the missile attack was the work of al-Qa'ida. Hoag and Kinlaw thought otherwise. With only sketchy information about the attack, they went to work and discovered that the missile and warhead did indeed come from Iran. The mission to launch it, however, was a coordinated effort of many diverse terrorist organizations.

In spite of that information, Israel's leaders remained determined to strike at the root of the problem by launching an all-out missile attack against Iran to eliminate Iran's nuclear capability. By then, however, President Hedges was convinced there was even more to the problem than had yet been revealed and did his best to convince them of the truth. But they were determined to launch, right up to the last minute....

1

OFFUTT AIR FORCE BASE
OMAHA, NEBRASKA

WITH PETE RIOS LEADING THE WAY, David Hoag and Jenny Freed hurried across the street to the central office complex. A guard opened the door and held it for them as they approached. They moved quickly inside and made their way downstairs to the situation room in the basement.

Created at the height of the Cold War as an alternative command center for the nation's strategic bomber force, the situation room at Offutt had been continually upgraded and was even better equipped than the one at the White House. Yet with key government officials now working in close physical proximity, more people clamored for inclusion in the handling of each crisis. By the time Rios, Hoag, and Jenny arrived at the command center downstairs, the room was packed with officers and cabinet officials who under typical conditions in the past would never have been included.

Rios squeezed through the tightly packed crowd to stand beside Hoyt Moore, director of the CIA. Hoag and Jenny wedged their way in between an air force colonel and two men from the Treasury Department. Hoag leaned close to the colonel and whispered, "What's going on?"

"NORAD has detected Israeli preparations for a missile launch."

Hoag was concerned but not surprised. "What kind of attack?"

"Nuclear."

Hoag arched an eyebrow. "Did we know this was coming?"

"Apparently not," the colonel shrugged.

"What's the target?"

"Iran."

"Which sites?"

"All the sites."

Hoag's mouth fell open in a look of surprise. "They're hitting every nuclear installation in Iran?"

"No." The colonel shook his head. "Every military site." He looked grim. Hoag frowned. The colonel nodded. "They're hitting them all."

Jenny took Hoag's hand and squeezed it tightly. Her palm felt clammy. He glanced down at her with a nervous smile.

The daughter of a prominent New York attorney, Jenny Freed grew up in Manhattan, where she lived a privileged life. She attended Yale with Hoag and Kinlaw, then joined the CIA as an analyst. Over the years since then, she and Hoag had an on-and-off relationship. It was back on at the time of the missile attack and when Hoag was sent to Offutt, she was assigned there, too.

A few feet away from them, President Hedges stood near an operator at a console in the center of the room, nervously pacing back and forth. "Is he on yet?"

"Yes, sir," the operator replied. "Prime Minister Oren is on the line."

Hoag looked over at the colonel once again. "Are they just now talking?"

"No. This is their second or third session."

"How's it going?"

"Not too well right now. They've been at it for a while."

"Mr. Prime Minister." Hedges' voice was firm but tense. "I thought we had agreed to delay a response."

"Mr. President ..." Oren sounded tentative. "I'm...in the midst of important—"

"I know what you're doing, David," Hedges countered, making no attempt to hide the irritation in his voice. "That's why I called. I need you to stop the countdown."

"They have sworn to wipe us off the map," Oren replied.

"I know. We've been following developments closely. But I need you to—"

"And they've tried to do that very thing. A missile launch from the desert. If they had succeeded, millions in Tel Aviv would be dead now. Would you still be urging restraint if they had succeeded?"

"I understand the threat, David, but you stopped them." Hedges' face was red, his fists clenched as he fought to keep his emotions in check. "We worked together, we stopped them. Your people, our missile system. It worked. You shot down everything they flew at you. The world knows what happened. And right now Iran is the villain. If you hit them with a missile attack, Israel will become the villain."

When there was no immediate response, Hedges turned to the operator once more. "Is he still on?"

"Yes, sir," she nodded.

"David? Are you there?"

"I am here, Mr. President. Perhaps you are right, but our people demand a response."

"We are not puppets, Mr. Prime Minister. You and I, we are not puppets. We are heads of state and we have been placed in our positions to exercise the wisdom given to us. This is a time for wisdom, not vengeance." Hedges paused to take a breath. "Give us time to respond to what is *really* happening. We will work with you. We will respond together to eliminate our *real* enemies, not just the ones who show their faces in public."

"You have information that you wish to share?"

"Yes, but I can't give it to you on the phone. Stop the launch sequence and I'll have someone brief you with the details."

There was a noise in the background from Oren's end of the call. Voices shouted. Hedges glanced around, an anxious look on his face. "What was that?" More voices were heard, shouting in Hebrew.

Someone in the situation room spoke up. "Sounds like they're going forward with the launch." A collective gasp went up. Murmuring wafted across the room.

"Shh!" Moore held up his hand for silence. "Mr. President, I believe they're actually standing down."

The prime minister's voice returned. "Mr. President, I have

ordered the missile command center in Dimona to suspend our launch sequence."

"Great!" Hedges beamed. "Thank you, Mr. Prime Minister."

"You will have someone brief me immediately?"

"Yes." Hedges glanced across the room and caught the eye of Lauren Lehman, the secretary of state. "We'll send someone within the hour. And the secretary of state will be in Jerusalem by morning."

"You and I need to talk."

"Yes," Hedges replied. "Secretary Lehman will arrange a meeting when she sees you."

A moment later, the call ended and a cheer went up from the room.

2

MOSSAD OPERATIONS CENTER
ASHDOD, ISRAEL

EFRAIM HOFI DROPPED INTO A CHAIR and leaned back, his eyes closed, his hands over his face, as news of the prime minister's order reached the room. He and a team of analysts had been listening in on the prime minister's conversation with Hedges. Now, as the crisis seemed to be under control, Hofi took a deep breath. "That was close."

Analysts seated nearby, who had watched and listened in silence, now began to talk again. "I thought we were launching that time," someone suggested.

"I did, too," another responded.

Tzipi Levanon spoke up. "We should have."

"Should have what?"

"We should have launched the missiles," Levanon answered. "The Iranians are a menace to the entire region."

"The entire world," someone added.

Leon Zukerman joined the discussion. "They are the ones who should be wiped off the face of the earth."

"Now you sound like them," Hofi replied.

"Some people," Levanon countered, "cannot be allowed to prosper."

Then a voice called from across the room, "Sir, we may have a problem."

"What are you talking about?" Hofi asked as he turned to see.

A few feet away, Naomi Tayeb was on her feet, pointing toward a screen on the wall at the opposite end of the room. "There, on the screen."

Hofi glanced up to see images from inside the Dimona missile command center. There, among the monitors and switches that controlled the launch of Israel's land-based missiles, many of which were armed with nuclear warheads, stood General Khoury with his arm around the neck of Yigil Ari, a launch control officer. A few feet in front of him, half a dozen men stood with their hands up, their bodies moving from side to side as if angling for an advantage. In his free hand, Khoury held an automatic pistol, which he pointed first at one man, then the other, keeping them at bay while the countdown clock on the wall continued to move toward zero.

"This can't be happening," Hofi gasped as he slowly stood. "They didn't stop the launch."

Levanon came to his side. "The countdown is still going?"

Hofi ignored her and turned to the operator seated at the console in the center of the room. "Can we hear what they're saying?" He gestured in frustration toward the screen. "Turn up the volume." The speakers crackled with sound but the words were inaudible.

"I'm working on it," the operator called in reply.

"Where are they in the countdown?" Hofi demanded. "How long until launch?"

"Less than a minute," Tayeb replied.

Cameras inside the Dimona launch center continued to provide a view of the scene as the men tried to flank Khoury.

A frown wrinkled Hofi's brow. "Any way to get inside?"

"No, sir," the operator answered. "The room was locked down when the firing sequence began. Only way to unlock it before launch is from the inside, where they are."

"Doesn't look like there's much chance of that happening," Zukerman quipped.

"Can we cut the power to the missiles?"

"No time for that. Has to be manually thrown at the site."

"The system has three backup sources," Zukerman added. "If the power is lost from one, the others will come online."

"Could unplug the missiles," another suggested.

"No time for that," Zukerman replied. "And even if you did, the missile has an onboard power supply. It'll launch itself."

Then the speakers crackled once more and voices from inside the launch center became audible.

"You cannot be serious," Ari shouted. "We have orders to stand down."

Khoury shook his head. "I do not know anything about any orders to stand down. All I know is those worthless Iranians want to destroy us. Only now, we have the chance to destroy them. And we are going to do it."

One of the men in the command center moved to the right. "This will never work."

"Of course it will work," Khoury said with a wry smile. "I may have to shoot you, but it will work. The launch sequence has been initiated. Computers are in charge now. Nothing can stop them but human intervention." He wagged the pistol. "And I am going to make certain that will not happen."

Another launch control officer spoke up. "There are six of us, and one of you."

Khoury brandished the pistol once more. "I have fifteen rounds. That is two for each of you. Do you want to be first?"

"But, sir," another shouted. "We have an EAM telling us to stand down."

"I don't care how many Emergency Action Memos we get. I'm not backing down this time. The Iranians have held those weapons over our head too long and we have a chance to end it. All we have to do is stand here and watch. So unless you want to die, back off!"

Suddenly, a man rushed toward Khoury from the right. Khoury wheeled in that direction, pointed the pistol, and squeezed the trigger. Flames shot from the muzzle and the man clutched at his chest.

In the Mossad control room, Hofi watched in horror as the wounded man staggered back. "He shot him," Hofi gasped. "Khoury just shot Yosi."

"You know him?"

"Yes. That's Yosi Gavriel," Hofi said, pointing toward the image on the screen. "I know him. I know them all. Khoury knows them, too. This is insane."

Khoury seemed as shocked by his actions as the others, and as he hesitated they lunged toward him. Yigal Ari wrenched free of Khoury's grasp and took hold of him from behind. One of the launch control officers pried the pistol from his hand. Khoury twisted one arm free and turned on Ari, but before he could land a single blow, Ari grabbed the receiver from the phone on the console and struck him in the head. Khoury fell to the floor.

"Hurry!" Hofi shouted, though no one in the launch center could hear him.

"Two men are required to abort the mission," Tayeb warned. "And they have to be identified by the biometric device."

As if listening to Hofi and the others, Ari grabbed Gavriel by the wrist and pulled his body to the control panel. With one of the officers helping, he pressed Gavriel's thumb against the biometric reader, then placed his own thumb there, too. A message box appeared on a control panel monitor. Ari entered the authentication code from the EAM into the message box on the monitor and pressed the Accept button. Almost instantly, a red light flashed on the panel and a message appeared that read, "Countdown aborted." On the wall, the countdown clock showed three seconds remained.

With the launch sequence aborted, doors to the command center automatically unlocked. Armed guards rushed inside and took Khoury into custody. Ari reached over the control panel and removed the launch keys from the switches. Then he glanced up at the camera and said in a terse voice, "Launch control is secure."

Hofi took a deep breath, then turned to the analysts watching the screen in the Mossad command center. "Okay, listen up." He paused a moment, making sure he had their attention. "Not a word of this to anyone, understand?"

"Sure," someone replied.

"We'd never mention a thing like this."

"I mean it," Hofi reiterated. "Not a word of this to anyone. Not even to your fellow analysts and certainly not to any American contacts. Until I tell you otherwise, no one standing inside this room is to talk about the things we have just witnessed to anyone else except among ourselves."

Levanon glanced at the others, then over to Hofi. "You think the Americans do not know?"

"I think there's a good chance no one knows except us, and the people at launch control. And I would like to keep it that way until we can determine exactly what happened."

3

OFFUTT AIR FORCE BASE OMAHA, NEBRASKA

MEANWHILE, HOAG AND JENNY LEFT the situation room and walked outside. As they came down the steps from the building to the sidewalk, she glanced over at Hoag. "You know, in spite of all the drama back there, the conflict with Israel was rather easy to contain."

"That's why your hands were sweaty?" he needled. "Not much too it?"

"You know what I mean," she said, jabbing him playfully in the ribs. "We actually have a phone line to Jerusalem."

"I know," Hoag nodded. "Would be nice if we had a phone line like that to Tehran."

"And someone who was willing to make that phone call."

"Or take it on the other end."

Just then, Hoyt Moore caught up with them and placed his hand on Hoag's shoulder. "Good work."

"I didn't do much back there," Hoag replied.

"I was talking about the situation in Europe. They tell me you had quite a trip to Germany."

"Yes, sir," Hoag smiled. "It was rather exciting."

"You can tell me all about it later," Moore continued. "Right now I need you thinking about something else."

"What's that?"

"With Peter Burke out, we need someone to take his job. So I'm designating you to be his replacement."

Hoag stopped dead in his tracks. "Me?"

"The president already signed off on it," Moore said reassuringly. "As of now, you are deputy director for Middle East Analysis." Moore gave Hoag a slap on the back. "Be in my office in an hour. We have a situation developing in China that will affect your area of responsibility." He turned away and walked toward an SUV parked nearby. Hoag stared after him.

Jenny hooked her arm in Hoag's and smiled up at him. "Just like that?"

"I guess so." Hoag watched as Moore got inside the SUV and drove away. Then he looked back at Jenny. "What does a deputy director do?"

"I think you'll figure it out." She tugged on his arm. "Come on. Walk with me. We never got to finish that conversation we started before you left."

"What conversation?"

"The one where you asked me to marry you."

Her arm was still hooked in Hoag's and he used it to pull her close to his side. "If we don't do it now, we'll never do it."

"Okay," Jenny said softly. "Then, in answer to your earlier question, I will."

Hoag gave her a blank stare. "You will what?"

"I will marry you."

"Great," he beamed and pulled her close.

She leaned against him as they walked. "But we still have to talk."

"What more is there to say?"

"There's something I have to tell you."

"Okay." The smile on Hoag's face melted. "Tell me about it."

"While you were away, in Germany," she began, "something happened."

"What are you talking about?"

"I was lonely and feeling sorry for myself. You were gone. Peter Burke was here."

Hoag had a solemn look. "What happened?"

"He took me out a few times, dinner, a ball game, and then the next thing I knew, he kissed me goodnight."

"And you kissed him back."

"Well," she shrugged, "it's rather difficult not to, even if you aren't interested in the person. And," she quickly added, "I was never interested in him. It just happened."

"Is that all?"

"Yes," she sighed. "That's all. I promise. Nothing more happened, but it made me feel like I'd failed you."

"It was a difficult time." Hoag stopped and pulled her close. Their lips met in a long, wet kiss. Then Hoag smiled at her. "Did he kiss you like that?"

"No," she blushed. "And neither did I."

"Good." He kissed her again, then they turned back toward the building. "Come on. I need to find out what Moore wants, and then we need to decide about a wedding."

"I don't want a wedding."

A frown wrinkled Hoag's forehead. "I thought you said you would marry me."

"I did. And I am. I mean," she explained, "I don't want a formal wedding."

"You want to elope?"

"Where could we go?"

"Las Vegas," Hoag suggested. "Reno. Downtown to the court-house. Pick a place."

"Reno is still open?"

"They weren't affected by the blackout."

"No friends? No family?"

"No friends. No family," Hoag said, shaking his head. "Just you and me."

"Okay," she smiled. "I like the sound of that. Just the two of us." She reached up to kiss him. "Now, you'd better get going. Hoyt Moore will be looking for you."

"Yeah," Hoag sighed. "I suppose he will."

"Any idea what he wants to talk about?"

"No. But whatever it is, it won't get in our way. We're going to

Reno," Hoag said emphatically. "Tonight."

She cut her eyes at him. "Promise?"

"Yes." He kissed her full on the lips. "I promise." Then he backed away and started up the street.

4

BERLIN, GERMANY

JOSEF MUELLER LEFT HIS RESIDENCE and crossed the Chancellery to the east wing where he kept a private study. Instead of entering the study, he turned down a narrow hallway that led to a locked door. He took a key from his pocket, unlocked it, and stepped inside.

Mueller had first entered German politics years before in a race for the governorship of Bavaria, his home province. Campaigning on a platform that stressed a more prominent leadership role for Germany in world affairs, he won a landslide victory that coincided with a resurgence of German nationalism among the populace. After two terms as governor, which saw unprecedented economic growth in his region, Mueller was elected by parliament to the office of chancellor, where he was expected to do for the nation what he had done for Bavaria. But one week after taking office, he was shot by a would-be assassin and gravely injured. Mueller was rushed to the hospital where he lingered near death until Gregor von Bettinger paid him a visit.

A mysterious ecclesiastical figure, Bettinger practiced a heretical blend of Orthodox Christianity and ancient Germanic religion, a practice that led the Lutheran Church to denounce him and the Orthodox Church to defrock him. While Mueller lay in a hospital bed, struggling to survive, Bettinger paid him a visit and prayed for his recovery. Almost immediately Mueller began to improve. When he emerged from the hospital three days later looking fit and ready for service, his followers proclaimed it a miracle and a sure sign that God was with them. Little did they know the true nature of the forces that lay behind what they had witnessed.

As chancellor of Germany, Mueller presided over a period of unprecedented prosperity, which made him popular both at home and throughout Europe. Behind the scenes, he used that popularity and the power it brought to orchestrate an ambitious plan not only to dominate Europe, but to rule the world.

When terrorists exploded a nuclear device over Washington, D.C., and the United States was forced to turn its attention to domestic issues, Mueller stepped onto the world stage, filling the international power vacuum with a German presence and asserting himself as the leader of the West.

With the free world looking to him for guidance, he struck a bold deal to acquire all of Iran's oil production, for which Germany would act as broker to the world, guaranteeing Iran a favorable price while making Germany one of the largest oil nations in the world. With German prosperity as the fulcrum and oil as the lever, he intended to bring all the nations of the world under his control. But there was a catch to Mueller's plan.

Prior to the deal with Germany, Iran was China's largest source of foreign oil. Without it, the Chinese economy would grind to a halt, a consequence sure to provoke a military response. And that is what brought Mueller to the room near his study.

The room behind the locked door was lit by a single flame that flickered from a sconce on the wall. An altar table occupied the center of the room and on it was a single golden candleholder. As Mueller entered, a voice rumbled from the darkness behind the altar.

"Ostara greets you in all her majesty and glory." A hand appeared through the glare of the flame, its fingers wrapped around a candle, and when the wick was touched to the flame the glow lit the room in soft light, revealing the hand of Gregor von Bettinger. Clothed in a hooded black robe, Bettinger moved behind the altar table and placed the candle in the holder. The flame from the wick rose straight up, casting a shadow across a large sun wheel that hung on the wall behind him. An ancient German pagan symbol, the wheel had an open circle in the center with ten spokes that extended in jagged lines to an outer rim.

Bettinger stood behind the table and gestured for Mueller to come forward. Mueller did so and knelt on the front side of the table, his hands folded together, fingers laced in a reverent pose.

"Spring rises from the dead of winter," Bettinger began.

"And brings forth the bloom of summer," Mueller replied.

"The cold darkness of death gives forth light."

"And out of the light comes power and strength."

"The earth embraces strength and victory."

"But devours the weak and cowardly."

"Indeed," Bettinger continued, "the weak inherit the dirt on which they stand."

"And with the labor of the weak, we build a nation for the strong."

Bettinger touched him lightly on the shoulder. "Rise and ask of Ostara what you will."

Mueller stood and bowed his head. "I have but one wish for my day and that is to obey Ostara in all that I say and do. What message does Ostara have for me today?"

Bettinger closed his eyes and took a deep breath. He stood there in silence a moment, as if lost in a trance, and then he spoke, "I see a ten-headed beast, nine small heads ruled by one large one. There is a bit in the mouth of the largest head with reins made of leather. A man sits atop that beast, riding on its back. His chest ripples with muscles, his arms are large and powerful. In one hand he holds the reins of the beast and in the other Klandenets, the magical sword. And on his forehead is the sign of Germany. With the reins he guides the beast, directing it where he wills, and with the sword he slays all who oppose him. Together, beast and man move as one, swaggering across the globe like proud conquerors."

Mueller smiled with pleasure. *Klandenets, the magical sword of Russian folklore.* That was the answer he'd been seeking. Germany need not fear the Chinese, or any other nation. The Russian army would be their foil, an arm of the emerging German empire. A vassal under a different flag, but a vassal nonetheless. The wonder and beauty of that answer infused every fiber of Mueller's body with a sense of rapture and ecstasy that all but overwhelmed him. Germany would truly dominate the world, and he would dominate Germany.

For his part, Bettinger seemed not to notice Mueller's reaction.

Instead, he held out his hand. "You have the medallion?" Mueller reached into his pocket and took out a small sun wheel medallion, about the size of a two Euro coin and shaped like the large one that hung on the wall. He leaned forward and placed it in Bettinger's palm.

Bettinger passed the medallion through the flame of the candle and laid it on the table. Then he lifted up his hands, "Draw near, all who seek to serve and please Ostara, and accept her gifts and power." Mueller reached out his hand and placed it atop the medallion, then Bettinger placed his hand over Mueller's.

"Ostara of Spring will bring you power to lead your people in strength and might. All who oppose you will be crushed beneath your feet. With your right hand you will slay our enemies and with your left you will tame the beast on which you ride."

5

NEAR ISHKASHIM, AFGHANISTAN

AT THE MOUTH OF THE WAKHAN CORRIDOR, a narrow strip of land that connects Afghanistan to the Chinese border, Lo Gai Zong and three men from his platoon made their way down a steep mountain trail. Ahead of them was Siddiq Kamran, an Afghan who regularly guided Chinese patrols in the region.

A little way down the trail, Zong and his men followed Kamran through a narrow passageway between two boulders. As they emerged on the opposite side, Kamran held up his hand for them to stop. Then he dropped to the ground and crawled out onto a ledge that overlooked the valley below. A moment later, he glanced over his shoulder and gestured for Zong to join him.

When they were together, Kamran leaned near Zong's ear and whispered, "This is the American base we were telling you about. They operate patrols from here up the valley all the way to the border."

"This is their only permanent location?"

"Yes," Kamran nodded. "The only location of any kind in the area. Our people should shoot the Taliban on sight, and the Taliban know it. So, not much happens up here. Consequently, the Americans have no need to keep a strong presence here."

Zong took another look over the edge, then glanced back at the others standing behind him and gestured for them to come as well.

They joined him, and the four men lay side by side on the ledge, studying the scene below.

Beneath their position, on a flat near the banks of the Wakhan River, two dozen steel cargo containers were arranged in a circle around eight huts. Made of wood and canvas, the huts provided shelter and work space for a contingent of thirty to forty US Marines. Gai took a notepad from his pocket and began taking notes. The others did as well, and for the next five minutes they worked in silence as each of them sketched the scene below.

When they were finished, they slid back from the ledge and retreated into the rocks. From there they followed Kamran up the trail toward the crest of the mountain. As they retraced their earlier path, the men talked among themselves. Zong walked ahead of them but listened intently to their conversations.

"I still do not understand why we do this," one of them said.

"We were ordered to," another answered.

"Not that," the first one countered. "I understand why we draw the maps and make notes. I am talking about the larger plan. It seems as though we are preparing for a major operation, but why? What is the whole plan?"

"What whole plan?" the second man asked. "We were told to draw maps, we draw maps. That is all we know of the plan."

"Don't be so naïve," a third man added. "We are going to Iran."

"Who told you we were going to Iran?" the first man asked. "And it is not naïve to follow orders."

"It is when the order is not right."

"What have we been told to do that was wrong?"

"You miss the point," the third man added. "This is all about oil."

"Does it matter what the point is? We have orders."

"The satellites cannot always see the details clearly," the first man continued to argue. "But we can see things clearly. That is why they send us on these patrols. It is the only way to verify the truth. Just like asking questions. It is not wrong to question our leaders. It is the only way to find the truth. Asking questions of our leaders is proper Mao Zedong thought. That is what he taught us in his book."

Near the top of the trail Kamran came to a halt. Zong and the others gathered with him. They stood in silence, watching as Kamran glanced back over the valley one last time. "This has been the home of my ancestors for thousands of years," he noted with pride. "And in that time, many foreigners have come and gone, but we remain the same as we've always been. Just like this valley." He stared down at the valley a moment longer, then turned aside and started toward the trail that led to the opposite side of the crest. "We should get moving. The light will fade soon and we do not want to be exposed against the setting sun."

When Kamran had his back to them, Zong drew an automatic pistol from the holster on his belt. He stepped forward and placed the muzzle against Kamran's head, then squeezed the trigger. In an instant, a bullet ripped through Kamran's skull, spraying bone fragments and blood through the air. For a moment, Kamran stood motionless, as if frozen in place, then, as the sound of the gunshot echoed through the mountains, his knees buckled and his body crumpled to the ground. Two of the men from the patrol caught hold of his legs and dragged the body off the trail, then tossed it over the side and watched as it tumbled down the mountain.

"The Americans will find it," one of them said.

"But they will not know what happened."

"If they examine the body closely, they will know the bullet was made in China."

"Everything is made in China," another chuckled. "And in this area, the natives all carry Chinese weapons."

Zong returned the pistol to its holster. With his eyes still fixed on the mountainside below, he said quietly, "We draw maps because we are told to draw maps. Information we gather assists in the planning of missions. Those missions are part of tactical decisions designed to achieve a larger strategy that we need not understand or debate." He squared his shoulders and turned to face them. "It is correct that questioning our leaders is proper Mao Zedong thought, but those who question must be prepared to pay the price of a revolutionary, as did Chairman Mao and the leaders of old, some of whom lost their lives in the effort." Without waiting for a response he turned away and started down the trail. "Come. We must return to camp at our scheduled time."

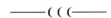

When Zong and the patrol arrived back at camp, Commander Luo Li-Jen was waiting for them. "You were successful?"

"Yes." Zong handed Li-Jen the maps and notes they prepared while on the ledge. Li-Jen glanced at them briefly. "This is the Americans' only position?"

"Yes," Zong nodded. "We patrolled the river valley from the border to Ishkashim. This is their only location."

"Very good." Li-Jen looked back at the notes. "And what of your guide?"

"As you suggested, he is no longer with us."

Li-Jen had a pained expression. "We have many guides who know the mountains well," he sighed. "But I do not like the practice of terminating them."

"Are we not under orders?"

"You will learn that orders must always be read with an eye for the goals of the greater strategy. Orders are tactics."

"And the tactic of removing the guides is an attempt to maintain secrecy of our mission."

"That is what they tell us." Li-Jen looked over at Zong. "But unless you wish to remain in the infantry your entire career, you will learn to think not only of tactics but of strategy as well. In the end, the ultimate goal is all that matters." Li-Jen turned aside. "Come with me to the tent and we will enter this information on the map."

Li-Jen's tent was larger than the others in the camp, measuring ten meters long and almost as wide. It served as his sleeping quarters and the command center for multiple patrols that monitored American and NATO activity in the northernmost Afghan provinces.

Inside the tent was a small table. Behind it was a large board that rested on an easel. A map was tacked to it and on the map were red and blue flags that denoted military positions discovered by the patrols. Li-Jen stood before the map and placed a new flag on the location of the American encampment Zong and his men had seen that day.

"As you have observed," Li-Jen offered, "the Americans are few in number. We could take them with few problems and leave no survivors. But do you know why we do not?"

"Someone would eventually learn of our actions and the Americans would view it as a provocation."

"Right," Li-Jen nodded. "And then they would interfere with our tactical plans and that would disrupt our efforts to achieve our strategic objectives."

"But we would be far from here by then and no one could stop us. They cannot stop us even now."

"But we have no quarrel with the Americans. So why waste the energy?"

"Perhaps you are correct."

"Always remember the goal. Our quarrel is not with the Americans and there is no advantage to us from picking a fight with them." Li-Jen flashed a smile at Zong. "At least not now."

6

MOSCOW, RUSSIA

VLADIMIR VOSTOK WALKED down the broad corridor of the Kremlin Senate's east wing. Commissioned by Catherine the Great, the building was once home to the Russian legislature. Now it housed offices for the Russian president, a position Vostok had held for the past three years. As he made his way through the building, Anatolyn Luzhkov, his chief of staff, came to join him.

"Good morning," Luzhkov smiled at Vostok.

"We have meetings today?" Vostok replied in a tone that belied his contempt for the mundane matters of daily government business.

"Yes, but before we get to that, Vasily Kerensky would like to brief you."

Vostok's countenance brightened. "What is it about?"

"A developing situation in the Middle East."

"When does he want to see me?"

"Now. He is waiting in your office. That is why I came to find you, so you could avoid him if you wished."

"No," Vostok shook his head. "I should hear what he has to say."

"But I should also tell you," Luzhkov added, "Kerensky is not alone."

"Who is with him?"

"Mikhail Mirsky."

"Ahh," Vostok grimaced. He ran a hand through his hair. "I have to see them both at the same time?"

"Yes."

"Very well."

Moments later, Vostok entered his office and found Kerensky, the foreign intelligence service chief, seated in a chair on the far side of the room. Mikhail Mirsky, the foreign affairs minister, stood near Vostok's desk. They gathered at the center of the room as Vostok entered.

"Take a seat, gentlemen."

Vostok continued around the end of the desk to a chair that faced them, and got right to the point. "I understand you have news from the Middle East."

"Yes," Kerensky began. "A source inside the Chinese government has told one of our agents in Beijing that Chinese troops are amassing along the border with Afghanistan."

"How many troops?"

"We do not know an exact number, but our contact talked in terms of divisions."

"Divisions." Vostok leaned back in his chair. "That is a sizeable force."

"Yes," Kerensky nodded. "Too large to ignore."

"What do the Chinese say is the reason for these troops?"

"Officially they say it is only a military exercise, but our information seems to indicate otherwise."

Mirsky spoke up. "As you are aware, Germany recently made a deal with Iran to acquire all, or substantially all, of its oil production."

"Making themselves an oil broker to the world," Vostok nodded.

Mirsky continued. "Apparently, Chinese leadership is not willing to let Iran ignore its commitment to supply them with that same oil."

"Or," Kerensky added, "to allow Germany to gain leverage in the world oil market."

Vostok struck a contemplative pose. "Do they have the strength to do anything about it?"

"Militarily," Kerensky explained, "China could occupy the Middle East from its border with Afghanistan all the way to Turkey. And they could do it without much problem at all. In fact, many in the region would welcome their presence as an alternative to both the Taliban and the Americans."

"If they seize Afghanistan, Iran, and Iraq," Mirsky added, "they would control billions of barrels of proved oil reserves."

"Unless we get there first," Vostok moved his hand to his cheek in a thoughtful pose. "We should verify this report about their troop movements. Do we have satellite images of the area?"

"I assumed you would ask that." Kerensky opened a briefcase and took out three photographs, which he laid on Vostok's desktop. "These were taken yesterday." He pointed to a spot on the first photo. "Our analysts say those bare spots are indications of troop placements. Based on the condition and debris accumulating there, they appear to have a large number of men on the ground, but not much in the way of equipment."

Vostok had a questioning look. "What does that mean?"

"Unless they intend to march through the region on foot, they're still some distance from being prepared to invade."

"That gives us time to act," Vostok responded.

"Yes," Mirsky hesitated, "but we could not confront them in Afghanistan without running afoul of the Americans."

"But we could occupy Iran before the Chinese get there," Vostok countered.

"Yes," Mirsky nodded, taken aback by the abruptness of the suggestion but filled with pride at the notion of the Russian army once again asserting its power in international affairs. "Yes," he repeated, "we most certainly could."

"And what would be the favorable route for doing that?"

"We should get the army involved in that discussion," Mirsky suggested.

"We will. But just between us, thinking about this now, what would be the most favorable route for invading Iran?" He paused a moment, his eyebrows arched, eyes wide open. "That sounds ominous, merely mentioning it."

"It *is* ominous," Mirsky nodded. "Which is why I suggested we defer this discussion until we can do it with knowledgeable representation from the military."

"Without question," Kerensky ignored Mirsky's suggestion that they wait. "The quickest way to attack would be through Azerbaijan, send our army down through the passes in the mountains of northern Iran."

"What about simply traversing the Caspian Sea with an amphibious assault?"

"That would require a massive flotilla. It would be much too obvious, and the lead time would give the Iranians ample opportunity to prepare. Our military advisers could brief you on the specifics, but I think we'd be far better off moving troops into Azerbaijan and attacking from there."

"But," Mirsky interjected, "the Azerbaijanis would be sensitive to our army's presence in their country. Memories of the Soviet Union are still strong."

"I think we could manage any dissent," Kerensky argued. "We could disguise the whole thing as a military exercise," he chuckled. "Just as the Chinese are doing now."

Vostok leaned forward and rested his elbows on the desk. "If we took this course of action, we would need to accomplish it in a matter of months, if not weeks."

"We could simply ask them, I suppose," Mirsky suggested. "Bring the army onboard and have them pass the request for joint exercises up the chain of command."

"I've actually thought about this issue," Kerensky offered. "Our trade agreement with Azerbaijan is coming up for renewal next year. We could push for a discussion of the matter now, saying the process might be long and arduous and we want to get started early to give us additional time. Then once we have them engaged, we give them what they want on trade in exchange for military access to conduct these exercises. And then sell it to the public by saying we weren't as far apart as we thought, we've reached a good deal for all parties, and we are going to renew now."

"I like that idea," Vostok smiled. Then he turned to Mirsky. "Mikhail, I want you to get down there and make it happen. Give them what they want on trade, but get a private agreement that allows free passage for our military."

"Just like that?" Mirsky had a troubled look. "Without vetting the idea through other agencies? With no other input?"

"We need the option such an agreement would provide," Vostok explained. "I'm not cutting anyone out of the process. I'm including you, our foreign minister, the appropriate official with whom to discuss such a measure. Get down there and talk to them. Use that famous Mirsky charm. Make sure they understand we're not taking over. We just want permission to position troops along their border with Iran." He looked at them with a twinkle in his eye. "Who knows? We might never need to take any further action. But if we don't get started now, we might live to regret it. If we have to counter a Chinese threat quickly, without such an agreement, we'd have to fight our way through Azerbaijan to the Iranian border, and that would be a waste of men and time." Vostok glanced over at Kerensky. "Are we expecting to hear again from our contact in China?"

"Our agent in Beijing can meet with him as we need."

"Good," Vostok nodded. "Ask him to obtain more information." He stood as if the meeting was over, and the others rose from their chairs as well. "Mikhail," Vostok mused as he came from behind the desk, "perhaps these discussions with the Azerbaijanis would go better for us if we talked to them on our soil."

"Perhaps," Mirsky nodded. "You wish to invite them here to Moscow?"

"No," Vostok shook his head. "Invite them to a meeting in Sochi where we can wine and dine them. Better yet, send some of your people to Baku for meetings with their staff, then you and your counterpart ..." He had a puzzled frown. "I can't remember his name...the Azerbaijani foreign minister."

"Jalil Qurbani."

"Yes," Vostok nodded. "You and Qurbani could meet separately in Sochi for talks on a ministerial level. Work this on two levels simultaneously. That would keep most of the staff occupied and out of the way. Maybe it will speed things along."

"Good idea," Mirsky agreed.

"And," Vostok added as he guided them toward the door, "have our satellites monitor the border area."

"They are already doing that," Kerensky replied. "I agree with Mikhail, though. We should get others involved in this before it goes much further. A matter of this nature should involve Garasimov."

"General Garasimov is coming in later to discuss our policy toward the army reserves. I will bring up the matter with him then."

"Good," Kerensky smiled. "Having the secretary of defense involved now would be to our advantage."

7

OFFUTT AIR FORCE BASE

WHEN HOAG ARRIVED for the briefing with Hoyt Moore, he found Jerry O'Connor, an analyst from the Middle East Section, seated near Moore's desk. Moore stood near the window, staring out at the street behind the building. He turned as Hoag entered the room.

"I think you know Jerry," Moore said with a nod.

"Yes. We've met a few times."

"He's in your section now. You two ought to get acquainted." Moore took a seat behind the desk and looked over at O'Connor. "David will be running Middle East Analysis from now on, replacing Peter Burke, but we just appointed him today and he doesn't know about what you've been following. Bring him up to speed on what we've found so far."

"Yes, sir." O'Connor turned his attention to Hoag. "One of our operatives in Xinjiang province, in the far northwestern corner of China, observed several Chinese military patrols working across the border inside Afghanistan."

"Which part of Afghanistan?"

"Wakhan Corridor."

"Okay," Hoag nodded. "Go ahead."

"We reviewed recent satellite images and found several locations that appear to be military encampments."

Moore leaned back in his chair and folded his hands behind his head. "David," he said, interrupting, "I wanted you to meet with us and let you know that Jerry and I have been monitoring this situation behind Peter Burke's back."

"Okay," Hoag hesitated. "You had a reason for that, I suppose."

"Peter was a good man when he first came onboard," Moore continued, "but in the last few years things just went downhill for him and I didn't think I could trust him to get this right. I think I can trust you and I want you and Jerry to get to the bottom of it. See if there's anything to this activity out there."

"Any reason they would be there other than to put down unrest in their own province?"

"None that we know of. But tell me again what you learned from the Germans about their oil situation."

"That they've made a deal with Iran to buy their entire production."

"That's not possible," O'Connor interjected. "They have a strong economy but it's not *that* strong."

"Actually, the deal works more like an exclusive brokerage. The Germans pay as they take delivery."

"But Iran is China's largest supplier of oil. Without that oil, the Chinese will be in a world of hurt." Moore leaned forward in the chair. "And that's what bothers me about these Chinese troops on the Afghan border. Quickest way to solve this problem, from a Chinese point of view, would be to invade through Afghanistan. Nothing there to stop them except us and we couldn't do much more than wave at them as they went by." He stood. "You two see what you can find out about it and get back to me, but work quickly. I'm not sure we have a lot of time."

O'Connor rose from his seat and started toward the door. Hoag stood as well and turned to leave. Moore called after him. "I didn't like doing that to Peter, but he left me little option."

Hoag turned back to face him. "I understand."

A smile turned up the corners of Moore's lips. "You taking Jenny to Reno tonight?"

Hoag felt his cheeks blush. "How do you know about that?"

"I'm the head of the CIA," Moore grinned. "I know lots of things." He folded his arms across his chest. "When you get back, I need you to get right on this business with China. See if the folks at Langley have anything on it. Maybe check around with some of our people in other places."

"I hear Winston Smith has Langley up and running now."

"Winston is a good man," Moore replied. "But you already know that."

"Yes," Hoag nodded. "I do."

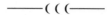

When the meeting with Moore ended, Hoag walked across the base to Jenny's apartment. He found her seated on the sofa with a suitcase standing nearby.

"What's that?" Hoag asked playfully.

"You said we were eloping," she smiled. "Change your mind?"

"No," he grinned and reached down to take her by the hand. "Come with me while I pack."

Two hours later, they were on a plane headed to Reno. When they arrived, a taxi drove them to Chapel of the Bells and, after a quick trip down the street to obtain a license, they were married. They spent the night at the Atlantis Resort and awakened the next morning a little after sunrise.

Hoag rolled on his side to face her. "What are you thinking about?"

Jenny had a sheepish grin. "You won't like it."

"Try me."

She turned to face him. "I was thinking about the other ship."

"Other ship?" Hoag frowned. "What other ship?"

"They sent three. The *Panama Clipper*, the *Amazon Cloud*, and the *Santiago.*"

"Yeah," Hoag said and rolled onto his back. "The ships."

"See?" Jenny grinned. "I said you wouldn't like it." She slid next to him and rested her head on his chest. "I'm sorry. But I woke up thinking about it."

"It's okay," Hoag said softly. He ran his fingers through her hair. "That's been your assignment. Find the other ship before it launches a missile against another target."

"I should have been thinking about how blessed I am to be your wife."

Hoag cut his eyes at her. "Now you're being funny."

"Actually, no, I'm not. I am blessed." She leaned over him. "But I wasn't thinking about it."

He lifted his head and kissed her. "We finally did it," he whispered.

"I know. We should have done this earlier."

"But we have now," and he pulled her down against him.

Later that morning, they sat on the balcony outside their room, enjoying a cup of coffee and a panoramic view of the nearby golf course. Hoag took a sip from his cup and looked over at Jenny. "You know," he returned to their earlier conversation, "we've been searching for that missing ship, asking everyone about the *Santiago*, but maybe that isn't the name anymore."

A puzzled expression wrinkled her brow. "What do you mean?"

"Smugglers rename ships all the time. It's one of their favorite tactics. Rename the ship, fly a different flag. It's an effective way to throw investigators off their trail. Some of them carry templates for extra names and flags from a dozen countries. Out on the high seas, hundreds of miles away from the nearest port. No one around to see them. Very easy to change the name on the hull of a ship. If I were captain of a cargo ship carrying a missile with a nuclear warhead, and I knew everyone in the world was looking for me, I might paint a new name on the side of my ship."

Jenny rested her cup against the armrest of the chair. "Now that you mention it, I suspect a number of agencies have databases for that sort of thing."

Hoag looked over at her again. "Why didn't we think of this before?"

"We were a little busy with other things," she quipped. "Blackout in the east. The second ship off the coast of Virginia. Panic in the streets. You running around Germany trying not to get killed."

"We need to check those databases."

"I know," she sighed. "But I don't want to go back to Nebraska this soon." She glanced around at the scenery. "This is beautiful out here."

"I don't want to go back now, either," Hoag agreed.

"Don't you need to get back and work on the stuff Moore gave you yesterday?"

"Jerry can take care of it for now."

"Who's Jerry?"

"One of the analysts."

"I thought you didn't like the analyst group at Offutt."

"They're rather weak, but Jerry actually knows what he's doing." Hoag took another sip of coffee. "Want to go to Langley?"

A broad grin spread across Jenny's face. "That is the best idea you've had since we got out of bed."

Hoag grinned at her. "I knew there was a reason I married you."

She stood. "Come on. Let's get out of here."

"Think we can find a flight?"

"You're a CIA deputy director. We're going to Washington on official business. I think you can call for a plane to take you anywhere you want to go."

8

JERUSALEM, ISRAEL

AS PROMISED, SECRETARY OF STATE Lauren Lehman flew to Israel, where she was met at the airport without public ceremony by David Oren, Israel's prime minister. They chatted amicably in the car on the ride from the airport, then met for formal discussions at a secure facility near the Knesset building on the west side of the city. She spent an hour outlining what US intelligence agencies knew about the attack on the United States and the follow-on attempt against Israel.

The ships—*Amazon Cloud*, *Santiago*, and *Panama Clipper*—were owned by a Karachi-based company originally financed by members of the bin Laden family. All three of the company's newest ships had been specially constructed to accommodate oversized shipping containers and built with a single mission in mind—to transport three mobile missile launchers, one on each of the ships, to locations off the east and west coasts of the United States from which the missiles, armed with nuclear warheads, would be launched against key population centers. Money to fund the operation came through two Saudi Arabian charities. The missiles, warheads, and launch technology were supplied by Iran. Al-Qa'ida and the Haqqani network furnished men who were trained to operate the missiles and then placed aboard each ship. They and the captains of each of the ships, also specifically recruited for this job, were responsible for shepherding the missiles to their ultimate destinations.

Oren seemed unconvinced. "You do realize, of course, that if what you say is correct, we'd be talking about the Sunnis and Shias working together. That's never happened before."

"I understand that."

"They view each other as the equivalent of the infidel. They despise each other as much as they despise Israel and America."

"I realize that," Lehman continued. "Which is why this is all the more troubling. But we are certain from documents seized at Osama bin Laden's compound that he was involved in planning these attacks long before we got him. And we've researched the corporate history of the company that owns the ships. There's no doubt about its connection to members of the bin Laden family."

"And you really think that Saudi charities funneled money to these people without the royal family knowing about it?"

"We have found no direct links to the royal family. They didn't supply money themselves. But it's difficult to see how all of this could have happened without their knowledge."

"But," he said with a sarcastic tone, "America will never address the issue of their participation, no matter how tangential it might be."

"Probably not," she acknowledged, then moved on. "The missile that actually exploded was detonated as a high-altitude burst for the deliberate purpose of disabling our electrical and communications grids. The other two were to follow immediately after that in a precisely timed and coordinated attack designed to wipe out the population centers in and around New York City and Los Angeles."

"What happened to prevent it?"

"The *Amazon Cloud* was disabled by the electromagnetic pulse from the first blast. We found it adrift off the Virginia coast. It had been fitted with defensive measures that should have prevented loss of its electrical system, but for some reason those measures failed. The *Santiago* never reached the West Coast. We aren't sure why or what happened to it."

Oren looked concerned. "You don't know where it is now?"

"No."

"This is troubling."

"Yes," Lehman agreed. "It is very troubling. But it's part of a much larger issue, David. Iranian missiles on ships. Missiles launched against Israel from the Egyptian desert. They are merely symptoms of a fundamental problem we both face. And one we have to address."

Oren leaned back in the chair and crossed his legs as if anticipating what she might say next. "Which problem do you see as fundamental?"

"The current state of relations between Israel and every other country in the Middle East," she replied. "They hate you."

"And that is our problem? *They* hate *us* and *we* are the ones who have to change?"

"It might not be your problem in the moral sense, but it becomes your problem in a practical sense when they launch missiles at your cities. And it becomes a problem for both of us when they start lobbing them at Washington, D.C."

Oren tilted his head to one side in an imperious pose. "Do you know why they hate us?"

"For many reasons, I suppose, but the chief one is your stance on the Palestinian question."

"There is no Palestinian question," Oren said with indignation. "That is merely a cover for their real reason."

"And what is that *real* reason?"

"They hate us for who we are. Simply because we are Jews. We could give them everything they've asked for—in fact, we offered it to them at Camp David—and still they would refuse to acknowledge our right to exist. And the sole reason for doing so is simply because we exist. We are Jews and we exist, and they hate us for it with a hatred so engrained in their psyche that it is beyond their capacity to accede to even the idea that we have rights of sovereignty equal to their own, much less actually negotiate in good faith about it."

Lehman's eyes darted away. "I'm not sure it's that systemic."

Oren gave a sigh of frustration. "And that right there is the issue between us." He jabbed angrily with his index finger for emphasis. "That is the central issue between America and Israel and the reason why our two nations are at odds on this issue. We recognize that people will never accept us. You do not."

Lehman had a cynical frown. "We don't recognize that people will never accept us?"

"Yes," Oren said with a nod of his head. "They hate you for the same reason they hate us."

"Because we're Jewish?" Lehman gave a dismissive chuckle. "We're not Jewish."

"No," Oren continued, undeterred by her response. "Not because of that. America is not a Jewish nation. They hate America because you are Americans. They hate you simply for that. It has nothing to do with your support of Israel, or your stance on the historicity of the Holocaust, or your love of individual freedom and a lifestyle they see as profligate. That is merely Islamic propaganda—an attempt to clothe their hatred in the garments of civilized dialogue and the language of religious devotion. Beneath that veneer of reason, civility, and moral superiority, the fundamental force driving their policy toward America is simply their hatred for the fact that you exist."

"You may be right about that," Lehman conceded, "but we have to solve this Palestinian situation—whether we call it a question, an issue, or whatever. We have to resolve it. We'll never get anywhere on the tactical problems until we overcome this bigger issue."

"We would be happy to resolve all our differences with them if they would acknowledge that we have as much right to exist at they do. Instead, they use every instance, every occasion to assert their belief that we should cease to exist. They have been carving us up since the day of our formation. Chipping away at our edges. Always moving the line."

"Israel has moved the lines a few times, too," Lehman countered.

"Only in an effort to preserve our historic boundaries," Oren argued. "When the British Mandate was first partitioned, Syria, Lebanon, and Jordan were reserved for the Arabs. The rest was reserved for us. Now they argue that the Palestinians need their own place, too. But the Palestinians do not exist as a separate people."

Lehman had a questioning look. "What do you mean by that?"

"They portray themselves as if they are the indigenous people of this region—as if the so-called Palestinians of today were the Canaanites of old, or some more ancient group that first occupied the area—but they are not. They are simply Arabs, like the people living in Jordan, Syria, and Lebanon. Descendants of people who invaded the region a thousand years ago, which was more than eight thousand years *after* our ancestors first came here. If they want their own state, they should go talk to the Syrians, or the Lebanese, or the Jordanians."

The discussion continued into the night and spilled over to the following day. They made little progress on the issues of Palestinian statehood and relations with countries in the region, but they agreed to cooperate more fully and to share intelligence openly. For the United States, that meant providing Mossad with live feeds of satellite images without need of further request or acknowledgement, and access to surveillance aircraft operating in the Mediterranean basin, both as a source of intelligence and for targeting, without question from the United States as to the ultimate purpose. Israel agreed to give US intelligence agencies, primarily the CIA and NSA, unhindered access to its communications intercepts and unedited reports of Mossad agents in the field at various locations around the region. Both sides knew neither was being completely transparent, but they came away with a renewed sense of mutual commitment to a future in which their separate interests were better served by cooperation, not conflict.

9

JERUSALEM, ISRAEL

A FEW DAYS LATER, EFRAIM HOFI stared out the side window as his car sped along the highway toward Jerusalem. He'd been summoned there by David Oren and was certain he knew what the meeting was about.

Since the disruption in the Dimona missile command center that almost resulted in an unauthorized launch of nuclear weapons, members of Oren's administration had worked feverishly to contain the story. Personnel at the command center had been threatened with arrest if they talked about the incident to anyone other than authorized investigators, and no less than three official but top-secret inquiries were underway in an effort to determine how and why General Khoury was able to gain control of the launch process. A separate effort was being readied to develop appropriate countermeasures to ensure that it didn't happen again.

Hofi had been worried, too, but for very different reasons. General Khoury wasn't merely a general to Hofi.

The summer after graduating from college, Hofi joined the Israel Defense Forces. He rose quickly through the ranks, eventually attaining the level of colonel. But in the battle at Bint Jubail during the First Lebanon War, a grenade exploded near his bunker. He was wounded in the leg, chest, and arms by shrapnel and knocked unconscious from the concussion of the blast. Blood poured from Hofi's wounds. Everyone in the bunker was dead and no one was there to care for him.

While the battle raged, Tomer Khoury fought his way into the bunker, found Hofi alive but unconscious, and carried him to safety. The two had become inseparable friends after that in a relationship that only grew deeper as their careers continued. Hofi was certain their friendship was the reason David Oren asked to see him.

When they reached Jerusalem, the driver made the turn onto Balfour Street and was waved through the gate into the driveway outside the prime minister's residence. Moments later, the car came to a stop near the front entrance. Hofi opened the car door without waiting for the guards and climbed out of the back seat. He was cleared through security and ushered inside to a reception room. An aide led him to a parlor on the second floor where Oren was waiting to see him.

"Efraim," Oren rose from the sofa. The two men shook hands. Oren gestured to a chair a few feet away. "Have a seat. Can I get you something?"

"I am fine, thank you." Hofi took a seat in the chair.

Oren returned to his place on the sofa. "Did they give you a summary of my visit with Lauren Lehman?"

"Yes." Hofi knew that wasn't the reason for this visit and wanted Oren to get to the point. "They briefed me on it."

"I thought it was better not to include anyone else in the meetings," Oren said by way of explanation. "The fewer involved, the less chance there is of a slipup. Not that it's an issue with you. It's just that we can't risk details getting out about what Khoury did in the control room. We don't need anyone worrying about whether we can restrain our own generals right now."

"I understand."

"CIA and NSA are supposed to give us live feeds from their satellites and unquestioned access to surveillance aircraft operating in the region."

"Good," Hofi answered. "We could have used that a few weeks ago."

"Right," Oren nodded. "I let them know that, as well."

"They said you wanted to see me and that I should come quickly." Hofi hoped to move the topic of conversation toward the point of the visit. "I came as soon as I could."

"Right," Oren nodded. "And I am also sure that as the director of Mossad, you already know it has nothing to do with Secretary Lehman's visit."

Hofi nodded. "This is about Tomer Khoury."

Oren had a tight-lipped smile. "He is your friend."

"Yes, he is." The strain in Hofi's voice belied the tension he felt inside. "One of my best."

"Which is exactly what I was hoping you'd say."

Hofi disliked small talk and wanted to get to the heart of the matter. "How may I be of service to you?"

"I need to find out what happened at the Dimona launch center."

"You have at least three different investigations underway right now."

"But none of them is mine," Oren objected. "And you know how investigations go. What you learn from them is more a reflection of the investigating agency's own agenda, and its internal politics, rather than the unvarnished truth."

"I doubt you'd get the unvarnished truth about this from anyone, sir."

"Why is that?"

"This was a serious breach of operating procedure," Hofi offered. "The unvarnished truth would prematurely end more than one career."

"I don't care about that," Oren shook his head. "This was an unacceptable event."

"But it was also an extremely tense moment," Hofi argued. "Tense and unique. We'd just undergone a missile attack that threatened our very existence as a country. One so severe that you ordered a nuclear counterstrike in response."

Oren looked away. "And I withdrew that order, too."

"Yes, sir," Hofi nodded, mindful of the strong-arm effort from the United States that made him do it.

"What happened in that launch control room," Oren continued, "was a major breakdown in our most critical defense system. I need to know what actually happened and how to prevent it from ever occurring again. And for that, I need to know why General Khoury disregarded a direct order, took hostages, and killed a man in the course of it."

"I understand the seriousness of this situation, but shouldn't the IDF be the ones to investigate this? He's one of theirs."

"IDF is conducting an investigation. And, under any other circumstance, I might leave it at that, but as you pointed out so well, this is nothing like anything we've ever faced before. Those missiles were armed with nuclear warheads."

"Yes, sir," Hofi nodded. "And they were within seconds of being launched."

Oren's forehead wrinkled in a frown. "What made him do it?"

"I have no idea," Hofi shrugged. "None at all."

"He's had a long and illustrious military career," Oren lamented. "The best training anyone could receive. But something motivated him to act contrary to all of that." He paused, a pained expression on his face. "What could possibly bring him to do such a thing?"

"I am certain he thought he was doing what was in our best interest."

"Well," Oren bristled, "he doesn't get to make that decision. Not under these or any other circumstances." He sat up straight on the sofa. "He's your friend. I want you to talk to him and find out what happened."

"You are asking me to use our friendship to coerce him into talking about things that he would be better off not discussing."

"I know," Oren nodded, his voice sounding increasingly impatient. "And I know this is difficult for you. But I need to know why he did what he did. He's not going to tell the investigators, but he might tell you."

"And how will you keep what he says from becoming public?"

"We are here," he said, gesturing to the room around them. "Two people having a private discussion in my private residence. There are no recordings. No records of any kind. Just you," he said, pointing to Hofi, "and me."

Hofi shook his head. "I need some kind of privilege or immunity."

Oren frowned. "For yourself?"

"For me. For him. I do not want to be compelled to testify against him."

Oren shook his head. "I'm not giving him immunity. This was the worst breakdown of command in our nation's history. He'll have to answer for that, regardless of what we find. And he killed a man in the process. I'm sure he'll have to answer for that as well. There's no doubt about the actions he took, only about why he did it." Oren rose from his seat on the sofa. "Find out what he says about why he did it and report back to me and me alone. I assure you, nothing will come of it."

Hofi stood and turned toward the doorway. "I doubt he will talk, even to me."

"Just do your best." Oren walked with him as far as the steps that led downstairs. "And don't tell anyone I asked you. Just go visit him as his friend and see what you can find out."

"I'll do that."

Oren continued to talk as Hofi moved slowly down the steps. "Everyone in the operations center knows to keep this quiet? You've made sure of that?"

The question made Hofi angry and he turned to glare up at Oren. "You doubt my integrity or that of my analysts?"

"You have my complete trust, Efraim. You know that. But I have to ask the question. We have powerful enemies who would use this against us and I fear it would be very effective in shaping the opinion even of our friends. We have to keep this information from them."

"I have already taken steps to ensure that we have no leaks." Hofi was at the bottom of the steps by then. "And I reminded them of this before Khoury was removed from the launch center."

"Good. Make seeing him a priority," Oren smiled. "Report back to me. Verbally. No written report of anything."

"Right." Hofi reached for the door to step outside.

The car was waiting on the driveway when Hofi left the residence. He climbed into the back seat and slammed the door shut. The prime minister had asked him to do a favor. He couched it in simple terms, as if what he asked was a task easily fulfilled, but for Hofi it presented a choice. Ask his friend to reveal motives behind what he did, and thereby get him to admit things he should keep to himself. Or, resign now, before he visited Khoury. As the car turned from the drive onto Balfour Street, Hofi once again stared out the window, lost in thought.

10

REUTOV, RUSSIA

ALEXANDER NEVSKY WAITED FOR THE TRAIN to stop. When the doors opened, he stepped out on the platform at the station off Fryazevskaya Street and started toward the sidewalk. A few blocks later, he turned left and came to the police station on the south side of town.

When Nevsky graduated from high school, he entered the Russian army. After six years of active duty, he was discharged and came home to Moscow. Not long after that, he reconnected with his childhood sweetheart and they were married. The following year, his wife gave birth to a daughter.

At first, Nevsky hoped to find a job that would utilize the skills he'd learned in the army, where he operated telecommunications equipment. But private businesses wanted people with better credentials—formal training in technical schools, if not a college degree. Nevsky had no hope of attaining that. Instead, he opted to join the army reserve and substituted his meager pay with part-time work. Four days each week he worked as a patrolman with the Moscow police department, patrolling a region east of the city that covered most of the suburbs. When he wasn't doing that, he worked as a private security guard for a department store downtown.

As he entered the station that day, someone called to him. He glanced in the direction of the voice and saw his supervisor, Oleg Repin, seated at a desk in the corner. He held a white envelope. "This came for you," he said with a smile, waving the envelope from side to side. "I think the army is looking for you."

"No," Nevsky grinned, taking the envelope. "They just want to make certain my address has not changed. I get something from them every three or four months." He tore open the flap, removed a letter from inside, and began to read. Nevsky read it quickly but with each line he felt his chest tighten. The smile faded from his face.

"Bad news?" Oleg asked.

"Yeah," Nevsky replied slowly. "This is not good."

"What does it say?"

"It says I'm being called to active duty." Nevsky looked up, his eyes open wide, his jaw slack. "They want me to report in the next three days."

"What?!" Oleg exclaimed. He rose from his chair and came from behind the desk. "Let me see that." He snatched the letter from Nevsky and quickly scanned it. "You're right," he whispered. "They want you back on active duty. Why would they recall a telecommunications officer to active duty?"

"Maybe they recalled the entire unit."

"But why? You are support. They only need you on active duty if they have mobilized much larger units." Oleg looked over at Nevsky. "This doesn't sound right."

Nevsky took the letter and slid it back inside the envelope, then stuffed it into his pocket. "Well, I don't know why they want me, but they want me," he sighed. "This won't go well at home."

"Milla will not like it?"

"She will like the increase in pay, but she will not like that I am away."

"No one to help her change diapers?"

Nevsky's shoulders slumped. "That is the hardest part of all. Leaving Elizaveta behind."

"Well, cheer up," Oleg said with a smile. "It could be worse."

"How's that?"

"It could be me they called instead of you." Oleg laughed out loud. "That would be a sight, wouldn't it?" He patted his protruding stomach. "This body in an army uniform carrying a rifle."

Later that evening, after his shift was over, Nevsky rode the bus across town to the tiny apartment he and Milla had rented in one of the 1970s-era Soviet housing projects. Milla was waiting for him in the kitchen.

"I prepared supper." She smiled as she kissed him. "Sit down and I will get it." He took a seat at the kitchen table and waited while she took a plate from the cabinet and filled it with food from the pots on the stove. When it was ready, she set it before him and sat down in a chair on the opposite side of the table. "What is the matter, Alex? You look worried." She reached across the table and took his hand. "Tell me what is on your mind."

"Where is Elizaveta?" he asked softly.

"Asleep in bed."

"Did she have a good day?"

"Yes. She had a good day." Milla squeezed his hand tighter. "Tell me what is bothering you."

Slowly, Nevsky slid his hand into his pocket, drew out the crumpled envelope with the letter inside, and handed it to her. "This came today," he said grimly.

She peeled back the flap of the envelope, took out the letter, and carefully unfolded it. Then she began to read, her eyes darting back and forth across the page. Before she reached the bottom line, tears formed in her eyes and trickled down her face.

11

OFFUTT AIR FORCE BASE
OMAHA, NEBRASKA

WHEN HE HAD FIRST ARRIVED at the base, Jack Hedges and his presidential staff took over one of the duplexes on General's Row, a section of historic homes reserved for general officers. The house was the best the base could offer on short notice. President Hedges and his wife occupied one side of the structure; the security detail and essential office staff took the other. Hedges set up his office in the downstairs study. From the window near his desk he had a view through the trees of the parade grounds, which he enjoyed every morning while he sipped his cup of coffee.

In the ensuing months, engineers expanded and renovated offices and entire buildings all across the base to make room for cabinet officials and the executive branch bureaucracy. An elaborate presidential office was constructed in the building that housed the situation room, and numerous other accommodations had been made to suit the needs of assistants, deputy assistants, and minions of every stripe. Yet Hedges preferred the setting in the duplex, with its high ceilings, large windows, and hardwood floors, all of which seemed to hearken back to an earlier time, when government was smaller, issues better defined, and decisions much easier to make. Or so he thought.

As Hedges stood sipping his morning coffee, a white Chevrolet sedan came to a stop at the curb in front of the house. The driver's door opened and a tall, rawboned man stepped out. He wore a tan suit with a white shirt, string tie, and leather boots. With one hand he gripped the handle of a briefcase and with the other he pushed the car door shut.

Just then, Braxton Kittrell appeared in the office. "Mr. President, your next appointment has arrived."

"Who is it?"

"Cecil Zweifel."

"Our new economic adviser?"

"Yes, Mr. President."

"Good. Show him in."

Kittrell stepped from the room and returned with Zweifel in tow. Hedges greeted him politely from behind his desk. Zweifel took a seat across from him, and the conversation quickly turned to the topic at hand.

"As you know, Mr. President, several months have passed since the nuclear device exploded over Washington, D.C. Utility companies are rebuilding the communications and electrical grid in the eastern half of the country."

"With shielded cables this time," Hedges sniped. "I hope."

"Yes, sir. That's my understanding." Zweifel continued, "In doing that, they are finding that more of the system is intact than first thought. The electrical grid is coming online from the Gulf Coast working north. And from the west moving eastward."

"They've been over this with me before," Hedges said impatiently. "Where are we on this? What kind of progress have they made?" He looked over at Zweifel. "And why are you briefing me on all this? This sounds like something somebody else should be covering. You're the economics adviser."

"Yes, sir," Zweifel nodded with an amused smile. "This is context, sir. So the numbers make sense. As far as progress goes, most of Louisiana, Mississippi, Alabama, Georgia, and Florida are already up and running. The lights are on. Electricity is flowing. Western portions of Tennessee are operational. Illinois is coming back."

"So, we're getting the infrastructure back."

"Yes, sir. But that's not to say everything is looking great. The blackout from the blast's electrical impulse was a major disruption to the economy, both physically and psychologically. In the initial months after the blast, many people fled major East Coast cities, but not as many as first thought and those who have stayed in place have found ways to survive. But demand for consumer goods has dropped precipitously."

"Steeply?"

"Yes, sir. Steeply."

"That's not good."

"No, sir. It's not good for growth, but could also portend a long-term shift in trends."

"Caused by the blackout?"

"Yes, sir. Catastrophic events like this can not only disrupt economic patterns in the short term, but disrupt them in the long term as well."

"You mean, effect permanent change in buying patterns?"

"Yes, sir."

"Any data to support that?"

"Imports from China fell below the historic bottom. We broke way below the trend line. We haven't seen this level since before the great Chinese economic rush of the 1980s. Consumption is far below what it would normally be, even accounting for the interruption in availability. I'm not sure it's ever coming back."

"What's that going to do to consumer prices?"

"Difficult to say right now. Spot shortages in the East have created pricing anomalies that have skewed our numbers right now. But at the same time, imports have been dropping, and exports have decreased to near zero. Most of our production is now consumed internally with rebuilding infrastructure."

"We're using our own material to do it?"

"Yes, sir," Zweifel responded. "Current production is meeting current demand almost across the board. And demand for what we can't produce isn't really significant enough to increase import levels much above current levels."

"What about food?"

"That is actually the bright spot right now," Zweifel smiled. "Food stocks have risen and exports of farm products are on the rise."

Hedges leaned forward. "Where does that leave our balance of trade?"

"Our trade balance is shifting to the positive for the first time in almost a century."

"Wow," Hedges grinned. "Farmers must be doing well."

"That's just it," Zweifel said with a troubled look. "They're having great success in coaxing the ground to produce a crop, but financially they're in a bad spot."

"How so?"

"The price of oil has skyrocketed. Gas, fuel, and fertilizer prices are through the roof."

"That's not good," Hedges grimaced. "What are farmers saying? Have you talked to them?"

"No, Mr. President," Zweifel replied. "That's not really what I do."

"You're a numbers man."

"Yes, Mr. President. I study the numbers, make projections, that sort of thing."

"You need to talk to some farmers. I do, too." Hedges leaned back in his chair. "Braxton!" he called in a loud voice.

Braxton Kittrell appeared at the door. "Yes, Mr. President."

"I need to get out of the office. I want to meet some farmers. Cecil does, too."

"Yes, Mr. President," Kittrell replied, trying to catch Zweifel's eye for a hint of what was happening. "We can arrange a trip."

"No. I don't want to arrange a trip. I want to see some farmers." Hedges looked over at Zweifel. "Where could we go?"

Before he could answer, Kittrell spoke up. "I'm sure we could find—"

Hedges pushed back his chair and stood. "Get the car."

"Sir?"

"I said, get the car."

"Mr. President," Kittrell protested, "we have a schedule. Meetings. Some of them planned well in advance."

"Cancel them," Hedges barked as he rose from the chair. "I'm going to talk to the farmers. Get the car. And no press. This is a working trip. I want to talk. Not for the media." He started toward the door and glanced over his shoulder. "Come on, Cecil. Let's see what we can find out."

Zweifel moved to stand, but Kittrell laid a hand on his shoulder. Zweifel hesitated. "Mr. President," Kittrell called gently.

Hedges turned to face him with a look of disgust. "What is it now?"

"You have a meeting with Secretary Lehman in an hour, about China. And Director Moore wants to brief you. They both said it was urgent. You slotted them into the schedule after your meeting with Mr. Zweifel. We can't run off on a tour of the countryside just yet."

Hedges' shoulders sagged. "Okay," he groused, looking over at Zweifel. "I have to do these things."

"Yes, Mr. President." Kittrell removed his hand from Zweifel's shoulder, and Zweifel stood. "I understand."

Hedges lumbered back toward the desk. "I'll have them call you when we get it set up."

"Certainly, sir." Zweifel picked up his briefcase and walked quickly from the room.

Hedges came around the end of the desk and took a seat. "Some days," he grumbled, "I hate this job."

12

MOSSAD OPERATIONS CENTER ASHDOD, ISRAEL

LATE IN THE AFTERNOON, there was a knock on the door of Efraim Hofi's office. Then the door opened and his assistant, Mara Moss, appeared. Hofi looked up from the file that lay on his desk. "You need something?"

"This came for you," she stepped toward the desk and handed him an envelope.

Hofi took it from her and glanced at the return address in the upper left corner. It had been sent from the office of General Grossman, chief of general staff for the Israel Defense Forces.

"I guess we know what this is," he sighed.

"Yes, sir," Mara nodded. "I suppose we do."

Inside the envelope, Hofi found a memo responding to his formal request to visit General Khoury. The memo noted that Khoury was being held in solitary confinement at Nevatim Air Force Base, near Beersheba. Hofi glanced at his watch, then rose from his chair and reached for his jacket. "I need a car and driver."

"It's late," Mara replied.

"This can't wait," his voice had a note of urgency. "Get the car and driver."

Ten minutes later, Hofi came from the building and found his car waiting on the driveway. He opened the rear door and ducked inside. Moments later, they were speeding south from Ashdod on Highway 6 that led to Beersheba.

Out the window, the Israeli countryside zipped past, but in his mind Hofi was far away as he recalled again the day years before when the grenade exploded outside his bunker. Memories of the pain, with the blood trickling from his wounds, seemed more real than ever. The sense of relief as Khoury lifted him from the ground, more profound than any day since. A kinship was born between them that day. And here he was, off to betray that relationship, to use the bonds of trust that had grown between them to manipulate Khoury into telling him things better left untold.

Perhaps it will not come to that, Hofi thought. *Perhaps Khoury has no secrets to tell, but only honest, clear motives for his actions. Perhaps he will say the shooting was an accident, and admit nothing incriminating.* The thought of that possibility filled him with hope and confidence for a moment, but the elation it brought lasted only until he remembered his conversation with David Oren.

Oren held out no possibility that there were no secrets behind Khoury's conduct. He assumed there were, and that Hofi would sacrifice anything to have them revealed. And not for the sake of the truth. *No,* Hofi thought, *this was an effort solely to cover Oren's own decisions and actions.* Oren had been ready to launch the missiles himself, right up to the moment President Hedges talked him out of it. Now he was prosecuting Khoury for the same thing. It all left Hofi feeling disgusted and bitter at Oren, the IDF generals who did Oren's bidding, and most of all, with himself. He should have resigned on the spot, right there at the prime minister's residence.

While he was still lost in thought, the car came to a stop at the main gate to the Nevatim base. They were cleared through the security checkpoint and continued across the base to the detention facility on the far side of the complex. After a phone call to verify Hofi's permission, he was escorted to a visitation room.

Walls of the room were painted white. The floor was tiled with a smooth finish. Three stainless steel tables were arranged an equal distance apart in the center, each bolted to the floor with benches attached to the frame on either side. Hofi took a seat and waited.

A few minutes later, a steel door to the left creaked open and General Khoury appeared. Dressed in an orange jumpsuit, his hands were shackled at the wrist with manacles that were attached to a thick leather detention belt cinched tightly around his waist. Manacles fastened to his ankles were connected by a short but heavy chain that kept his feet less than half a meter apart, making his gait halting and awkward. A guard accompanied him and as Khoury took a seat across the table from Hofi, the guard moved to the corner of the room, where he stood watching them from a distance. Hofi glanced in his direction. "Wait outside, please."

"Not allowed," the guard replied tersely.

"I'm not afraid of him."

"Doesn't matter. Prisoner's under solitary confinement. Only allowed outside the cell with special permission. Someone has to be with him at all times."

"Do you know who I am?"

"Yes, sir," the guard nodded. "I know who you are. That's the only reason you're in here."

"This place has cameras in every corner. They capture everything that goes on here." Hofi gestured with his thumb pointing over his shoulder. "Someone is monitoring the activity in here constantly. I'll assume responsibility for my own safety."

"It's against regulations."

Hofi stood and turned to face the nearest security camera. He waved his hands over his head and spoke in a loud voice. "Could you radio your guard and tell him it's okay to step outside, please? I would like to speak to General Khoury without anyone present."

Moments later, the radio on the guard's hip squawked. He pressed a button to answer it, listening through an earpiece connected to the radio by a thin white cord that snaked across his chest. He said something Hofi could not understand, then moved away from the corner and started toward the door. When he was gone, Hofi returned to his seat opposite Khoury and looked his friend in the eye.

"You really created a big mess." Hofi's eyes narrowed. "A really big mess."

"I know," Khoury nodded. "But it was unavoidable."

"What were you thinking?"

"That I was fulfilling my oath."

"Your oath?" Hofi had a look of disbelief. "What oath?"

"As an officer," Khoury insisted. "As a soldier. My oath. Your oath. The oath we all took." He leaned over the table, his eyes focused, and in a low, tense voice he said, "Masada shall not fall again."

Hofi refused to be moved by the display. "How is disobeying an order and shooting a co-worker serving your country?"

"The Iranians hate us."

"They have always hated us," Hofi shrugged.

"Yes," Khoury agreed, "but now they have nuclear bombs and missiles to deliver their hatred. Now they give them to their terrorist proxies and they shoot those missiles and bombs at us. You were there. You saw how close they came to striking our cities. They have the means to fulfill their dream of driving us into the sea. It's no longer a dream for them." He slapped the table. "They can do it!"

Again, Hofi forced himself to show no emotion. "And you thought shooting Yosi would change that?"

Khoury leaned back from the table. "Shooting Yosi was a mistake," he sighed. "They tell me he is dead."

"Yes," Hofi nodded. "He was dead before they got the door open. From the wound he received, they think he was probably dead before his body reached the floor."

Khoury's eyes darted away. "I have known him a long time."

"You made his wife a widow," Hofi said, unwilling to let the moment pass with simply a casual remark. "His children are orphans."

Anger flashed across Khoury's face. "It was tragic! Okay?" he shouted. "If I had it to do over again, I might not do it that way. Okay? But am I sorry I tried to prevent them from terminating the launch? No." He clasped his hands together and rested them on the tabletop. "I am not sorry for that." Then, before Hofi could respond, Khoury leaned forward and lowered his voice. "Listen to me, Efraim. This was our last opportunity to destroy Iran."

"You don't know it was the last."

Khoury leaned away. "We could have done it right then and no one would have denied they had it coming."

"It was based on faulty information."

"The quality of the information does not matter," Khoury argued.

"This was God's moment for defending us and preserving our future."

"Those missiles would have killed many innocent civilians."

"A cost of living in such a godless land. And they are not so innocent as you suppose." He leaned forward once more. "If they are not destroyed, Efraim, they will destroy us. Forget about me. Forget about what they plan to do to me. This is about our nation. About God and His purposes in history. They cannot be allowed to live."

"Perhaps so," Hofi sighed. "But the world will not tolerate a preemptive strike of that nature from us."

Khoury folded his arms across his chest. "Then God will raise up another who will destroy them." Hofi had a puzzled look. Khoury continued. "It is true," he insisted. "The Iranians are our enemy, and that makes them an enemy of God. They cannot be allowed to prevail. He will not allow them to suppress us." He unfolded his arms and pointed with his finger for emphasis. "We are His chosen people. The people of a covenant-keeping God. I was not crazy when I took control of that room, and I am not crazy now. You will see. God is fulfilling His prophecy. As the prophet Samuel said of David, 'He shall build a house for my name, and I will establish the throne of his kingdom forever.' God will bring it to pass."

"That was a long time ago. And David is long since dead and gone."

"You don't really believe that."

Hofi ignored his last comment. "So you think blowing up Iran has something to do with that?"

"It has to do with keeping us alive, and *that* has everything to do with the fulfillment of prophecy."

They talked a few minutes longer, then Hofi signaled for the guard. He waited while Khoury was led from the room, then he walked down the main corridor, through the security check station near the front door, and stepped outside.

On the sidewalk, Hofi paused and raised both hands above his head, stretching as high as he could reach. He held them there a moment and took a deep breath, filling his lungs with air. Then he let it slowly escape.

What he'd heard from his friend left his head feeling tight and his soul deeply disturbed. Was Khoury insane? Had he lost touch with reality? Or was he more right than ever before? Years had passed since Hofi had attended synagogue. Longer than that since he last read Torah. And even longer since he prayed. Still, the suggestion that ancient prophecy might somehow come true in his lifetime left him intrigued. Perhaps there was more to their situation than he'd noticed. "Or perhaps," he mumbled to himself, "Tomer Khoury just got to me, and now I'm being sucked into his insanity."

Just then, the car turned onto the drive and came to stop before him. Hofi, with his hands still high in the air, suddenly felt self-conscious. He lowered them quickly to his side and stepped from the curb to the pavement. Minutes later, he was once more on the highway, staring out the window from the back seat as the Israeli countryside zipped past the speeding car.

13

BERLIN, GERMANY

DRESSED IN A GRAY RUNNING SUIT, Josef Mue ogged across the darkened chancellery grounds. The night air felt cool as his sweat-soaked shirt pressed against his skin. Behind him, his security detail trailed at a distance, and in his mind he escaped to places only he could imagine. This was his time, cloaked in the dark of night, with the sidewalks devoid of daytime foot traffic, as alone as a head of state could possibly get.

As he turned a corner near the river, Karl Murnau, an assistant from his office, appeared on the sidewalk up ahead, shattering the anonymity of the evening. Reluctantly, Mueller came to a stop beside him. He leaned forward, both hands on his knees, and took deep breaths as he waited for Murnau to speak.

"They need you in the situation room," Murnau had an air of urgency.

"Like this?" Mueller gestured to his shirt. "I'm a mess."

"They said it was urgent."

Just then, a member of Mueller's security detail stepped forward. "Sir, they need you in the situation room. Right now."

Mueller pushed himself up to a standing position. "Very well." He reluctantly followed them inside the chancellery building and down to the basement.

The situation room was located on the opposite end of the building from where Mueller entered. He made his way there down a long, underground corridor. When he realized how far away it was, he glanced over at Murnau. "I might as well keep jogging." Then he picked up the pace and trotted on ahead. Members of the security team rushed to keep up and fanned out in front of him, blocking intersecting hallways as he approached. Murnau lagged behind, then finally disappeared altogether.

A few minutes later, Mueller turned from the corridor into a hallway that led to the right. Doors to the situation room were at the end. A guard posted there snapped to attention and opened the door as they approached.

At the far end of the room was a large projection screen. Television monitors were mounted on either side. The screen in the center showed a map of the world. News from Berlin, New York, and London played on the monitors beside it.

A conference table occupied the center of the room. Around it were seated Georg Scheel, the Foreign Office minister; Konrad Hölderlin, head of German Foreign Intelligence; and representatives from the German army, navy, air force, and the Federal Police. They all came to attention as Mueller entered. He acknowledged them with a nod and pulled a chair from the end of the table. "Take a seat, please." Everyone sat. Mueller looked around at them. "I understand we have a situation."

Hölderlin rose from his chair at the table. "Sir, earlier today our operatives working from a site in a remote corner of northeastern Afghanistan intercepted cell phone transmissions from an area in southern Tajikistan." A map appeared on the main screen behind him. Hölderlin stepped closer to it and pointed. "The phone calls originated from this area here, near an area known as the Wakhan Corridor."

Mueller looked perturbed. "You called me down here for a phone call?"

"No, sir," Hölderlin replied quickly, "we called you down here because of what that phone call was about."

"It better be good," Mueller grumbled.

"The parties to those calls were discussing the body of a man they found at the base of a mountain that borders the Wakhan River. The dead man was Siddiq Kamran." Hölderlin paused while a photograph appeared on screen. "An Afghan who lives in the region and has been working recently as a guide to Chinese troops patrolling the area."

"So, we're here tonight because of a phone call about a dead Afghan who worked for the Chinese army."

"Yes, sir. He's one of half a dozen men our teams have located in the area over the past six months."

"Located?"

"Yes, sir. Located their bodies."

"All of them were dead?"

"Yes, sir. A single gunshot to the head. All shot with Chinese rounds manufactured especially for the Chinese army. We think Chinese patrols are using locals for guides. Work with them awhile, then shoot them in the head to keep them from talking."

Mueller frowned. "Keep them from talking about what?"

"That's the unknown. But whatever it is, they want to keep it a secret and we want to know about it."

"So why am I here?"

"We'd like to send a couple of UAVs over the area to find out what's going on."

"Aren't the Americans out there also?"

"They have one group of Marines located at a base near the mouth of the Corridor. The area sees very little Taliban or rebel activity."

"What about NATO satellites. Do they have images of the area?"

"We're working on that now, but we'd like to evaluate this situation for ourselves, before we bring them in. Our teams in Afghanistan already have UAVs they can deploy within the hour. They've asked permission to send them into the Corridor. To do that, we need to give them a prompt response. We wanted you in the decision loop because we need to alert the Americans to what we're doing, so they won't shoot it down."

"It's nighttime. Wouldn't this be better in the daylight?"

"Less chance of being seen at night. And the thermal imaging works better at night. Higher degree of temperature contrast."

Mueller thought for a moment, then gestured to the others gathered at the table. "I understand your interest. But why are all these people here, too?"

"Given the nature of our recent agreement with Iran regarding oil supplies, which runs counter to China's heavy dependence on Iranian oil, we wanted to include all areas that might be potentially affected by a Chinese military response."

"You think this is a Chinese military response?"

"We don't know. But we think we ought to find out."

"Very well," Mueller replied. "Send in the UAVs." He pushed back from the chair. "Anything else?"

"No, sir."

"Good. Then I'll get on with my jog." He stood and started toward the door. Those seated at the table rose as he departed.

Outside the room, Mueller made his way down the hall to the corridor and turned right, toward the nearest exit. As he stepped outside and broke into a trot, he was met by General Erhard, commander of the German air force. "Sir, if I may?"

Mueller stumbled to a halt. "What is it now?"

"I wanted to speak with you about the issue in Afghanistan."

Mueller glanced around suspiciously. "Some reason you didn't bring this up in there just now?"

"Sort of. Our aircraft have participated in reconnaissance missions over the area as part of the joint NATO forces in Afghanistan. I'm sure we have images from the area in our database. My analysts can work up a separate review for you, if you like."

"Why not just give them to Hölderlin? Let him give us a single answer that addresses all the information."

Erhard looked uncomfortable. "Hölderlin likes to run whatever show he's part of. If I tell him about the images, he'll want his analysts to review them and if our images conflict with the position his analysts have already taken, he'll just bury the photos." Erhard smiled. "It's just pride, I suppose, but that's how I feel. I'd rather have our people work up our information."

Mueller grinned. This was precisely the kind of internal suspicion and rivalry he treasured. Erhard would come in handy one day. He reached out with his right hand and slapped him on the shoulder. "Nothing to be ashamed of. Get me those images and whatever your crew has to say about them. And don't let anyone else see them first."

"Yes, sir," Erhard nodded with a satisfied smile. "I'll get them for you by the end of the day."

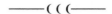

The following morning, General Erhard came to Mueller's office, briefcase in hand. Mueller looked up as he entered. "You have something for me?"

"Yes, sir." Erhard crossed the room to the desk. He set the briefcase on a nearby chair and opened it, then took out a large manila envelope. In it were five photographs. "These were taken by our pilots about a month ago. We forwarded the digital files to NATO headquarters and to the Americans, but kept a copy for ourselves." He laid the first photo on the desktop.

Mueller studied it a moment and saw only mountains, boulders, and here and there a few scraggly trees. He leaned back in his chair, a puzzled look on his face. "That means nothing to me."

"No," Erhard replied. "I don't suppose it does." He took a second photograph from the envelope. "This was taken two weeks earlier." He placed the second photograph next to the first, then leaned over the desk and pointed with his finger. "This flat place right here that looks like a bare spot in the later photo isn't in the earlier one."

Mueller hunched over the desk for a second look. "Okay," he nodded. "I see that. But what does it mean?"

"Ah," Erhard smiled. "Good question. Which is answered by this." He placed a third photograph on the desk. "This is the most recent photograph in the database." He pointed to the same location on it. "That is a formation of soldiers standing in rank on that same spot."

"What kind of soldiers?"

"Our experts say they are Chinese."

"Is this location within China's border?"

"No," Erhard shook his head. "It is in an extreme corner of Afghanistan."

Mueller leaned back from the desk once more. He propped his elbows on the armrest of the chair and laced his fingers together. "Is this a problem?"

"Only because of their location and what appears on these last two photographs." Erhard took the final pictures from the envelope and placed them near the others on the desk. Mueller moved forward to see. "These are similar groups of soldiers in the same region." Erhard pointed to the last photograph. "That is a survey team. The transit is there." He moved his finger. "The rod man is down here." He moved his finger again. "These dots back here, and here, and here, appear to be stakes."

"You can take pictures that clearly?"

"The cameras have wonderful lenses."

Mueller tapped the photograph with his finger. "What are they doing? Mapping?"

"In another location, perhaps," Erhard offered. "But the troops we've observed are located in an area that leads directly down a gentle slope to the Wakhan River valley. The only place of its kind." He looked over at Mueller. "We think the surveyors are following the easiest and most convenient path for a road into that region. From the look of it, a very broad highway."

Mueller nodded thoughtfully. "What do you think the Chinese are up to?"

"If I were a betting man, based on my experience, I would say they are preparing for a major military operation."

Mueller scooted back in his chair and looked up at Erhard. "Why do you say that?"

"Just a hunch." Erhard shrugged. "I've been in the military a long time. I've seen buildups by the Americans in Saudi Arabia, Panama, Nicaragua. I saw how the Russians gathered their troops to invade Afghanistan and how the Americans did it there and in Iraq." He tapped a photograph with his finger. "This is somewhat crude by Western military standards, but the Chinese are a labor-intensive society. We prefer one machine to ten men. They would rather use ten men in place of one machine. I think this is big."

Mueller nodded toward the photographs. "Mind if I keep these to study?"

"I brought them for you." Erhard laid the empty envelope on the desk beside the photographs and turned to close his briefcase. "When Hölderlin brings you the latest from his UAVs, you can compare these to what he shows you."

"Think his information will bear this out?"

"I hope so. If it does, you'll know you're getting some good intelligence."

"Yes," Mueller nodded. "I guess so. Do the Americans know about this?"

"They have the photographs, obviously. But I don't think their analysts have paid them any attention. The Americans are mostly looking for the Taliban, and remnants of al-Qa'ida. They are not thinking about the Chinese."

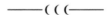

Late the following evening, Hölderlin came to Mueller at the Chancellery residence. Like Erhard, he brought photographs with him. Mueller, dressed in pajamas and a satin robe, met him in the parlor. "A little late for this, isn't it?" he frowned. "Or is it early?"

"Because of the time difference, we worked on it most of the day. I wanted you to have the information as soon as possible."

Mueller took a seat on the sofa. Hölderlin sat in a chair a few feet away. A coffee table was between them. "Okay," Hölderlin began as he laid his first photograph on the table. "This is what we found today." He pointed to the picture. "Trucks here and here." He moved to a different spot. "These are troops in formation here." He laid a second photograph on the table. "This is a close-up. As you can see, these are Chinese regular troops. Not reservists. Not civilians in uniform."

"Right," Mueller nodded. He rubbed his eyes with his fingertips. "What else do you have?"

Hölderlin produced a third photograph. "This one shows a tent we believe is their command center. From the size of it we're sure they're running a company-size unit out of this location." He spread four more photos on the table. "These are four additional sites, just like the one I showed you. Two are located in the Wakhan Corridor. Two are south of that location, inside Pakistan."

Mueller's eyes opened wider. "In Pakistan?"

"Yes."

"Do the Pakistanis know about it?"

Hölderlin smiled as he showed yet one more photograph. "This is a close-up of one of the command locations in Pakistan." He tapped the photo with his index finger. "That man right there is Dorab Haleem. Director of the Joint Intelligence Bureau for Inter-Services Intelligence."

"ISI is supporting them."

"This is a Chinese operation with Pakistan's blessing. I think they're planning something really big."

"Any indication the Americans know about this?"

"I'm sure they could know about it if they wanted to. I suspect they do, but they aren't worried about the Chinese. In fact, they like having the Chinese army in the vicinity. It's a way of backstopping their operation. They don't have to worry about Taliban fighters slipping over the border into China because if they do, the Chinese will kill them on the spot. They have enough trouble from their own indigenous population."

So, what should we do with this information?"

"We'd like to continue drone flyovers. Keep the UAVs operational. See what we can pick up."

"If you had to guess?"

"Based on activity in the region, there's no reason for the Chinese to be there."

"Is it a training exercise?"

"No." Hölderlin leaned back in the chair. "If it is, it's not like any we've observed before from them."

Mueller gestured toward the photos on the coffee table. "Mind if I keep these awhile? I'd like to study them a little more."

"Certainly." Hölderlin stood.

Mueller stood as well. "Perhaps we should consider sending a few more operatives into the area."

"I've already ordered a dozen of our personnel to the region. Don't want to increase our presence too much, but a few more eyes would help."

"Keep me informed."

"Yes, sir. I will."

When Hölderlin was gone, Mueller picked up the phone and called General Erhard. In spite of the late hour, Erhard answered the call on the first ring.

"Come see me," Mueller ordered. "I have a job for you."

"Yes, sir. I'll be right over."

Mueller leaned back on the sofa, closed his eyes, and remembered the words Bettinger had spoken over him just a few days earlier. "*With the reins he guides the beast, directing it where he wills, and with the sword he slays all who oppose him."* Klandenets, a magical sword. A Russian sword. A smile spread across his face. "This will work out nicely," he whispered.

14

SOCHI, RUSSIA

ADNAN KARROUBI SAT ON A CHAISE LOUNGE near the pool at the Grand Hotel and Spa. From his chair he had a splendid view of the Black Sea and the attractive brunette lounging across the way. She had a knowing smile and waved at him while she sipped from the glass in her hand. Karroubi rested his head on the seatback and closed his eyes, his mind filled with thoughts of the night before. Like many privileged male Muslims from Iran who traveled aboard, Karroubi enjoyed a lifestyle outside the country that was quite different from the way he lived at home.

In Tehran, he was head of Iran's Assembly of Experts, an elected body of Islamic scholars charged with choosing the country's Supreme Leader and monitoring his activities. That position forced him to follow strict Sharia law, remembering always to wear the proper garments, adhere to traditional Muslim dietary restrictions, bow at the proper times, and greet others with the proper salutation and blessing. And he never missed prayers on Friday. His life while traveling outside the country, however, was another matter.

Abroad, he dressed in Western garb, preferring a gray suit with white shirt, muted tie, and fashionable leather shoes. He consumed liquor in large quantities and indulged an acquired taste for the finest wine. He also enjoyed beautiful women. The woman waving to him from across the pool that day had been with him the night before.

For tonight, he had designs on a blonde he'd seen in the bar. As he lay there, eyes closed, imagining what he might do with the blonde, he heard a familiar voice from behind. He rolled onto his side and looked in that direction. Near the door to the hotel he saw Mikhail Mirsky, the Russian foreign minister.

Karroubi had first met Mirsky years before when Russian engineers and physicist helped fledgling Iranian scientists construct the nation's first nuclear reactor. Back then, Mirsky was one of many employees from the Russian Foreign Ministry who accompanied the engineers. They came, supposedly, to observe and assist. But most people understood they were in Iran as spies, to make certain the nuclear technology program was used only for peaceful purposes. Karroubi was there to convince the Russians they had nothing to worry about. Very quickly he leaned that Mirsky and he shared a common hatred of America. That shared interest became the seed of friendship that had grown stronger and stronger as the years went by.

Standing with Mirsky was Jalil Qurbani, the foreign minister from Azerbaijan. Karroubi knew him only by sight and reputation. He was known in the region for his deceptively benign persona that masked a remarkable intellect and keen eye for details.

Karroubi watched for a moment, then ducked out of sight behind the seat back to avoid being seen. Even from a distance, he could tell they were engaged in a serious discussion.

Later that afternoon, Karroubi found Mirsky seated in the hotel lobby. Mirsky glanced up as he came near. "Ahh!" he exclaimed. "Adnan. I didn't know you were here."

"Just up for some relaxation and sunshine," Karroubi answered with a smile.

"Not enough sunshine in Tehran?"

"We have sun, but no beach. And certainly no relaxation." Karroubi took a seat in a chair beside him. "Will you be here long?"

"A few more days."

"Great. We should have dinner. Are you free this evening?"

"I would enjoy visiting with you," Mirsky said apologetically, "but I have a meeting tonight. Perhaps tomorrow. It's been a long time since we talked. Much has happened."

"Yes," Karroubi nodded. "Much has happened."

Just then, Jalil Qurbani entered the lobby, surrounded by an entourage of aides and bodyguards. Mirsky rose as they approached. Karroubi stood, too. Mirsky introduced them, then said good-bye and walked with Qurbani across the room and out the front door. Karroubi stepped to a window and watched as the two men climbed into the back seat of a limousine.

That evening, about ten o'clock, the phone in Karroubi's room rang. The call was from Mirsky. "We could not have dinner, but what about a drink in the hotel bar?"

"Sure," Karroubi replied. "I'll be right down."

The hotel was crowded with vacationers but the bar was mostly empty. They took a table in the corner and sipped on a drink while they talked.

"I noticed a number of high-ranking people here from Azerbaijan," Karroubi observed. "Many of them I have not seen in years."

"Yes," Mirsky nodded. "More than I imagined."

"Something going on?"

"We are meeting with representatives from Azerbaijan. I suppose the others gathered in an attempt to find out what those meetings are about." Mirsky glanced over at Karroubi. "Is that why you are here?"

"Not at all," Karroubi smiled slyly. "Finding you here was purely coincidental."

"Adnan," Mirsky laughed, "I have always enjoyed your sense of humor."

"Were you happy to see that someone finally hit the Americans hard enough to make them hurt?"

"I thought of you when I saw the reports."

"Purely coincidental, I'm sure."

Mirsky laughed again and reached for his drink. "We should see each other more often. I miss our evenings together in Tehran. Those were some great discussions."

"I thought we were planning."

"Yes. That, too."

"So, you are here to meet with Qurbani?"

"Yes," Mirsky nodded. "Our countries have enjoyed a pleasant relationship since we severed political ties. Not always true with some of the others, but with Azerbaijan, we have had a good result. Our trade agreement is coming up for renewal next year and we decided to get an early start."

"How is that going?"

"Actually, we have made much better progress than we thought."

"I can't imagine there would be much to argue about."

"Surprisingly, none at all," Mirsky nodded. "We are about to conclude our discussions. Just covering last-minute details."

They talked until late in the night, neither of them actually saying much of anything important. But Karroubi was skeptical of Mirsky's explanation about the visit. He was a Russian minister, much too high in rank to be handling mundane diplomatic tasks like last-minute details in a trade agreement. If he was involved, Karroubi was certain something big was in play.

15

BERLIN, GERMANY

GENERAL ERHARD SAT IN THE BACK SEAT of a Mercedes limousine and watched as Gennady Panova stepped from a taxi and walked toward the Adlon Kempinksi Hotel, a five-star hotel on Linden Street near the parliament building. As Russia's ambassador to Germany, Panova had grown accustomed to the luxuries of life. The mistress he kept upstairs in the hotel was just one of the many pleasures he enjoyed. Erhard smiled as Panova made his way past the doorman and into the hotel lobby. Things were going just as he knew they would.

On the seat beside Erhard was a manila envelope. In it were the photographs he had brought to Mueller, along with several gleaned from those taken by Hölderlin's UAVs. Erhard's mission, straight from Mueller himself, was to deliver those photos to Panova. "But do it in a way that makes him think he's getting something important," Mueller had said. "Make him believe it. The future of our nation depends on it." Erhard had accepted that assignment with delight and after only a day of following Panova, he knew exactly how to play him.

As Panova disappeared through the hotel doors, Erhard threw open the car door and stepped out. He walked quickly across the street and up to the hotel entrance. He ignored the doorman and pushed his way into the lobby. He hurried past the front desk to the elevator and rode up to the sixth floor, arriving at the hallway just as Panova reached the door to his mistress's room.

Erhard spoke up as he stepped toward him. "A moment of your time, Mr. Ambassador."

Panova wheeled around, startled that someone recognized him. "I was just going in for the night. It's been a long day."

"Yes," Erhard grinned. "And I'm sure it will be even longer once you get inside that room."

Panova looked perturbed. "What can I do for you?"

"I was wondering if we could talk a moment."

"Talk?" Panova looked puzzled. "What is this about?"

Erhard glanced around warily and lowered his voice. "I'm in a little bit of a bind, if you know what I mean."

"I am sorry." Panova shook his head. "I have no idea what you're talking about."

"Oh. I think you do," Erhard nodded confidently. "And I think we can both help each other."

Panova frowned. "Each other?"

"Sure. I need some financial assistance. And you need for your wife not to find out where you really go when you work late."

"Hush," Panova said nervously. "What do you want?"

Erhard gestured with a wave of his hand. "Come with me."

"Where?"

"Come with me. I will show you. It will only take a moment." Erhard turned away and motioned again for Panova to follow. He led the ambassador down the hall and around the corner to a room. When they were inside, he turned to face Panova. "As I mentioned, I am in a financial bind. You wish for your secrets to remain secret. I wish to sell you some of mine."

"You want to sell me secrets?"

"Yes," Erhard nodded in response.

"What secrets?"

"I will show you one. You may have it for free." Erhard opened the manila envelope he'd been carrying and produced a single photograph. "This is my gift to you," he said, handing the picture to Panova.

Panova took it from him and studied it a moment. "This is useless," he shrugged. "I have no idea what it is, or what it means." He tapped it with his finger. "This is a photograph of barren wasteland."

"Yes," Erhard nodded. "Barren wasteland along the Afghanistan border with China. Go on," he said, gesturing. "Take another look." Erhard pointed. "That right there is a tent. A Chinese tent serving as a command center for patrols into the Wakhan Corridor. You know where that is?"

"Yes," Panova nodded. "I know about the Wakhan Corridor. What does this mean?"

"If you had the other photographs, you would know. Or, at least your analysts back in Moscow could tell you."

"And what would they tell me?"

"That the Chinese are gathering troops on the Afghan border for a major military operation."

"What kind of operation?"

"Many think they are preparing to move against Iran."

"That's absurd."

"Is it?" Erhard held the envelope a little farther from his body. "I know you are interested. And I know others in your government have been asking questions about this very matter. What I have in my hands can make you a player among them."

"Is this some twisted idea of yours about how to extort money from me?"

"I am not extorting you. I am merely suggesting that I have something you want, and you have something you want no one to know about. I need money. You need silence." Erhard pulled open the envelope just enough to see inside. "I'll give you a peek," he said playfully. Panova leaned over to look, but as soon as he did, Erhard turned the envelope away. "That's all," he smiled. "Just a peek."

"How much do you want for them?"

"A hundred thousand Euros."

Panova's mouth dropped open. "A hundred thousand. You're out of your mind. I'll give you ten thousand, and you can pray I don't turn you in."

"No," Erhard shook his head slowly. "I'm afraid ten thousand Euros would not keep photos like these from your wife." He reached inside his jacket and took out a photograph showing Panova with a young woman, neither of them dressed. He glanced at it, then handed it to Panova. "It was taken with a telephoto lens, but I think your wife will still recognize you, don't you?"

"Where did you get this?!" Panova demanded.

"Same place I got these." Erhard took a smartphone from his pocket, pressed a button, and held it up for Panova to see. "Recognize the couple in that photograph?" Panova's eyes flashed with anger and he reached for the phone. Erhard jerked it away. "I see you do recognize them." He looked down at the screen. "That's you and, oh my, I do believe that's your current mistress. The blonde." He stared at the picture a moment longer, then glanced up at Panova, his face and voice suddenly serious. "A hundred thousand Euros for the photos in my envelope." He gestured with the phone. "Or the photos in this phone arrive in your wife's inbox before you can grab my wrist."

"Okay," Panova snapped. "A hundred thousand Euros. When do you want it?"

"Tomorrow. At noon. Meet me in front of the Reichstag building. I'll be waiting on a bench outside the main entrance."

"I suppose next you'll say come alone," Panova snarled.

"I don't care whether you come alone or bring a crowd," Erhard said as he started toward the door. "Just bring the money."

16

OFFUTT AIR FORCE BASE
OMAHA, NEBRASKA

IN SPITE OF HIS ATTEMPTS to keep things simple, finding time in Hedges' schedule to visit a farm in the Nebraska countryside soon became a major task. Braxton Kittrell insisted on conducting preliminary screening interviews of area farmers and sent assistants to scout potential locations before setting a place for the president's on-site visit. Once that process got started, the Secret Service wanted to conduct background checks on all private citizens who might come into direct contact with him. After the initial planning was finally complete, Hedges selected three sites west of the city, but he was frustrated that an idea as simple as driving down the road to say hello to a farmer had now become a public relations event.

When the day for the trip finally arrived, three SUVs came to a stop at the curb outside President Hedges' duplex on General's Row. Minutes later, Hedges came from the building with Braxton Kittrell beside him. Cecil Zweifel, the economic adviser, trailed behind and all of them were shadowed by the Secret Service detail.

Hedges strode down the walkway toward the first SUV, glad to be free of the office and hopeful that he might finally find some answers to his lingering questions about agriculture and its importance to the country's economic future. As he reached the SUV, one of the agents opened the door and Hedges climbed into the seat behind the driver. Kittrell opened the door on the opposite side and ducked low to crawl inside. Before he was seated, Hedges stuck out his hand and wagged a finger. "Put Cecil up here with me. I need to pick his brain while we ride."

Kittrell climbed into the back seat while Zweifel got in next to Hedges. When they were in place, an agent closed the door. Ron Hanks, the driver, caught Hedges' eye in the rearview mirror. "Where to today, Mr. President?" he asked with a smile. Hedges and Braxton had been arguing about the trip for days. Their running sometimes-not-so-friendly banter became a source of amusement for the staff.

"I wanted to drive out in the country and stop at the first farm we find," Hedges groused in a less than playful tone. "But I'm sure Braxton already gave you a schedule with everything planned to the minute."

"Yes, Mr. President. I'm afraid he did." He put the car in gear and started forward.

"But thank you for trying." Hedges turned his head to one side and spoke over his shoulder. "I like this driver, Braxton. We need to keep him around in case I want to break out of the compound for a trip into town."

"Take us west, Ron," Kittrell called from the back. "Take this side-show west. And whatever you do, make sure you follow the schedule."

"It wasn't a sideshow when I first suggested it," Hedges countered. "It wasn't supposed to be planned and orchestrated like all those other events you get me into. It was supposed to be just Cecil and me visiting with a farmer."

"We manage events because image matters, Mr. President."

"I need information, not events." Hedges turned toward the front and gestured with a wave of his hand. "Pick up the pace, Ron. I can't sit here talking to him all day."

As they drove away from the base, Hedges picked up his conversation on the economy with Zweifel from where they left off several days before. They talked at length about farm policy, prices, and the ability of the market to apportion resources equitably, but by the time they turned onto County Road B near Valparaiso, west of Omaha, the conversation began to lag. Hedges glanced out the window and in the distance saw a two-story house sitting back from the road. Behind it was a large wooden barn. Metal buildings stood to the right and left and beyond them were three grain bins that towered in the sky. "Hey," Hedges called, pointing out the window. "This looks like a good place."

"Not on the list," Kittrell replied from the back seat.

"Not on the list?" Hedges did little to hide his frustration. "Why not?"

"We have an appointment, Mr. President." Kittrell took a paternal tone. "Just stick to the schedule."

Hedges slid forward on the seat and leaned over Ron's shoulder. "I'm the president of the United States. You work for me. Turn into the driveway at that house up there."

"Yes, Mr. President," Ron grinned. Gravel crunched beneath the tires as he made the turn from the pavement and rolled slowly up the driveway.

"We don't have time for this," Kittrell complained.

"That's your schedule," Hedges retorted. "Not mine." Kittrell closed his eyes and collapsed against the seat.

The SUV came to a stop alongside the house and Hedges stepped out. "Come on, Cecil," he called. "Let's find someone to talk to who hasn't been vetted and sanitized."

As they came from the SUV, the side door of the house opened and a man appeared. Dressed in blue jeans and a red work shirt, he was about six feet tall with broad shoulders and a muscular chest. His skin was tanned and weathered, and gray hair poked out beneath the edges of a green cap that sat atop his head. His boots were scuffed and unpolished and he walked toward them with an uneven gait, a scowl on his face. "Hey," he called. "I already told you not to come out here without calling first."

Quicker than he could react, Secret Service agents flanked him on either side, each with a hand on their sidearm. Hedges strode forward, determined to intervene and avoid a confrontation. "It's okay," he said, gesturing to the agents. "He's not going to do anything." The agents relaxed and Hedges looked over at the man who'd come from the house. "I'm sorry for the interruption, but whoever you thought we were—we're not them."

A puzzled frown wrinkled the man's forehead. He reached up with one hand and grasped the cap by the bill, adjusting it nervously. Then his face softened. "President Hedges?" he asked with a slack jaw.

"Yes," Hedges stuck out his hand. "I'm Jack Hedges."

"John Cannon," the man replied, still puzzled. "What are you doing here?"

"I was wondering if we could talk for a few minutes."

"Yes, sir," Cannon nodded slowly. "I reckon so. What did you want to talk about?"

"Farming."

Cannon gestured over his shoulder. "Maybe we should go inside."

"Actually, I'd rather have a look around. Mind if we walk and talk at the same time?"

"Sure," Cannon agreed. "What would you like to see?"

Hedges pointed toward the barn. "How long has that been here?"

"My grandfather built that barn. It's more than a hundred years old."

"That's a nice building."

"Yes, sir." They started in that direction and Cannon continued to talk. "We put in these other two buildings back here. The barn was built mostly for storing hay and raising cattle. We don't do much of that anymore and we needed space for the combines."

"What do you grow?"

"Corn mostly." Cannon pointed to a field in the distance. "That's soybeans over there beyond that fence, and behind it is some wheat, but not too much."

"I'd like to see it up close."

"It's a little far to walk all the way out there."

A pickup truck was parked nearby. Hedges pointed to it. "Is that your truck?"

"Yes, sir."

"Take me for a ride." Hedges opened the passenger door and turned toward the agents who were following them. "You men can ride in back if you want to. But not up front." He looked past them. "Come on, Cecil. Ride with us."

Zweifel hurried past the agents and crawled onto the seat of the truck. Hedges got in beside him and shut the door. Two agents climbed in back and they started from the barn with Cannon at the steering wheel.

Hedges leaned forward to see around Zweifel. "Did the blackout back east slow you down this year?"

"No, sir." Cannon drove the truck past the barn to a field road that was rough and uneven. "We've had all the electricity we need."

"What about everything else? Seed and fertilizer."

"Yes, sir. Our production capability has been pretty much unaffected by the blackout in the east. Most of the country's farming has always been west of the Mississippi River. But even Illinois and Indiana weren't affected much." Cannon glanced over at Hedges. "Is there something in particular you were trying to get at?"

"Well," Hedges began, gesturing toward Zweifel, "Cecil here tells me exports of farm products are rising and prices are high."

"Yes, sir. We're getting a good price for the wheat. Corn looks good right now. Just hope it'll hold up until the end of summer when we start harvesting."

"Could you do more?"

"More?"

"Yeah. Could you grow more, produce more?"

"He means," Zweifel explained, "are you operating at full capacity?"

"We're doing something every day from daylight to dark," Cannon answered. "But we could always hire another man and farm twice the acres we have right now."

"Then why don't you?"

"Only thing holding us back is the cost of fuel and fertilizer."

Hedges had a questioning look. "Getting the land's not a problem?"

"No, sir. We can get all the land we need. Good land. Top soil's three feet deep. It'll grow anything we ask it to."

"But you need fuel and fertilizer."

"Yes, sir," Cannon nodded. "That's about the size of it."

"If farmers in America had that, affordable fuel and fertilizer, could America be self-sustaining?"

"Self-sustaining? You mean grow enough to feed our own country?"

"Yes," Hedges nodded. "Think American farmers could still do that?"

"We're doing it," Cecil added. "We're exporting because we have excess capacity and there's a market for it overseas."

"Mr. President," Cannon continued, "if you can get us cheap fuel and cheap fertilizer, American farmers can feed the world."

By then they'd reached the soybean field. Cannon let the truck roll slowly along the fencerow. Hedges propped an elbow on the window ledge and looked out with a smile. "That's a beautiful field."

"Our crew does a good job keeping the rows clean. The plants do the rest."

"How much will that field produce?"

"We'll get about fifty-five to sixty bushels per acre."

Hedges glanced over at Zweifel. "Is this giving you a context for all those numbers you quoted to me?"

"Yes, sir," Zweifel nodded. "I've got a pretty good grasp of it."

"Me, too," Hedges looked over at Cannon. "If you can take us back to the house, I think we've found what we were looking for."

Cannon turned the truck around at the end of the field and started back in the same direction they'd come. In a few minutes they came to a stop by the SUVs still parked on the driveway. Hedges opened the door and stopped out. He came around the rear bumper of the truck and thrust out his hand once again. "Mr. Cannon, I appreciate your time."

"Glad to have you, Mr. President." They shook hands and Cannon gestured over his shoulder. "Sure you won't come in for a cup of coffee?"

"I'd love some coffee, but I need to get back to the office."

Kittrell stepped forward. "Mr. President, we still have those two stops to make."

"Not today, Braxton."

"But, sir—"

Hedges ignored him and turned toward the SUV. "Let's go. We need to get back to the office."

"We can't just ignore the appointments," Kittrell argued. "We've spent all this time arranging these visits and people are expecting to see you."

"That was your idea." Hedges leaned against the open door of the SUV. "This right here was what I wanted. And now that I've been here, I've seen what I needed to see and heard what I needed to hear."

"What does that mean?"

"It means I know what to do." Hedges slid onto the seat of the SUV.

Kittrell stood in the open door and continued. "Which is?"

"We're going to Washington."

"They're not ready for us yet."

"Tell them to get ready. We're going to the White House. I've got things to do and I can't do them from anywhere else but there." Hedges looked past Kittrell to a Secret Service agent. "Let's go." The agent closed the door. Zweifel was already seated on the other side. Hedges called up to the driver, "Ron, let's go home. I have some business to attend to."

17

ASHDOD, ISRAEL

SINCE THE DAY HE VISITED General Khoury in the detention center, Efraim Hofi had been unable to escape the words he heard. *"The Iranians are our enemy,"* Khoury had said, *"and that makes them an enemy of God."*

As a child he had heard every week in temple how—of all the people in the world—God chose to reveal himself to the Jews. Over and over again he heard the ancient stories of Abraham and Moses, Joshua and David, Elijah and Elisha. Moving, powerful stories of God at work in the history of their people. Of prophets foretelling the things to come, and living to see it happen. But that all seemed so long ago and as the years went by and he grew older, he'd come to wonder if any of it was real, much less whether it might happen again. Now, after seeing Khoury, he found one question inescapable. Could it be that in his lifetime he was seeing God actually at work in human events?

Night and day, Hofi wrestled with this question and no matter what he was doing, whether at work or at home, it was always on his mind. He read Torah and the prophets searching for an answer, but still the question remained. He read books by rabbis and books on prophecy by Christian authors, and still the matter was unresolved. Everyone seemed to agree that God had moved through events of the past, but no one could say whether events happening now had any connection to some greater plan He might be orchestrating.

All of this struck Hofi as strange—to ask such a question and search for the answer among ancient texts and religious writings. He was the director of Mossad, the nation's intelligence agency. His daily routine brought him cold, hard facts and brutally real circumstances. The world where he worked was filled with technology and armaments, secrets and threats no one should know. It was a place with little room for God and the unresolved mysteries of Man and of heaven.

And when he wasn't thinking of what Khoury said, he was remembering again the look in Khoury's eyes when he said, *"I was not crazy when I took control of that room, and I am not crazy now. You will see. God is fulfilling His prophecy. As the prophet Samuel said of David, 'He shall build a house for my name, and I will establish the throne of his kingdom forever.' God will bring it to pass."*

After days of preoccupation and nights buried in stacks of reading material, Hofi did what he was certain was an act of desperation. He called Mordecai Riskin, the rabbi he'd known for most of his life. Riskin agreed to see him in private. They met in an office off the sanctuary at Tiferet Yisrael synagogue on Herzl Street.

When he arrived, Hofi found Riskin seated at his desk. He rose as Hofi came through the door and, after a greeting, guided him to a sofa across the room. Hofi took a seat and Riskin settled into a chair across from him. "I was delighted when you called," he began. "It is always a pleasure to hear your voice."

"Thank you for agreeing to see me."

Riskin's forehead wrinkled in a questioning look. "You are well, Efraim?"

"Yes," Hofi nodded. "As well as can be expected. And you?"

"I am fine. Of course, it would be better to see more of you. We still have Sabbath services, you know."

"It has been a long time since I was at temple."

"Yes," Riskin nodded slowly. "It has been years."

"I know."

"But enough of that," Riskin said with a kindly smile. "Tell me, what is on your mind?"

"I've been wondering about prophecy lately."

"Oh?" Riskin arched an eyebrow. "Is this something from your work?"

"Not exactly. Sort of."

"I see."

"It's just, there was a situation and I had to talk to a friend about something he did. And he told me that if he hadn't done the thing he did, God would raise up someone else to do it for him. Like God was fulfilling ancient prophecy today in the events of our time. And I was wondering if that's true."

"You would have to tell me the facts for me to answer that particular question. And I am sure you cannot do that."

"No. I can't."

"Well, tell me this. Are you really wrestling with the notion of God at work in human history? Or are you wrestling with the notion of God at work in the life of Efraim Hofi?"

"I'm not sure I understand what you mean."

"Oh, I think you do. This person was a friend?"

"Yes. A good friend."

"I see from the look in your eyes he was more than just a friend."

"He saved my life once."

"From an accident?"

"No. We were in the IDF together. I was wounded and bleeding to death. He fought his way to me and kept me alive."

"Yes," Riskin nodded. "He is more than a friend. And when you talked to him, you saw a man who was convinced that God was working through his life. Right?"

"Yes."

"And that troubled you."

"Yes. It did. I thought he was crazy."

"Did it trouble you because you thought your friend was crazy? Or was it because you knew in your heart he was not crazy?"

"I never thought about it that way."

"I think your problem is much more personal than you've realized."

"Maybe so."

"But as to the question you asked, is God working in history? Of course He is. The fact that our nation exists is a testament to His work in human history. The fulfillment of His promise to Abraham. His promise to David."

"Those are stories from a long time ago."

"They aren't just stories. They were accounts of prophecies given and prophecies fulfilled."

"How do we know they were prophets?"

"Prophets always dealt with the truth. They spoke the truth as God showed it to them. And that is how a prophet was judged. If his words came to pass, he was seen as a prophet. If not, he was stoned for blasphemy."

"Are there any prophets now?"

"Most people believe the age of the prophet has passed, and that we are in the age of the rabbi. The teacher."

"That's good for you."

"Yes. I suppose so."

"Christians seem to talk about this more than we do."

"We talk about it a lot. You just aren't here to hear us when we speak."

"So, if the prophet's words come true, we know he is a prophet?"

"Yes," Riskin replied. "God always operates in the realm of truth, and the truth about any situation will always point us to God."

18

BERLIN, GERMANY

AS PREVIOUSLY ARRANGED, General Erhard arrived outside the Reichstag building a little before noon. Throngs of tourists, government officials, and members of parliament scurried about seemingly in every direction. Erhard, for his part, walked slowly to a stone bench on the far side of the plaza outside the building's main entrance. When he reached the bench, he dropped onto it as if settling onto the sofa in his living room, propped one arm along the top of the back, and wedged himself into the corner next to the armrest. The warm noonday sun made him drowsy and soon his chin bobbed against his chest. He kept shifting positions on the bench in an effort to remain awake.

A few minutes later, Gennady Panova approached. Dressed in a gray suit with white shirt and red tie, he looked as if he'd stepped from the pages of a fashion magazine. As he came near, he eased onto the bench next to Erhard and spoke without turning his head. "You brought the pictures?"

"Only if you brought the money," Erhard replied dryly.

Panova reached inside his jacket and took out a brown envelope, which he laid on the bench between them. Erhard thrust out his hand toward it but Panova blocked him with a forearm. "The pictures first," he insisted quietly.

Erhard took an envelope from his pocket and handed it to Panova. Panova opened it and glanced inside to see a dozen photographs.

"These are all from the same location as the one you gave me?"

"Yes," Erhard replied.

"You can't give me an electronic file?"

"You should be glad to get this much. No one else is offering you photographs of your arch enemy, are they?" He glanced in Panova's direction, as if awaiting a reply. When none came, he continued. "I am sure your analysts will find them interesting. You showed them the other one I gave you?"

"We transmitted it to them last night."

"Imagine that was painful," Erhard chuckled.

A puzzled expression appeared on Panova's face. "How so?"

"Going back to the office to transmit a reconnaissance photograph to Moscow," Panova explained, "when you could have been at the hotel with the blonde."

"Yes," Panova grinned. "That part was difficult to explain."

"Oh?" Erhard's eyes opened wide. "She was there when you returned?"

"Of course," Panova answered in a matter-of-fact tone. "Where else would she go?"

"A kept woman."

Panova ignored the comment and gestured with a roll of his wrist. "You do not wish to count your money?"

"I have seen it," Erhard smiled. "That is enough for me."

"What if I cheated you?"

"You would never do that."

Panova had a questioning look. "Why not?"

"Because I still have my phone with all those pictures inside." Erhard said, patting the chest pocket of his jacket. Then he leaned closer to Panova and lowered his voice. "And I still know how to find your wife."

19

CIA HEADQUARTERS
LANGLEY, VIRGINIA

TRAVELING TO WASHINGTON proved more difficult than Jenny and Hoag first imagined. When he called the office from the hotel room to schedule a flight, he learned that Jerry O'Connor, the analyst working on the China situation, had uncovered information that required immediate attention. Addressing it meant a return to Nebraska. They arrived that afternoon, hoping to make it a short stay, only to find the analysis section, which Hoag now directed, in disarray. Straightening that out took several days.

The lengthened stay meant their housing arrangements had to be changed right away rather than later. They had planned to combine their belongings into a new apartment, but had hoped to put that off until they returned from Washington. Instead, they were forced to do it now. Getting comfortable living together as husband and wife, surrounded by each other's belongings, quickly became a complex and challenging task.

Finally, after convincing Jerry O'Connor to take charge of day-to-day scheduling for the analysts, order was restored in the section, and the quality of their work product began to improve. Only then, after two weeks of delay, Hoag and Jenny boarded a CIA Gulfstream for the flight back east.

The jet landed in northern Virginia at Dulles International Airport, just west of the District of Columbia line and not far from CIA headquarters in Langley. With a car at their disposal, however, Hoag and Jenny decided to ride through the city rather than driving straight to the headquarters building. Both of them wanted to see how recovery was progressing.

Much to their surprise, they found the city coming back to life. Traffic lights were operational. Subway and commuter trains were functioning on most lines, and people were going to work, eating in restaurants, and getting back to their typical routines.

When they arrived at the CIA, Hoag and Jenny were cleared through building security, then made their way downstairs to the lower level of the basement. At the far end of the hall, they entered the Operations Control Center.

Like most government command centers, large video screens covered every square inch of available wall space. Across the room, workstations were arranged in successive arcs forming a semicircle around a central operator's station. Atop each desk were computer screens, keyboards, and phone sets. Bright young analysts busily pecked away at keyboards, headsets on, fingers flying over the keys. They all seemed to talk and chatter at the same time and the sound of it filled the room with an endless stream of conversation.

Near the operator's station stood Winston Smith, dressed in a blue blazer, khaki pants, and white shirt—just as Hoag remembered him. The collar of the shirt was open. His tie hung loosely against his chest. With his hands resting on his hips, he looked more like a basketball coach than a CIA control officer.

For a man of his rank and stature, Winston Smith was an oddity. Unlike most senior operations officers, he was not a graduate of an Ivy League school or a prestigious prep school, and his parents were not wealthy. Instead, he came to Langley from the University of Kentucky, where his proficiency in languages caught the attention of a professor with connections. Fluent in Spanish at the age of twelve, he taught himself French and German while enrolled in public high school. At the university he picked up Arabic, Chinese, and Hebrew. That language skill, along with good timing and dogged determination, propelled his career forward at a rapid pace. Now, more than twenty years later, he was supervising teams of fresh-faced analysts half his age and working on the agency's most intractable issues. He looked up as Hoag and Jenny entered the room.

"Hey, you two," Smith flashed a surprised smile. "Thought you were off on a honeymoon."

"Well, you know," Hoag shrugged, "you can only enjoy so much of a good thing."

Jenny elbowed him in the ribs. Smith leaned over and kissed her on the cheek. "If you need me to whack him in the head, just tell me."

"I will," she grinned.

Hoag spoke up, changing the subject. "What are you working today?"

"Got a little activity in Baku, Azerbaijan," Smith explained, turning to face the room, "and a meeting in Sochi, Russia."

"Related?"

"Yeah," Smith nodded quickly. "Looks like it."

"Baku," Hoag observed. "That's not far from the Iranian border."

"Got a source in Tehran claiming they don't know anything about it. We'll see," Smith had a knowing smile. "Lots of mid-level Russian diplomats in Baku, and high-level ones in Sochi." His eyes were alive with energy. "Looks like a two-step setup. Staff in one place. Major players in another. Decision makers isolated from too many distractions. I'd say they're up to something big."

"That's interesting."

"Yeah," Smith agreed, nodding again. "It's made everyone curious. We've spotted agents and operatives from every major intelligence network there. They even have—"

The door opened, interrupting them, and Dennis Kinlaw entered the room. Born and reared in North Carolina, Kinlaw had worked his way through Yale, earning a degree in Near Eastern History. That's where he and Hoag met. After graduation, they enrolled at Harvard Law School where they were roommates. During their final year at Harvard, they were recruited by the CIA and eventually sent overseas as field officers. They had worked together at every step of their careers until just a few months earlier when terrorists detonated a nuclear device above Washington, D.C. Damaging the electrical grid and forcing the president to move his offices to Nebraska. Since then, Hoag had been at Offutt Air Force Base while Kinlaw remained in Langley with Smith, rebuilding the analysis and operations sections at headquarters.

As Kinlaw entered the room, Hoag grabbed him in a bear hug. It was an instinctive reaction. Kinlaw was his friend and they had not seen each other in almost a year. But there in the command center, with everyone watching, Hoag's spontaneous display of emotion created an awkward moment and he felt Kinlaw instantly recoil from his embrace. Almost as quickly as he grabbed him, Hoag let go and patted Kinlaw on the shoulder. "So, how are you doing?" he smiled, taking a step back. "It's great to see you."

"I'm doing fine." Kinlaw gave Jenny a polite hug. "I would have come to the wedding if you'd told me sooner."

"I know," she nodded. "But we just wanted to be alone."

"Yeah," Kinlaw grinned. "I can understand that." He turned to Hoag. "So, what brings you here?"

"We wanted to try again to find the *Santiago*."

"Strange form of entertainment for your honeymoon. Didn't they make you a deputy director?"

There was a hint of tension in Kinlaw's voice, but Hoag let it pass. "Yeah," he said. "They did. You know. Same old story, though. Different title, more hours at the office."

"Yeah, but don't you have teams of analysts back in Nebraska for this kind of thing?"

"You know," Hoag shrugged evasively, "once you're in, you're in." He looked over at Smith. "Think we could use a desk?"

"Yeah," he nodded. "Jenny's old office is empty."

A few minutes later, they left the operations center and headed in that direction. When they were down the hall, Jenny turned to Hoag. "What was that between you and Dennis?"

"I don't know. He just didn't seem like himself."

"I think he missed you and doesn't know how to say it."

"I was wondering if he was jealous about the promotion."

"That hardly seems like him."

"I know, but he's never reacted to me like that before."

"He never spent a year away from you, either," she added.

"Well it's not like we haven't been talking on the phone. I mean, we Skype two or three times a week."

"Still," she smiled at him playfully. "I think that has something to do with it." Then she nudged him in the side. "You two are like a couple of old maids."

At the opposite end of the hall they came to a door with a biometric lock. Beyond it was the operations section where Jenny worked before the move to Nebraska. She slid her key card through the reader to activate the system, then placed her thumbs on the print panel and leaned forward to let the scanner check her retina. A moment later, the lock on the door clicked and she pulled it open. Hoag followed her inside as they made their way past rows of cubicles to the space she previously occupied.

"I don't think anyone has used this desk since I left." She pulled open a drawer and took out a hairbrush. "This is mine." She held it up for him to see. "I wondered what happened to it."

"Can you get on the system?"

"I'm sure I can." She closed the desk drawer and glanced over at him. "Are you that eager to get to work?"

He leaned forward and kissed her. "Not really," he kissed her again. "But that was the reason for coming out here."

"No," she smiled. "That was the excuse for coming out here, remember?"

"Yes," he grinned. "I remember. But we need to find that ship."

"Right," she agreed coolly. She turned aside and moved the chair away from the desk.

"What did I say?" Hoag protested.

"I was just enjoying the moment," she replied. "Excuse me for thinking you would, too."

"I did." He leaned over the desk and kissed her again. "And I'll show you how much tonight, when we're alone."

She plopped down on the chair and looked up at him with a playful pout. "Promise?"

"Yes."

"Where are we staying?"

"The agency has an apartment on—"

"No way," she interrupted. "I'm not spending the night in any apartment the agency owns. No telling how many monitoring devices they've installed."

"Okay," Hoag grinned. "We'll stay at a hotel." He backed away from the desk. "But for now, we need to get busy."

"Sure thing, boss," she groused. With a few strokes of the keyboard, she logged on to the system and glanced up at him once more. "Where would you like for me to begin?"

"Start looking for ships of a similar size and tonnage as the *Santiago*. Don't worry about the name of the ship or the flag it's flying. Just concentrate on similar physical descriptions."

"What are you going to do?"

"Find a desk and get busy, too."

20

TEHRAN, IRAN

A FEW DAYS AFTER KARROUBI RETURNED from Sochi, Maziyar Shokof, director of the Iranian Ministry of Intelligence and National Security (VEVAK), came to see him at Golestan Palace. They met at a shaded bench near the pistachio grove at the far side of the grounds. Karroubi preferred seeing disagreeable guests outside, rather than in the palace study. This was his favorite location for those meetings. Shokof was by far his least favorite person.

Shokof was born in Rafsanjan, a city in south central Iran, about halfway between Tehran and the Gulf of Oman. His father, Yadollah Shokof, was a *qadi*, an Islamic judge. By Islamic law and tradition, qadis were held to a strict ethical standard that prevented them from holding any business interests that might conflict with their public duties. Yadollah, however, disregarded that restriction and many others and, instead, engaged in profit-making ventures both large and small, using his position as judge to enhance his business interests, often at the expense of innocent individuals. With the money he made and the wealth he thereby accumulated, Yadollah provided a luxurious and opulent life for his family. Karroubi hated him for it and sat on the committee that recommended his execution.

Years later, when Kermani took office as president, he asked Karroubi for advice about filling appointments in his administration. The request was publicized as a necessary nod toward Karroubi's importance, but he knew what Kermani was really after. He wanted Karroubi's blessing for Shokof's appointment to his current post. Karroubi advised against it.

When he arrived at the palace for their meeting, Shokof was met by Karroubi's assistant, Hasan Dirbaz, who escorted him to the bench near the pistachio grove. Karroubi was already seated and waiting. Shokof came near and bowed.

"Asaluma alaykum."

Karroubi replied with the traditional response, "Wa alaikum assalam wa rahmatu Allah." He patted the bench beside him. "Come. Have a seat." When Shokof was seated, Karroubi looked over at him. "Your message said you wished to ask me a few questions."

"Yes. But I had expected we would meet in your office."

Karroubi was certain that meant Shokof was wearing a wire and he was glad he'd decided to meet him outside. The bench was located at a spot to one side of the palace grounds, but the neighboring property put it as far from the street as possible, making it more difficult for others to monitor the low-frequency transmissions emitted by monitoring devices. That way, Karroubi could enjoy a measure of privacy, and avoid the need for physically searching visitors upon their arrival.

"I prefer the outdoors," Karroubi smiled. "The heavens provide a far more pleasing roof than any ceiling ever could." His eyes bore in on Shokof. "What did you want to ask me?"

"One of our agents saw you in Sochi."

Karroubi's face gave no hint of emotion. "You were following me?"

"No, we were there on other business. But one of our agents saw you meeting with Mikhail Mirsky, the Russian foreign minister."

"And that is a problem?"

"You were with him in the bar, having drinks. Our agents were not prepared for such a meeting and could not hear the conversation. What did you discuss?"

"We're old friends," Karroubi replied calmly. "We talked about many things."

"Did you travel there to meet with him?"

"If I did, wouldn't you already know that?" Karroubi's words were delivered evenly but with just enough tension to make them bite. "I was there," he continued without waiting for a reply, "for a brief vacation.

Just to get away. Relax."

"And the Russian foreign minister just happened to be there," Shokof said sarcastically, "so the two of you had drinks together. Is that what I'm supposed to believe?"

"You may believe whatever you wish. That is precisely what happened."

Shokof seemed not to believe him but kept going. "Why was he there?"

"Why do you care and why did you have agents in Sochi?"

"We were following someone who works for the president of Azerbaijan."

Karroubi's eyes opened wider. "Tahir Shahat was there? I did not see him."

"I didn't say we were following Shahat," Shokof countered. "Only that we were following someone who works for him."

"We are spying on the Azerbaijanis now?"

"We are always interested in our neighbors."

Karroubi ran his hand over his chin. He wanted to simply end this conversation and walk away. If Mirsky was that important, Shokof should have found a way to intercept his conversations. The fact that he didn't meant that he couldn't. More to the point, it was yet another indication of just how incompetent Shokof really was. Any information Karroubi gave him would only bail him out of an apparently awkward situation. Still, Karroubi thought, there might be some advantage to helping him. "Mirsky told me," he explained finally, "that he was there to discuss renewal of Russia's trade agreement with Azerbaijan. I think they purposely engaged the staff in one location, Baku, while he and Jalil Qurbani met at a separate site, away from the others. That is my opinion. He did not say that directly."

"And you believed him?"

"I have no reason not to believe him. It seemed plausible to me. I saw him earlier with Qurbani, at the hotel in Sochi." Karroubi had a thin smile. "But I am sure you know all about their meeting if your men were there."

"We had a team in place." Shokof was defensive but not rude. "What did Mirsky say about his discussions with the Azerbaijanis?"

I was right, Karroubi thought, *he has no idea what happened at those meetings. This is why he came to see me. He is hoping to garner enough information from me to cover his mistake.*

Karroubi cleared his throat. "He said the talks were going quite well. Better than expected, I think. Thought they would conclude them earlier than expected and sign a new treaty as soon as the text is formalized."

They talked awhile longer, but at last Karroubi grew weary of the conversation. He rose from the bench and Shokof followed. Together they walked back to the palace and bid their good-byes from there.

When Shokof was gone, Karroubi entered the building and moved down the hall to his first-floor study. Hasan Dirbaz was waiting near the door when he arrived.

"I have an assignment for you," Karroubi continued toward his desk. Dirbaz followed him and waited while Karroubi took a seat. "Mikhail Mirsky was recently in Sochi, Russia. I was there and visited with him briefly. Unknown to me, VEVAK had a team following Mirsky. Find out who was on that team and why they were there."

"Individual names of agents on the team?"

"Yes," Karroubi nodded. "Agents, operatives, whatever they call them. Make certain no one knows that I am the one asking."

"Very well," Dirbaz said, then disappeared from the room.

Three days later, he returned with an answer. "VEVAK sent a team of ten men to Sochi. They were there to monitor Mirsky's contact with Qurbani, and to test the authenticity and integrity of information provided by an informant."

"What information?"

"No one would disclose the information or the informant's name."

"No one?"

"No one. Not without disclosing your identity."

"Hmmm," Karroubi sighed. "Anything else?"

"The agent in charge of the detail was Ruhollah Tabrizi."

21

BERLIN, GERMANY

JOSEF MUELLER SAT AT HIS DESK in the Chancellery office and stared across at Max Brody and General Erhard, who were seated before him. As head of Germany's central bank, Brody's cooperation was essential for all of Mueller's plans for Germany's role in the world. Erhard, as Mueller's primary military adviser, knew more than most just how far those plans went. Mueller caught Erhard's eye but gave no hint of what he was thinking.

"So," Brody concluded a mind-numbing review of European financial statistics, "I say all of that to say, there's trouble in Spain, perhaps also in France."

"What kind of trouble?"

"Economic trouble," Brody replied with a puzzled look. "That is why I gave you all that information."

"I heard you." Mueller rested his arms on the desktop and folded his hands together. "But what I'm asking you now is precisely what kind of problem does Spain face? Monetary, fiscal, fundamental? Which is it?"

"All of the above," Brody answered. "They have not followed sound fiscal or monetary policy. They have overspent and funded it with debt. Their central bank failed to keep the monetary consequences in check, and now they face both rising inflation and rising interest rates that are beyond their ability to curtail. And they face fundamental economic weakness across the board."

"A recession."

"A depression. And it may not be limited to Spain. We see signs that trouble may not be far off for France. Even our own position is weakening."

"How so?"

"We overestimated our ability to absorb the negative economic effects of the attack on the United States."

"In what way?"

"We assumed the US economy would collapse from the catastrophe and that the Treasury refinance date that followed shortly after the attack would destroy their international credibility. Neither of those occurred. Their economy took a severe hit from the consequences of the attack, but the permanent destruction was not as widespread as first indicated and much of the nation is well on the way to recovery. They handled their Treasury bond refinance internally and have emerged in much sounder fiscal condition than anyone could have predicted. The real economic weight of the attack has fallen on the Chinese."

"Due to the drop in US imports you were mentioning earlier?"

"Yes. A drastic drop in US demand for cheap manufactured goods is rapidly shrinking the Chinese economy. They are in serious decline, which is cascading across the globe with devastating effect on weaker economies."

"Can we help with Spain?"

"We have options."

"And not just financial options," Erhard added. "As you will recall, agreements that facilitated both the 2008 and the 2010 bailouts gave us broad powers to intercede both from a monetary perspective and a military one as well. Direct concessions from the affected countries—Greece, Spain, and Portugal, in particular—as well as concessions from the European Union as a whole gave us virtual control of the collective economies. We also gained the right to intervene militarily if necessary to protect the EU's economic interests."

"So," Mueller asked, "where are we?"

"The Spanish central bank wants money," Brody replied grimly.

"Do we have a request from their bank?"

"We have been in discussions with them."

"What about the president, Bayona? Has he filed a formal request for assistance?"

"No," Brody shook his head. "He has not asked, yet."

"But the country is on the verge of disintegration," Erhard interjected. "Riots are already a problem. If they continue to grow, Spain will need troops to maintain order."

"I don't know," Mueller mused, leaning back in his chair. "I think we should consider our options carefully. Perhaps wait a little longer. We don't want everyone to think that they can do as they please and when the consequences hit hard, come running to Germany for a handout."

"Accountability," Erhard smiled. "They must not forget accountability."

"Perhaps," Brody said with a look of concern. "But the longer we wait, the more likely we are to feel the effects of their situation in our own economy."

"We can weather this a little longer," Mueller dismissed Brody's worries. "We are not as weak as some might think."

The discussion continued awhile longer, then Mueller rose from behind his desk to escort them from the room. As Brody stepped outside to the hallway, Mueller took Erhard aside. "You were successful with our friend Gennady Panova?"

"Yes. Very much so."

"I'm sure you were," Mueller smiled knowingly. He patted Erhard on the shoulder. "I asked you to take a risk. The reward of that risk is yours."

"Thank you," Erhard beamed as he turned to join Brody in the hallway. "I would take a risk like that anytime."

When they were gone, Mueller sat alone at his desk, relishing the thought of Spain twisting helplessly in the economic wind. *I will leave them to dangle until just the right moment. Then I will act. And things will work out just as Bettinger predicted.* A grin spread across his face. *The first step in asserting control over the mighty EU beast.*

22

OFFUTT AIR FORCE BASE
OMAHA, NEBRASKA

AS WITH DAVID HOAG'S ATTEMPT to get back to CIA Headquarters, Jack Hedges ran into delays with his plan to return to Washington. First, the Secret Service was concerned his return might provoke another attack. When Hedges dismissed their worries as absurd, especially in light of the time that had passed since the first attack, they raised issues about the adequacy of tests conducted on White House security systems. But Hedges wasn't concerned about safety or security. All he could think about were the things he heard and saw during the visit to John Cannon's farm. That phrase, *"We could feed the world,"* kept playing over and over in his mind.

Agricultural production, Hedges was convinced, was the key to America's return from the brink of economic collapse, the path forward from the devastating effects of the attack. With just a little help, America could become the world's breadbasket. We could easily become grain merchant to the nations, he thought. And he knew precisely how to make that happen.

While he argued with his staff and security detail, Hedges met with William Nunnally, the secretary of agriculture. For the better part of two days they reviewed crop progress reports prepared by the National Agricultural Statistics Service and after hours spent working through that information, Hedges was convinced Cannon was right. American farmers really could feed the world, if only they found a source for cheap fertilizer and fuel. It was a realization that opened his eyes to a systemic problem for the American economy.

For decades, concern over pollution and global warming had driven government regulators to tighten the noose around the country's industrial base, requiring progressively cleaner emissions into the atmosphere and discharges into the rivers and streams. With each new requirement, the nation's economy took a hit, and the long arm of the federal government reached deeper and deeper into the heart of the American economy. For agribusiness, that meant tighter control of farmland runoff from crops and livestock, increasingly expensive fertilizers, and weaker versions of crop chemicals, all of which increased costs and reduced productivity. And it was a scenario repeated in almost every sector of the economy.

Hedges knew how to change that economic model. He knew how to set the economy free from constraint and let it run its own course. A course set by the market, rather than by the government. But to do that, he needed to convince key players to participate without resorting to more regulation, and without turning to Congress. *I can't force them to go along,* he kept thinking to himself. *For this to work, I have to lead them out.* And for that, he needed a change of location.

In the months following the terrorist attack, Hedges remained always the American president. Even with all that had happened no one questioned the legitimacy of his constitutional authority, or the decision to move the executive branch away from Washington. But in Nebraska, living and working within the confines of a heavily guarded air force base, he was a weak president. More a government official than charismatic leader and even then an official hiding in a bunker, cowering in the face of challenges while the rest of the nation bravely soldiered on through adversity and danger, or so it seemed to him. Power and authority could be conferred by a document, and he had both. What he needed was the aura and force of leadership, and for that he had to return to the traditional seat of presidential power—the White House—the one place that exuded the kind of presence he needed to turn things around.

Finally, after days of deliberation over endless details with the Secret Service and his own staff, Hedges decided it was time to act. He rose from behind his desk in the office on General's Row and walked out to Braxton Kittrell's office near what had been the front living room. He leaned through the doorway and said calmly, "Is the plane ready?"

Kittrell looked up with a puzzled frown. "The plane?"

"The airplane. Air Force One. Is it ready?"

"Yes, sir," Kittrell replied. "I suppose it is. Why do you ask?"

"We're flying to Washington."

Kittrell glanced down at the file on his desk. "When?" he asked, not bothering to look up.

"Now," Hedges answered.

Suddenly Kittrell was alert and focused. "Now? Why?"

"We're going back to the White House."

"Yes, Mr. President." Kittrell stood and came from behind his desk. "They're working on that. We have a few more—"

"No," Hedges said sharply, cutting him off. "We're going now, Braxton. Today."

"But we can't," Kittrell protested. "The White House isn't ready. They haven't finished testing the security system. No one knows for sure if all the electrical systems work."

"They can test it all they want. Just tell them to do it with me there."

"I would advise against it."

"I know," Hedges nodded. "You've been telling me that for days." He backed away from the door. "Bring a sleeping bag. We might be sleeping on the lawn."

Hedges turned aside and started toward the front door. Kittrell called after him, "Mr. President, are we going now?"

"I'm going next door to pack. I suggest you do the same, right after you tell them to have the plane ready." Hedges stopped and turned to face him. "And Braxton, if the plane isn't ready, I'm driving myself." He pushed open the door to step outside. "And call Mooney," he added over his shoulder. "Tell him I want him to fly back with us."

Kittrell hurried to the front door. "Mooney?"

"Yeah. Tell him to bring that report."

"What report?"

"He'll know." By then Hedges was at the entrance to the residence next door. "We talked about it the other night."

"What other night?"

"They came over for dinner. Tell him to bring it and meet me at the plane. Get moving." Then Hedges opened the door to the residence and disappeared inside.

"Mooney" was Bobby Mooney, the secretary of energy, and the report was the *Annual Energy Review*, a study produced by the Energy Department's Energy Information Administration. Later that afternoon, aboard Air Force One, Hedges and Mooney holed up in the president's suite and worked through data from the report on the nation's energy production and consumption.

Several hours later, the plane carrying Hedges and a sparse entourage touched down at Andrews Air Force Base. They came from the plane to a row of black SUVs waiting on the tarmac. An hour later, they arrived at the White House and Hedges stepped onto the drive at the entrance to the West Wing. It was an unceremonious occasion, no bands or dignitaries there to hail his return, and Hedges wasted little time gazing at the building or pausing to savor the moment. Instead, he moved quickly inside and made his way down the hall toward the Oval Office. Kittrell followed close behind.

For the most part, the office complex appeared unchanged. Lights were on, telephones appeared to be working, and computer monitors at each of the desks were up and running. But the building seemed unusually quiet and unusually empty. And then he realized the reason. Very few of the staff manned the desks. Senior aides and most of the essential office staff were all back in Nebraska.

As Hedges made his way down the hall, those few who remained rose from their desks and clapped. Some cheered loudly. Others wept openly. Touched by their devotion and kindness, Hedges paused to speak to each of them and lingered in the area longer than usual.

When he finally reached the Oval Office, Hedges glanced over at Kittrell. "We should see that they get some kind of recognition."

"For what? Greeting you on your arrival?"

"They stayed behind when the rest of us cut and ran."

"We didn't cut and run."

"Sure feels like it."

"We stood our ground, too. Just in a different location."

Hedges gestured toward the door. "Try selling that line to them. They know the truth. They saw us hightail it out of here at the first sign of trouble."

Kittrell closed the door and returned to stand near the desk. "All right," he had a matter of fact tone. "Is that what this is all about? You facing down your own feelings of inadequacy? Is that why we came back here in a rush?"

"No," Hedges retorted. "We came back here in a rush because that was the only way to get out of that prison you put me in." His face was red and he was shouting. "I can't live like that, Braxton. And I sure can't lead like that."

"What was it you wanted to do that couldn't be done from Nebraska?"

"I've been reading this." Hedges picked up the *Annual Energy Review* from the desk. "There's a lot of information in it about just how high our energy prices are right now, and exactly why. And I intend to do something about it."

"Gas prices are high. We got hit by terrorists with a nuclear bomb and gas prices are high," Kittrell argued. "There's not much more to say about it than that, and there certainly isn't anything we can do about it in the short term."

"Oh, there's plenty more to say about it," Hedges arched his eyebrows. "And there's way more we can do than sitting on our hands. We have enough energy to meet all our demands. Enough and more," Hedges continued. "We just need to shift our use from one kind to another in certain strategic sectors of the economy."

Kittrell took a deep breath and let it slowly escape, then lowered his voice. "So, what are you saying?"

"I'm saying our high fuel prices are due to the current political unrest, both here and elsewhere. Much of that has been caused by the fact that Germany now controls Iranian production and is diverting most of it to Europe and elsewhere. And because the world is waiting to see what effect that has on places like China, Russia, and South America. I'm not waiting. We're going to get the nation to a state of energy independence just as quickly as possible."

"That's part of our plan for a second term."

"No," Hedges wagged his finger. "We're doing it now. Before the end of the year."

Kittrell shook his head. "Can't be done."

"Well," Hedges insisted, "we're gonna show the world differently." He looked toward the office door. "Is there a secretary out there?" he called in a loud voice.

"No one's there," Kittrell pointed out dryly. "You left Mrs. McMahan in Nebraska."

"I know. But don't they have the desk manned?"

"Not if you aren't here."

"Well, I'm here now." Hedges came from behind the desk and started toward the door. "I'll get someone myself."

"We could just return to Nebraska where we belong."

Hedges wheeled around with a glare as cold as stone. "This is where we need to be. This place. This hour. This time. The country needs a leader, not a government in hiding on an air base. A leader. And if you don't want to be part of that, you can quit anytime." Then he turned away, jerked open the door, and stalked out to the staff secretarial pool.

A thin brunette with intelligent eyes looked up as he approached. When he stepped into the cubicle, she scooted back her chair and stood. "Mr. President, what can I get you?"

"A name."

"Yes, sir," she nodded. "Whose name do you need?"

"Yours."

"Oh." Her countenance dropped. "I'm Anna Lester."

"I apologize," Hedges continued. "You work for me even though you're assigned to the staff and I should know your name. But I don't. Or, I didn't until now. And I'm sorry."

"That's quite all right."

"I have a new assignment for you, Anna. Whatever you're working on you'll have to give it to someone else." He gestured with a wave of his hand. "I'm sure they won't mind picking it up for you."

"Yes, sir. What do you need?"

"I need a new secretary."

"Certainly. I'll call personnel and they'll send over some candidates. I'll just—"

"No," Hedges cut her off. "I don't want personnel. I want you."

Her mouth fell open. "Me?"

"Yes." He turned away from the cubicle and stepped toward the hall. "Come on, you're my secretary."

"Yes, sir." She followed after him. "But what about Mrs. McMahan?"

"I left her in Nebraska. Only hired her because my wife thought it was a good idea. Never really liked her." He glanced over his shoulder. "Mrs. McMahan, that is. I never really liked *her*. I like Mary, my wife, just fine."

"Yes, sir," Anna chuckled.

Hedges led her to a desk outside the door to the Oval Office. "This is it," he pointed. "You'll work in here now."

Anna hesitated at the end of the desk. "I'm not sure I'm right for this job."

"Ms. Lester, in another time and under other circumstances, you might be correct and I might agree with you. But right now, in this place, at this time, you're perfect. Have a seat." She moved around the end of the desk to the chair and sat down. "I'll contact personnel and tell them what we're doing. I'm sure there's a raise in it for you. You'll be working for a cranky guy. They ought to pay you the highest salary in the building, but for now that one's mine."

"Yes, sir."

"Now, here's your next assignment." She looked up expectantly. Hedges continued. "I need you to set up some meetings."

"With whom?"

"The CEOs of Chevron, Exxon, Royal Dutch Shell, and as many other oil companies as you can find."

"Now?"

"As soon as possible."

"That's a lot to coordinate and I've never done this before."

"Well then," Hedges smiled, "let's keep it simple. You get them on the phone and tell them we're meeting here at the White House in three days to decide whether they get to keep their companies and that it would be in their best interests to attend. It'll be a morning meeting. Set it for ten o'clock."

"Yes, sir. I'll get started right now."

"And when you finish that, set up the same meeting the following day with executives from all the major coal companies."

"Perhaps someone at the Department of Energy should get involved."

"No," he snapped. "Whatever you do, don't call over there. I don't want anyone to know about this except you and me. Understood?"

"Yes, Mr. President."

"And when you get the meetings set with the coal companies, do the same the next day with CEOs from all the major electrical companies."

"Just the CEOs? I suspect they travel with their staff."

"No staff. I want them to come alone. And I need them here quickly."

"Yes, sir."

23

BAKU, AZERBAIJAN

AFTER THEIR INITIAL ROUND of discussions on bilateral trade in Sochi, Mikhail Mirsky, the Russian foreign minister, met again with Jalil Qurbani, his Azerbaijani counterpart, to address the Russian request to locate troops in Azerbaijan. They gathered without staff members in a rambling French-style villa built by members of the Rothschild banking family during the oil boom of the 1800s. Located high in the hills overlooking the Caspian Sea, the villa was now owned by the Azerbaijani government and used as a retreat for state guests. Mirsky and Qurbani sat at a table in a room just off a first-floor parlor where they talked over coffee.

"Trade concessions are not a problem," Qurbani began. "You have been more than accommodating and the terms are very much in our favor."

"Then what is the delay?"

"Politics."

Mirsky frowned. "What do you mean?"

"It is bad politics to allow the Russian army here."

"We aren't coming here to take over."

"Yes, but as you are aware, appearances are more powerful than substance these days. The sight of Russian troops—large numbers of Russian troops—would bring back memories of the Soviet days, and that would not be good."

"That is merely public relations," Mirsky said with a dismissive tone. "It is nothing that cannot be handled."

"It is not that easy," Qurbani countered. "And it is far more than mere public relations. Our president faces strong opposition both in the National Assembly and in the coming elections. In such a highly charged partisan environment, something like this—simply granting permission for Russian troops to return to Azerbaijan—would be unthinkable."

Mirsky leaned forward. "Are you saying that President Shahat is refusing to accommodate our request?"

Qurbani's eyes danced. "I am saying Tahir Shahat cannot allow you this gratuitous concession."

Mirsky leaned back, a puzzled look on his face. He picked up his cup from the table and sipped from it as he attempted to decipher Qurbani's last statement. *Gratuitous concession.* Precise, well-chosen words. Was Qurbani suggesting they needed something more to close this portion of the deal?

After a moment, Mirsky set his cup aside and looked across the table. "We are not asking for a gratuitous concession. As you have already conceded, we've been more than generous in our trade proposals."

"This is not about trade," Qurbani replied. "This is about the military and that is quite a different matter."

"You realize," Mirsky countered with a smile, "we only want to conduct exercises, not occupy your country."

"Come now," Qurbani smirked, leaning back from the table, "we both know this isn't about military exercises."

Mirsky was surprised by the remark but he kept a straight face. "What do you think this is about?"

"China," Qurbani answered slowly. "Iran. The oil deposits that lie between here and the Gulf."

They know more than we realized, Mirsky thought. *But how much?*

"That's the craziest thing I've ever heard," Mirsky feigned an indignant response. "And I've heard a lot of crazy ideas on this trip."

"No," Qurbani shook his head. "The oil deal between Iran and Germany was crazy." He rested his hands in his lap. "How much is Kermani making off of that deal?"

"From what I understand, the Iranians are making—"

"No," Qurbani interrupted. "Not the Iranians. Kermani. How much is he making?"

A frown wrinkled Mirsky's brow. "You think he has a personal stake in their arrangement?"

"If Kermani made a deal like that," Qurbani continued thoughtfully, "risking confrontation with China and the wrath of the world, he must be making a fortune. Personally. At least enough to allow him to leave Iran and never come back. Because that is what he will have to do."

"I don't know about all that," Mirsky shrugged. He moved closer to the table. "Look, what is it going to take to get this done?"

"What will it take?"

"Yes. What would it take to make this deal politically palatable for President Shahat?"

Qurbani struck a contemplative pose and gazed into the middle distance, as if lost in thought. Then he said finally, "Ships. Ships... and airplanes. And not just any airplanes," Qurbani added. "We want fighter jets."

"Okay," Mirsky nodded slowly. "I think we can do something with that."

"But not just *any* jets. Those new Russian T-81s would make our people very comfortable."

"Now, *that* might be a problem."

"Oh?" Qurbani said with a playful lilt. "How so?" He seemed to be enjoying himself as he squeezed Mirsky for more and more items.

"The 81 employs our latest stealth technology. Things not even the Americans have thought of. I don't think Moscow would let them out of their control."

"Well, you'll have to explain it to them in a way that helps them understand the situation. And when you do, make sure they know we will need them to train our pilots and technicians to operate and maintain them."

"Assuming I could do that," Mirsky mused, "would we have an agreement?"

"With one more thing."

"What is that?"

"Your army leaves behind whatever it brings into our country."

"Whatever it brings?" Mirsky looked confused. "I'm not sure I understand what you mean. You want them to walk back home?"

"I mean all the surplus. Arms, ammunition, temporary housing, troop transports. Whatever extra they bring. If they don't use it, they leave it here."

"I'm not quite sure how that would work out," Mirsky demurred, "but okay. The things we don't need for the trip back home, we'll leave behind."

"And," Qurbani added, "you will prevent retaliation against us by Iran."

"Now, that I cannot do," Mirsky responded.

"Oh?"

"First of all, I'm not sure what you think they might retaliate about. But even if I knew, the Russian government has no way of preventing them from taking some future military action."

"But you do have the means to protect us."

"Yes," Mirsky nodded. "We have the means."

"And you will agree to do that."

"Yes. We'll agree to protect you."

"Good." Qurbani sat up straight in his chair. "Then I think we can reach an agreement."

24

CIA HEADQUARTERS LANGLEY, VIRGINIA

AS THE DAYS PASSED, Jenny and Hoag continued to work on locating the *Santiago*, but with records and video available from thousands of ports around the world, the task quickly proved overwhelming and far more complex than they had first imagined. With Winston Smith's help, they enlisted analysts and support staff from operations to assist in culling the data and information. Their effort quickly dominated every available cubicle in the basement.

At the same time, Hoag moved into an office upstairs from which he monitored events and activities taking place at the facility in Nebraska. Then one day, Hoag looked up to see Hoyt Moore standing in his office doorway.

"Director Moore! Surprised to see you here."

"As am I to see you. I thought this was going to be a short trip."

"I thought so too, but finding the *Santiago* has turned out to be a little more than we imagined."

"And who's running the analysts in Nebraska while you're out here?"

"I'm keeping tabs on them," Hoag assured. "And Jerry O'Connor is handling the day-to-day assignments."

"Yes," Moore nodded. "I know about that part of it."

"Is that a problem?"

"Well, not as long as the quality of the work product isn't suffering."

"I don't think it is."

"No," Moore agreed. "I don't either. O'Connor's a good man."

"He's an excellent man."

"In fact," Moore continued, "I'm thinking of giving him your job."

"Oh." Hoag shifted positions in the chair. "That doesn't sound good."

"You're not a supervisor, David." Moore came from the doorway and dropped onto a chair in front of Hoag's desk. "Budgets and work-load allocation aren't the things that interest you."

"Well," Hoag began defensively, "I admit they aren't my first choice, but I can learn."

"That would be a waste of good talent." Moore grinned. "Relax," he added with a wave of his hand. "I'm not firing you. And I'm really not even demoting you." He looked Hoag in the eye. "I'm thinking about something else."

"What's that?"

"Sending you back to Georgetown where you belong."

Hoag's face brightened. "Will they take me back?"

"Ha," Moore chortled. "They've been harassing me about you and Kinlaw since they got the electricity turned on."

"But I'd also like to see this *Santiago* thing through to a conclusion."

"You will," Moore said as he pushed himself up from the chair. "It'll take some time to work this out." He started toward the door. "So, don't tell O'Connor about it just yet."

"Yes, sir."

When Moore was gone, Hoag grabbed his jacket and hurried to the elevator. He rode down to the basement and went straight to Jenny. He found her seated at her desk, combing through yet one more set of ship records.

"You'll never guess what just happened," Hoag blurted.

She glanced at him with a distracted look. "Did you know they have records for every move of every ship? Not just from port to port but from berth to berth. If they move a ship across the harbor, they have a record of it. And in all of that, not one mention of the *Santiago* or anything like it."

"I know. It's frustrating. But listen ..."

"It's almost like someone—"

"Listen!" Hoag snapped. "I'm trying to tell you something."

"Okay," she said coolly. "But don't yell at me." She leaned against the armrest of her chair. "What is it?"

"Hoyt Moore is here."

Jenny frowned. "Is that a problem?"

"No. It's not a problem. But guess what he told me."

"I have no idea what you're talking about."

"He wants to send me back to Georgetown."

She sat up straight, her face flush with anger. "He's firing you?"

"No, no, no," Hoag tried to explain. "He found out we came back here to look for the ship and that I've been running the section long distance from here, so he said supervision was a waste of my talent."

"He's right about that," she sighed. "Did that hurt your feelings?"

"No," Hoag shook his head from side to side. "Not one bit. I hate it."

"I know."

"You know?"

"Yeah," she smiled. "You haven't been comfortable since he gave you that job."

"Georgetown has been after him to send me and Dennis back to our old positions. We'd be professors there again and consultants here."

"Will you still have tenure?"

"I don't know. We didn't get into the details. He's still working it out." Hoag grinned. "But we'd be back at Georgetown."

Jenny stared up at him with a satisfied look. "You haven't smiled like that in a long time."

"I know." He leaned over the desk and kissed her. "And I haven't felt like this about work in a long time, either." He turned to leave. "I'm going to tell Dennis."

"He might not be as excited as you are," she warned.

Hoag paused and turned back to face her. "What do you mean?"

Before Jenny could answer, someone called out from down the hall, "Hey! I think I found something!"

Hoag started in the direction of the voice. Jenny rose from her desk and followed as they moved toward a cubicle near the opposite wall. There they found Jimmy Coleman, a young analyst recently hired from

Centre College. He looked up as they appeared. "I think I've found the *Santiago*." He pointed to the monitor on his desk. "Only now it's called the *Vasco Nuñez*."

Hoag came behind him and looked over his shoulder at the picture on the screen. "You sure this is it?"

"It's a container ship of exactly the same size and weight."

"Where is it?"

"Tunis."

"Tell me about it."

"Flies a Liberian flag. Been to a number of places. Bangkok, Kuala Lumpur, Yangon."

"Yangon?" Hoag asked.

"A port in Myanmar."

"Those are all obscure places."

"And perfect locations to hide out if you think someone's looking for you."

Jenny stood near the doorway. "What makes you think it's the *Santiago*?"

"This ship is the exact size and configuration as the *Santiago*. That's how I found it. Then I traced it backward as far as Bangkok. Port records indicate it arrived there from Singapore. When I checked in Singapore, they have no record of a ship called *Vasco Nuñez*, either arriving or departing. But they do have records for a ship called the *Santiago* setting sail the exact same date as indicated on the *Vasco Nuñez* records when it arrived in Bangkok."

"That looks convincing," Hoag conceded, "but is there any way to prove for a fact that it's the *Santiago*?"

"Not without getting onboard and inspecting it."

"And it's in Tunis now?"

"Yes. Arrived about a week ago."

"Any departure date?"

"None scheduled. It's just sitting there."

"We need to get over there and take a look."

Kinlaw appeared in the hallway outside the cubicle. "Someone needs to go, but not you."

Before Hoag could respond, Smith arrived. "Go where?"

"Tunis," Kinlaw answered.

Hoag spoke up. "We think we've found the *Santiago*."

"Where?" Smith elbowed his way past Kinlaw and into the cubicle. "Let's see what you have."

Coleman pointed to the image on the monitor. "Best I can determine, that's the ship formerly known as the *Santiago*."

"What's it known as now?"

"*Vasco Nuñez*."

"Okay, someone needs to check it out." Smith glanced at Hoag. "But not you."

"Why not?"

"Because you're our boss now. This isn't a job for a deputy director."

"I'll go," Kinlaw volunteered.

"Maybe we should get a younger guy," Smith replied dryly. "Someone who's been to the field sometime in the last three or four years."

"Look, I was in this from the beginning," Hoag argued. "I want to see it to the end."

"I know," Smith grinned. "That's one of the things I like about you. You never quit. But if you go and get caught, it's an international incident. If an operative with no past gets caught, it's just some freelance corporate guy or a Greenpeace activist looking for trouble. You can't go."

"I was part of this from the beginning, too," Kinlaw offered. "Hoag and I found the first ship together. If he can't go, I'll go and finish it for us both."

"All right," Smith sighed. He looked over at Kinlaw. "You can leave tonight."

Kinlaw turned away from the cubicle and disappeared up the hallway. When he was gone, Hoag turned to Smith. "Why do I feel like you just took over this operation?"

"Because I did," Smith had a matter of fact tone. "That's my job. You're not an operative anymore. You're not an analyst, either. You're a deputy director, and the sooner you realize that the better off we'll all be."

"Well, that's about to—"

"Okay, everybody!" Jenny shouted. "We need to change our task." She moved up the hall to a spot from which the others could hear her.

"Coleman is sending all of you the latest information we have on a ship called the *Vasco Nuñez*. We think this may be the *Santiago*. I want all of you to stop whatever else you're doing and dig into this ship. We need to know everything about it. Coleman will brief you in the conference room in five minutes." She walked back to the cubicle and gestured to Coleman. "Get moving. They're waiting for you. Tell them what you know and get them started."

Coleman stood and came from behind the desk. "I've never done this before."

"I know," Jenny said. "But you're the one who knows the most, so you get to tell them."

While Coleman went to join the others, Smith slipped out to the hallway and made his way to the exit, leaving Hoag and Jenny alone in Coleman's cubicle. Hoag glanced at her. "You think we need all of them on this?"

"I think you need to keep quiet about the move to Georgetown and let Hoyt take care of it."

A smile spread across Hoag's face. "You did that just to keep me from telling Winston?"

"Just looking after you." She kissed him quickly on the lips. "And us."

25

DIMONA, ISRAEL

INSTEAD OF REPORTING IMMEDIATELY to the prime minister after his meeting with General Khoury, Hofi decided to expand the scope of his inquiry and include others who were present in the missile command center when Khoury tried to take over. To do that, he reviewed video footage from the incident and prepared a list of those who were present at the time.

The first person on Hofi's list was Yigal Ari, the man who wrested the pistol from Khoury's grip after Yosi Gavriel had been shot. Hofi talked to him in a detainee interview room at the air force base in Dimona. They sat across from each other at a small table, Ari with his hands resting on the tabletop, Hofi with a pen and note pad, ready to take notes.

"You were in the missile command center the day we were preparing to launch the missiles."

"Yes," Ari nodded.

"Describe what happened."

"Where should I begin?"

"Back up to the beginning. When you came on duty."

"Okay. I came on duty and reported to the data center. We had received an order directing us to include additional targets in the targeting package. They were already working on it before I arrived."

"What did that entail?"

"We have predetermined targeting packages, but none of them had these locations in it. And, they wanted the missiles to strike simultaneously at all locations, so we had to add coordinates and data for each of those new locations to the existing package. Which meant we had to first ascertain the locations, encode the data, and load it into the system."

"That sounds tedious."

"It was. And that's not the end of it. After it was all entered, we ran a printout from the program for the entire package and went through it by hand to make certain the coordinates in the guidance system were correct. When we got that straight, we then checked to see that the information in the guidance system was accepted by the target acquisition computer for each of the twelve missiles."

"You do that every time you prepare to launch? Even in a test?"

"Normally, we use one of the preselected target packages for tests," Ari explained. "We update those packages based on the latest intelligence, but never in a rush."

"This was a rush?"

"Yes. Very much so."

"What happened after that?"

"After I determined the information in the system was correct, I went to the launch control room."

"The missile command center?"

"Yes."

"Do you normally go there?"

"No. But this wasn't normal. I knew we were going to launch and I knew what we were going to hit. I wanted to be there when it happened."

"Who was in the room with you?"

"There were two weapons technicians monitoring the board, the instruments along one wall of the room. They provide data from each of the missiles. Yosi Gavriel was the launch commander that day. He was seated at one of the workstations."

"And General Khoury was there?"

"Yes. He was present but he was not directly involved with the launch procedure. He's not part of the regular staff."

"Was it unusual for him to be there?"

"Not under the circumstances. Under normal conditions he might observe an exercise. I've seen him in there on a number of occasions. But knowing what I did about what was about to happen, I didn't think it was unusual."

"You knew we were going to launch?"

"Yes. Like I said, I supervised the addition of extra targets for the package. I knew what was going to happen."

"Did anyone else in the room know?"

"As far as I am aware, the only people who knew were General Khoury, Gavriel, and me. Everyone else appeared to be conducting themselves according to their normal, daily routine."

"Okay. You loaded the targeting information and went into the room. What happened next?"

"Not long after I entered the control room, an alarm bell rang for the EAM."

"Emergency Action Memo."

"Right."

"Was it written?"

"No," Ari shook his head. "It's announced over the command center's intercom system. Everyone in the room heard it."

"It's always delivered that way?"

"Yes. So everyone can hear it. Nothing happens in secret there."

"What did it say?"

"The first part is an authentication code, a series of numbers and letters, which must match the code for that day in the written code book. We have a book on the desk, updated periodically. The authentication from the message has to match the code in the book."

"You have that in the room?"

"Yes. We all write down the code and compare it with each other, and then to the one in our book. If it checks out, we know we have an authentic message."

"And this one checked out."

"Yes."

"Then what?"

"Gavriel and one of the officers working with him unlocked the safe and took out an authentication card. It's about the size of a credit card with a series of letters written across the front. The letters on the card have to match the first letters of the code from the EAM."

"And these matched?"

"Yes. These matched. It's just another step in the safety process, to make sure nothing happens either in secret or inadvertently."

"Okay. The codes matched. Then what?"

"So, Gavriel handed the message, the EAM they had written down, to one of the technicians monitoring the electronic panel. He entered a series of letters and numbers from the second half of the code in the EAM."

"Now, wait," Hofi said, holding up his hand. "Let me ask this before you go on. The EAM isn't actually a written memo, it's announced. If I heard it, all I would hear is a series of numbers and letters?"

"Yes. That's correct," Ari answered. "The first part is the authentication code. The second part is the launch code to enter into the system. It corresponds to a code assigned to the targeting package already loaded in the system. The two have to match. Again, for safety. If you get past all the other checkpoints, you still must have a code that matches the code imbedded in the specific targeting software package that was already sent to the computers onboard the missiles."

"Okay." Hofi paused while he scribbled a note, then he looked up and nodded. "Go ahead. They entered the code ..."

"The technician entered the code, and the missiles began taking on fuel."

"Once the code was entered into the system, the system took over and the fueling process began?"

"Yes."

"How long would that take?"

"Thirty minutes."

Hofi frowned. "That's as quickly as we can respond?"

"These are not defensive weapons," Ari explained. "They are offensive weapons. Our missile defense system can respond instantly. The order is given, the process starts, but there's a built-in time gap in which the launch can still be aborted."

"So, you just waited?"

"Pretty much. With the code loaded in the system, Gavriel pressed a button to start the launch sequence, and then we waited. Spent most of our time staring at the countdown clock on the wall."

"And that was about thirty minutes?"

"Yes."

"Did anyone say anything during that time?"

"General Khoury said something." Ari's eyes darted to one side. "I don't remember exactly."

Hofi pressed the issue. "What did he say?"

"I told you," Ari's voice held a hint of anger. "I don't remember."

"But you know generally what it was about."

Ari sighed. "He said something about visiting the wrath of God on our enemies."

"How did that make you feel?"

"To tell you the truth, it made me feel good."

"Good?"

"Yes," Ari insisted. "Good."

"You realize millions of women and children would have died if that launch had actually occurred."

"And all the better," Ari was defiant. "Kill the men, you kill one generation. Kill the women and children, you wipe out many generations. Why should our children live in fear of their children if we can end it now?"

"If you felt this way, then why did you interfere to stop the launch?"

"We had an order."

"An order?"

"We had an order to launch, followed by a valid, authentic order to stand down. General Khoury was attempting to disobey a lawful, valid order. And then he killed someone in the process. If we don't follow orders, even when they are difficult, we are no better than our enemies."

26

REUTOV, RUSSIA

EARLY IN THE MORNING, Alexander Nevsky rolled out of bed and tiptoed to the bathroom. After washing his face and shaving, he came back to the bedroom and dressed. Milla was awake and peered out at him from beneath the covers, her eyes following his every move.

"We could leave," she said quietly.

"And where would we go?"

"The countryside. You could get a job in the east. On an oil rig."

"And we would be fugitives for the rest of our lives."

"But we would have a life."

He pulled the trouser legs down over the tops of his boots. "You will look after Elizaveta?"

"Of course I'll look after Elizaveta. Why do you ask such a thing?"

"I am going to the army now. Who knows when I will be back? I worry about these things."

"You are being placed on active duty. There is no war."

"But there is trouble. Always, there is trouble. They would not have called me up if something was not planned."

"Who knows what they think?"

He came to the side of the bed and leaned over, taking her in his arms. "I love you," he whispered.

"And I love you." Tears streamed down her face.

He held her there a moment and kissed her, then kissed her again.

Finally, he eased her back onto the bed and stepped away. "I must be going." He slipped on his coat and turned to the doorway.

"Wait," she called. "I almost forgot." She stood and opened a dresser drawer. "I want you to take this with you," she said, handing him a red scarf. "It will remind you of me."

"I do not need a scarf to remind me of you. But the scent of you will be one of my few pleasures." He picked up a backpack from the floor and stuffed the scarf inside it. As he did, he caught sight of a photograph of Elizaveta on top of the dresser. He held it in his hand and glanced at Milla. "May I?"

"Certainly," she nodded. He tucked it into the pack with the scarf and kissed her once more, then stepped out into the hallway. He paused at the door to Elizaveta's room and watched her for a moment, sleeping safe and sound in her bed. Then he tiptoed softly, leaned over carefully, and kissed her on the forehead.

Finally, and with a heavy heart, Nevsky plodded down the steps from their apartment to the sidewalk out front. From there he turned and headed up the street to the bus stop. An hour later, following the instructions in the letter he'd received, he arrived at an induction center in Moscow. Only men were present, no women, and no other members of his unit.

Nevsky found an empty chair in a meeting room down the hall and took a seat. While others gathered there chatted and talked among themselves, Nevsky sat quietly to one side and thought of home, the path his life had taken thus far, and why the army would want him on active duty.

Several hours later, a young officer appeared and directed the men outside. Three buses were parked at the curb and they were herded aboard in no particular order. Nevsky sat by a window near the front and waited while the others filed down the aisle past him to their seats. In a little while, the buses were loaded and began to inch forward through the tangled web of Moscow traffic. They crawled along slowly for the first several blocks, then the pace quickened and soon they were traveling at highway speed away from the city.

Late that afternoon, they drove through the entrance of a decommissioned air force base near Voronezh, a city located four hundred kilometers southeast of Moscow. The bus lumbered along the crumbling pavement of untraveled streets as they wound their way past empty and abandoned buildings.

Near the center of what once had been a sprawling modern complex, they came to a paved and lighted runway. When they reached it, the bus turned left and idled across the tarmac, then came to a halt outside a rusted, decaying hangar.

Moments later, the door near the driver opened and the same young officer appeared once more. "Off the bus!" he shouted. "Everyone fall out and form up in ranks."

Slowly, the men rose from their seats, shuffled up the aisle, and stepped down to the pavement. No one said a word as they moved away from the bus and assembled in ranks of fifteen soldiers each.

In a little while, a captain appeared. He strode to a spot equidistance from either end of the formation and spoke with a loud voice. "I am sure you are wondering why you have been selected for active duty at a time of apparent peace. I assure you, this is not an exercise. This mobilization will assist our great republic in facing the direst circumstances of her long and glorious history. Few men are privileged to live in such times, to have the opportunity and honor of serving their country in time of need. You should be pleased to give your service to her now." He pointed to the hangar behind them. "Inside this building you will find stockpiles of the basic goods of war. Tents, portable latrines, and mobile kitchens." He squared his shoulders and thrust out his chin. "They may seem like lowly objects to you, but I assure you, no man goes to the battlefield without using these essential items every day. And that is your assignment."

"Ah," someone groused. "We're in logistics."

"Say it like you mean it!" the captain shouted. "Logistics!" He said it with gusto, expecting them to repeat it the same way and when they did not he became indignant, shouting even louder. "LOGISTICS."

"Logistics," the men repeated weakly, in voices barely above normal conversation.

The captain stepped to the first man in line and without hesitating struck him with his fist, landing it squarely on the young man's chin. His knees buckled and he collapsed to the pavement as the captain roared, "Once more, like you mean it."

"LO-GISTICS!!!" they shouted in unison.

"Much better," the captain announced calmly. "For the next two weeks, you will train with these items and you will become proficient in using them and deploying them. You will familiarize yourselves with each detail of how they operate. And you will set them up and take them down until you can do it on your own with your eyes closed. Is that understood?"

"Yes, sir."

"Very well. Fall out and assemble inside."

As Nevsky wandered with the others toward the hangar, a man next to him spoke up. "This is crazy."

"That captain is crazy," someone else offered.

"Supply," another groused. "I'm not a logistics officer. I'm in communications."

"Me, too," Nevsky added.

"Why do they have us out here doing this? This is basic infantry stuff."

"I'm sure it's just another exercise."

"Do they really call up reservists for exercises?"

"But what if that's the exercise?" someone offered.

A skinny guy with a pale complexion laughed out loud. "An exercise in being called up for an exercise?"

An older man spoke up. "I heard this is serious."

"Yeah?" someone chided. "How serious?"

Before the older man could answer, someone else chimed in, "It's always serious with the army. Did you see how much that captain was into this stuff?"

"Sorokin is his name," someone offered. "Captain Sorokin."

"It's more like Captain Latrine or something," another suggested.

"Ha," they all laughed. "Captain Latrine."

The others continued talking and laughing as they moved on toward the hangar, but Nevsky lingered behind and walked with the older man who'd spoken up earlier. "So, where do you think we're going?"

"I have a friend who's stationed at a base in Ukraine. He says we're going to Azerbaijan."

"Azerbaijan?" Nevsky frowned. "Why would we go back there?"

"I don't know," the man shrugged. "But that's what he says."

"Besides not liking the place, it does lack one essential thing for a military deployment."

"What's that?"

"Trouble," Nevsky said with a smile. "There's no trouble there."

"Not now."

"What does that mean?"

"Who knows what's in the works."

"One thing is for certain. The Azerbaijanis would never ask us to come back, not after working so hard to get us out."

"Maybe they didn't ask. Maybe they aren't being given that option."

"Well, I know where I would like to be going," Nevsky added.

"Where?"

"Home."

27

THE WHITE HOUSE
WASHINGTON, D.C.

PRESIDENT HEDGES SAT AT HIS DESK in the Oval Office and stared across the room at the men gathering there before him. Dressed in the finest suits available, most of them handcrafted, they filled the room, one by one, as Anna Lester ushered them to the chairs that had been arranged for the gathering. CEOs of the nation's largest oil companies, all of them male, all of them titans of an industry that held the keys to the country's future, keys Hedges was determined to wrest from their grasp.

Historically speaking, the American oil industry was long the domain of a limited group of companies known as the Seven Sisters—Anglo-Persian Oil Company, Gulf, Standard Oil of California, Texaco, Shell, Standard Oil of New Jersey, and Standard Oil of New York. Following decades of mergers and consolidation, that group was now down to just three—ExxonMobil, ConocoPhillips, and Chevron. Hedges invited CEOs of mid-majors to the Oval Office meeting, but in reality, he only needed the cooperation of the three largest companies to effect his goal without resorting to force.

In a typical meeting with influential executives, he would move to an armchair near the center of the room. They would sit on the two sofas that normally occupied the space directly opposite the desk. The meeting would begin over coffee while they chatted about nothing at all, then turned to more serious matters after everyone was relaxed and egos had been sufficiently stroked. But this time, Hedges omitted coffee and pushed the sofas against the wall, brought in additional chairs and arranged them in successive arcs that spanned the room, each one carefully planned to seat key officials in strategic locations. And while they filed into the room, he sat quietly behind the desk, waiting as they took their seats.

When everyone was present, Hedges scooted closer to the desk and began. "I called you here today because I want the price of gasoline, diesel fuel, and chemicals—particularly fertilizer and farm chemicals—to fall immediately and I don't mean by just a few cents. I want prices at or below pre-1980 prices by the end of the year." He delivered the statement with a straight face and let his eyes bore in on them while he awaited a response.

"Ha," someone laughed from the back of the room. "That's funny."

Others joined in, scoffing at the suggestion. "Like that could ever be done."

"Nice try, Mr. President."

"Never happen."

John Daniels, president of Chevron, was seated on the front row. "Mr. President," he said courteously. "That is not possible. I mean, even if we wanted to do it, we couldn't. The market simply doesn't permit it."

Hedges was unmoved by the derisive response he received. "John," he said evenly, "this *can* be done and it *will* be done. The times require it. The nation requires it."

Milton Allen, seated next to Daniels, spoke up. "Mr. President, I think what John is getting at is this: Oil sells on a global market. The price is set by worldwide supply and demand."

"I know that," Hedges nodded. "That's how it's been in the past, but not anymore."

The room was now silent as the exchange up front continued. "What do you mean?" Allen asked.

"I mean," Hedges continued, "from right now going forward, oil produced from leases within the borders of the United States and its territories will be sold only in the United States."

"That's illegal," someone called.

Hedges looked up in the general direction of the voice. "It's not illegal if you do it by agreement."

Dudley Jackson, the man who'd spoken out, stood up. "Mr. President, if we could sell our oil on the world market at a higher price, why would we agree to something as ridiculous as what you're suggesting?"

"Because the nation needs it," Hedges answered solemnly.

"Where was the nation when we invested in those leases?" Jackson argued. "Where was it when we drilled countless dry holes? Did our nation step forward to help pay the expense for that?"

"Listen, we have to do this. And we're going to do this. Now, I'll waive environmental rules on drilling, refinery operations, and new refinery construction."

Billy Glover, from ConocoPhillips, shifted and caught Hedges' eye. "You'll waive the environmental impact statements and studies on all of that?"

"Yes. I'll approve whatever it takes to get mothballed refineries currently in existence back online, and I'll approve construction of any you want to build. You can drill wherever you can get permission from the landowner or leaseholder. We'll open up federal lands that have heretofore been closed and you can bid on the leases there so long as you drill the wells immediately upon award." He looked out at them once more. "We are going to achieve energy independence and we're going to do it by the end of the year, if not sooner."

"Mr. President," Daniels spoke up again, "we still have one major problem."

"What's that?"

"Even if we do all that you say, based on the geological information now available, we don't have enough oil in the ground to do it."

"We do," Hedges argued, "if we shift non-transportation energy consumption away from petroleum-based products into other types of fuel. The facts and figures are in the latest energy report. We have enough energy. We just have to change the way we use it."

"You mean use coal and natural gas?"

"Among other things."

"I don't like it," Simpson Carter called out from the second row. "It just sounds like a federal takeover of the industry."

"You don't have to like it," Hedges replied. "You just have to make it happen."

"Now, that sounds like a threat," Carter retorted.

"No." Hedges shook his head. "It's not a threat. It's a promise."

"Of what?"

"Unless you want to be out of a job," Hedges said sternly, "I suggest you stop talking and get busy making it happen."

"Out of a job?" Now Carter was angry. "What are you talking about?"

"Under martial law," Hedges explained, "I have the authority to nationalize your entire industry."

"We aren't under martial law."

Hedges opened a desk drawer, took out a blue folder, and turned back the cover to reveal a memo, neatly typed and prepared on White House stationery. "We are in the midst of a national emergency, gentlemen. The agriculture sector can lead us away from an economic abyss, but they need cheap energy and cheap fertilizer to do it. We can get it with you, or without you." He took a pen from the inside pocket of his jacket. "What's it going to be?"

Carter was on the verge of losing control. "I never heard of such a thing! You can't possibly think—"

Daniels turned in his seat and raised his hand, interrupting Carter. "Hold on for a minute, Simpson. Just have a seat and hold on." Then he turned back to face the desk. "Before we get to the ultimate question, what about ethanol?"

"What about it?"

"We're required by law to add it to our gasoline products. Assuming we went along with the idea of limiting sales of US products solely to the United States, we still can't control the cost of ethanol."

"And emissions standards for gasoline generally," Allen added. "Our refined products have to meet federal standards."

"And some state regulations as well," Glover added. "Our stations in California require different components from the rest of the country. That adds cost, too, and requires special runs in our refineries."

"We're scrapping ethanol," Hedges announced flatly. "We'll end it today if you guys agree to what I'm proposing."

Carter slowly settled onto his chair. "Scrapping it?"

"Ending it."

"What about the farmers?" Daniels asked. "Ending that program will destroy the price of grain."

"They'll trade it for cheaper fuel and chemicals. Farm prices are rising. Global demand is rising. The world has a shortage of grain. We have a surplus and we haven't even begun to push our productivity capacity yet."

"But we still have the problem of emissions standards," Carter noted.

"I'll waive that," Hedges replied.

"Now, wait a minute," Glover was grinning from ear to ear. "You'll end the ethanol program, give us carte blanche on drilling and refining, *and* you'll waive emissions standards?"

"You'll have to continue making unleaded products," Hedges responded. "You can't go back to using lead, but I can make the emissions standards vanish with the stroke of a pen. Right now." He opened the desk drawer again and took out another blue folder. "Do we have an agreement?"

They looked at each other a moment and started nodding. Then Daniels stood and addressed the room. "Gentlemen, I know many of you aren't accustomed to being addressed this frankly, but I think it's true. Our nation is in crisis. What President Hedges is proposing only applies to US operations. You can make and sell as much product overseas as you like, at any price you like." He paused and glanced back at Hedges. "That's correct, isn't it?"

"Yes," Hedges nodded. "As long as it doesn't come from US leases."

"So, speaking for our company, we're onboard. I'm not sure how we'll sell it to the directors, but so long as I can get them to agree, I'm in favor of this. I don't know how this will work out in terms of profit and loss, but I'm onboard."

"Yes," Allen agreed. "We're in."

"As are we," Glover said, standing. "Let's have a show of hands to make it official." He raised his hand and waited while those in the room lifted theirs, and then he turned to Hedges. "Mr. President, I believe we're unanimous."

Hedges suppressed the urge to smile as he opened the blue folder that held an executive order waiving emissions standards and temporarily halting the requirement to use ethanol in automobile gasoline. He signed the order with a flourish, then looked up at those in the room. "Just make sure the price drops quickly."

28

BEIJING, CHINA

MING SHAO CAME FROM HIS PRIVATE RESIDENCE in the Zhongnanhai compound and walked down the corridor toward a conference room in the office annex. Located near the Forbidden City, the compound was composed of six residences arranged around a man-made lake. Most of the structures were completed before the year 1500, when the site was first constructed as an imperial garden. More recently, two modern office buildings were added when the area became the official state residence for China's most important leaders.

Awaiting Ming in the conference room was the Central Military Commission, an inter-service working group comprised of leaders from the major branches of the Chinese military, along with the civilian Minister of National Defense and the chief of Foreign Intelligence. Together, they were charged with executing China's military policy.

A contentious collection of egos, during his tenure as president and party chairman Ming had made the Commission both his collaborator, when situations posed difficult political choices, and his servant, when an easy and decisive victory seemed at hand. Thus, he shifted all the blame for failure onto the Commission, while reserving for himself sole credit for their successes. Playing one side against the other, for his own benefit, was a skill Ming had honed and perfected over years of public and party service.

Ming became active in Chinese politics following graduation from Beijing University. He rose quickly through the ranks, becoming party secretary for Guizhou Province and later regional secretary for the Tibet autonomous region. After two years in Tibet, he was elected vice president and, following the death of Jiang Biwu, was confirmed as president by the National People's Congress and elevated to the position of general secretary of the Communist Party. Holding both positions solidified his control over the government, but it had required years of hard work and cunning deception, an effort that left him exhausted. Maintaining his grip on power required constant vigilance against possible intrigue. Many around him who posed as friends and allies desired his position. Some of them would take any risk to wrest it from him.

As Ming entered the conference room, he found Commission members gathered around an ornate conference table that occupied the center of the room. Made of teak and mahogany, it had been a gift from peasant farmers to Dong Zhuo, third emperor of the Han Dynasty. Prior presidents used it for a dining table, but when Ming came to office he had it placed in the conference room.

Assembled that day were Hu Chang, commander of the People's Liberation Army; Quan Ji, chief of Foreign Intelligence; Li Chengfei, commander of the Second Artillery, China's strategic missile arsenal; Admiral Xian Linyao, commander of the navy; and Jin Ping, the Minister of National Defense. They stood as Ming entered the room and waited while he took a seat at the head of the table. When he was in place, they sat and Ming began.

"I called you here today to review our troop buildup along the Afghan border and our readiness for the pending invasion of the Middle East. Before we get to that, I would like to know where we are on our oil reserves." Ming looked down the table to Jin Ping. "Do you have the latest figures on that?"

"According to available data, our strategic reserve remains untouched, which gives us a four-week cushion at current consumption levels. But excess supply in the system is dwindling faster than expected. We estimate no more than a six-month window before rationing will be required."

"Six months," Ming frowned. "Let us hope that is long enough."

He turned to Hu Chang, commander of the People's Liberation Army. "Where are we on troop preparation?"

"We have two hundred thousand men at or near the border. All of them put in place without detection," he added proudly.

"How did we achieve that?"

"We reverted to tactics used by the honorable chairman Mao Zedong. Out of love and devotion to their country, they have eschewed modern conveniences and live in caves and huts. They walk instead of ride. And they are dispersed over a larger area than we first planned."

"Still," Linyao spoke up, "they must be visible when they assemble to train and drill."

"Ah," Chang grinned, "they conduct most of their training at night."

"And you have no tents?" Linyao pressed. "I thought you were constructing villages of tents."

"We scrapped the tent cities idea and only have a few near the border that we use for command centers. For the patrols." Chang turned back to address Ming. "And we are using very few trucks or mechanized equipment in order to keep our presence small, so as not to draw attention to ourselves."

"Very good," Ming nodded, turning to Quan Ji, chief of Foreign Intelligence. "Are you able to confirm that the Americans do not suspect our presence?"

"As far as we can tell," Quan replied, "they know nothing of our presence." He glanced in Chang's direction. "But your operations must change soon to stay on schedule, mustn't they?"

"Yes," Chang nodded. "We will need trucks and equipment in order to be fully ready."

Ming pressed his point with Quan Ji. "And you are certain the Americans have not discovered us yet?"

"There is no indication the Americans know of our presence," Quan reiterated. "But there is chatter from our sources suggesting the Russians are preparing to move large numbers of troops into Azerbaijan, supposedly with the permission of the Azerbaijani government."

"Any indication why they would do this?"

"Rumors indicate they are being located there for the purpose of invading Iran."

Others at the table murmured in response. Ming raised his hand in a gesture for silence and the room became quiet. His eyes bore in on Quan with a troubled look. "You heard news that the Russians were gathering for an invasion of Iran, and you did not think to alert us?"

"They are rumors, Mr. President," Quan answered defensively. "We hear rumors all the time about many things."

"Have you undertaken to ascertain whether these rumors are true?"

"We are doing that now."

"I should like to have known this as well," Chang added, doing little to hide his growing anger. "If my troops are to face the Russian army, I would like to know it *before* we reach the Iranian border."

"I am concerned the Russians know what we are doing," Linyao offered.

"How could they?" Quan questioned. "I do not think it possible."

"You must find out precisely how much they know," Ming said.

"If they know what we are doing," Chengfei interjected, turning to face Quan, "we must consider the possibility that you have a spy somewhere in your agency."

"You should have thought of that ahead of time," Linyao added, "and been diligent to see that it didn't happen. Then you would know if these rumors are true."

"I will find out," Quan snapped. "I will find out if they are true."

"See that you do," Ming commanded tersely." Then he turned to Chang. "You will notify me when you must move the mechanized equipment to the front?"

"Yes," Chang nodded. "Of course."

"Do not do so until I approve."

"Certainly. We will notify you when the time arrives and await your order before moving."

The meeting continued as Chang reviewed plans for moving troops through Afghanistan to the Iranian border. Several questions were raised about the timetable but everyone seemed satisfied with the progress they had made thus far. When the meeting ended, Quan lingered behind as the others left the room. Finally, he was alone with Ming. "I did not like the way you treated me just now. You knew about the Russian rumors. We discussed them three weeks ago."

"I know, but when you mentioned them in the meeting, I could not protect you without appearing to undermine the authority of the Commission."

"You would destroy my credibility to maintain yours?"

"If I had protected you," Ming snarled, "they would direct their anger toward me. I am president and secretary of the party. I will not be made to appear weak. In the future, if you do not wish to have your conduct reviewed by the Commission, do not bring it up. Keep your private briefings private. I was appalled that you mentioned it in the first place. Were you *trying* to make me look weak?"

"You asked me about our sources. Just now. In the meeting. You asked. I thought you wanted me to tell."

Ming frowned at the suggestion and shook his head from side to side. Quan had stumbled upon the truth—Ming wanted Quan to reveal the Russian rumors so he could humiliate Quan before the group. Quan had been much too assertive since the troop buildup began. Ming was determined to keep the intelligence community under control, but he was not about to admit that now. "In the future," Ming ordered coldly, "if I ask you questions in the Commission meeting, you should assume I am not asking about the contents of your private briefings. Understood?"

"Yes, Mr. President," Quan bowed. "I understand."

29

THE WHITE HOUSE
WASHINGTON, D.C.

LATE IN THE EVENING, President Hedges walked up the hall to
Kittrell's office. Kittrell was seated at his desk, hunched over a file.
He pushed back his chair to stand as Hedges entered the room.

"Keep your seat, Braxton," Hedges instructed with a wave of his
hand. He flopped onto a chair near the desk and crossed his legs.
"Think our friends in the oil industry will keep their promise?"

"We'll give them no choice, sir," Kittrell replied.

"You didn't like my idea before. Are you onboard now?"

Kittrell pushed aside the file that lay on his desk and leaned
back, his arms folded behind his head. "I said what I thought about
it, but you are the president. I serve at your pleasure. Whatever you
say is what we will do."

"Yeah. Well, somehow we seem to be doing less and less of what
I want to do and more and more of what everyone else thinks is
right."

"Is that what this is about? You asserting yourself as president?"

"No, Braxton. It's about saving the country."

"Well, then, I gave you my counsel only in an effort to assist you
in making that decision, but the decision is yours. After that, it's my
job to bring the executive branch into line behind you."

Hedges rested his hands in his lap. "You still sound a little miffed at the whole idea."

"I'm coming around," Kittrell smiled. He moved his hands from behind his head and leaned forward, propping his elbows on the desktop. "If this works, and we can actually bring down the cost of energy, while thriving solely on energy produced from within our borders, you'll go down as one of the greatest leaders in the history of the republic."

"And if not?"

"You'll be the guy who presided over the demise of the republic."

"Thanks for the encouragement," Hedges quipped.

"You're welcome," Kittrell smiled.

"If we don't do something, we'll be bankrupt by the end of the year. We can't keep refinancing our debt eternally. People will only take worthless paper for so long."

"I wouldn't go that far," Kittrell grimaced. "It's not totally worthless. It still has the backing of the finest military in the world."

"And we could be the world's strongest economy, in spite of what Mueller and the Germans think. But we still have to get the electric companies to agree."

"They'll come around."

Kittrell glanced down at the file on his desk and turned a page. A television sat at eye level on a shelf in the bookcase across the room. News reports played constantly throughout the day, though Kittrell kept the sound muted. Hedges pointed to the images on the screen of demonstrators clashing with police. A caption at the bottom of the screen indicated the news report was from Madrid, Spain. "What do we know about this?" Hedges asked.

Kittrell looked up. "Riots in Madrid? They've been going on all day."

"Yeah," Hedges nodded. "I know. They told me about it this morning in the briefing. What's going on?"

"The Spanish banking system is about to collapse."

"From what?"

"Well," Kittrell began, leaning away from the desk once more. "It's mostly more of what Zweifel was talking to you about a few weeks ago. Our weak demand and shift to internal consumption put a strain on the Chinese economy. Forced them to cash out many of their investment holdings to pump up their own economy and cover the loss they incurred from not selling manufactured goods to us. That, in turn, had a negative effect on banks everywhere, which caught Spain at a vulnerable time. The Spanish economy was weak to begin with and their housing market was overextended. This just made things worse."

"Sounds like us in 2008."

"Except that they never had that strong of an economy to begin with."

"Germany should fix it," Hedges said.

"Sources indicate the president of Spain is mulling over a trip to Berlin now."

"Germany should have fixed it sooner."

"Maybe so."

"They're the only country in Europe strong enough to do something about it."

Kittrell nodded. "Which is ironic, isn't it?"

Hedges had a questioning look. "What do you mean?"

"The way Europe turns to Germany for help now. First the Greeks, then the Italians. Now apparently the Spanish. Not too long ago, we were all trying to destroy Germany in World War II."

"Not so much the Italians," Hedges sighed, "but that was a different generation. This one doesn't even remember the Nazis, let alone understand what they did—or why. And it's probably just as well, I suppose."

Kittrell looked stricken. "Mr. President, you can say that to me, in here, with the door closed, but you can't let a comment like that get out of this building."

"Relax," Hedges waved with a dismissive gesture. "I just mean if they remembered the Nazis and what Germany tried to do to Europe in 1939, they might be reluctant to seek help from them. And they have nowhere else to go. If Germany doesn't help them, they're sunk. So it's just as well they don't remember."

"Maybe so," Kittrell cautioned, "but don't mention the Nazis in public."

30

BEIJING, CHINA

AT NOON, PAVEL MANAROV came from the Russian embassy and walked up the street. Listed on the roster as a business liaison officer for the Foreign Ministry, he was, in fact, an officer with the SVR, the Russian Foreign Intelligence Service.

Several blocks from the embassy, Manarov came to a busy street intersection. An apartment building stood on the opposite corner, diagonally from his position. Like a scene from a cheap spy movie, he lingered there as if waiting for the bus, but all the while his eyes moved up the wall of the building, counting the floors as he went. At the fifth floor, he counted over to the third window from the end. The window shade was up and the curtains were tied back, exposing the window to a full view from the street. On the ledge was a clay flowerpot, positioned in the center.

When he saw the flowerpot, Manarov turned away from the corner, crossed over, and continued up the street. Three blocks later, he came to a park with a lush green lawn and towering trees. A walkway led from the street and he followed it until he came to a fountain surrounded by a large paved plaza. A bench stood to the right. He took a seat on it at one end, leaned to one side in a restful pose, and waited.

In a few minutes, Chen Hongsheng appeared from the far side of the plaza, carrying in one hand a white paper bag with a brightly colored logo on the front, and in the other a soft drink. When he was closer, Manarov saw the bag was from a McDonald's restaurant.

Hongsheng continued across the plaza, nonchalantly avoiding eye contact with Manarov as he walked. Then, without greeting or acknowledgement, he took a seat at the opposite end of the bench and opened the bag. His hand slid inside and there was a rustling sound as he removed a hamburger, unfolded the paper wrapper that held it, and put the sandwich to his mouth. He sipped from the soft drink between bites while he ate.

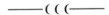

Twenty yards away, Robert Whilden sat on a bench with a novel in his hand, pretending to read while he kept his eyes trained on Pavel Manarov's every move. So far that morning he'd followed Manarov from his apartment to the embassy, then the walk up the street to the corner, and now the noontime meeting in the park. It was nothing new. Manarov had repeated the routine so often it was almost a weekly ritual, but the more Whilden learned about his subject, the more intrigued he became.

Whilden had begun the task of shadowing the Russian diplomat almost seven months earlier when Manarov approached Linda Brown, a member of the US embassy staff assigned to the cultural attaché. He claimed to have compromising photographs of her with a man who was not her husband. When he offered to keep quiet about those photographs in exchange for classified information, she came straight to the embassy security staff.

Manarov's information about Brown was only partially correct. She was with a man, and they were engaged in private activity, but Brown was not married. Under normal circumstances, the matter might have ended there, Manarov was known among Foreign Service officers for his bungling attempts to turn them, but Brown was not a typical employee. She was a CIA employee working at the embassy under temporary cover. That Manarov chose to approach her raised a few eyebrows. People in Washington wanted to know more. Whilden and a six-man team were assigned to investigate. So far, they had observed four meetings between Manarov and Chen

Hongsheng, an employee in the Chinese Foreign Intelligence Service.

After Manarov's first meeting with Hongsheng, additional agents were assigned to follow him. Through electronic eavesdropping devices planted in his apartment, and hours spent following his numerous trips around the city, they learned that Hongsheng had contacts that reached to the highest levels of China's military leadership. That piece of information was enough to convince Whilden that Hongsheng was selling Chinese military secrets. From the envelopes Manarov brought to the meetings, he was certain the price was quite high. When the meetings and payments continued, he knew the information was solid, reliable, and serious.

From high atop an office building one block away, Cam Fong and Chong Han, agents from the Ministry of State Security, watched as the scene in the plaza unfolded. Cam Fong viewed it through the telephoto lens of his video camera. Chong Han held a highly sensitive laser microphone through which he listened to movements and conversations from the park.

As Hongsheng took a seat on the bench, Cam Fong pressed his eye closer to the viewing lens of the camera and spoke softly, "Both men are together now. Some distance from the noise of the fountain. Point the microphone at the bench. See if we can hear them this time."

Chong Han did as he was told and listened through headphones to the sounds coming from below. "Much better. I hear birds. And the sound of footsteps."

"Someone is passing the bench now," Cam Fong noted. "Hold it steady. I think you have it exactly where we want it."

"Now there is the sound of crumpling paper," Chong Han continued.

"I see him," Cam Fong said with a hint of impatience. He adjusted the focus of the lens. "He has a paper in his hand. The wrapper from a hamburger." He tilted the camera down at a slightly steeper angle. "That is what you hear."

On the bench below them, Hongsheng finished the hamburger and wiped his mouth on a paper napkin. Then he took a sip of soft drink and sat quietly for a moment. Finally, he wadded the paper wrapper from the hamburger into a ball, dropping it into the bag. Casually, in a way that drew no attention from those walking nearby, he set the bag on the bench, and stood.

Cam Fong picked up a radio from beside him and keyed the microphone. "Get ready. He is about to move."

"We see him," a voice replied.

While Cam Fong watched, Hongsheng turned aside and casually walked toward the fountain, moving at a slow and deliberate pace in the direction he'd come. Behind him, the paper bag sat on the bench. Cam Fong keyed the microphone once more. "He is walking back toward the fountain. But he left the bag on the bench."

"I don't see it," someone answered on the radio.

"Do you see it?" someone else asked.

"I do not."

"Hey!" a second voice shouted. "That guy has it. The one walking away."

Cam Fong swung the camera around to see what they were talking about, and there was the bag, sitting on the bench, next to the Russian.

A voice from the radio announced, "We have him in sight. Should we take him into custody?"

"No," Cam Fong warned. "Do not apprehend him. Just follow him and see where he goes."

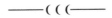

While Chinese intelligence agents followed Hongsheng across the park, Manarov picked up the paper bag from the bench and started back toward the street. He continued past the corner near the apartment building and down to the Russian embassy.

In his office, he dumped the contents of the bag on the desk, then checked the outside for marks. A matrix barcode was located on the bottom. Manarov took an iPhone from his pocket and scanned the code. Within seconds, a web page opened on the screen with pictures showing rows and rows of military transports, tanks, and missile launchers with missiles loaded in place. Next to the pictures was a link, which he clicked. A video message opened, showing a man wearing a mask, standing before a blue wall. Manarov's understanding of the Chinese language wasn't great, but he knew enough to know that the message indicated China was preparing to move large numbers of men and equipment to the border with Afghanistan.

Manarov copied the link for the page and emailed it from the phone to an account accessible through the embassy's computer system. Then he created a report about what he'd seen and heard, attached the link, and emailed all of it over a secure web link to Moscow.

31

MOSCOW, RUSSIA

VASILY KERENSKY LEANED OVER THE SHOULDER of an intelligence analyst and squinted at yet one more image on the monitor. "That one is too soft," he complained. "Can you enhance it?"

"We can compensate for it some," the analyst replied, "but I'm not sure we can do enough."

"How is it that the Americans get such good pictures, while ours are all so poor?"

"The Americans spend ten times more on defense than we do."

"I wonder what happens to the difference we save," Kerensky quipped.

"Good question."

"Work through the rest of these. Get me something I can use. Pick out the best." Kerensky turned toward the door. "I'll be in my office. Phone me when you have the results."

For days it had been the same, each pass of the satellites over the Afghan-Chinese border produced images too poor to analyze. The software in the operating system of the satellite, and in the computers the analysts used, could make the images sharper and the details more distinct, but there were limitations and Kerensky knew full well what they were. He was on the committee that approved the purchase of the satellites. And the computers. And the software. No one had to tell him how cheaply they were made, or where the money went.

When Kerensky reached his office, he found Gennady Panova seated near his desk. Panova turned in the chair to face him. "Vasily," he grinned. "You look tired."

"I am tired." Kerensky trudged across the room toward the desk. "I thought you were staying in Berlin. Never coming back to Moscow."

"You know," Panova shrugged. "Once in a while the president likes to see me in person, not just by teleconference."

"Something up in Berlin that I don't know about?"

"I should hope not."

"You were seen with General Erhard the other day," Kerensky continued without missing a beat. "The two of you seated on a bench outside the Reichstag building."

"Erhard and I were merely getting acquainted."

Kerensky had a skeptical expression. "You should know that he is Mueller's closest confidant. Whatever you say to him goes directly to Mueller's ear. It's like an implant, these two are so close. One of Mueller's ears implanted in the side of Erhard's skull."

"I know," Panova chuckled. "He thinks he is so suave."

"There's a lot of that going around," Kerensky groused. He continued to the backside of the desk and dropped into a chair. "So what brings you here, Gennady?" He looked over at Panova. "The Russian ambassador to Germany does not show up unannounced in my office without coming on business."

Panova reached inside his jacket and took out an envelope, which he tossed on the desk. "Recent images from German drones flying over the Afghan–Chinese border."

Kerensky's eyes opened wide. "How did you get these?" he whispered as he removed the photographs from the envelope.

"You know," Panova shrugged. "You can get anything from a German if you offer him the right bribe."

"We wondered what was in the envelopes you and Erhard exchanged. You bought these?" Kerensky asked, gesturing with the photographs in his hand.

"Yes."

Kerensky shot Panova a look. "Where did you get the money?"

"Don't ask."

"I just did."

"You don't want to know."

Kerensky laid a photograph flat on the desktop, then opened the drawer and found a loupe, which he placed on the picture. He leaned forward, placed one eye to the lens of the loupe and studied the image carefully, moving the device along barely a centimeter at a time. "This is from the Wakhan Corridor," he commented without looking up. "Why did the Germans send their drone into that region?"

"From what I can determine," Panova explained, "they intercepted cell phone calls from the area in which people were talking about the body of a man who had been discovered there. He'd been shot in the head."

"People are shot every day in Afghanistan," Kerensky commented, still focused on the picture. "What made this one so special?"

"Single gunshot to the head. Using a bullet manufactured solely for the Chinese army."

"What were Chinese soldiers doing there?"

"No one seems to know. But the Germans think they used the Afghans for guides."

"Perhaps," Kerensky mused. "Use them, then kill them to keep them from talking?"

"Yes."

"Dead men tell no secrets. These pictures are very good. If quality of product meant anything in war, the Germans would have won every war they entered."

"They are very good at sophisticated, high-end manufacturing."

"Their products were always far superior to those of everyone else. It just took them too long to make each item." Kerensky gestured to Panova with one of the photographs. "Any possibility you can get us some more like these?"

"I don't know. Maybe. You want me to try?"

"That would tell you if he was selling them to you, or feeding them to you," Kerensky replied.

Panova frowned. "Feeding them?"

"The Germans do this all the time. They want someone to have a piece of information—might be good information, might be disinformation—whatever it is, they want to get it in the hands of someone. A foreign government or intelligence organization. So they find a way to leak it to them, or better yet, sell it to them."

"To who?"

"Someone like you," Kerensky explained without a smile, "who wouldn't know if the photographs were current or not."

"Are they current?"

"I think so."

"Why do they do that?"

"Do what?" Kerensky asked.

"Sell it like that."

"To make you think you've got something special."

Panova pointed toward the photographs on the desk. "Is that special?"

"Yeah," Kerensky nodded. "It's special."

"Then why did they let me have it?"

"I don't know. But they didn't let you have it." Kerensky looked straight at him. "They sold it to you."

"I still don't understand."

"It's all about what they want to happen to the information at the next step. They sell it so it will be injected into the intelligence stream quickly. But what we want to know is whether they are trying to influence our intelligence operation, our military policy, or just turn you into one of their operatives." Kerensky stood and picked up the photographs. "I have to get these downstairs." He came from behind the desk and patted Panova on the shoulder as he walked past. "Always good to see you, Gennady. Next time, see if you can get them as a digital file." And then he started for the door.

32

TUNIS, TUNISIA

USING AN ALIAS and traveling with an Egyptian passport, Kinlaw boarded a commercial airline flight from Washington, D.C., and flew to Frankfurt, Germany. From there, he caught a connecting flight that took him to Cairo. Finally, almost two days after leaving the United States, and carrying all his possessions in a backpack slung over one shoulder, he arrived in Tunis, posing as an Egyptian writer on a trek along the North African coast as preparation for writing a book about the city of Carthage, now a suburb of Tunisia, and its fall during the Punic Wars. In reality, he was there solely and only to locate the *Vasco Nuñez* and, hopefully, to locate the cargo container with the third missile still inside, a fact he was set to confirm by measuring radiation levels with the handheld dosimeter stuffed in the bottom of the backpack.

From the airport, Kinlaw rode the bus around Lake Tunis to an area of the city that lay along the coast, facing the Gulf of Tunis and the Mediterranean Sea beyond. The bus let him off in front of a mosque on Bourguiba Avenue and from there he walked to the harbor.

Still with the backpack slung over one shoulder, he made his way to the container port entrance and waited while a truck pulling a trailer loaded with a cargo container drove by. Not far beyond where Kinlaw was standing was a gate that led onto the dock. By the time he reached it, the truck was stopped there for an inspection. Officers came from a guard shack and checked the seals on the rear doors, then walked along the driver's side to the cab. While they were at the front of the truck, Kinlaw hurried forward, approaching from the rear, and crawled beneath the trailer chassis. He found a space between the rear tires and the undercarriage and wedged himself into it. Moments later, the truck started forward. He held on tightly, his legs just inches from the turning wheels, his body only a few feet above the pavement.

The truck started forward and only a few minutes later came to a stop on the pier. Kinlaw waited until he heard the driver's door of the cab open, then he dropped from the undercarriage and crawled out on the opposite side. He dusted off his hands, adjusted the backpack on his shoulder, and walked calmly toward the ships that were tied along the dock.

Locating the *Vasco Nuñez* proved to be a simple task. It was tied at the dock directly in front of where the truck had stopped. Workmen were busy with an overhead crane, offloading a portion of the ship's container cargo. Kinlaw took the iPhone from his pocket and snapped a picture, making sure to capture the flag flying from the stern, then sent it as a text message to Hoag. While he waited for a reply, he climbed up the gangplank and boarded the ship. To his amazement, no one tried to stop him.

On the main deck, he threaded his way past tie-down clamps and coiled cables, then wormed his way between the rows of containers that lined the ship's deck. To the rear of the cargo area, near the ship's superstructure, he found an oversized container with a crescent moon and star painted in the upper corner of one door.

Kinlaw glanced around nervously, making certain no one was watching, then he ran his fingers along the seams of the container, checking for an opening near the corner from which he could get an air sample. After a quick search, he located a crack in the metal near a hinge on the right side of the door. He dug out the dosimeter from the backpack and held it near the opening, then pressed a button to activate it and waited. Almost instantly, the meter emitted a loud beep. He checked the screen and saw it had registered the maximum amount detectable by that device.

Just then, Kinlaw heard the sound of footsteps approaching. He ducked out of sight around the end of the row of containers, then peeked out to see a man at the opposite end of the container stack. Not quite six feet tall, he was abnormally thin and his eyes were sunken deeply into their sockets. His cheeks were hollow and his skin had a pallor that made him appear sickly. He had lesions on the backs of his hands. While Kinlaw watched, the man checked the lock on the container box then took out a key and opened it. With great effort, he pushed back the door and disappeared inside.

With the man out of sight, Kinlaw turned away, leaned against a container, and sent a cryptic text message to Hoag that read, "Dinner in the oven. Don't be late."

A creaking sound came from the stack, and Kinlaw leaned out to see that the man had emerged from the cargo container and was pushing the door closed. It slammed shut with a loud bang, then he slipped the lock in place and checked to make sure it was fastened.

Just then, a man appeared at the railing on the deck above. He was dressed in dark pants, white shirt, and wore a black captain's hat. "Babak," he called down to the man on the deck. "Is the door secure?"

"Yes," Babak nodded. "It is closed and locked."

"You are sure?"

Babak gave him a wry smile. "You want to see for yourself?"

"No," the captain replied, shaking his head and smiling. "I'll take your word."

"I thought so."

"I will be glad when we get rid of that thing," the captain continued. "Killed two men already and we haven't even launched it."

"They knew what they were getting into," Babak droned in a gravelly voice.

"Yes, well, they are dead and you don't look so good, either."

"I am fine," Babak replied. "I am fine."

With the doors closed, Babak wandered toward the far end of the stack and disappeared. The captain took a pack of cigarettes from his pocket, stuck one in his mouth, and lit it. For the next ten minutes he stood at the rail, staring out at the cargo hold. From the look in his eyes, he was lost in thought.

When the captain finally finished his cigarette and moved from the rail, Kinlaw came from his hiding spot and walked quickly up to the cargo container. He shrugged the backpack from his shoulder and

opened it, then took out a small electronic tracking device. He placed
it behind a reinforcing plate at the corner of the container, where the
catch on the trailer chassis fastened to the box. Satisfied it was out of
sight, he slipped off the ship and made his way across the dock.

In town, Kinlaw located a café and ordered coffee. Then he sat at a
table in the back corner and placed a call to Hoag. "It's there," he said
without introduction when Hoag finally answered.

"You're sure?"

"Pegged the meter," Kinlaw said dryly.

"And it was on the ship?"

"Yeah. Right there in the stack on the deck."

"We have the right name?"

"That's what it's called today. From the look of its crew, it might be
called something else tomorrow."

"Any idea where it's going?"

"I was hoping you could tell me that."

"We'll check."

"You got a fix on it?"

"Yeah. The device is working fine. We're watching it."

33

BEIJING, CHINA

CAM FONG SAT AT HIS DESK in an office on the fourth floor of a nondescript office building located off Guangningbo Street, near the Ritz Carlton Hotel. Again and again he replayed the video from Hongsheng's meeting in the park with the Russian, Manarov. Each time he checked a different area of the background to see if Hongsheng really was alone. When he was satisfied of that, he tightened the image on Hongsheng and watched as he appeared near the fountain. He noted Hongsheng's gait, the way he held his hands, the shirt on his back and the pants he wore. And he noted his shoes. Nothing appeared out of the ordinary.

He let the video play on as Hongsheng took a seat on the bench and ate the hamburger from the bag. Once again, he reviewed the images, moving through one frame at a time. He tightened on the wrapper, which Hongsheng kept around the sandwich while he ate. A watch on Hongsheng's wrist caught his eye and for a while he focused his attention on it. The time on the watch face showed 11:41 and he compared it to the time stamped on the video. They were within seconds of each other.

The video continued to play as Hongsheng picked up the sack and placed the used wrapper inside. And then he caught sight of something on the bottom. He tightened the frame and zoomed in closer, let the video move forward, and finally caught a clear view.

"A matrix barcode," he whispered.

Fong captured the barcode image and scanned it into the computer system. Moments later, a web page opened with images of Chinese military equipment. He clicked on the link for the video message and listened as a man wearing a black mask told of the thousands of troops already gathered along China's border with Afghanistan, the manner in which they had been moved there undetected, and the many hundreds of thousands of troops waiting to join them. Fong's heart rate quickened at the sight of it. For weeks he'd heard rumors that a major military operation was in the offing, but no one in his section knew any details about it and no one with clearance above him would discuss it. Now he had evidence on his computer screen that the operation existed, and that an informant inside the government was intent on letting the world know what was about to happen. "A mole," he said to himself, copying the Western expression. "叛徒" he snarled. "A traitor."

Using a forensics program that decoded metadata and other information from the web page, Fong learned that the server hosting the site was located in Bangladesh. He hacked into the server and followed a circuitous electronic trail that led to a computer assigned to a location on Yuanbei Road in Baodi, a village to the east of Beijing. He alerted Chong Han and the team that had been with him at the park and ordered them to the address. Then he picked up the phone and called Quan Ji, the chief of Foreign Intelligence. They arranged to meet within the hour in Quan's office.

When Fong arrived, he found Quan seated at his desk, smoking a cigarette. A gray cloud hung over the room and the smell of smoke stung his nostrils.

"So, you have figured out why Hongsheng was in the park with the Russian?"

"Yes, sir," Fong bowed. "We have figured it out."

"Very well," Quan paused to take a long drag on the cigarette he held between his fingers. "Tell me what you have learned."

For the next few minutes, Quan listened patiently as Fong described what he had discovered from the barcode on the bag, the website, and the team he already deployed to the location from which the website information originated. Then Quan said calmly, "You can prepare a report of all this?"

"Yes. I will write it up and have it for you later today."

"Good. I think you should continue to analyze the information. Not all things that can be known are revealed at once. Often they must be discovered through meticulous attention to details. Only then will the relationships of information reveal themselves."

"Yes, sir. Should I have the team in Baodi search the location from which the information arose?"

"Do we know anything about this location?"

"Only the address."

"I see," Quan nodded. "Do we know anything about the people who are involved?"

"Only about Hongsheng."

"Perhaps we should learn more of the people in Baodi who might be involved, before we move on the location."

"Very well," Fong nodded.

"Have the team monitor the location, but do not have them enter it." Quan gave a thin smile. "At least not yet." He paused again and took another drag on the cigarette. "We must learn all we can about this person." He exhaled smoke in the air above his head. "Or persons, as the case may be, before we respond. Observe carefully, but under no circumstances should they allow him to escape."

"Very well," Fong turned to leave.

"Tell me," Quan spoke up. "We hear chatter regarding the meetings the Russian foreign minister conducted in Azerbaijan."

"Yes." Fong turned back to face him. "Apparently these were high-level negotiations."

"President Ming Shao would like to know if we can confirm the exact nature of those talks."

"You think the two are related—the Russian discussions with the Azerbaijanis and this traitor's meeting with the Russian in the park?"

"I do not yet know, but many who are knowledgeable in these matters feel they might be." Quan looked over at Fong. "We cannot risk ignoring the potential for a connection. You can find out the details of those meetings?"

"We have one person inside Russia who can probably find out what this was about. But it may take a few days to contact him and forward the request."

"Then you should contact him immediately. Instruct him to find out what the Russians were doing in Azerbaijan, and what they know about our troop movements along the Afghan border." Quan took another long drag on the cigarette. "Perhaps, if the two are related, we will learn how deeply this traitor has damaged us with the secrets he is passing to the Russians."

34

LANGLEY, VIRGINIA

WHEN HOAG FINISHED THE CALL with Kinlaw, he left his office, took the elevator to the basement, and walked down the hall to Jenny's cubicle. She glanced up as he appeared. "I was just thinking about you," she grinned.

He came around the end of her desk and leaned over to kiss her. Then he moved his lips near her ear and whispered, "Dennis called."

Jenny struck him on the thigh with her fist. "Not exactly the words a new bride wants to hear from her husband."

Hoag kissed her again, then moved back to her ear. "You don't want to know what he said?"

"Is he okay?"

"Yeah." Hoag moved away and dropped onto a nearby chair. "He put the device on the container. Can you track it?"

"Yeah, I should be able to get it."

Using the terminal on her desk, she logged on to the tracking system for the device Kinlaw used and waited while it loaded the location. Moments later, a map appeared on the screen. A red dot blinked on the port at Tunis. "There it is," she pointed to the screen.

Hoag rose from his chair and stood behind her. "Good," he nodded. "Do we have coordinates for that location?"

Jenny moved the cursor over the screen to the red dot, and a text box appeared with the coordinates. She scribbled them on a scrap of paper and handed it to him. "What do we do now?"

"I'm not sure. Let's go talk to Winston."

Together they walked down the hall to the operations center where Smith was still pursuing details from the meetings that had taken place earlier in Baku. Hoag motioned for him to step outside and they talked in the hall.

"Dennis called," Hoag began. "He found the ship."

Smith was all business. "Is he sure it's the right one?"

"Yeah."

"What about the container?"

"Dosimeter hit the limit."

"You have a fix on its position?"

"Yes, he put a tracking device on the container. We can track it through the system."

Smith looked over at Jenny. "You know that for sure? You checked the system?"

"Yes," she nodded. "We logged on and made sure."

"Here." Hoag reached into his pocket and took out the scrap of paper. "These are the numbers."

Smith glanced at the coordinates. "Okay," he nodded. "What do you want to do next?"

"I'm not sure. That's why I came to you."

"You're the boss," Smith said with a sly smile. "That's your call."

"I know it's my call," Hoag said with a hint of frustration. "I just don't know if we should take the ship now or wait."

"Do you have any assets in the area?"

"Not really. Not enough to seize it and get the container out of there before the Tunisians interfere."

"Well, maybe that's your answer," Smith suggested. "Either way, you had better tell Hoyt Moore what you know. And you better do it now."

Hoag arched an eyebrow. "Me?"

"You're the deputy director," Smith chuckled. "Not me." Then he pushed open the door to the operations center and disappeared inside.

When he was gone, Hoag looked over at Jenny. "So, I tell Hoyt?"

"Absolutely. We located a ship that poses a major threat to our nation and the world. He has to know. The president has to know." She leaned forward and kissed him, then swatted him on the behind. "Get moving."

From the basement, Hoag took the elevator upstairs and walked into Moore's suite. His assistant sat at a desk near his office door. "Is he in?"

"Just a minute," she replied. "I'll check."

Hoag continued past her and pushed open the office door. Moore was seated at his desk, hunched over a file, his back to a large window that looked out on the courtyard below. He looked up with a frown, not at all pleased by the interruption. "You don't believe in knocking?"

"We've located the *Santiago*," Hoag announced.

Moore closed the file that lay before him and leaned back in his chair. "The missing ship with the other missile?"

"Yes, sir."

"Where is it?"

"Tunis. Only the ship's not called the *Santiago* now. They renamed it the *Vasco Nuñez*. It's flying a Liberian flag."

"Makes sense," Moore nodded. "Smugglers do that all the time. You're sure this is the ship?"

"Yes, sir. We sent someone over to make sure."

"Who did you send?"

"Dennis Kinlaw."

"I remember him. Your friend from Yale."

"Yes, sir."

"Didn't realize he was still in field ops."

"He's not. But he volunteered for this."

"Do we know if the missile is there?"

"He found the container. Just like the other two. Hit a maximum read on the dosimeter."

"He was onboard the ship?"

"Yes."

"Interesting," Moore observed. "Is the ship still in port?"

"Yes. Dennis placed a tracking device on the container. We're monitoring it downstairs."

"Okay. What do you think we should do now?"

"We have no assets in or near Africa who could seize the ship, offload the container, and get it out of the country. If we bring in the

Tunisian government, they'll stall us while they warn whoever's controlling the ship, and the container will be gone before we can act. With the tracking device in place, we can monitor the container's movement. So I think we should continue to do that and wait until the ship puts out to sea. Once it reaches international water, the president should order the navy to seize it."

"Good," Moore rose from his chair behind the desk. "That's exactly what I would say."

"There's just one thing."

"What's that?"

"The tracking device is on the container. Not the contents."

"You mean, they could unload the missile and leave the container behind?"

"Yes."

"We can't control that now. And we have little option but to wait until they are out of port." Moore glanced at Hoag and pointed. "Adjust your tie."

Hoag had a puzzled look. "My tie?"

"Yeah. It's not straight. You can't go in there looking like that."

"Go in where?"

Moore came from behind the desk and slipped on his jacket. "The White House."

"The White House?"

"We've located a ship carrying a missile armed with a nuclear warhead. One that is identical to the missile that struck our nation's capital and identical to a second one we've already seized. We can't sit on information like this and wait to see what happens. I have to brief the president. You have to go with me."

Moore started toward the door, but Hoag stood there frozen in place. He'd never participated in a presidential briefing like this. His mind whirred with images of the Oval Office and the president turning to him, looking for answers to direct questions.

"Well, come on," Moore called impatiently from outside his door. "We have to go."

35

MOSCOW, RUSSIA

DOWN THE HALL FROM HIS OFFICE, Vladimir Vostok sat in a private dining room enjoying a quiet lunch, sharing the room only with the steward who stood near the kitchen door, always ready to fill his glass or serve the next course. On the table, just beyond Vostok's plate of smoked salmon and caviar, lay a newspaper open to the center section. He read from it between bites, pausing now and then to turn the page or straighten the crease in the fold.

Halfway through the entrée, the door to the hallway opened and Anatolyn Luzhkov, Vostok's chief of staff, entered the room. He came quickly to the table and stood to one side.

"Vasily Kerensky is in your office," he announced with a business-like tone.

Vostok did not look up from the paper. "What does he want?"

"He has news from China."

Vostok lifted his head, suddenly focused on the moment. "What has happened?"

"It's not like that," Luzhkov waved in a reassuring gesture. "He's reporting back to you on the issues you discussed earlier. When he and Mikhail Mirsky came to see you."

"Right," Vostok nodded thoughtfully, turning back to the newspaper.

"Shall I have him wait, or assign him an appointment?"

"Have him join me," Vostok said, not looking up.

"Now?" Luzhkov asked.

"Yes."

"Very well."

Luzhkov crossed the room from the table to the door and stepped out to the hall. A few minutes later, he returned with Kerensky, the Foreign Intelligence Service chief, in tow. Partway to the table, Luzhkov backed away and gestured for Kerensky to approach the table alone. Vostok saw him coming, moved the newspaper aside, and gestured to a chair across from him. "Have a seat."

"Yes, Mr. President," Kerensky eased into the chair. "I didn't mean to interrupt your lunch."

"Quite all right," Vostok smiled. "Anatolyn said you had news from China."

"We reached our contact in Beijing. He has informed us—"

Vostok gestured for Kerensky to stop, then caught the eye of the steward standing on the opposite side of the room. He motioned to him with a nod of his head and the steward left the room. When he was gone, Vostok looked over at Kerensky. "You were saying ..."

"We reached our contact in Beijing," Kerensky began again. "His source says the Chinese are now prepared to move large numbers of troops and equipment to the Afghan border."

"Did he say why?"

"No, but these movements, if made, would be important. Not as an indication of their underlying reasons for the deployment, but as it relates to their next step. The sequencing of events in a mobilization is designed to build toward a launch date and as that date approaches, the doing of whatever they have planned takes on a certain inevitability."

"They reach a point of no return?"

"Exactly," Kerensky nodded. "Troops and equipment require logistical support. Amassing sufficient numbers for an operation of size poses significant supply chain issues which affect the sustainability of that chain."

"Which means?"

"They can't keep large numbers of troops at the border for long. They'll have to move forward with whatever their plan is, or recall them to their fixed barracks."

"So this latest information indicates a shortened time window?"

"Yes, Mr. President, I think so."

"How long before they would have to act?"

"Weeks."

"Not months?"

"I do not think so. This is a remote area in a remote region. Everything would be a great distance from their border position."

Vostok took a bite of salmon. "Movements like these would be the kind others would notice, would they not?"

"Yes."

"Is our source reliable?"

"He has been in the past."

"You are not concerned that this is erroneous information given to us on purpose?"

"No." Kerensky recalled his earlier conversation with Panova. "Our confidence level in this information is high."

"So," Vostok paused to wipe his mouth on a napkin, "if they do this, if they move these forces to the border, they will incur limitations imposed by logistics."

"Yes," Kerensky nodded.

"And the American satellites will see them, which means the element of surprise will be lost."

"That is correct."

"Any indication of whether the Iranians are aware of these pending movements?"

"No, sir. The Iranians have no military satellites and no real intelligence network inside China. In the past, they have known of these kinds of things only because we have informed them."

Vostok looked across the table at Kerensky. "And we're not telling them now?"

"No, sir." Kerensky leaned forward. "Did you want us to brief them?"

"No!" Vostok barked sharply. "You are to share nothing with them." He looked Kerensky in the eye. "Understood?"

"Yes, Mr. President. I understand."

"Give the Iranians nothing," Vostok repeated. He took a sip from the water glass that stood beside this plate and wiped his mouth once more. "I want you to task a satellite to verify the information. We need confirmation from another source before I decide what we should do."

"We have pictures," Kerensky offered.

"From our satellites?"

"From multiple sources." Kerensky took a smartphone from his pocket, loaded pictures onto the screen, and handed the device to Vostok. "These are from our source in China. If you scroll through the images you'll come to a video link at the end that includes a message about the troop movements."

Vostok took the phone from him and began looking through the pictures. "Where did we obtain these images?"

"From our contact in Beijing."

Vostok frowned. "He sent us a video link?"

"He gave us a paper bag with a scanable barcode on it."

Vostok had a pained expression. "Scanable barcode?"

"The bag was from McDonald's," Kerensky explained. "The barcode was on the bottom. When scanned with an iPhone it links to a website. That's where the photos and video message were located."

"And that's how we received the information?"

"Yes."

"Whatever happened to drop boxes and actual photographs?"

"This is much more anonymous."

"Much more," Vostok said with a hint of uncertainty, "but not totally?"

"Not completely," Kerensky confirmed. "Identities can be discovered with the right research software. Our computer technicians are following the electronic trail now. Trying to locate the source of that website. It appears to be hosted on a server somewhere in or around India."

Vostok glanced through the pictures, then handed the phone to Kerensky. "We discussed earlier using our own satellites to confirm their activities in the region. Do we have anything from that?"

"Yes. Our analysts are working on those now. The best of those images show a significant buildup of troops. Would you like to see those photographs?"

"You have them with you?"

"No, but I can have them sent over."

"That is not necessary," Vostok deferred. "But I think you should ask our contact in Beijing for more details."

"Details?"

"Numbers. Description of the equipment. Anything he can provide."

"Yes, Mr. President. I will get right on it."

36

JERUSALEM, ISRAEL

AFTER A LONG DAY IN ASHDOD, Hofi rode in his car to Jerusalem for
a meeting he both wanted and dreaded. In spite of all he'd heard and
read, and even after visiting with Rabbi Riskin, he still could not escape
the things General Khoury had said that day when he interviewed him.
And it wasn't even so much the words, but the intensity with which
Khoury said them.

Hofi knew he should have pushed the whole thing aside and
simply reported to Oren about their conversation. He had a job to complete and it had little to do with understanding ancient prophecies,
or believing in his friend Khoury, but try as he might he could not
stop thinking about it. When he lay down at night, he remembered
the lessons he learned as a child and the stories he'd heard about the
ancient prophets who wrote of Israel as a people chosen by God for a
unique purpose in history. In the daytime, when he wasn't busy with
something else, his mind returned to the stories he heard growing up
about how the modern state of Israel came into existence. Now, in a
desperate attempt to resolve those issues, he turned to the one place
he thought he would never consult—the Christian church. With a few
phone calls, he arranged for an audience with Clemis Michael Shimon,
a priest at St. Mark's Monastery, a small Syriac Orthodox church on
Ararat Street in the Armenian Quarter of the old city.

Formed inside the ancient walls of Jerusalem, the Armenian

Quarter was the smallest of the four central city sections. Its narrow streets—most of them no wider than sidewalks and paved with cobblestone—wound through a confusing jumble of buildings that had been constructed over the past thousand years, and which now occupied every square inch of available space.

With the streets much too cramped for a motorized vehicle, Hofi traveled by car as far as the Jaffa Gate. There he alighted from the back seat and, accompanied by two bodyguards, walked the rest of the way on foot. Clemis Michael was waiting in the sanctuary when he arrived. They stood near the altar table and talked.

"Thank you for seeing me," Hofi injected.

"I was told you are a man of honor," Clemis Michael replied. "I am pleased to give you my time. How may I help you?"

"This is...a little awkward for me." Hofi warmed to the subject of his visit. "I handle many things in my job. Critical things. Things that often are crucial to the continued survival of our country."

"I am aware of who you are and the job you perform."

"So then you know following orders is very important to me and to the work I do."

"As it should be," Clemis Michael nodded in agreement.

"The other day someone did not follow the orders. And not just anyone, but someone who has been in the military for a long time."

"You knew this person?"

"Yes," Hofi replied. "Very well."

"He was your friend?"

"Yes."

"Very well. Please," Clemis Michael gestured. "Continue with whatever you have to tell me."

"Well, in fact," Hofi picked up where he left off, "he not only disobeyed an order, he took steps to do the very opposite of that order. If he had succeeded in his disobedience, millions of people would have died."

"So, what happened to him?"

"He was stopped, of course, and taken into custody. Then they sent me to talk to him. When I asked him why he did that, he said it was his duty. That the Jews were God's people and that our enemies must be wiped from the face of the earth. That they cannot be allowed to prevail. And if we refuse to destroy them ourselves, another nation will appear and wipe them away instead. And when I asked why he felt that way, he said it was because of the prophecies of old and how they would be fulfilled."

"And you have a question for me?" Clemis Michael asked with a smile.

"Yes. No one can tell me if that is true. No one can tell me if the prophecies of the past have all come true, or will come true, or even that they will never come true."

Clemis Michael folded his arms across his chest. "And you are wanting me to tell you?"

"I was hoping you could help."

Clemis Michael thought for a moment, his head down staring at the floor. Then he looked up with a kindly smile. "Answer me this. Are you looking for information that will resolve a theological or spiritual dilemma, or are you looking for permission to destroy your enemies?"

"I don't know," Hofi was taken aback by the abruptness of the question. "I never thought of it that way."

"Perhaps you should. I sense in your voice that you find your friend's conduct courageous and somehow you feel that sense of courage is lacking in yourself."

"He is a very brave man." Hofi's eyes darted away, avoiding Clemis Michael's gaze.

"But what did you think of the things he did? The acts of disobedience. What did you think when he told you those things?"

"I thought, 'This man is a hero,'" Hofi answered with a hint of defiance. "We shouldn't have incarcerated him. We should have given him a medal."

"Would you have done what he did?"

"No." Hofi shook his head. "I would not."

"Yet, isn't that the real question you are asking? Aren't you really searching for the courage to finish what he began? And if not the courage to do it, then a reason to justify it?"

"I suppose I am," Hofi answered lamely. "But should I?"

"Ahh," Clemis Michael's eyes opened wide. "That is an entirely different question. I can tell you that the prophets of old spoke for God. And in every sense they told the truth. You need only look at the words they said and the things that followed to know this. But as to the course of conduct one human should take, I cannot say. But I can tell you this: No act of courage will ever set you free from the person you already are."

Hofi looked puzzled. "No act of courage can ever set me free ..."

"... from the person you already are," Clemis Michael finished the sentence. "Courage can make you feel better about yourself for a time, but it cannot set you free. Courage is an act that arises from freedom, not one that gives it."

"So how do I find freedom?"

"The truth," Clemis Michael explained, as if declaring the obvious. "That is what sets us free. The truth. And in that sense, we come into agreement with the prophets of old. They spoke the truth. We get to live it."

They talked awhile longer about prophecy, both Jewish and Christian, but Hofi had found his answer. His problem wasn't that he didn't always believe the prophecies. His problem was that he lacked the courage to live from the convictions he already held. And yes, he was looking for a reason to justify completing what Khoury had attempted. But now that he knew that, he no longer needed to do it.

37

THE WHITE HOUSE
WASHINGTON, D.C.

LATE IN THE AFTERNOON, President Hedges was once again seated at his desk in the Oval Office with rows of chairs arrayed before him. One by one, his assistant ushered executives into the room, this time CEOs from the nation's electrical utilities. Like the oil industry, a handful of key power producers controlled most of the generating capacity, but unlike the oil business, distribution of power across the grid was relegated to thousands of companies, co-ops, and municipalities. In response to Hedges' request, representatives from the largest of those entities dutifully filed into the room and took a seat.

When everyone was in place, Hedges looked out at them and began. "I'm sure by now you've heard of my earlier meeting with oil company executives and their agreement to get us moving toward energy independence and lower energy costs. So I'll get right to the point of my meeting with you." He paused for effect, then continued. "You're going to participate in that effort, too."

Lee Roebuck, from Southeastern Generating, spoke up. "You're going to force us to reduce our prices?"

"No," Hedges shook his head. "You're going to agree voluntarily."

"Why would we do that?"

"Because the future of our country depends on it."

"Pricing power below cost would bankrupt us in just a few months."

"Gentlemen," Hedges glanced around the room, "we have been dealt a severe economic blow. One that has changed not only our economy but the economy of the world. Most of the nations in the world think we're down for the count. We can get moving again and prove them wrong, but the key to our success lies with lowering our energy costs."

Dale Mills, from West Texas Power asked, "How much lower are you talking about?"

"Drastically lower. I told the oil industry they needed to reduce prices to pre-1980 levels by the end of the year."

Someone in the back of the room piped up, "And they agreed to that?"

"Yes," Hedges nodded. "They agreed."

"We can't do that," Mills offered. "We can't simply drop our prices."

"Yes you can. And you will. And I'll help you do it."

Roebuck folded his arms across his chest in a defiant pose. "Or what?"

"Or I'll sign an order declaring martial law and seize your company." A wave of murmuring swept over the room. Hedges continued. "Now, before it comes to that, hear me out. We have enough energy available in this country to supply our own needs solely from our own domestic sources. But to do that we need to reallocate the use of those sources and how we consume them. According to the *Annual Energy Review*, we have about six hundred inactive coal-fired generators. Is that number accurate?"

"More or less," someone answered.

"Thanks to the declining cost of natural gas," another offered.

"And overregulation in the Obama years," someone else added.

Hedges pressed the point. "What will it take to get those plants back online?"

"Four years," Mills replied. "And a significant increase in demand. We closed those plants in part because of the cost of complying with regulation, but also because natural gas was cheap and readily available. It still is. So to get those coal-fired plants up and running, we'd need time to prepare the equipment and an increase in demand sufficient to justify both the expense and the cost differential between gas and coal."

"You don't have four years," Hedges stated flatly. "You don't even have two years. And we need those plants operating regardless of demand."

Roebuck frowned. "Why would we intentionally create excess capacity without demand?"

"To drive down the price," Hedges responded matter-of-factly. "That's the whole point."

"But that would kill our bottom line."

"This is not the time to guard your profit margin."

"Assuming our stockholders didn't revolt, how would we stay in business?"

"If your costs drop with the price drop, the decrease in revenue is only proportional," Hedges explained. "You would maintain profitability, just on a smaller scale."

"But our business capacity would increase in scale."

"Right. But the bottom line would work out." Hedges gave a dismissive wave of his hand. "Look, you can sacrifice your bottom line, find a way to make it work, or give up and sell out to one of your neighbors. I don't care. We have to have cheap energy and we're going to get it. And we're going to get it using local sources."

Red McCann, from New York Steam and Light, had a pained look. "You mean you're cutting off imports?"

"I mean you're agreeing not to import fuel of any kind from foreign sources," Hedges reiterated. "We'll use American coal to fire American generators."

"Well, there's still a problem," Mills suggested.

"What's that?"

"Most of those mothballed coal-fired plants have to be retrofitted to meet EPA emissions guidelines. The cost of doing that, and the time required, would destroy your financial model for this exercise we're discussing."

"I can solve that problem." A smile spread across Hedges' face as he opened a desk drawer and took out a blue folder. "I can solve it with an executive order rolling back and waiving those regulations."

Roebuck's eyes opened wide. "You're prepared to do that?"

"We are in a crisis of historic proportion, Lee. Right now the only bright spot in our economy is agriculture, and that's our way forward. We can become grain merchant to the world, but to do that our farmers need cheap fuel and cheap fertilizer. You're going to help us get it by reducing the price of electricity so we can shift as much consumption as possible into electricity. Cut your costs, drop your prices, and increase the volume. And you'll do it all while producing electricity generated from something other than petroleum products."

A hand went up in the back of the room. "What about nuclear plants?"

"You all have proposals pending for construction of a dozen new nuclear-generating facilities," Hedges responded, "and for the reopening of five existing plants shut down for inspection and repairs." Hedges reached into the desk drawer once more and took out another blue folder. "I have an order here that will wipe away regulatory obstacles to all of those new facilities and allow the old ones to operate under the least restrictive criteria possible."

"In turn for what?"

"Pre-1970s energy costs."

"I thought you said pre-1980s," Mills chortled.

"That was for the oil industry. We need more from you."

"What about going forward? How do we know you won't get us into this, only to reverse it three years down the road?"

Hedges gave them a serious look. "You don't."

"So we have to trust you."

"And I have to trust you. But I need those coal-fired plants up and running in three months."

"We would need six," McCann objected.

"I'll give you four," Hedges countered tersely, "if we have an agreement on my proposals."

Roebuck glanced around the room, checking the mood of the others, then turned back to Hedges. "Okay. We're in agreement. You'll roll back and waive the regulations. We'll get the coal-fired plants up and running. And those who have nuclear facilities will move forward."

Hedges reached into the pocket of his jacket and took out a pen. With a quick motion of his wrist, he signed his name to the executive orders and slid them to the edge of the desk. "Gentlemen, I think we can safely say you have saved the Republic."

"Let's hope we can now save ourselves," Mills grumbled.

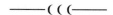

As the meeting with electric company executives broke up, Moore and Hoag were arriving at the White House. They met first with Kittrell in his office, then he took them to see Hedges. Kittrell led the way, followed by Moore, with Hoag lingering behind. They trooped into the room and stood in front of the president's desk.

"Mr. President," Kittrell spoke as they crossed the room, "we have a situation. Hoyt would like to brief you."

"Okay," Hedges sighed. "Should I sit down for this?"

"It won't take long, sir."

"Then I'll sit," Hedges sighed. "This may take a while." He settled onto the chair behind the desk and gestured with a wave of his hand. "Go ahead."

Moore began, "We have received news from one of our operatives confirming the location of the ship known as the *Santiago*."

"This is the one with the third missile?"

"Yes, sir."

"Where is it?"

"Tunis, sir. It is has been renamed the *Vasco Nuñez* and flies a Liberian flag, but we're certain it's the ship."

"And the missile is onboard?"

"It was as of yesterday."

"You've confirmed this?"

"We put a man on the ship. He found the container. Took a reading with a dosimeter."

"No doubt it's nuclear?"

"None, sir. Readings were off the chart."

"I thought there were two containers."

"The other ships had two containers each and it's likely there are two on this one as well, but the containers were stacked in a way that didn't allow our man to see the second container. Only the one."

"And you're positive this is the ship."

"Ship's tonnage, configuration, and description fit. Its log matches with port records. We're certain."

Hedges turned to Moore. "What are you suggesting we do?"

"Wait until the ship puts to sea. When it reaches international water, order the navy to seize it. Board the vessel. Take custody of the container."

"How do we know it will still be on the ship?"

"We can't guarantee it, but we have a tracking device on the container and we're monitoring it around the clock."

Hedges thought for a moment, then nodded in agreement. "Okay." He glanced in Kittrell's direction. "You'll inform the others on the national security team, get everyone up to speed on this?"

"Yes, sir." Kittrell checked his watch. "We'll meet in the situation room for a full briefing in half an hour."

38

BERLIN, GERMANY

AS THE EVENING TURNED LATE, Gregor von Bettinger came from the shadows and walked across the Chancellery campus. In the garden to the west of the building, he found a stone bench and sat down. The moon slowly rose above the trees, casting a silvery glow across the shrubs and bushes. He liked this time of night, after the sun had set and darkness was at its deepest.

After a while he heard the sound of footsteps approaching on the walkway that led back to the building. Moments later, a dark shadow appeared and as it drew nearer he saw Josef Mueller.

"I was just thinking of you," Mueller smiled. He took a seat on the bench next to Bettinger. "How did you get in here?"

"We have ways," he whispered. "And I knew you needed to talk."

"You always know things about me."

"That is my office. I could sense your troubled aura."

"Things have changed."

"Oh? I hadn't heard." Bettinger knew exactly what Mueller meant, but he wanted him to say it for himself. "And how is that?"

"Spain is now on the verge of collapse."

"In what way?"

"Financially. Their banking system is all but illiquid. Protestors are rioting in the streets."

"That is an opportunity for you." Bettinger was careful to smile. "Just as I foresaw."

"Yes, but we still have not heard from the Chinese."

Bettinger had anticipated this question. Mueller was intelligent and quick-minded. It was important to let him think he was in control. Bettinger feigned a look of concern. "You were expecting them to contact you?"

"I assumed when Iranian oil was no longer available to them, they would approach us directly. That they have not causes me concern."

"You *had* promised to help them, had you not?"

"I mentioned it," Mueller smiled. "But that was in relation to US bond sales. We wanted them to stay out of the auction."

"Which they did."

"Yes."

"So that was the arrangement and that time has passed. Perhaps they are silent now because they have nothing to say. Why do you bring this up?"

"We have authority from prior dealings with the European Union that allows us to send our troops into troubled countries and impose order. It was part of our arrangement when we bailed out the banks in 2008. To protect our investment, we took back the right to impose order."

"I remember it well."

"And now we are preparing to send our troops to Spain."

"And so you are set."

"But if we do that, we will be somewhat vulnerable should China respond with force."

"To reach you, the Chinese must sail their ships around the world, or march their army across two continents. If they come, they will do so with emissaries."

"So our effort in Spain will succeed?"

"The ancients are with you. The spirits of the age are on your side. You can only fail if you do not act."

In Moscow, Yang Bao came from the Chinese embassy and started up the sidewalk. The night was unusually cool and he pulled the collar of his jacket tight against his neck. Cam Fong had called personally with explicit instructions. Things were changing in the Caucasus. Officials at the highest level were concerned. Quan Ji himself had made the request. Recent meetings—some in Sochi, others in Baku—supposedly addressing trade relations between the Russian Republic and the government of Azerbaijan, had sparked interest from almost every intelligence agency in the world. Quan Ji wanted to know details. Those in the Zhongnanhai Compound were asking questions. Time was of the essence.

At the corner, Bao turned and walked to a café near the center of the block. His contact, Rolan Buldakov, was seated at a table in the corner. Bao made his way in that direction and dropped into a chair across from him.

"You look cold," Buldakov observed.

"I *am* cold!"

"Most Chinese last at least until Christmas before they start shivering."

"I prefer summer."

Buldakov gestured to a waiter and ordered a cup of tea for Bao. Their banter continued until the tea arrived and Bao had his first sip, then the expression on Buldakov's face turned serious. "You said it was important. We can't sit here long."

"There have been a series of meetings in Sochi," Bao spoke softly between sips of tea. "Perhaps they are still occurring. That part is not clear."

"Sochi is a long way from here," Buldakov offered. "You have no one there who can help you?"

"No one as reliable and thorough as you."

"Ah, I have a reputation."

"The Russian foreign minister met in Sochi with the foreign minister from Azerbaijan. At the same time, staff members from each official met with their counterparts in Baku."

"How much do you want to know?"

"We want to know why they were meeting and what they discussed."

"I'll have to go there to find out that information. No one on this end will talk."

"Very well." Bao set the cup aside, reached inside his jacket, and withdrew an envelope. He laid it on the table and pushed it toward Buldakov. "This should be enough to cover your expenses."

Buldakov picked up the envelope and tucked it in his pocket. "This will be enough to get started," he smiled. "But this trip will cost more than the others."

"We need the information quickly."

"And that will cost even more."

"Cost is not a concern." Bao picked up his cup for another sip.

"For you."

"Nor for you. We will cover your expenses, and your fees, but we need the information as quickly as possible."

Buldakov pushed back his chair and stood. "I'll be in touch."

"And I will be waiting," Bao replied.

39

MEDITERRANEAN SEA

TWO DAYS LATER, the *J. Lee Gifford*, an Independence-class littoral combat ship from the US Navy, patrolled in international waters one hundred fifty miles off the coast of Tunisia. Running at less than a quarter of its top speed, the ship lumbered through the waves, its bow rising and falling as it plowed through first one crest, then the next.

Up top, in the integrated command and control center, Captain Rutledge, the ship's commander, stared out the window and watched, his eyes scanning the horizon for any sign of a ship. Eight days earlier they'd put to sea from a refueling stop in Gibraltar. They were patrolling off the Moroccan coast, working on drug interdiction, when they received a call about a container ship headed north from Tunis. The president wanted it seized. Rutledge took the briefing alone in his quarters. Since then, they'd been loitering in the area, hoping to find it. No one else onboard knew the true nature of their mission.

A few feet away, Michael Henderson, the ship's Intelligence, Surveillance, and Reconnaissance officer, stared at the center screen on the instrument panel in the ISR suite. Moments earlier, something from the onboard radar scan caught his eye and now he wanted a closer view. He switched to an area radar scan provided by a nearby Joint-STARS aircraft patrolling off the Libyan coast. Seconds later, a detailed image from the aircraft appeared on a screen to his right.

Sure enough, there it was—a ship of the size and configuration they were searching for. "Sir," he called out, "we have a bogie."

With a few quick steps Captain Rutledge entered the ISR. "What do you have?"

"Container ship." Henderson pointed to the screen. "About thirty miles out."

"What is it?"

"A self-loading Feedermax."

"Does it meet our profile?"

"Yes, sir. Fits it perfectly."

"Can you get an image of it?"

"Yes, sir." With a few strokes of his fingertips on the instrumentation keyboard, a satellite image appeared on the screen to the left. Henderson tapped the image from the shipboard radar on the screen in the center and a message box appeared with coordinates for the ship's location. A tap of the box sent the information to the ship's computer. Moments later, the satellite image tightened on the container ship's location and produced a picture of it.

"There it is," Henderson pointed.

"Is that real time?" Rutledge asked.

"Yes, sir. That's the ship as she sits right now."

"Tighten down on it some more and see if you can read the name on it."

Again, Henderson's fingers moved across the keyboard, and the image drew tighter and tighter until they could see a crewman walking along the ship's deck. Using his fingertip as a stylus, Henderson adjusted the image on the screen to move forward. As the bow came into view, his eyes lit up. "Look at that, sir," he said, pointing once again.

At the bow of the ship, ropes dangled over the railing and three men were suspended there, a few feet below deck level. Two of them appeared to be holding a template in place while a third man repainted the name of the ship. Of the name *Vasco Nuñez*, only the word Nuñez remained clearly visible.

"Very well," Rutledge replied, then turned to the helmsman. "Make your heading 2-1-0 degrees."

"Aye, captain. Make my heading 2-1-0 degrees."

"All ahead flank speed."

"Aye, captain. All ahead flank."

Down below, the engines rumbled as they increased in speed from an idle to a high-pitched whine. At the same time, the bow rose in the water as the ship picked up speed, then planed on the surface. Twenty minutes later, a rooster tail of sea spray rose in the air from behind the stern as the ship roared across the water at fifty-five knots.

In the White House situation room, President Hedges sat at the head of the table, watching and listening. Braxton Kittrell sat next to him. Around them were gathered members of the national security team—Lauren Lehman, secretary of state; Carl Coulliette, secretary of defense; Bob Lewis, secretary of the navy; Harry Giles, director of national intelligence; and Hoyt Moore, director of the CIA. Admiral Scott Marshall, chairman of the Joint Chiefs of Staff, stood at the end of the room opposite the president, near a wall covered with monitors and video screens. David Hoag was seated in the corner near the admiral. They'd been gathered there since Captain Rutledge's call to the Pentagon's National Military Command Center alerted them that the *Vasco Nuñez* had been found.

"Mr. President," Admiral Marshall informed, "the boarding party is closing on the ship now." He pointed to an assistant seated next to Hoag. Seconds later, images appeared on one of the video screens that hung on the wall. Taken from a camera on the bow of a launch deployed by the *J. Lee Gifford*, the video feed showed the container ship as it loomed ahead. Paint, hastily applied to change the name on the bow of the ship, drizzled down the side.

Hedges pointed to the screen. "Are we going to board from this boat?"

"No, sir." Marshall gestured to the assistant, and the image on the screen switched to an aerial view. "This is from one of two helicopters deployed from the *Gifford*, sir," Marshall explained. "The primary landing force will rappel down to the deck from above. The launch in the water is there to retrieve any of the ship's crew who jump overboard, and to assist if necessary. We have audio to go with the team's video feed." He nodded to the assistant once more, and the speaker in the corner of the room crackled.

"Go, go, go!" a voice shouted over the roar of the helicopter's engine.

A camera mounted on the helmet of a Navy SEAL captured the action as members of the boarding party dropped onto the deck of the ship, landing near the bow, then slowly worked their way toward the superstructure at the stern. The deck was empty as they moved past rows of cargo containers stacked three levels high.

When the team reached the end of the container stack, a door to the bridge, located three levels above the main deck, opened and a man appeared. Dressed in dark pants, white shirt, and wearing a cap, he stepped to the railing and stared down at them.

"Hands in the air!" someone shouted.

The man raised his hands above his head. "I am unarmed," he called. "I am unarmed."

Team members on the deck took up defensive positions, while three SEALs climbed the steps that led up the right side of the super-structure. When they reached the bridge deck, they worked their way to the open door where the man stood. In quick order, they patted him down, shoved him back through the doorway, and disappeared inside.

Moments later, Admiral Marshall's assistant handed him the phone. He listened intently, then turned to the president. "Sir, we have the ship stopped."

"Great," Hedges nodded. "Now what?"

"Now we search the ship," Marshall replied.

"Will that take a while?"

"It'll take a while to complete the entire ship, but it won't take long to locate that container."

"The one with the missile?"

"Yes, sir. With the locator on it, we can go right to it." Marshall glanced to his assistant, then pointed to a screen on the right. "Actually, we have that right there." On the screen, images of a cargo container appeared with members of the boarding team standing to either side of it.

Hoag leaned forward in his seat to watch. The camera moved from side to side, but even with the motion, the symbol at the top of the door—the crescent moon all but surrounding a star—was plainly visible. "That's it," Hoag called out loud.

Hedges glanced in his direction. "Excuse me?"

Hoag felt his cheeks turn warm. "Sorry, sir," he said sheepishly.

"Something you want to add here?"

"The symbol on the door, sir," Hoag explained. "It was on the other two containers."

Hedges turned back to watch the screen. Moore shot Hoag a disapproving look. Hoag shrugged in response. The president had called on him. He had little choice but to respond.

On the screen, someone appeared with a bolt cutter and snapped the lock from the container door latch. A hand came into view and lifted the handle. Slowly, the door swung open revealing the space inside the container was stacked to the ceiling with cardboard boxes. Members of the team stepped back and a man appeared with a handheld dosimeter. He stood near the first row of boxes and took a reading with the machine.

"Got anything?" someone asked.

"Trace amounts, sir."

"Trace?"

"Yes, sir."

"Get those boxes out of the way."

Two men stepped forward and began unloading the cargo container, passing the boxes hand over hand to those who stood behind them. In a matter of minutes, they worked their way through the first row. Then the man with the dosimeter returned and once more took a reading.

"Still only trace amounts, sir."

"Eagle One, this is Strike One."

"Eagle One. Go ahead."

"We're only finding trace readings here."

"Roger that. We see you on the video. What's in the boxes?"

Images on the screen jumped from side to side as the camera jiggled with the team member's movement. A ripping sound came through the speakers, then a voice. "Eagle One." The tone was flat and lifeless. "We have tractor parts."

"Tractor parts?"

"Affirmative."

"Stand by."

Hedges looked angry. "Tractor parts?" he blurted. "I thought this thing had a missile in it. We diverted a combat ship from drug interdiction to stop a container ship carrying tractor parts?"

Just then, the assistant working near the video screens took a call. He handed the phone to Marshall who listened for a moment, then turned to Hedges. "Mr. President, the team onboard the ship wants to know what they should do."

Hedges took a deep breath and seemed to force his body to relax. "They've confirmed it's really tractor parts?" he asked with a hint of sarcasm.

"Yes, sir."

"I don't know," Hedges shrugged. "At this point, what do you suggest?"

"Sir, I suggest we take the crew into custody and search the rest of the ship."

Hedges glanced at Kittrell. "What difference does it make now?"

"This will be fine, Mr. President," Kittrell said calmly. "Let them search the vessel, see what evidence we can find. Maybe they'll develop some intelligence about where the missile is now."

"I suppose," Hedges groused.

"Mr. President," Marshall offered. "They're floating adrift on the high seas."

"Right," Hedges nodded. "Take the crew into custody and search the ship. Let me know what you find." While Marshall returned to the phone call, Hedges stood to leave. Everyone in the room stood in response.

As Hedges turned away, his eyes fell on Hoag, seated in the corner. "This was your idea, wasn't it?" He pointed his finger at Hoag in an accusing manner. "I know it was, because you briefed me on it."

Before Hoag could respond, Moore spoke up. "Mr. President, I reviewed the information and concurred in the analysis. We'll make a thorough inquiry and find out what happened."

Hedges turned to Moore. "See that you do."

When Hedges was gone, Moore came to Hoag's side and took him by the elbow. "Find out what happened."

"Sir, I'm sure we had the—"

"I don't care what we had before," Moore cut him off tersely. "These things happen. Nobody's blaming anyone. That's the nature of our business. It's not a perfect world. But we have to react now, so find out what happened and find out now."

As the situation room emptied, Hoag stepped out to the hallway and placed a call to Kinlaw. He began without introduction. "The container was loaded with tractor parts."

"Did it still have the tracking device?"

"It was right there on the box."

"You're sure?"

"Yeah I'm sure," Hoag growled. "I was in the room when they hit the ship. They went right to it. I saw it."

"And you're sure it was the same one?"

"We've been tracking it for days. Of course it's the same one."

"I'll find out," Kinlaw said and ended the call.

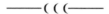

After locating the *Vasco Nuñez* and the cargo container on its deck, Kinlaw rented a room in a run-down hotel on the north side of Tunis, a few blocks from the beach. He had spent most of his time lounging on the bed and waiting. But when he finished the call from Hoag about the contents of the container, he stuffed his things in his backpack, walked downstairs, and made his way back toward the container port facility.

As he approached the gate, he slowed his pace and glanced over his shoulder hoping for an oncoming truck. Finding none in sight, he lingered near the corner opposite the gate until one approached. When it rolled past, he hurried after it and was within a few feet of the rear bumper when it came to a stop at the main gate guardhouse. While security guards checked the driver's documents and confirmed the seal number from the load, Kinlaw crawled beneath the frame at the rear wheels, wedged himself into the tight space near the axle, and repeated the trick that got him inside before.

Up and down the dock, cargo containers were stacked at each berth. Standing in rows that were often four boxes high, they shielded Kinlaw from view as he worked his way down the pier, watching, listening, thinking. As he did, he came to the conclusion that one of two things happened. Either the ship's crew had offloaded the container and exchanged it for one with tractor parts, or the contents had been removed and placed inside a new container. As he thought of the size and configuration of the deck, Kinlaw did not think removal of the contents was an option. But neither was removal of the container—it was buried in the stack when he found it. Still, he had to locate the box and do so quickly. Mistakes like this, however unintentional, could be career ending.

At the far end of the pier, Kinlaw came to a small, single-story office building. He studied it from a distance, watching through the windows as people arrived and left. As best he could tell, only one person was inside, a woman who worked in a room on the side to the left of the door.

Moving quietly, he made his way to the door, opened it carefully, and slipped inside. Without making a sound, he crossed to the other side of the building and into an office with an unoccupied desk. He made his way around it and dropped into a chair. A monitor sat to one side and with a few efficient keystrokes, he hacked into the port's operating system. From there, he created an account and accessed the security system. With persistence, he located a link for the video cameras and scrolled through them until he found one providing images of the berth where the *Vasco Nuñez* had been moored. A few minutes later, he found archived video from that camera and began looking through it.

Ten minutes later, he came to an image of the *Vasco Nuñez* still sitting at the pier. Playing files from that camera on fast-forward, he watched until the ship set sail. He played it in reverse and caught a glimpse of the crane returning to the ship just before it departed. He slowed the replay and tightened the image. As he did, he noticed the same man he'd seen on the ship's deck now standing on the pier beside it, watching as the overhead crane lifted two containers from the ship and set each of them onto waiting trailers. When both containers were in place, the man walked to the passenger side of the first cab and climbed inside.

Just then, a woman appeared in the office doorway. "What are you doing in here?" Kinlaw glanced up with a smile. "I was just leaving."

The woman backed away and ran toward the door that led outside. "Security!" she shouted. "Security! Someone call security!"

Kinlaw ran up the hall to the door and darted outside. Running as fast as his legs would carry him, he crossed the pier on foot and out through the main gate. As he reached the street, sirens wailed behind him but he kept running and soon found himself in a dark and empty alley not far from the sea. He slumped to the ground to catch his breath and once more took out the phone to call Hoag.

"What did you find?" Hoag asked as he took the call.

"They removed it from the ship."

"They removed the container?"

"Yes," Kinlaw replied. "The whole thing. I watched it. Took both of them. The missile and the launcher."

"Are you sure? The box we found looked like all the others."

"Yes, I'm sure," Kinlaw insisted. "I saw it on the video."

"You got into their system?"

"Yeah."

"Any idea what they did with it?"

"No. They just lifted it off, put it on a trailer, and hauled it away."

"We should have thought of this."

"Maybe. But I didn't think they saw me."

"Well, apparently they did."

"I'll find them," Kinlaw reassured. "I'll find them and then we can end this part of the story."

"Leave it," Hoag huffed. "We'll do it another way."

"There is no other way."

"Yes, there is. Just come home."

"No," Kinlaw snapped. "I'll find it." And he abruptly ended the call.

40

MOSCOW, RUSSIA

WHEN MIKHAIL MIRSKY RETURNED from Baku, he notified Vostok's chief of staff, Anatolyn Luzhkov, and requested an appointment to brief him on the trip. Instead of meeting at the Senate building inside the Kremlin, they met over tea in the solarium at Novo-Ogaryovo, a sprawling two-story mansion on the west side of Moscow that Vostok used as his private residence. Seated at a small table in the center of the room, they had a commanding view of the gardens and grounds. A butler served them from a porcelain service that had once belonged to Czar Nicholas I. The pastries were from Vostok's favorite bakery in the heart of old Moscow.

"So," Vostok began when they were alone, "I assume you had no trouble."

"None."

"And where do we stand with the Azerbaijanis?"

"To begin with, they know this isn't really about trade and it isn't about finding a location for a military exercise."

"Really?" Vostok looked surprised. "What do they think it is about?"

"They know about the deal between Iran and Germany."

"That is nothing new. The entire world knows about it. The only real question has been how and when the Chinese will react. That is the true question."

"Well," Mirsky sighed, "they know that Chinese troops are gathering on the Afghan border. They're certain the Chinese will respond by invading Iran."

"That...changes...things," Vostok said slowly.

"Perhaps," Mirsky nodded.

Vostok reached for a teacup. "Getting past the Azerbaijanis peacefully," he took a sip, "will cost us more than a military invasion."

"Not really," Mirsky shrugged. "It is just a matter of the terms."

"So how is it that they know about the Chinese?"

"That part is unclear. Perhaps the Germans told them. It would not be unlike Mueller to do just that. He has been playing all sides against the middle for some time."

"Or even the Chinese," Vostok suggested, "to maintain a neutral northern border and forestall an unwarranted response from the Azerbaijanis."

"Perhaps," Mirsky nodded, "but the Azerbaijanis pose no significant military threat to anyone. I would not see them reacting regardless of whether they had advance notice or absolute surprise."

"Yes," Vostok nodded thoughtfully. "I see your point." He paused to take another sip of tea, then continued. "Do the Iranians know what the Chinese are planning?"

"Apparently not."

"Do they know what *we* are planning?"

"They didn't before we met in Sochi."

"And now?"

"Adnan Karroubi was there," Mirsky explained.

"You talked to him?"

"We met for drinks."

"You think that was wise?"

"It was unavoidable. He and I have known each other a long time. I did not realize he was there until we ran into each other at the hotel. He saw me with Jalil Qurbani. After that, there was no avoiding the fact. Ignoring him would have raised even more suspicions than talking to him."

"So he knows we are talking to the Azerbaijanis."

"Yes. I told him we were negotiating terms of a new trade agreement."

"Did he believe you?"

"He has no reason not to believe me. But I suspect he realizes more is at stake than mere trade."

"How so?"

"I am a minister. Qurbani is a minster. Preliminary negotiations for these kinds of agreements are handled at the staff level. That they have moved to a ministerial level signals something more."

"So if he doesn't know about our military interests, he's curious."

"Yes."

"He'll figure it out."

"Probably. He's quite intelligent. At the least, he will find a way to probe the edges of the issue until he learns enough to satisfy his curiosity."

"If the Germans had only minded their own business," Vostok sighed. "All this could have been avoided."

"Ah," Mirsky nodded in agreement. "That is the lesson of Russian history. One can never trust a German."

"Yes," Vostok said with a smile. "We have learned that at a very great price."

Conversation lagged for a moment and both men ate in silence. Then Mirsky set aside his cup and wiped his hands on a napkin. "So, Mr. President, what shall we do now?"

"The Azerbaijanis will agree to give us access?"

"Yes. In the end they will grant us access, but it will cost us more than we expected to pay."

"And what does that get us?"

"Speed in the form of an unhindered advance to the Iranian border. And a measure of obscurity. Not absolute secrecy, but not the notoriety of an invasion of Azerbaijan, to which the world would react with outrage."

"Then I see no choice but to proceed. We'll gather the security council and brief them. If we're doing this, we have to get them onboard with us. We can't let the Chinese gain control of the entire region."

41

CIA HEADQUARTERS
LANGLEY, VIRGINIA

WHEN HOAG RETURNED FROM THE WHITE HOUSE situation room, he went downstairs to the basement operations section. "Okay," he said as he entered Jenny's cubicle. "We have a problem."

"The missile wasn't in the container," she acknowledged without looking up.

The answer caught him off guard. "You know?"

"Word travels."

"How did you find out?"

"Information still gets disseminated," she replied in a sarcastic tone.

A frown formed on his forehead and turned to a look of concern as he dropped onto a chair near her desk. "What's the matter?"

"What's the matter?" she railed. "Your analysis evaporates in front of the president and the entire national security team, and I'm not your first call?"

"I wanted time to think."

"About what?"

"I don't know," he whined plaintively. "I just needed time to think."

"And lick your wounds."

"That too." He looked over at her. "It was bad." His voice was low and he looked as if he might cry. "The president, everybody. Right there in the room. And it just fell apart."

"I know," Jenny said softly. "I know." She came from behind the desk and took a seat in a chair beside him. "How about if we get to work finding the missing container."

"I know." His eyes darted away. "I just wanted to think."

"You mean Dennis isn't here to bounce ideas off of, and you feel lost without him."

"I guess." Hoag turned to her. "Yes." His voice was almost a whisper. "I miss sitting across from him and working our way through a problem."

"Well," Jenny reached out to take his hand. "I'm here. Talk away."

"Won't be the same," he shook his head.

"Give it a try," she urged. "The meeting fell apart. Everyone left. What did you do?"

"I...called Dennis...from right there in the White House."

"What did he say?"

"He was upset. After we talked, he went back to the container facility and hacked into their security system."

"How did he do that?"

"He didn't say. I didn't ask."

"You talked to him? A second time?"

"Yeah. He says people at the port removed the containers from the ship before it left Tunis."

"So they found the locator."

"Yeah. Apparently someone on the ship saw him and figured out what was going on."

Jenny let go of Hoag's hand and slid low in the chair. "So how do you get a container off a ship? One that's already loaded and ready to sail."

"That's not how we do this."

"What do you mean?"

"Dennis and me. That's not how we bounce things back and forth."

She gave him a questioning look. "How do you do it?"

"I say, 'So the ship was loaded and ready to go.' And you say…" He gestured for her to continue.

"Then…" she said haltingly, "at the last minute, someone calls the dock supervisor and says, 'We need to get one of those containers off that ship.'"

"And not one container, but two."

"Someone has to approve it," she continued.

"The crane has to be moved," he added. "Truck chassis have to be ordered in place."

"Other containers have to be rearranged."

"And the manifest has to be amended."

"Which means people on the docks know about it."

"And the ship's captain."

"Who alerted them?"

"Someone had to look for it."

"And all of this means more than one person on that ship knew about this. The captain had to know. How else would the container get off? A mere crew member on the ship couldn't surreptitiously persuade the captain to remove the container. It's too much of a disruption." Hoag's eyes opened wider. "The captain knows about the container and its contents. We have to brief whoever's interrogating him."

"They sent an FBI team over to handle it."

"Why FBI?"

"I don't know," Jenny shrugged. "But that's what they did."

"We need our own people there, too."

"So, Dennis saw the security camera video?"

"Yes."

"We need to look at it, too."

Hoag stood. "Get everyone working on this. Find the security footage, traffic cameras, whatever they have."

"Won't have much. This is Tunis, you know."

"Whatever they have, find it." Hoag turned toward the door. "I'm going upstairs to talk to Hoyt."

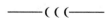

When Hoag returned to the basement later that day, he found Winston Smith in the operations command center. Around him, analysts worked at a frenetic pace. Hoag came to Smith's side. "What's going on?"

"Trying to find your missing container."

"Anything new?"

"Jenny and the guys down the hall found this," Smith pointed to a screen on the wall. Hoag turned in that direction and watched as video footage showed two trailer trucks at the container port. "Those are your missing containers," Smith continued. "On their way out of the container port in Tunis on a truck."

"Where did this footage come from?"

"Container port security cameras."

"This is what Dennis saw."

"Yeah," Smith nodded in agreement. "I'd say so."

"Think we can find the trucks?"

"Oh yeah," Smith nodded again. "We'll find them. Only question is, will we find them in time?"

"No way to track them," Hoag observed with a skeptical tone. "Like looking for the needle in the haystack."

"Yeah," Smith said deferentially. "Maybe. But we have options." He had a twinkle in his eye. "We're not out of plays yet."

"What do you mean?"

"I mean we have satellites now that cover the entire globe. This isn't the 1980s. We're sorting through that and —"

"Got it," a voice called from across the room.

Smith turned in that direction. "What do you have?"

Bob Webster, an analyst seated across the room, pointed to the monitor at his workstation. "Satellite images from the port at the time they off-loaded those containers." Hoag followed Smith across the room to see. Webster gestured to a picture on the screen. "That's it right there." He tapped a key on the keyboard. "It runs for just a few seconds." A series of images showed the containers being lifted from the ship's deck and placed onto waiting truck chassis.

"How far can you go with this?" Smith asked.

"I haven't followed it."

"Well, do it," Smith snapped. "Fill in the gaps. Work this out as far as you can take it."

"Okay, but it'll take a while. We have to switch from—"

Smith ignored the rest as he backed away from the workstation. "Okay," he called. "Listen up. Bob has the images we've been looking for. He's sending them to you now. We need a current location for the trucks. To get there, you have to compile the images in succession, following the trucks every step of the way. You'll have to use multiple satellite passes to do it. Don't short-cut it. Just begin with the satellite information Bob is sending you and put it together." The room was quiet while he spoke. When no one moved, he clapped his hands. "Let's go. Get busy. We have to find these trucks. And when you're finished, put the final product on the main screen."

Suddenly the room came alive again as the analysts went to work. Smith turned to Hoag. "We'll have a result in a little while." He looked Hoag in the eye. "Maybe you should take a nap. You don't look so good."

"I'm all right."

"How long since you slept?"

"I don't know."

"Take a nap," Smith insisted. "You're no good to anyone when you're this tired. We'll come get you when we know something."

Smith turned back to the task at hand, moving from workstation to workstation, answering questions, offering suggestions. Hoag watched for a moment, then stepped to the door and moved out into the hall. As he came from the command center, he met Jenny coming in his direction. "They gave you the update?"

"Yeah. They found satellite images for the container port. They're working on a timeline for the trucks now."

She took his hand in hers. "You're exhausted."

"I'm pretty tired," Hoag admitted.

"Good," she had a wry smile. "Come with me." She let go of his hand and hooked an arm in his. "I can take care of that."

"Where are we going?"

"You'll see."

Jenny led the way down the hall and around the corner. On the opposite side of the building, they came to a door marked Private and guarded by a digital lock. She entered the code for the lock and pushed open the door. Inside the room, two cots, pushed side-by-side, sat along the wall. A small table with a lamp sat nearby. She led Hoag inside and pushed the door shut. "Now," she said softly. "No one will bother us until something happens. And we can get some sleep." She leaned forward and kissed him. "In a little while."

42

CIA HEADQUARTERS LANGLEY, VIRGINIA

SOMETIME LATER, a knock on the door roused Hoag from a fitful sleep. He rose from the bed, pulled on his pants, stumbled across the room, and opened the door just wide enough to see Bob Webster standing in the hall outside. "What is it?" Hoag asked, squinting against the stark light that streamed into the room.

"They need you in the command center."

"What for?"

"Mr. Smith said to get you," Webster replied.

"I'll be there in a minute."

Hoag closed the door and switched on the light. Jenny rolled over to face him. "What time is it?"

"I don't know. Winston found something."

"Want me to come with you?"

"No," he leaned down to kiss her. "Go back to sleep."

Ten minutes later, Hoag arrived at the command center. "Did you sleep?" Smith asked, arching an eyebrow.

"I think so."

"You look rough."

"I need some coffee. What time is it?"

"About four hours later than when you were in here before."

"Okay," Hoag yawned. "What do you have?"

Smith pointed to a video screen on the wall. "This is the image we had before. Shows them taking the containers from the ship." He moved closer to the screen and pointed. "You see that man standing right there?"

Hoag took a few steps back and let his eyes focus on the spot Smith indicated. On the screen, barely discernible to the naked eye, was the image of a man standing next to the cab of the first truck. "Yeah, I see him. What about it?"

Smith gestured to the operator at the control station in the center of the room. "Show the next frame." The picture changed to show the first truck leaving the berth with the second truck lagging behind. Smith pointed again. "The man is gone."

"Yeah."

"He'd been standing by the first truck in the first picture. Then he was gone and the truck was moving in the next frame. We think he was riding in the first truck."

"Any way to tell for sure?"

"Not to a scientific certainty," Smith replied. "As you know, these images were composed from multiple satellite passes, traveling in low-earth orbit. They take a hundred frames per second but they're moving while they do it. National Reconnaissance Office puts it all together in images we can use, but it's a compilation."

"Right," Hoag nodded. "So where did the trucks go?"

Smith motioned to the operator, and the picture on the screen changed. "That's them leaving the container port." A new image appeared. "Headed down the street."

"Which direction?"

"This is west," Smith replied as the image changed again. "Here they've reached A4, the road that leads across town and becomes the highway to Bizerte." The picture changed again, showing a highway intersection. "And here they split up. First truck keeps going. Second truck turns off."

"That's a problem," Hoag groaned.

"Maybe. Maybe not." Two more pictures appeared in quick succession. "First truck continued on to the far side of town," Smith narrated. "And turned into this." An image appeared showing the truck stopped outside a warehouse. "And then the other one arrived." The image changed once more to show the first truck entering the warehouse and the second truck following close behind it.

"That's an industrial area," Hoag observed. "Think they have any security cameras we can use?"

A grin broke over Smith's face. "You're never going to leave research and analysis, are you?"

"I hope not," Hoag smiled.

"We're looking for the video now."

"Great. Get me the location of that warehouse."

"Already got it." Smith handed him a slip of paper. "You sending Dennis out there to find it?"

"I don't have much choice. He won't come home until this is over anyway. Better to send him and get it over with now than to drag this out while we wait for someone else to get there." Hoag took the cell phone from his pocket and scrolled down the contacts list for Kinlaw's number.

It was almost sunup in Tunis when Kinlaw received the text message from Hoag. By then, he'd been holed up in the hotel for three days. He checked the screen and found the message contained only a series of numbers. "This looks like map coordinates," he mumbled to himself.

With a tap of the screen, the GPS app on the phone loaded a map. A red dot highlighted the location—a building on a street in an industrial area west of town just off highway A4, in a neighborhood known as Cebalat. He rose from the bed, stuffed his belongings into his backpack, and started downstairs. When he reached the first floor he found the front desk was unoccupied. He reached over it and laid a twenty-dollar bill on the ledge by the cash drawer, then placed the key on top of it.

On the street out front, he found a street vendor just moving his cart into place. He bought an orange and ate it while he walked. It was the first real food he'd eaten in days.

At the corner, he turned left and continued four blocks to the beach. Regardless of the season, cars filled every available parking space as tourists flocked to the coast to swim or walk on the sand, and this season was no exception. Kinlaw glanced through the windshield of the parked cars as he walked nonchalantly up the street.

The first few were locked, but finally he came to one that wasn't. He looked around cautiously to make certain no one was watching, then opened the driver's door and slipped inside. The car he'd selected was an older model, a 1968 Opel Kadett. He felt beneath the dash and found the ignition wires, then touched them together and the engine came to life. With the wires twisted together to hold them in place, he put the car in gear and steered it way from the curb.

Using the iPhone for a guide, Kinlaw made his way south of the beach to the highway and turned right. A few minutes later, he reached Cebalat where the GPS system on the phone took him to a large metal building, to which successive additions had been cobbled together to form a rambling structure that covered most of a city block. From the lettering painted on the side, it appeared once to have been part of a soap factory.

Kinlaw drove past it, turned the corner at the next cross street, and checked the building from the backside. Weeds grew along the foundation, and sand was piled in a drift two feet high against one corner. From all he could see, it had not been occupied in years.

A block away, Kinlaw turned into an alley and parked the car alongside a furniture factory. He left it there and, with a strap of the backpack hooked over one shoulder, started back toward the warehouse, coming toward it from the west. When he reached it, he circled around to the back and found a door. It was unlocked and he eased it open, then went inside.

Beyond the door was an office and across from it a hallway. He followed the hall, feeling his way forward in the dim predawn light, as it meandered past several large rooms littered with trash and black steel drums. Finally, he came to a doorway that opened into the main part of the building. Two trailer trucks were parked there and seated beside them on the floor was the man he'd seen on the ship, only now, in the soft morning light that filtered through an overhead window, he appeared in worse health than before.

He held a cell phone, his thin, bony fingers quickly working the keys as he sent a text message. The sight of it reminded Kinlaw of his own phone and he took it from his pocket, switched off the power, then tucked it into a pocket on his backpack. He watched a moment longer from the doorway, then backed slowly up the hall to find a place to hide.

43

BAKU, AZERBAIJAN

WHEN THE AIRPLANE ROLLED TO A STOP, Rolan Buldakov rose from his seat, took his bag from the overhead compartment, and started toward the door. With a smile to the flight crew, he moved quickly down the steps and made his way across the tarmac toward the terminal. Posing as what he was, a Russian businessman prospecting for new investors and clients, he entered the building and joined a line waiting for clearance at the customs and immigration checkpoint. When it was his turn, Buldakov showed the inspection officer his passport and visa. The officer glanced at both documents briefly, stamped the visa with an entry date, and waved the next person forward. The entire process took less than twenty minutes.

From the airport, Buldakov took a taxi downtown to the Four Seasons Hotel. He checked in and was assigned a room with a commanding view of the old city and placed a phone call to Jafa Vahid, an investment broker who helped him find investors for his projects. Buldakov, an oilman of sorts, made his living buying undeveloped leases on the fringe of depleted oil fields. Azerbaijan, once the world's leading producer of crude oil, had many depleted fields. The two men arranged to have dinner that evening and spent most of the time discussing several of Buldakov's pending transactions.

When dinner was over and Vahid was gone, Buldakov walked up the street to the Red Lion Bar and took a seat at a table in the corner.

He ordered a drink of Russian vodka and sipped it while he waited. Thirty minutes later, he was joined by Murtuza Nagiyev, an assistant who worked in the office of Jalil Qurbani, the Azerbaijani foreign minister. He came to Buldakov's table and took a seat with his back to the window.

Buldakov raised his glass in a mock toast. "I was wondering how long it would take you to find me."

"I noticed you when you arrived at the hotel, but it was not a good time for me. And then you had dinner with that idiot Vahid. Why do you continue to do business with him?"

"He is a good man."

"He is a crook."

"I have conducted business with him for a long time."

"Without you running interference for him, we would have turned him over to the authorities long ago."

"I need him."

"Like you need a headache."

"He has access to people no one else can reach."

"That's because most people have sense enough to steer clear of him," Nagiyev cut his eyes at Buldakov. "And the people he knows," he added.

"You seem in an unusually cheery mood. Need something to drink?"

"Ahh, it's just these meetings. And no," Nagiyev gestured. "I don't want anything to drink."

"What meetings?"

"With the Russians. The ones you asked about." Nagiyev chuckled to himself. "It seems strange talking about them in the third person. The Russians. You're a Russian."

"But I am not like them."

"Maybe a little," Nagiyev shrugged.

"What do you mean?" Buldakov protested. "Maybe I can only see as far as the end of my nose. But they cannot see at all. And that, my friend, is a very big difference." He paused to take a sip from his glass. "So, tell me about these meetings."

"A few weeks ago we were contacted by the Russian foreign minister's office. I think he may have placed the call himself."

"Mirsky? Interesting. What did he want?"

"He wanted to get started on negotiating a new trade agreement with us. The current one expires next year. Talks were scheduled to begin in six or eight months, but he was wanting to do it now. We thought it was strange, but we agreed to meet. No harm in talking, right? Then he proposed this fast-track arrangement. Staff in Baku. Ministers in Sochi. I didn't like it. No one liked it. But Qurbani agreed."

"Why the rush?"

"Ahh," he grinned. "That's the key. The rush. Turns out they weren't really interested in the trade agreement at all. They gave us everything we wanted and more." Nagiyev's eyes were wide with interest. "What they really wanted was a military agreement that allowed them to place their troops on our soil."

"Permanently?" Buldakov asked, feigning outrage.

"No. The cover story is that the troops are there for training exercises."

"But that is not true?"

"No. They're pre-positioning them in anticipation of making a move on Iran."

Buldakov frowned. "A move against Iran? Why?"

"Your pals in Moscow are worried," Nagiyev explained.

"About what?"

"Iranian oil."

Once again, a frown wrinkled Buldakov's forehead. "The deal with the Germans?"

"That too, but right now they're worried about what might happen if control of Iranian oil falls into the hands of the Chinese."

"The Chinese," Buldakov mused. "They know about what the Chinese are doing?"

"Yes. They know about the Chinese troops gathering on the Afghanistan border."

"How do they know that?"

"I don't know. They have satellites. Not as many as the Americans, and not as good, but for whatever reason, they know."

"Will they get their military agreement?"

"Already done." Nagiyev took an envelope from his pocket, laid it on the table, and pushed it toward Buldakov. "Vostok will be here in a few days to sign it. There's a big ceremony planned. You should come. Might meet some new investors you and Vahid can swindle."

"Yes. Perhaps I shall."

"Now," Nagiyev changed the subject. "I have answered your questions; tell me what you know about mine."

"Ah, yes," Buldakov nodded. "You asked about the Americans. So far as we can determine, they do not intend to involve themselves with these things."

"They are not interested in a region with the world's largest supply of oil?"

"My sources tell me the Americans are convinced they can supply their own oil."

"But we supply the price."

"I think they have decided that none of that matters now."

"What do you mean?"

"Take a walk with me." Buldakov pushed back his chair and stood. "I'll tell you about it when we are outside."

44

BEIJING, CHINA

AT THE RUSSIAN EMBASSY, Pavel Manarov was busy at his desk, reviewing a file, when an assistant handed him an envelope. "This came in the pouch from Moscow." He took it from her and opened it to find a note written on plain white paper that read, "We need more details about pending Chinese movements." Manarov glanced at it and sighed.

As a career diplomat, he'd been doing this a long time, working first from the embassy in Washington, D.C., then from London as an intelligence liaison, and it was always the same. A field agent located a potential source of critical intelligence and discovered a personal weakness that made the source vulnerable. Manarov stepped in to develop a relationship with the source that exploited that weakness, then used it to gain access to information deemed vital by his superiors. Often his work supplied information from the target country's darkest secrets. Then Moscow, with a voracious appetite for gossip, pushed for more and more details until either the source cracked under pressure or the source's body turned up in a dumpster.

"Why don't they just check the satellites?" Manarov grumbled to himself. But he already knew the reason why. They couldn't. Most of the time, the cameras malfunctioned and even when they worked the images they produced were often grainy and of limited value.

Using a Blackberry to avoid compromising the embassy's official system, Manarov prepared a text message that read, "Feeding the birds in the park?" Then he pressed a button and reluctantly sent the message to Chen Hongsheng. Moments later, Hongsheng sent a response. "I'm watching the fish today."

Manarov knew what that meant without asking more. Hongsheng would take lunch that day at noon outside the aquarium, an attraction built next door to the Beijing National Stadium, site of the 2008 Olympics opening ceremonies. Unlike the park with a fountain where they usually met, the aquarium was a public place, often crowded with visitors. The change in location—park to aquarium, secluded to very public—did not go unnoticed, but Manarov had little choice but to follow through with the meeting. He checked his watch and saw it was just now ten o'clock, plenty of time yet to reach the aquarium by noon. He put away the phone and did his best to concentrate on the work at his desk.

Across town, in a nondescript building occupied by the Ministry of State Security, Chong Han sat at a workstation dutifully staring at a computer monitor. All day long he'd been sitting there waiting, watching, and listening to the voice and message traffic that moved into and out of Chen Hongsheng's cell phone. The calls that day were from family, friends, and a woman who appeared to be Hongsheng's lover. Nothing from work. Not even a call for a wrong number.

Then a text message caught Han's eye, a frequent caller from an unlisted number asking about a visit to the park, followed by a reply indicating Hongsheng planned to be 'visiting the fish.' Mention of the park struck Han as particularly curious.

They'd been tracking Hongsheng for months, certain he was passing secrets to the Russians. In that time, the park near his apartment had been the sole rendezvous location for meetings with his handler. This text message represented a change in location and Han wondered why. For an answer, he leaned back in his chair and looked toward Cam Fong, who was seated across the room. "You should take a look at this."

Fong came from his desk and leaned over Han's shoulder, quickly scanning the text message. "Feeding the birds in the park?" he mumbled. "I'm watching the fish today." Fong backed away, repeating the phrases aloud as he struggled to connect the two. Then he looked over at Han. "They're changing the meeting place from the park to the aquarium."

"But why? That's a long way from his apartment. He'll have to take the bus."

"Apartment?" Fong seemed surprised. "He's not at work?"

"No." Han pulled up a separate screen on the monitor with a map of Beijing. "There," he pointed. "The cell phone is right there." A white dot blinked to indicate the location on the map.

Fong had a worried look as he ran a hand across his chin. "This is not good. There are only a few reasons to change the location. The most obvious would be for security, which would suggest he knows that we're watching. But in the entire time we've been following him they've never met anywhere else than the park and he's never seemed worried about anyone noticing."

"And the change is not for convenience. This is inconvenient, even to his work."

"Right," Fong nodded. "The only other reason is because they have something important to exchange and he wants to make sure it is not compromised." His eyes widened. "This is a preemptive move on his part. He's protecting something."

"Did we scare him?"

"I don't see how. We didn't do anything."

"What should we do?"

"We have to stop him." Fong took a cell phone from his pocket.

"Stop him? From what?"

"From leaving the apartment."

"But why? He's done nothing yet."

"Like I just told you," Fong insisted. "He's about to make the drop."

"We don't know that for certain. He might simply be changing the location to see if he is being followed. But we know the location," Han argued. "We have a team following him. We can add more people. They can stop him from making an exchange."

"No," Fong shook his head from side to side. "That didn't stop them from making the exchange before. We may know the agreed-upon destination, but if he gets on that bus, the drop could happen anywhere between his apartment and the aquarium."

Fong scrolled down the contacts list on the cell phone and placed a call. Moments later, he reached the team following Hongsheng. "This is Fong. Take him out." The words were terse and pointed. Hongsheng was to be eliminated. And just like that, the order was given. Fong ended the call and returned the cell phone to his pocket.

Han looked astounded. "Don't you need to call someone before doing that?"

"No. I have all the authority I need. Our military is in the critical stages of a major operation. He was about to share vital information. We cannot let that occur."

Shortly before eleven, Manarov left his desk and took the elevator to the embassy garage, located in the basement beneath the building. There he requisitioned an unmarked automobile from the motor pool and climbed inside. A check of his watch told him there was plenty of time. No need to rush. He steered the car from the garage into traffic and started across town.

Using backstreets and alleys, he avoided most of the traffic congestion and arrived at the aquarium shortly before noon. He made the block once around the facility, checking faces in the crowd and vehicles along the street for anything suspicious. Satisfied the location was safe, he parked the car in a parking deck two blocks away and walked back to the aquarium's front entrance.

Benches lined both sides of the broad walkway that led from the street to the entrance doors. Tourists of every race and nationality lingered there, forming a constant flow of traffic into and out of the building. Manarov did his best to blend in and made his way to a bench on the right.

Thirty minutes later, Hongsheng still had not arrived. Established protocol suggested that they break off the attempt and establish contact again later, but Manarov often ignored protocol. Instead of leaving, he took the Blackberry from his pocket, created a text message containing only a question mark, and sent it to Hongsheng's number.

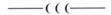

Half a block away, Robert Whilden sat behind the steering wheel of a gray Honda Accord parked at the curb on a cross street between the aquarium and the garage where Manarov left his car. From his position, Whilden had an unobstructed view of the front entrance to the building and access to Manarov's most probable route of escape. As he scanned the scene before him, a taxi came to a stop not far from the corner. The rear door opened and Chen Hongsheng climbed out. He paid the fare and started across the street, angling in Whilden's direction as he crossed in the middle of the block.

As he neared the sidewalk on the far side of the street, a black Audi sedan approached. It slowed as it came alongside him, and a passenger in the rear seat pointed an automatic pistol in his direction. Whilden saw a silencer fitted to the muzzle. Moments later, a bullet struck the fender of a car parked to Hongsheng's left. Another struck the car to his right. Then a red blotch appeared in the center of Chen's back, and his arms flew up in a reflexive motion. An instant later, his head snapped backward and a gaping hole appeared at his right temple. Hongsheng took two steps forward, carried mostly by momentum, and fell face first onto the sidewalk.

Whilden snatched a radio from the console and keyed the microphone. "Their man is hit."

"I saw them," someone replied.

"I know the driver," another added.

"Stay on task," Whilden replied, doing his best to sound calm. "Stay with our man. Is he okay?"

"He's right here on the bench," a voice murmured quietly. "I'm looking straight at him."

Ten minutes later, when there was still no reply to his text message, Manarov rose from the bench and started back toward the car. As he neared the corner at the cross street, he noticed a crowd gathered midway down the block. Emergency vehicles were parked there. He was headed in that direction anyway and was curious to see what caused the commotion. At the corner, he drew abreast of the crowd and saw uniformed policemen standing on the sidewalk and in the street, holding back the crowd and forming a circle around the body of a man sprawled across the curb. His arms were spread out wide and blood trickled from a gaping hole in his head. Then he realized the dead man was Hongsheng.

A policeman looked in Manarov's direction and for a moment their eyes met. Then Manarov glanced away, crossed the street to the opposite corner, and continued toward the car. In the parking deck, he took out the keys to unlock the car door, but his hands shook uncontrollably and he had to work to fit the key in the lock. Finally he succeeded in opening it and flopped down behind the steering wheel. His mind reeled as he thought of what he'd just seen.

Hongsheng was dead. Most certainly someone knew what they were doing, which meant they knew about him, too. His first instinct was to run, but that was only fear and he pushed the notion aside. Instead he forced himself to think logically through the situation. If the work had been compromised, Moscow needed to know. Vasily Kerensky, the Foreign Intelligence Service chief, insisted on being informed of such events. "I've been reviewed by him twice," Manarov mumbled. "He'll remember me, and that isn't good."

Manarov took the Blackberry from his pocket to send a message and saw the note indicating his text to Hongsheng had failed. A sinking feeling swept over his chest. If they knew Hongsheng had been passing classified information, then they knew about the cell phone calls and text messages. The Blackberry was no longer a tool of his trade. It was now a link that connected him to an operation gone awry—a link that needed to be broken. He opened the back cover of the phone, removed the SIM card, and slid it into his pocket. Then he laid the phone on the seat beside him and backed the car from the parking space.

At the ground level, he steered the car into traffic and picked up speed. Two blocks later, a garbage truck was stopped in the far left lane and workmen emptied refuse cans into it. Manarov moved the car to the left and lowered the window. He slowed as he approached and, as the car rolled past the truck, tossed the phone into the growing refuse pile and sped away.

45

TEHRAN, IRAN

ADNAN KARROUBI SPENT THE MORNING at his desk in the study at Golestan Palace, reading a book that bore the title *Life of God's Messenger*. It had been found recently in the library of Qom, and all of Islam was excited by the possibility that a work of such monumental value, written in the year 767 by Ibn Ishaq and previously thought to be nonexistent, might now be available. From the moment of its discovery, debate raged among scholars regarding its authenticity, many of it heated. When the controversy spread to members of the Assembly of Experts, Karroubi took upon himself the task of authenticating the manuscript. He'd been working on it almost nonstop since shortly after returning from Sochi.

At noon, he left the study in search of his assistant, Hasan Dirbaz. The desk outside the study door, where Dirbaz normally sat, was unoccupied and Karroubi continued past it to the hallway. From behind him, he heard a cell phone ding with a signal indicating a new text message was available. He turned back from the hallway and saw a cell phone resting on Dirbaz's desk. Karroubi checked the screen and saw no message, but when he scrolled through the list of recent calls, he noticed several international phone numbers. *This cannot be good,* he thought.

As his assistant, Dirbaz saw everything that crossed Karroubi's desk. Every memo, research paper, letter, and formal governmental proposal. He also knew the names of every visitor to the palace and every person Karroubi entertained at over a dozen private residences located across the city. Dirbaz knew everything, and the fact that he was in contact with foreign nationals made Karroubi deeply suspicious.

After a moment, he set the phone aside and returned to his own desk, still wondering about Dirbaz's foreign contacts, when he caught sight of his cell phone lying atop a stack of books. He checked the screen and saw a new text message had arrived. It was from a number not on his contacts list, but the message made his heart skip a beat. "Babak holding item. Original address unavailable. Send instructions."

When Karroubi and Nabhi Osmani first devised the scheme to build container ships, load them with missiles carrying nuclear warheads, and sail them to America, they knew that selecting good men would be the key to success. The *Panama Clipper* had been assigned to Zaheden and had worked precisely as designed, delivering a nuclear explosion above Washington, D.C., that, in turn, produced an electromagnetic pulse that disabled the electrical grid for the eastern half of the country. That single blast spread havoc to millions of Americans and in a single stroke reduced their lifestyle to that of a jungle village in Africa.

Sirjan, however, aboard the *Amazon Cloud*, had proved utterly incompetent and a complete failure. The ship had been disabled as a result of the EMP from the blast of the *Panama Clipper* missile. Everyone knew that could happen, but they also knew the electronics in the missile and the launcher would still be functional. Yet rather than launching the missile as the ship drifted aimlessly south, Sirjan had allowed the missile to be captured by the Americans, compromising the entire operation.

Babak Tabas, onboard the *Santiago*, was supposed to bring the same destruction upon the West Coast with an explosion high over Los Angeles. As in the east, no buildings would be destroyed and not a single person injured by the blast, but the resulting misery would show the world the strength of Islam and the resolve of Allah's people to see their cause vindicated. The ship, however, had been delayed leaving China, one of its last ports of call before sailing to the United States. The delay put it behind schedule, meaning it would have arrived off the California coast after the blast in the east, and long after the Americans moved to a heightened alert. Capture would have been far more likely than success. Instead of risking such failure, Babak ordered the ship to an alternate route. Crew and cargo simply disappeared. Now here it was at last, a nuclear missile on a launcher, fully operational, and at Karroubi's exclusive disposal. The only decision remaining was when and where to use it. And that, he could not say just yet.

Karroubi's fingers trembled with excitement as he typed in the reply, "Instructions soon." He sent the message and laid the phone on the desk. Then he moved to the chair and sat down, lost in thoughts of what might have been and how the world would look if they'd succeeded in working their plan.

Sometime later, he heard Dirbaz return to his desk. Karroubi glanced up and saw his assistant checking the messages on his cell phone. Karroubi's mind turned again to the number he'd seen on Dirbaz's call log and he did not like it. A cloud descended over his face as he thought of the possibilities, and of what he would do to Dirbaz if the worst turned out to be true.

46

MOSCOW, RUSSIA

WHEN VASILY KERENSKY, chief of Russian Foreign Intelligence, received news of the events involving Pavel Manarov in Beijing, he telephoned President Vostok and requested a meeting of the principals involved in planning the incursion through Azerbaijan. Vostok agreed to meet within the hour. Briefcase in hand, Kerensky arrived at Vostok's office and was ushered to the president's private study, where the meeting was less likely to attract the attention of others in the building.

By then, military operations against Iran had moved beyond the speculative phase and the secretary of defense, General Garasimov, had been brought into the discussion. He joined Kerensky, Vostok, and Mikhail Mirsky, the foreign affairs minister, for the meeting. They gathered around an antique table and after they were seated, Vostok turned to Kerensky. "You wanted to brief us on events in Beijing."

"Following decisions made at our last meeting," Kerensky began, "we instructed our agent at the embassy in Beijing to contact his source once again, requesting greater detail about Chinese troop movements toward the Afghan border. Contact was made and a meeting arranged, but as the Chinese source was approaching the meeting location, he was shot in the head."

Mirsky appeared incredulous. "In broad daylight?"

"Yes," Kerensky nodded. "Our agent saw his body lying in the street."

Vostok looked concerned. "Any indication who did it?"

"None, officially," Kerensky replied. "However, we made inquiries of others in China and learned that the source has been under observation for quite some time by the Ministry of State Security."

General Garasimov nodded thoughtfully. "Any way to know if that investigation affected the quality of the information your source supplied to us?"

"No," Kerensky shook his head vigorously. "To the contrary, the information he supplied and the information he was prepared to give us at that last meeting was apparently deemed vital to the Chinese cause. So much so that they killed him rather than merely apprehend him."

"They were sending a message to us," Garasimov suggested.

"Perhaps. But why they did not attempt to corrupt it is a mystery, but we have confidence in what he gave us."

"And you have double-checked the information this source gave you?"

"Yes." Kerensky opened his briefcase and took out a folder. "These are the latest satellite images." He opened the folder, removed a photograph, and laid it on the table. "This came from one of our best satellites." He pointed to the picture. "That is the Afghan border six months ago." He took out another photo. "And that is it today. We see troops here in large numbers. They are obscured in some places by the shadows of the mountains, but our analysts think there are several hundred thousand men there now."

Vostok was taken aback. "Several hundred thousand?"

"Yes." Kerensky turned to another picture. "And this is more troubling. This is an equipment yard approximately one hundred sixty kilometers from the border. In this photograph, taken four months ago, it is empty." He picked up another photograph. "And in this one, the equipment yard is full." He tapped the photo with his index finger. "Our analysts say those are trucks carrying tanks."

"That certainly supports the information conveyed earlier by your source," Mirsky agreed. "But why did they kill him?"

"I suspect that the first of those information transfers occurred before the Chinese became suspicious. He was very inventive in the way he did it, and even after they became suspicious I don't think they knew what he had or how he was giving it to us. Until that last exchange. I think that's when they realized how serious his breach of security had become and realized they had to stop him, at any cost."

Garasimov had a quizzical look. "You said he was inventive?"

"Yes," Kerensky grinned. "The most recent transfer was actually given to us from a website that we accessed through a barcode printed on the bottom of a McDonald's bag."

"Times have changed," Garasimov sighed.

Kerensky gestured to the pictures. "I think they had him killed because he was undermining their entire military operation."

Vostok leaned back with his hands in his lap. "Is that your guess, or are you basing that on some additional information?"

"That is my guess, and the guess of our secondary sources inside the Ministry of State Security. They think the Chinese were slow to realize what he was doing and when they finally did, they were shocked."

"Can you tell us about those secondary sources?"

"They are multiple. One of them was a member of the detail assigned to investigate the source."

"So, there is no doubt this is serious," Mirsky offered.

"It also indicates that time is short," Vostok added. "We need to speed things up, faster than planned."

"If we do that," General Garasimov countered, "we'll create a larger footprint. So far, we have justified our troop movements as merely a redeployment of personnel from base to base. We've called up some of the reserves, but only those that could be justified as necessary to cover vacancies during this readjustment. They all expect to return home soon. If we move troops to our border with Azerbaijan, we will need tents and temporary housing. It will become a major operation, not merely from the trucks on the highway transporting our troops. The United States will surely notice. And when our reservists do not return home as expected, word will begin to leak out as to what we are really doing."

"I do not think that matters now," Vostok pointed to the photographs on the table. "This puts us on a different timetable."

"But what will we tell the families?" Garasimov asked. "What will we tell the public?"

"We'll tell them it's part of an exercise," Vostok chided.

"That story is getting a little old," Garasimov groused.

"Most people know it's just a cover," Mirsky added.

"Most people won't ask," Vostok responded. "And if it makes you feel better, put some of our men in Azerbaijani uniforms." His voice grew louder and he gestured with his hands as he talked. "Fly their flag in some of the locations. Make it appear to be a joint operation. I don't care. Just position our troops so they are ready to move into Azerbaijan as soon as we sign the agreement."

By the time Vostok finished, he was shouting. They sat at the table in silence, the others somewhat cowered by his outburst.

"Very well, Mr. President," Garasimov agreed finally. "We will be on the border and waiting."

"Good," Vostok snapped, and he bolted from his chair.

When he was gone, Garasimov looked over at Mirsky. "I hope he realizes we can't possibly move the entire force there by then. Isn't he going to Baku day after tomorrow?"

"Yes," Mirsky nodded. He agreed with Garasimov but wanted no part of any dissension against Vostok's role as president and leader of the nation. "Just do the best you can," he added, avoiding the point of Garasimov's comment, "and be ready to give an explanation for it."

47

BERLIN, GERMANY

FOUR BLACK MERCEDES SUVS rolled quietly to a stop on the driveway outside the main entrance to the Chancellery. Guards formed a security cordon from the vehicles to the steps and opened the rear door of the first SUV. Juan Gomez Bayona, the president of Spain, climbed from the car and started toward the building. At the top of the steps, Georg Scheel, the German foreign minister, waited to greet him. After a brief word of welcome, Scheel ushered Bayona inside.

When Bayona and Scheel entered the Chancellery, Max Brody, head of the German central bank, appeared on the steps. The rear door of the second SUV opened and Luis Aragon, head of Banco de España, emerged from the car. He shook hands with Brody and the two moved quickly into the building.

A little way down the corridor, President Bayona waited with Scheel. Brody and Aragon caught up with them. Aragon caught Scheel's eye. "Everything is ready?"

"Yes," Scheel nodded. "We are set. I forwarded your document package to the chancellor's office last week and we are set to discuss it today."

"Good. We need assistance immediately."

Scheel had a cautious smile. "Then let us hope things turn out well."

Surrounded by staff and security agents, the four men moved down the hall to Mueller's office. Mueller was seated at his desk when they arrived. He stood and shook hands with Bayona and Aragon. When the formalities of an official greeting were satisfied, they took their seats—Bayona and Aragon in front of the desk, with Scheel and Brody in a row behind them, Mueller in his chair between the desk and the window.

"You wanted to see me about your request for assistance," Mueller began.

"Well...yes." Bayona appeared awkward and ill at ease. "As you can see from the documents, our banking system is in trouble and very much in need of an infusion of liquidity."

"The documents you submitted paint a rather grim picture."

"We thought full disclosure was the better approach," Bayona smiled. "All we need is enough to get us past this moment, until our economy can recover."

"It's worse than that," Aragon interjected. "We are facing a severe liquidity crisis, but we also have fundamental problems. Our entire banking system is on the verge of collapse."

Bayona's face turned red in a flare of anger. "We already agreed that we would—"

Mueller ignored him and focused on Aragon. "What sort of problems?"

"Our banks own a significant portion of the federal debt. And they have held far too many subprime mortgages. To make matters worse, in an effort to protect against the risk of mortgage default, they purchased default swaps—agreements that transferred the risk of default to another institution in exchange for a cash payment now. Most of those swaps were purchased from Spanish banks rather than from outside financial intuitions."

"Creating a house of cards."

"Yes."

Bayona glared at Aragon but Aragon ignored him and continued. "In addition to that, there were certain irregularities in the way various transactions were treated for accounting purposes."

"Such as?"

"Such as, mortgage packages that were sold by the originating banks to related institutions under repurchase agreements. They were treated as arms-length sales but all of these transactions occurred in the last month of the quarter. Every participating bank exercised its buy-back option in the first month of the next quarter, allowing them to book it as a sale in one quarter and an investment in the next quarter."

"They cooked the books," Mueller added.

"Well...yes," Aragon reluctantly agreed. "They treated these transactions as favorably as possible, but the net effect was to shield the true financial condition of the banks from public view."

"And this reached the central bank?"

"We did not participate in the mortgage transactions, but at the direction of the current administration and parliament, we acquired nonperforming loans from various banks in order to avert their earlier collapse. Those nonperforming assets are now on our books."

Mueller looked over at Bayona. "You knew about all this when you made that decision?"

Bayona turned sideways in the chair. "I did not come here to receive a scolding."

"Why did you come here?"

"Because we're desperate. We need nine hundred fifty billion Euros and there's no one else who can lend us that kind of money."

"Did you apply for assistance from the European Stability Mechanism? We established it for just such an occasion as this."

"We thought of that," Bayona replied in an imperious tone, "but they would require severe austerity measures that our people would not accept."

"You mean," Mueller bristled, "if you took their money you'd be forced from office."

"They do not get to determine who is the president of Spain," Bayona retorted. "That is for the citizens of Spain to determine."

"But your bank can't survive without it," Mueller offered.

"We need those austerity measures," Aragon interjected.

"I told you not to say such things," Bayona snapped.

"There's no sense in covering it up now," Aragon argued. "We have fundamental problems which I think should be addressed. This is the most opportune moment to fix them." He looked over at Mueller.

"President Bayona thinks we can patch this up and get past the crisis, then the economy will revive and everything will be fine, and he won't have to risk his office to correct the problem."

"That won't work if your banking system is part of the problem," Brody suggested.

"Exactly," Aragon agreed.

Bayona stood in a huff. "I don't have to sit here and take this kind of treatment."

"Yes, you do," Mueller responded, pointing to the chair. "Sit back down."

Bayona glared at him. "You cannot treat me like a beggar."

"I treat you like a beggar because that's what you are." Mueller's tone was stern but not caustic. "Sit down." Bayona hesitated, then dropped onto the chair. Mueller rested his elbows on the desk. "You're asking me to approve an injection of one trillion Euros into your banking system. Okay," he nodded. "I understand you're in a bad spot financially. Now tell me about the riots in the streets of Madrid."

The talks with Bayona and Aragon continued for well over two hours, much longer than anyone anticipated. They concluded, however, without a firm commitment from Mueller. When Bayona and Aragon were gone, Mueller asked Scheel and Brody to remain and invited General Erhard and Konrad Hölderlin, the head of German Foreign Intelligence, to join them. Scheel outlined the discussion to bring Erhard up to date. When he was finished, Erhard just shook his head. "They have serious problems and not a clue how to fix them."

"I think they know how to fix it," Mueller corrected. "They just don't want to pay the political price for doing it."

"And neither of them wants to give any ground," Scheel added.

"I didn't realize their government was so dysfunctional," Mueller sighed.

"And they didn't even tell you about Bayona's private investment accounts," Brody observed.

Mueller frowned. "He has accounts?"

"Yes," Scheel nodded. "He's accumulated almost a billion dollars US in accounts in New York, the Cayman Islands, and Moldova."

"Good thing that didn't come up." Mueller turned to Erhard. "They've formally requested our assistance with quelling the riots and propping up their banking system. Brody tells me we have the financial capacity to help their banks, but I don't want to send in our troops if they're just going to become part of the problem. At the same time, I don't want to spend the money if the country is going to collapse. From a military perspective, can we do this? Can we effectively restore order?"

"As we discussed before," Erhard began, "we have the authority to act. But I don't think we can be effective as long as Bayona is in power. He has become the face of Spanish anger toward the government. If we go in there, even to merely restore order, it will appear as though we are supporting him."

"Which we would be doing," Scheel added. "We would be relieving him of public pressure and, in effect, propping up a regime that most of the citizens would like to end."

"I agree," Brody chimed in. "He has proved to be wholly ineffective, inept, and, as we've alluded to here already, corrupt."

"But do we have the economy?" Mueller asked.

"We might encounter inflation later," Brody answered. "But yes, we can do it. Both fiscally and financially. We can manage it for now."

"All right," Mueller sighed. "We'll worry about the economic consequences later. You know how to do this in a way most advantageous to us?"

"Yes," Brody nodded. "Is that the approach you wish for us to take?"

"If we're doing this, we're doing it for ourselves as much as anyone," Mueller added, then he turned to Erhard. "Have our forces prepare an assessment of the situation in Spain and draft a plan for deployment with the rules of engagement."

"Yes, Mr. President."

Mueller turned to Hölderlin, who'd been silent throughout the meeting. "Konrad, we need a plan to move Bayona out of office."

"I've just been sitting here thinking about that very thing,"

Hölderlin offered. "I believe we can do that without risk of life at all."

"Oh?" Mueller had a quizzical look. "How so?"

"We'll buy him out," Hölderlin said with a straight face.

"But him out?" Scheel chuckled. "You'll just call him up and offer to buy the presidency?"

"Something like that," Hölderlin smiled. "Leave the details to me. We will move him out."

With that, the meeting broke up. As the others left the room, Mueller took Scheel aside. "You are comfortable with our authority to do this?"

"Yes. Very much. General Erhard is correct. We have the authority under prior agreements. Things are getting out of hand in Madrid."

"I agree. And I think many in the world would be glad to see us do this. But just the same, we need to get a message to the Americans."

"The Americans?" Scheel had a puzzled look. "Do they matter now?"

"Perhaps not. But we do not want them to speak out against us. They have a habit of becoming both a rallying point and a point of alienation, all at the same time."

"Why not just call Hedges yourself?"

"I would rather give President Hedges and myself a little space on this. German soldiers on the streets of Madrid, suppressing Spanish citizens, might be…historically sensitive. And who knows what Hölderlin will do to move Bayona out of office. We may all want some distance from that."

"Yes," Scheel nodded. "I see your point."

"You will get a message to President Hedges?"

"Yes, sir. Jürgen Stabreit is in Washington now. I shall contact him immediately."

"But the president is in Nebraska," Mueller corrected.

"Not anymore. He has returned to the White House."

"Interesting." Mueller had a faraway look in his eyes.

"Yes," Scheel nodded. "It is very interesting. Did you need something else?"

"No," Mueller returned to the moment. "That is all. Just make sure the message is delivered promptly."

48

BAKU, AZERBAIJAN

THE FOLLOWING DAY, Doug Bergen left the Baku Hilton on Azadlig Avenue and hailed a taxi for the ride to a building on Nizami Street once occupied by the Caspian-Black Sea Oil and Trade Society. Now it was to be the site of the official signing ceremony for the renewal of the multiyear Russian-Azerbaijani Trade Agreement.

Two blocks from the building, the street was clogged with traffic. Bergen paid the fare, climbed from the taxi, and covered the remaining distance on foot.

At the front entrance to the building, he flashed press credentials from the *New York Register* and was waved inside. A security screening station stood just past the doors. He made his way through it and followed signs down the building's central corridor to a reception hall. Security guards lined the way and docents offered assistance, but he'd been there before, studying every inch of the building, and knew where to go.

In the reception hall, a table with two chairs stood to the right. On either side of it was a podium. Rows of chairs sat facing it, most of them already full. Guards directed Bergen to an area on the opposite side of the room that had been roped off for journalists. A similar area was designated along the near wall for photographers. Television cameras were set up with a view toward the table. Bergen did as he was told and found a place among the journalists.

In a few minutes, Tahir Shahat, the Azerbaijani president, entered the room. Two steps behind him was Vladimir Vostok. Both men walked to the table and stood, waving at the crowd but ignoring each other. As applause subsided, Vostok moved to the podium on the far side. Shahat stood at the one nearest the door. As the host, he spoke first.

"We are delighted today to announce the renewal of our bilateral trade agreement with the Republic of Russia, our most important trading partner and our ally to the north." The audience applauded loudly. "Through the cooperation of President Vostok and with his enthusiastic support, we have reached this accord fully one year ahead of schedule and look forward to a long and vibrant trading relationship with Russian businesses." He continued for another five minutes. Then it was Vostok's turn.

"Today we join with President Shahat and the people of Azerbaijan in taking this momentous step forward in securing the vitality of our business relationship and, indeed, in securing the freedom and prosperity of the entire Caucasus region. We are delighted to have reached such an historic agreement with our most strategic and important ally and look forward to enjoying the fruits of that association for years to come."

Bergen listened intently as both men spoke. Nothing in either speech hinted at anything more than a cordial and mutually supportive relationship between the two nations. And nothing belied the true reason for that accord. Rumors had been running rampant since the meetings in Sochi between Mirsky and Qurbani, suggesting there was more to the agreement than trade, and insinuating the parties arrived at that accord after bitter and acrimonious negotiations which bordered on coercion, including the threat of an armed Russian invasion. But that day, in the room at the Caspian-Black Sea Oil and Trade building, the language was only conciliatory.

With their remarks concluded, the two leaders sat at the table. Assistants brought leather folders and opened one before each of them. Vostok and Shahat signed their separate copies, then exchanged them and signed again. When they were finished, they stood and shook hands.

The crowd stood in response and applauded enthusiastically,

with shouts of approval interspersed. While they continued, a guard removed the rope restraining the photographers and they stepped forward, forming a line across the room, snapping picture after picture in quick succession.

As the applause died away, Bergen's phone rang with a single ping. He took it from his pocket and saw a text message that read, "L'Aparté Café on the corner." He returned the phone to his pocket and headed toward the door.

When he reached the café he found Murtuza Nagiyev seated at a table in back, reading a magazine. Bergen made his way across the dining room to the table and sat down.

Nagiyev laid the magazine on the table and looked up with a smile. "Buldakov came to see me."

"Buldakov," Bergen scoffed. "What did he want?"

"Same thing everyone else does."

"Did you tell him?"

"Yes," Nagiyev nodded. "I told him the same thing I told you. Iran made a deal to broker their oil through Germany, effectively cutting off the Chinese from one of their primary foreign sources. The Russians are afraid the Chinese will make a move to take the oil by force. They want to be ready to invade Iran for themselves, if it comes to that. To do that, the Russians need to stage troops here, in our country. That's what the meetings were about in Sochi and that's what the signing today is about."

"That's all you told him?"

"Yes. I explained that to you yesterday." Nagiyev leaned forward and lowered his voice. "Listen, I know your country was hit hard by the attack, and I'm sure by now you've figured out it was the Iranians all along. But we need your intervention here to prevent a war."

"You think we should intervene to protect Iran, a nation that tried to destroy us?"

"You still have the world's most powerful navy," Nagiyev argued. "You can make a difference." He leaned back in his chair. "And this is still the most vital region for the world's economy."

"I'm not so sure about that," Bergen replied. "And I'm not sure Washington has the will for a war right now. Or the country, for that matter. And anyway," he shrugged, "I'm just the messenger."

"Yeah, I know." Nagiyev's tone became lighter and more pleasant. "You still enjoy sports?"

"Sure."

Nagiyev slid the magazine across the table. "There's an article in here you might enjoy. I marked the page for you."

Bergen took the magazine and rolled it together. "Good. I'll read it tonight when I get back to the room."

"You should probably look at it before then." Nagiyev pushed his chair back from the table and stood. "It's always good to see you, Doug."

"You too," Bergen responded as Nagiyev moved away from the table.

Bergen waited a few minutes, then left the café and took a taxi back to the hotel. In his room, he opened the magazine and found a four-page document tucked inside. Even from a quick scan, he could see this was a photocopy of an agreement, signed by Vostok and Shahat, permitting Russian troops to pass unhindered through Azerbaijan and camp along the Iranian border. Bergen spread the pages on the bed and took a picture of them with his iPhone. He checked to make certain the photos were readable, then prepared them as an attachment to an email and sent them to a cell phone number assigned to Winston Smith.

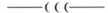

Meanwhile, down the street from L'Aparté Café, Ruhollah Tabrizi, an agent with VEVAK, the Iranian intelligence service, sat in the front passenger seat of a van watching as Nagiyev came from the café. Two men trailed behind him as he walked back toward the Oil and Trade building. When Nagiyev reached the corner, Tabrizi took a radio from the console and keyed the microphone. "Take him."

Seconds later, a car pulled alongside Nagiyev and screeched to a halt. The two men who'd been following him closed rapidly, grabbed Nagiyev by the shoulders, and shoved him into the back seat. Then they slid onto the seat beside him and closed the door. The driver pressed the gas pedal and the car shot forward.

"Got him," came the reply from the grab team.

Tabrizi nodded to the driver of the van and they started forward. Twenty minutes later, they arrived at a warehouse on the outskirts of town. A large rollup door opened as they approached and the van idled slowly inside the building. It came to a stop alongside the car that had been used to grab Nagiyev.

A few feet beyond the car, Nagiyev was seated on a wooden chair, his arms tied behind his back and a hood over his head. Two men, Kia Athari and Ali Farjami, stood nearby. Tabrizi leaned against the front of the car. "You are Murtuza Nagiyev?" he asked.

"If you know who I am, why do you ask?"

"And do you know who we are?" Tabrizi continued.

"From the sound of your accent," Nagiyev replied, "I would guess you are Iranian."

"Do you know what we want?"

"I have no idea."

"You met with a Russian earlier. The swine, Rolan Buldakov. Then you met with an American just now. We want to know what you told them. Tell me now and things will go much better for you."

"I think we both know things will not turn out so well for me no matter what I say."

"Perhaps. Perhaps not." Tabrizi came from the car and leaned near Nagiyev's ear. "Tell me what I want to know and you will at least spare yourself the pain of what will happen if you do not."

"They asked me where to find good women," Nagiyev chuckled. "I told them they should try the—"

Tabrizi slapped him across the face. "Do not play with me," he snarled.

"I told them what they wanted to hear," Nagiyev blurted.

"Which was?"

"That the Iranians are weak and useless."

With catlike quickness, Tabrizi struck Nagiyev in the face with his fist. "Do not insult me!" he shouted. Almost instantly, blood oozed through the fabric of the hood and it incited him even more. Suddenly passion inflamed him and he struck Nagiyev again and again until his arm grew tired and Nagiyev was slumped to one side. "Now," Tabrizi's words were punctuated by heavy breaths, "I will ask you once more. What did you tell the Russian and the American?"

"I told the Russian...what he wanted to hear," Nagiyev mumbled, "so he would pay me some money."

"And the American?"

"I gave him the same information for free."

"And what was that information?"

"There is still much oil in Azerbaijan."

Tabrizi kicked Nagiyev in the side, knocking him from the chair. Athari picked him up from the floor and returned him to his seat. "Tie him up," Tabrizi growled. Farjami brought a rope, which they used to secure Nagiyev's legs to the chair. Then they wound it around his waist to hold him in place, leaving his arms dangling at his side. When they were finished, Tabrizi took a pair of pliers from the trunk of the car and turned to Nagiyev. "Will you tell me what you told the Russian?"

Nagiyev could barely hold his head up. "I told him...Iranian women...were the best."

Tabrizi nodded to Farjami, who took hold of Nagiyev's hand and held it while Tabrizi gripped the fingernail of his middle finger with the pliers. In one quick motion, he yanked loose the fingernail. Nagiyev howled in pain.

"You will tell me what I want to know," Tabrizi grabbed the next fingernail. "Or you will die an agonizing death." Then he jerked the fingernail free.

Nagiyev continued to stall, giving evasive and inflammatory answers while Tabrizi removed the nails from each of his fingers, then his toes. When that did not produce the desired information, Tabrizi took the battery from the car and hooked leads from it to sensitive portions of Nagiyev's body. Shock after shock jolted him and the stench of burning flesh filled the air, but still Nagiyev did not speak.

Finally, they lifted him from the chair and drug him across the floor to a large steel vat that was filled with water. "I will give you one final opportunity," Tabrizi said in a solemn voice. "Tell me what you told the Russian."

"I told him as little as possible for as much money as he would pay."

Athari and Farjami grabbed Nagiyev by the head and shoved him into the water. Then they lifted him by the ankles and dangled him there upside down. When he stopped kicking and squirming, they jerked him out of the water, laid him on the floor, and revived him.

Tabrizi stood over him and glowered. "You wish to drown?"

Nagiyev shook his head in response as he gasped for breath.

"Then I suggest you start talking."

"Your mother...was a donkey. Your father a useless American. They bred like—"

Tabrizi kicked him in the head and gestured toward the vat. Once more, Athari and Farjami grabbed Nagiyev by the head and shoved him into the water. Then they lifted him by the ankles and dangled him upside down. When he stopped squirming, they jerked him out of the water, laid him on the floor, and revived him yet again.

"Okay," Nagiyev gasped. "I'll tell you." He paused to take a deep breath. "The Russians concluded a trade agreement with us. It was signed today."

"Everyone knows that," Tabrizi snapped. "Half the world was watching." He gestured to Fajami and Athari. They took hold of Nagiyev to lift him from the floor.

"No, no," Nagiyev protested. "Wait." Farjami and Athari hesitated. Nagiyev continued. "Everyone knows about the public ceremony, but what they do not know is that there was another agreement. A very private one that gives the Russian army the authority to cross our territory and camp near the border with Iran."

"Why do they want this authority?"

"Because they think the Chinese are about to invade your country."

"The Chinese! Do you think I'm an idiot to believe these stories you tell?"

"It's true," Nagiyev insisted. "The Russians think the Chinese are going to invade Iran to seize your oil."

"Why would they do that? They've been buying it for years."

"But not now," Nagiyev countered. "Not since the deal that brokers all Iranian oil through Germany."

"Even if that is so, why do the Russians care?"

"They don't want the Chinese to become a regional player."

"Do they have proof of these wild fantasies?"

"The Chinese are gathering their forces on the Afghan border even as we speak."

Tabrizi frowned. "You know this?"

"Yes."

"How do you know it?"

"The Russians have satellites."

"They told you?"

"I have many friends."

Tabrizi paused a moment, as if lost in thought, then stepped forward and lifted the hood from Nagiyev's face. His eyes were swollen almost closed and blood dripped from his nose. His teeth were loose and his lips split, but still he had a smile on his face. Tabrizi sighed. "I am sorry it has come to this," he said softly.

"I know," Nagiyev replied.

Then Farjami drew a pistol from the waistband of his trousers, pointed the muzzle at Nagiyev's head, and pulled the trigger.

49

CIA HEADQUARTERS LANGLEY, VIRGINIA

WINSTON SMITH STOOD WITH HOAG in the operations center. Together they'd been checking the latest satellite images from Tunis, hoping to find some new indication that the cargo container had not been moved, and that Kinlaw was alive and well. While they studied those images, a text message arrived on Smith's iPhone. He read it quickly, then handed the phone to Hoag. "How good is your Russian these days?"

Hoag's eyes grew wide as he read the attachment. "Who sent this?"

"Bergen. He was in Baku when Vostok signed the trade agreement. What you're looking at is the real reason they renewed the trade agreement."

"They just used that to buy their way into Azerbaijan."

"Yeah," Smith nodded. "When we found out Mirsky was involved from the beginning, I was pretty sure it had nothing to do with trade."

"Any indication that they're actually doing this?"

"Doing what?"

"Actually moving troops there. Or is this just an attempt to gain flexibility. You know, so they wouldn't have to solve access issues in a crisis."

"Read the message he sent with the document."

Hoag scrolled back through the pages to the message. "Chinese troops on Afghan border. Russians worried." As he read the words aloud a sense of dread swept over him. Smith noticed the change in his countenance. "You worried now?"

"I have a guy in Omaha who noticed this weeks ago."

"Noticed what? The Russians?"

"No. The Chinese. He's been watching them for a while. Began with suspicious patrols in the Wakhan Corridor. Last time we talked he tried to tell me about troop and equipment movements toward the Afghan border."

"That would be rather important information, wouldn't it?"

"Didn't seem like it at the time. We were worried about finding that ship."

"This is about oil. And oil is always important."

"Yeah."

"Sure you really want this job?"

Hoag gestured for Smith to follow him and they retreated to the back of the room. "I talked to Moore about that," Hoag whispered.

"The Chinese?"

"No. Me and this job."

"Oh? What's up?"

"He wants to send me back to Georgetown."

"That's the best idea I've heard in a long time. Who's he going to get to replace you?"

"Jerry O'Connor."

"I know O'Connor. Great guy. Tailor-made for running analysis. I suggested him to Moore the last time that job came open and he chose Burke instead." Smith laid his hand on Hoag's shoulder. "You are brilliant. And you have all my confidence. But sitting at a desk, shuffling papers takes a different perspective. You've spent your career engaged in the hands-on business of holding back the bad guys. It'll take some time to see administrative work as something equally important to what you've been doing."

"Yeah," Hoag nodded. "I suppose you're right."

"I know I am. This will all work out. Now come on," Smith urged. "We need to work this situation. I have something you should see." He led the way back to the operator's console in the center of the room and said something to her, then pointed to a screen as a picture appeared. "This is the road south from Rostov-on-Don. The main highway through southern Russia to the Azerbaijan border." The image on the screen began with a wide shot and tightened down to show the highway jammed with trucks from Rostov to Armavir. "We've seen lots of repositioning lately that could be explained as merely reassigning units from one base to another. That's a major task, relocating an entire division or brigade. But you *could* account for the earlier movements that way. This," he said with a wag of his finger toward the image on the screen, "is not relocation. This is a full-scale mobilization."

"So, we can assume the document is authentic. But can we assume the Russian troop movements and the Chinese troop movements are related?"

"I don't think we can afford to assume anything less."

"We should tell somebody about this. Get it in the president's daily brief."

"We will," Smith agreed. "But before we can take this upstairs, we need to flesh this out with some additional confirmable information. After that meltdown the other day, we'll need hard evidence to back up our analysis. Otherwise, they'll just ignore it."

"I'll get with Jerry and see if we can put this together better. Connect the dots."

"You should give it to someone else," Smith suggested.

"Why?"

"You're still in charge of Middle East Analysis. Give it to someone, put them with Jerry, and have them work it up for you."

"Yeah," Hoag chuckled. "I guess you're right. I should—" Just then, his iPhone dinged with a message. Hoag glanced at the screen and his countenance dropped.

"Something important?"

"Jenny," Hoag replied. He returned the phone to his pocket and looked over at Smith. "You think Dennis is all right?"

"I've known Dennis Kinlaw a long time," Smith said with a smile. "I'm not worried. A man who can survive the streets of Beirut can surely handle whatever Tunis could bring."

"I know," Hoag smiled. "But I was with him in Beirut. I'm not in Tunis."

Smith patted Hoag on the shoulder. "He'll be fine. Talk to O'Connor and see what he knows about the Chinese. We need to get moving on this." Then Smith turned to address the analysts in the room. "Okay. Listen up. We've got a new situation developing."

50

NEAR DERBENT, RUSSIA

LATE IN THE NIGHT, Alexander Nevsky lay sound asleep inside a tent pitched along a gently-rolling hill outside of town, not far from the shore of the Caspian Sea and less than one hundred fifty kilometers from the border with Azerbaijan. He was burrowed deep in a sleeping bag, the opening zipped all the way closed over his head to keep out the damp cold of night, Milla's scarf tucked under his chin.

Suddenly, a kick to his feet awakened him. He unzipped the bag and looked up to see Captain Sorokin standing at the tent flap. "Get your gear," Sorokin barked. "We're moving out."

Nevsky pushed himself to a sitting position and stood. As he did, Yury Turgenev, with whom he shared the tent, unzipped his sleeping bag and looked out. "What is happening?" he asked, still groggy and only half awake.

"We are moving," Nevsky answered. "Pack your gear."

They dutifully stuffed their belongings into their field packs, then rolled up the sleeping bags and tied them along the outside of the packs.

"Where are we going this time?" Turgenev asked.

"I do not know, but I do not think we shall ever return home."

"Perhaps you are correct. But if we make this our home, we shall be at peace now and surprised when we actually do get home."

"I do not share your sense of optimism," Nevsky hoisted his pack from the ground. "But maybe I shall give it a try." He pushed back the tent flap and stepped outside to find their camp was surrounded by large transport trucks. The headlights were on and in the glow of the beams he saw the others in their company were already awake and working feverishly to take down the hundreds of tents that just days before had lined the hills around them. Turgenev appeared at his side. "They're moving the whole place."

"Yeah," Nevsky sighed. "The whole place."

"Maybe you are right. Maybe we never will get home."

From behind them Captain Sorokin reappeared. "Let's go!" he shouted. "Get that tent down and on a truck, then report to the command post. We have to get it loaded and moved within the hour."

Nevsky set his pack aside and reached for a tent stake. "Come on," he grumbled. "The sooner we get it down, the sooner he'll leave us alone."

51

STATE DEPARTMENT
WASHINGTON, D.C.

IN ACCORDANCE WITH INSTRUCTIONS FROM BERLIN, Jürgen Stabreit, the German ambassador to the United States, contacted Lauren Lehman's office and requested an immediate appointment.

Like most of the cabinet level executives, Lehman returned to Washington from Nebraska shortly after the president returned to the White House. When Stabreit called, she was in the midst of meetings to address that transition. The chance to handle a diplomatic matter came as a relief and she readily made room for Stabreit in her schedule. They met in her office at the State Department shortly before noon. Lehman's assistant ushered him into the room.

"Ambassador Stabreit," Lehman greeted him from behind her desk. "Always a pleasure to see you."

"Thank you," Stabreit replied as they shook hands. "So good of you to see me on such short notice."

Lehman took a seat at the desk. Stabreit sat in a chair across from her. She propped her elbows on the armrests of her chair and looked over at him. "You indicated this was important."

"Yes. Of the utmost urgency." He paused to shift positions in the chair. "We have received a request from the Republic of Spain for assistance with their current monetary crisis. They would also like our help in addressing their growing problem with civil unrest."

"We have been monitoring developments there for some time."

"As well you should," Stabreit conceded. "We are reluctant to act on our own, but the safety and security of Europe seems to be in question, and someone has to take the initiative. Collapse of the Spanish economy would be a tremendous blow to EU stability, which would hurt us all."

"I agree," Lehman nodded, "as I am certain President Hedges does as well. In fact, he has said as much. Spain needs help, but if you're asking for our assistance, surely you can appreciate that we are not in a position to assist you right now. We're still trying to dig out from underneath our own crisis."

"Certainly. We understand completely and we aren't asking you to assist us, especially not at such a vulnerable time for your own country. We don't need your help, really. No offense intended."

"None taken."

"What we need is your silence."

A frown wrinkled Lehman's brow. "Our silence?"

"Yes. We expect that some in the international community will object to our actions. Some within our own party may, as well. What we need from the United States is simply an understanding that you will not publicly oppose us."

Lehman had a questioning look. "You thought *we* might?"

"The prospect of German soldiers patrolling the streets of Madrid brings to mind a certain kind of...mental image of the past that many wish to forget and others are ever too quick to use against us, no matter what we do."

"Shades of the past are always with us."

"Yes, but if we could get past this moment without the United States encouraging those dissident voices, it would be most helpful."

Lehman knew her response already but she didn't want to give it away too quickly. Instead she nodded thoughtfully. "Who made the request?"

"Juan Gomez Bayona came in person to see Chancellor Mueller."

Lehman arched an eyebrow. "That must have been a humbling experience for him."

"I am certain it was. Especially in light of the fact that he was accompanied by his arch enemy, Luis Aragon."

"Oh," Lehman grinned, "I would have loved to have seen that meeting. The two of them together with Josef Mueller."

"Yes," Stabreit had a thin, tight smile. "I'm certain the irony of the moment was quite obvious." He crossed his legs and rested his hands in his lap. "So, may I inform the chancellor that we shall receive your government's cooperation in this matter?"

"I will have to discuss this with President Hedges, of course," Lehman replied, "but as I said earlier, I don't think we would raise an objection to your efforts to assist Spain, even if it means sending German troops to control the crowds."

"Very good," Stabreit stood. "Then I shall be on my way and let you get on with your day."

Lehman came from behind the desk and walked with him to the door. When Stabreit was gone, she picked up the phone and called the White House.

52

BEIJING, CHINA

CHAIRMAN MING SHAO sat in an upholstered chair at a coffee table near his desk. Seated to his left was Geng Yun, minister of State Security. To his right was Quan Ji, chief of Foreign Intelligence. Yun avoided eye contact with Quan and instead looked directly at Ming.

"I asked for this meeting," Yun began, "because we have a serious problem within our government. One that threatens our work at State Security."

Ming nodded thoughtfully. "And what is that problem?"

"We have been conducting extensive investigations into the efficiency and integrity of State Security. While doing that—"

Quan interrupted him. "You have been investigating our Foreign Intelligence department?"

"Yes," Yun replied, still refusing to look in Quan's direction. "We had indications months ago that someone within the Foreign Intelligence department was passing secrets to the Russians. I authorized a full-scale operation to determine who that person was and to end their activities."

Ming looked over at Quan. "You were aware of this investigation?"

"Not at first," Quan replied.

"But then you later became aware of it?"

"Yes, Mr. Chairman. I did."

"And what did you do about that? How did you respond?"

"That's just it," Yun interrupted. "When he learned that we were investigating his department, he had one of his operatives within our department moved over to the investigating team. Within a few days, that operative was in charge of crucial aspects of our work. And all the while, he was sending reports and details back to Quan."

"That operative has a name?"

"Cam Fong."

"You know for a fact that he worked directly with Quan's department?"

"I know for a fact that he worked directly with Quan Ji himself."

"How do you know this?"

"We have logs for Cam Fong's telephone. And we have recordings of their telephone conversations." Yun pointed his finger toward Quan once more. "When Cam Fong got a break in the case, he went directly to him with the information. To Quan Ji," Yun cried. "Not even to his State Security supervisor."

"Your State Security agents are useless," Quan scowled. "They couldn't find their way home, much less find an informant."

"And it was his man!" Yun shouted. "His own agent who was giving away our nation's most sensitive secrets."

"Have we questioned this man?"

"No," Yun railed. "And we can't, because they killed him. Gunned him down on the street."

Ming turned to Quan. "Is this true?"

"Mr. Chairman, he was a traitor," Quan answered calmly. "He had already given the Russian top-secret information. And he was about to hand over even more crucial details of our mobilization against Iran. We shot him because he had to be stopped."

"And the only way you could locate him was to infiltrate State Security?"

"Not the only way. It was simply the method we chose." Quan leaned forward and looked directly at Yun. "We had no choice. Our own department was under suspicion. I did not know whom to trust. If we had conducted this investigation using our own people we might have been compromised from the beginning. So I used some of yours."

"You should have informed me."

"I would have, but, as I said, under the circumstances, I did not know whom to trust."

Yun's eyes opened wide. "You are accusing me of traitorous acts?"

"No, no, no," Quan gestured in a conciliatory manner. "I had no reason to suspect you, but I had to conduct an investigation that would give an authentic result."

Yun leaned back in his chair. "I do not—"

A knock on the door interrupted them as Ming's assistant, Yong Shu, entered the room. He came to Ming's side and leaned close. "Hu Chang would like to speak with you."

"Did he say what it is about?"

Yong Shu handed him a note, which read only, "Most urgent matters require a moment of your time."

Ming folded the note in his hand and stood. The others rose as well. "Please excuse me, gentlemen. This will only take a moment. Please continue your discussion privately while I am out."

Yong Shu led the way to the door and held it while Ming stepped to the outer office. He was met there by Hu Chang, commander of the People's Liberation Army. "I am sorry to disturb you, Mr. Chairman," Chang bowed his head.

"Think nothing of it," Ming replied. "How may I help you?"

"We have reached the critical point in our preparations," Chang said.

Ming guided him through a door to the left that led to a private study. When they were inside he shut the door and turned to Chang. "We are still on schedule with our mobilization?"

"Yes," Chang nodded, "but now we must move up the heavy equipment. Things that cannot be hidden. And we must increase our troop strength in the same way. We shall have to send truck convoys to the border and move forward deliberately. On a much larger scale."

"Very well. You may proceed with all haste. I will inform the others immediately. But do not cross the border until we give the order."

"As you wish," Chang bowed.

53

CIA HEADQUARTERS LANGLEY, VIRGINIA

HOAG CAME FROM THE OPERATIONS CENTER and took the elevator upstairs to his office. Jerry O'Connor might become the next director for Middle East Analysis, but not yet. Right now that job belonged to Hoag and he wanted to address O'Connor as a director speaking to a senior analyst. When he reached the office, Hoag took a seat at his desk and had his assistant place a call to Nebraska.

A few minutes later, with O'Connor already on the line and waiting, Hoag picked up. "Jerry, this thing with China has taken on a new dimension."

"Right," O'Connor replied. "Have you seen the latest images?"

"Not from Asia. I've been focused on Russia. What do you have?"

"Trucks, tanks, missiles. It's big."

"What are they doing with them?"

"Moving them toward the Afghan border. They were parked in a staging area about a hundred miles from the border last week. Now the latest satellite images show them moving toward the border. Are you in the office?"

"Yes."

"Check the file and you'll see what we have from National Reconnaissance."

Hoag turned to the computer terminal on the credenza behind his desk and logged on to the system. Seconds later, the file was loaded and he scrolled through the images. "When did you get these?"

"Last night. We just finished working with them this morning. I was going to call you."

"We really need to be in the same location."

"Yeah," O'Connor replied. "When are you coming back?"

"I don't think I am. The president is out here at the White House and it looks like he's going to stay. Moore's here. Everybody's up and running here without any problems."

"Man, I would love to be back at Langley. A lot easier to work out of our facility there."

"What about everyone else? Would they come back?"

"I think they're ready to go, too. Most of them, anyway."

"I'll talk to Moore about it. But listen, this thing has taken a twist."

"With China?"

"Yeah. When the Russians signed their trade agreement with Azerbaijan, they also reached an agreement that gives them the authority to move their military units through Azerbaijan, and to stage them in certain locations along the border with Iran."

"I saw the trade agreement. The military agreement might just be a formality. Something the Russians felt they had to ask from the Azerbaijanis because they had to give the Azerbaijanis more than they really wanted to."

"Except that the Russians are moving troops in that direction now," Hoag explained. "A source is telling us they're worried that the Chinese are going to invade Iran to seize their oil fields."

"We discussed that possibility before you left."

"Right," Hoag acknowledged. "But what I need to know is whether the Russian move into Azerbaijan is in response to the Chinese, or something else. Have you found anything that might point to a connection between Russian military moves into Azerbaijan and the Chinese buildup along the Afghan border? Is there a link between the two?"

"Only one, and it's just a link between the Russians and the Chinese."

"What's that?"

"We had a report a couple of weeks ago from Beijing," O'Connor began, "about a Russian diplomat who approached one of our people and tried to turn her. She reported the contact, and the mission chief initiated an investigation. That investigation cleared our person but in the process they discovered a Chinese employee who worked in their Foreign Intelligence service who was selling Chinese military secrets to the same Russian diplomat who tried to turn our lady."

"Who was the lady?"

"Linda Brown."

"I think I met her once. Who led the investigation?"

"Robert Whilden."

"We've crossed paths a few times. He's rather thorough."

"But here's the deal," O'Connor continued, "while they were working this up, the Chinese guy was killed."

"Killed? How?"

"Gunned down on the way to a meeting with the Russian. In broad daylight. Whilden was across the street from it. Saw the whole thing. One of his guys identified one of the people involved. Looks like they were State Security people."

"So, the stuff he was selling was good."

"Yeah. The Russians wanted it, and the Chinese were serious about preventing them from having it."

"Okay."

"You gonna show this to Hoyt?"

"I think I have to."

"I do, too."

When he finished with the phone call, Hoag went downstairs to the operations center. Smith was there, working with his team of analysts. "Anything more recent on the Russians?" Hoag asked.

"Yeah," Smith nodded. "Russian troops are moving south. They're in the midst of a huge force shift. Several of their northern bases are all but deserted." Smith nodded to the operator, and a map appeared on one of the wall screens. He pointed to it. "Lots of military transport traffic on the highways here, here, and here." He glanced over his shoulder to the operator. "Put up those traffic cam shots we have." Video appeared on a screen showing a line of military trucks on the road. "We hacked into these cameras out-side Volgograd. This is the highway south from the city."

"At this rate," Hoag mused as he studied the video, "they could have half their force in the southern region by the end of the month."

"Yeah," Smith nodded. "And some of their units have already crossed into Azerbaijan."

"O'Connor has similar indications from Chinese activity on the Afghan border."

Smith gestured with his thumb, pointing over his shoulder to the right. "Miller over there was just telling me about that. "They have a huge force amassed on the border with Afghanistan, and he thinks they have some units assembled farther to the east along the border with Pakistan."

"We better tell Moore."

"You better tell him," Smith corrected, pointing a finger at Hoag's chest. "You're the boss."

"You're right. I am the boss," Hoag grinned. "Which is why you're coming with me."

54

THE WHITE HOUSE WASHINGTON, D.C.

WHEN LAUREN LEHMAN ARRIVED at the Oval Office the door was closed. She stopped at Anna Lester's desk to wait. "Has something happened?"

"Not that I'm aware of," Anna replied. "He's with Mr. Kittrell."

Just then the door opened and Hedges appeared. "Lauren," he smiled, "come on in." He glanced back at her as she followed him into the office. "You said this was too important for the phone?"

"Yes. I wanted to talk to you about this in person so there's no question about it later."

"Sure," he smiled. "What is it?"

"The German ambassador, Jürgen Stabreit, came to see me just now to tell me that they are going to assist Spain."

"Great!" Hedges exclaimed. "It's about time. They should have done that earlier. Providing liquidity, I assume?"

"Yes. But there's more to it."

"Oh?"

"As I'm sure you've been following, Spain has a serious problem with civil unrest."

"Right," Hedges nodded. "They've been telling me about it in the morning brief, and I saw footage on the news the other day with

Braxton. Looks pretty bad."

"Apparently it's beyond their ability to cope. And I don't think the Germans want to send their money without sending enough other support to make sure the country doesn't collapse."

"Understandable." Hedges leaned against the front edge of the desk. "Were they asking for our help?"

"No. I told him we couldn't."

"Good." Hedges' eyes opened wider. "By the way, did Gomez ask for this?"

"He came in person," Lehman answered. "With Luis Aragon."

"Wow. Things must really be bad."

"That was my reaction as well. There is one thing they wanted from us."

"What's that?"

"Our silence."

"Our silence?" Hedges frowned. "About what?"

"They're worried about how this will look and the objections they might receive from the international community because of it."

"How it might look?" The frown on Hedges' forehead deepened. "This is a matter for the EU, not everyone else. Why do they think someone would object?"

"They're concerned this will look like the Nazis invading their neighbors and that others might use that imagery against them."

"I don't see that as a problem for us," Hedges shrugged. "Do you?"

"No, and I'm not convinced anyone will even make the connection. There aren't many alive now who remember what that was like."

"Right," Hedges agreed. "Only a textbook topic for most people."

"This was a huge step for Spain to ask for help. Might be what the EU needs to achieve stability—a true interdependence."

"Exactly. Tell Jürgen Stabreit that we won't object. And, if I get the chance, I'll say something to support them once they take action."

"Yes, Mr. President."

Hoag and Smith met with Moore in his office and outlined the developing situations with China, Russia, Iran, and the Middle East. Only partway through their presentation, Moore stood and came from behind the desk. "I've seen enough. Get your jacket."

Hoag looked surprised. "My jacket?"

"I've seen enough to know that we have to alert the White House. The president's in town. We'll call from the car and tell them we're coming."

Hoag didn't budge. "You think it's good for me to go?"

Moore had a puzzled look. "Why not?"

"After what happened before, with the cargo container and the ship, I'm not sure I'll be much help."

"Forget about it," Moore dismissed with a wave of his hand. "That happens in this business. As much as people want to think to the contrary, most of the time we give an approximate answer. And that's on a good day. At the pace things move, that's all we can do." He gazed at Hoag more intently. "Straighten your tie."

Hoag adjusted the fit of his tie against the collar of his shirt and brushed lint from the shoulders of his jacket. Smith grinned at him as they started for the door.

Forty minutes later, Hoag and Moore arrived at the White House. President Hedges was waiting with Braxton Kittrell in the Oval Office. They arrived just as Lauren Lehman was leaving. Moore described the situation for Hedges, then turned the details over to Hoag.

Hoag outlined the things they'd discovered—satellite images showing large numbers of Chinese troops gathering on the Afghan border, too many to account for as merely an exercise; the Russian military access agreement with Azerbaijan, followed by Russian troop movements toward the border; and reports of Russian concerns about the potential for military action by China, coupled with the death of a Chinese mole caught selling military secrets to them in Beijing. It was a lot to cover in just a few minutes but he edited the information carefully and kept the presentation succinct and to the point.

"You paint a grim picture of the Middle East," Hedges commented when Hoag was finished. "I should have kept Secretary Lehman around."

"The situation *is* grim," Hoag reiterated. "And I'll be glad to give Secretary Lehman the same presentation."

"You'll get your chance." Hedges paused long enough to nod in Kittrell's direction. Kittrell turned toward the door, stepped out to the hall, and disappeared. Hedges looked up at Hoag. "But tell me something," he said with a faint smile. "Is this information you're giving me now at least as accurate as the information you had about that cargo container?"

Hoag felt his cheeks turn warm. "We were going on the best information available at the time."

"But not the missile with the warhead," Hedges said, reminding him.

"We've located it," Hoag countered.

"I heard." Hedges looked over at Moore. "And then your agent went dark. Any recent information on what's happening with it?"

"Nothing new," Moore replied. "So far as we can determine, it's still right where they parked it."

Hedges had a dour look. "Tell me again why we didn't just go get the thing."

"Because we'd have to involve the Tunisians," Moore explained, "and they would tell whoever has the missile."

"And we'd arrive to find an empty cargo container one more time."

"Yes, Mr. President."

"You do realize, I hope, that our careers will be worthless if this thing gets away from us again."

"Yes, Mr. President. That thought occurred to me."

"They won't talk about our brilliant strategy for recovering it. They'll just remember that we let it—"

The office door opened and Kittrell appeared once again. "Mr. President, they're on their way."

Hedges stood and glanced in Hoag's direction. "Well," he sighed, "I guess we'll find out what everyone else thinks of your latest information."

Hoag had a questioning look. "Everyone else, sir?"

"You get to brief the national security team." Hedges shot Moore a look. "Think he can handle it?"

"Yes, Mr. President," Moore smiled. "I think he can."

Hedges patted Hoag on the shoulder. "I think he can, too. Come on. They need us in the situation room."

55

WHITE HOUSE SITUATION ROOM WASHINGTON, D.C.

HEDGES, KITTRELL, MOORE, AND HOAG walked together to the situation room. They were met by the rest of the national security team—Admiral Marshall, Carl Coulliette, Harry Giles, Lauren Lehman, and Russ Williams. When they were seated around the table, Hoag moved to the far end of the room, opposite the president, and stood in front of the screens that filled the wall. As images appeared behind, he talked his way through the latest satellite photos, comparing them to earlier ones and pointing out Chinese and Russian troop movements toward their borders; the former along the Afghan border, the latter toward the Azerbaijan border with Iran. Then he passed around copies of the access agreement reached between Russia and Azerbaijan. Finally, he walked them through details of the Hongsheng-Manarov matter in Beijing.

When Hoag was finished, Carl Coulliette turned to Hedges. "Mr. President, I think we face a very grave situation in the Middle East region. This information, with two super powers moving toward war, calls for a serious response on our part. We must get the parties together to discuss their respective issues."

"They don't have respective issues," Lehman countered. "They don't have any issue at all. At least, not directly between them. The problem is Iran and that agreement they reached with the Germans. It changed the balance in the entire region."

"An agreement," Williams added, "we think was designed to enrich Kermani at least as much as anyone else."

Coulliette pressed the issue. "We can't simply abandon the region, no matter what caused the problem. Especially not to these two countries. We need to deploy three more carrier groups to the Persian Gulf and Indian Ocean and ramp up our presence in Afghanistan. Will the Iraqis let us stage a force there?"

"You have to be kidding me," Lehman countered. "The Iraqis only just got rid of us." She turned to Hoag. "Are you certain about the Russian situation? Is this information reliable?"

"Yes," Hoag replied. "We're certain of it."

"Anything else to back it up?" Coulliette asked.

"Nothing beyond what I showed you."

Lehman gestured with her copy of the agreement. "How did we obtain this document?"

"When the Russians and Azerbaijanis began negotiating renewal of their trade agreement, we started hearing chatter that indicated there could be more to the agreement than simply trade. Based on that, we inserted several operatives in Baku and Moscow to monitor the situation. One of the operatives in Baku obtained the document I showed you earlier. Our experts have determined it's authentic."

"And the Russian army is there?" Giles asked. "In Azerbaijan?"

"Portions of it have crossed the Russia–Azerbaijan border," Hoag replied. "We think it's an advance force."

"Advance? Why couldn't it just as easily be all there is to the situation?"

"The Russians are in the midst of a major internal force realignment," Hoag explained.

"What does that mean?"

"They are in the process of moving as much as half of their army to the south, towards the border with Azerbaijan."

Hedges looked down the table at Giles. "What are you thinking, Harry?"

Giles glanced in Hedges' direction. "Mr. President, I think the Russians know that China is about to take Iran by force and they're about to become a second-class player in the international oil business. They can see the Chinese troop movements as easily as we can."

"Even without the oil," Williams added, "I doubt they'll concede their southern flank to Chinese troops without a fight."

"So," Hedges cut them off. "What should we do about it?"

"Mr. President," Hoag replied, "there is nothing we *can* do. The Chinese can field an army three hundred million strong. The Russians don't have that many troops, but they have sophisticated technology and a large nuclear arsenal. If those two armies clash, it'll be a war unlike any we've ever known before. If our army is in the middle, we'd be virtually defenseless."

Lehman was exasperated. "Why don't the Iranians simply sell the Chinese the oil?"

"I don't think they know this is happening," Giles answered.

"Probably not," Coulliette agreed. "The Russians and the Chinese are their usual sources of strategic intelligence and I'm sure neither of them is sharing anything right now."

"But he's right," Williams continued, gesturing to Hoag. "We can't possibly stop the Chinese. Once they start moving they won't stop. They'll just keep sending in more and more troops. This is precisely the mistake we made in Vietnam and the lesson we learned there. Both of these armies would be fighting in their backyard. We would be fighting as far from our country as possible against the largest armies in the world. It's a logistics nightmare."

"On top of that," Lehman offered, "we would be in the least favorable position possible, with the Chinese attacking from the east and the Russians from the north. We'd be caught in the middle."

"A recipe for Armageddon," Williams agreed.

"We have less than fifty thousand troops in the region," Hoag asserted. "We should get all of them out of there as fast as humanly possible."

"We may be small in number right now, but we can't just withdraw," Giles argued. "We have Chinese troops threatening Afghanistan, and the Russians lurking over Iran. The world is as unstable as it has ever been."

Hedges looked over at Lehman. "Have you briefed them on the Germany situation?"

"I was in the process of doing that when we got the call to come here."

"What's this about?" Giles asked.

"Bring them up to speed," Hedges suggested.

"A few hours ago," Lehman explained, "Jürgen Stabreit informed me that Spain has formally requested German assistance with its current banking crisis. They have also asked for help controlling the resulting civil unrest. Germany has agreed to provide liquidity for the Spanish banking system and assistance in managing the crowds in the streets."

"You mean," Williams said dryly, "Germany is sending troops to Spain."

"Yes."

Hedges spoke up. "I have instructed Secretary Lehman to inform the Germans that we will not object to this move."

"Mr. President," Coulliette responded, "I disagree. We should call off the Germans in Spain. Intercede with the Russians. Strengthen our troops in Afghanistan and force the Chinese to consider that any military action on their part in the region will place them in direct conflict with us."

"If we get between the Chinese and the oil they want," Lehman argued, "we'll have to use nuclear weapons to stop them and we'll be the bad guy."

"But what about the oil?" Giles asked. "We can't just let them have it. Prices will triple, at least. We don't have enough reserve to replace the market effects of a Chinese takeover in Iran."

"We have oil," Hoag interjected. The room grew quiet as all heads turned toward him. "We have oil," he repeated. "We just haven't developed enough of it and the oil we *do* pump goes onto a global market where it's priced according to international market forces."

"What are you saying?" Hedges asked.

"Embargo it," Hoag answered. "Make US oil companies sell US oil right here in the US. We have huge deposits of coal. Do the same with them, too. Embargo it. Most of what we mine is sold abroad. Use it right here. Adjust electricity production to burn more of it and less petroleum. We'll have all the energy we need and the cost of everything else will come down."

Coulliette looked intrigued. Giles spoke up. "If we burn coal, the environmentalists will go crazy."

Hedges exchanged a knowing look with Braxton Kittrell. "I think we're past that now," he said.

"Past what?"

"Past worrying about the environment." Hedges sat up straight in the chair. "Later this week we're announcing the rollback of environmental regulations on electrical generation facilities and oil refineries."

"You can do that?" Giles asked. "Just like that?"

"Already done. In exchange for lowered emissions restrictions, electric companies and oil producers have agreed to sell all US energy within the boundaries of the United States and its territories."

The room fell silent as the reality of what Hedges said slowly sank in. Hoag brought them back to the issue at hand. "Mr. President, we have to get out of Afghanistan now. Our troops will be crushed. They'll become prisoners of the Chinese. The technology we have in place over there will fall into Chinese hands."

Coulliette's eyes opened wide at the mention of the technology issue. "I agree, Mr. President. We have to get out...quickly...today."

Hedges nodded his head slowly. "I think you're right. The Germans should have moved on Spain sooner. Much of this trouble would not have happened if they had. And we can avoid trouble if we move quickly." He looked over at Admiral Marshall. "Evacuate the troops from Afghanistan."

"Yes, Mr. President." Marshall reached for the phone to pass the order down the chain of command.

"Evacuate?" Williams asked. "Don't you mean withdraw?"

"Evacuate," Hedges repeated. "Get them out as fast as possible. Destroy the classified information and software, but leave the trucks and heavy equipment behind. Bring home only the troops."

56

TEHRAN, IRAN

WHEN TABRIZI RETURNED FROM BAKU, he was debriefed by a case-worker who interviewed him at a secure facility maintained by the Ministry of Intelligence and National Security. The process took two days to complete. Under normal operating procedures, he would have been released for duty after that. This time, however, he was transferred to an apartment in a building on Nikooee Street, not far from Daneshjoo Park. He was met there by Maziyar Shokof, director of VEVAK. They sat at the kitchen table and talked.

"I understand your mission was successful," Shokof began.

"Yes," Tabrizi nodded. "We obtained the information you requested."

"And as we suspected," Shokof continued, "there is more to the Russian agreement with the Azerbaijanis than merely trade."

"The trade agreement was a cover." Tabrizi nodded again.

"Was there, in fact, a trade agreement? An enforceable agreement?"

"As far as we could tell, yes. They actually signed a trade agreement."

"But there was another agreement," Shokof suggested. "A military agreement."

"Right." Tabrizi nodded once more, but a puzzled look clouded his face. "All of this is in my report. We covered it in the debriefing interviews." He was worried about how far Shokof would delve into what he and the team in Baku actually did. And he was even more concerned about why Shokof was interested.

"Yes," Shokof acknowledged. "I read your report and the interview transcripts. I just want to get this clear in my mind and make certain nothing was missed." The comment struck Tabrizi as odd—the director taking an interest in the gritty details of a covert operation—but he kept quiet about it as Shokof continued. "Did you actually see a written document memorializing the military agreement?"

"No."

"But you were told about it."

"Yes." In an instant, images of the interrogation with Nagiyev flashed through Tabrizi's mind. "We were told."

"And what were you told? I want to hear from your own lips what you were told about this other agreement."

"The agreement gives the Russian army the right to travel across Azerbaijan, and to locate units as needed in the area south of Highway M2, which runs from Shirvan near the coast up to the Georgian border. They can position their units anywhere south of that east-west line."

"That would give the Russians control of the southern one-third of the country."

"Yes. Roughly."

"While you were in Baku, did you come into contact with any other foreign nationals?"

"No."

"But there were foreign nationals there. Correct?"

"Yes. Many. From any number of countries."

"Do you know if any of them obtained a copy of the written agreement between Russia and Azerbaijan? The agreement regarding military matters."

"It's my understanding that an American from the CIA received a copy."

"How did the CIA come to have a copy?"

"I believe they received it from the source we used."

"Your source gave them the document and told you about it verbally."

"Yes," Tabrizi nodded.

"I see."

"It was the nature of our relationship," Tabrizi explained. He was lying, of course, but he did not want to tell Shokof the truth—that he had no sources anywhere, only brutal tactless methods—so he lied. "We have worked together a number of years."

"And he always gives you information in this secondhand manner?"

"Three or four years ago," Tabrizi continued, elaborating as he went, "I learned that he was secretly supplying information from the Azerbaijani foreign minister's office to the Americans. He did not want anyone to know that. So I told him no one would know as long as he gave me the same information he gave the Americans. And that is how we have worked since then."

"Only he did not do that."

"What do you mean?" Tabrizi had a worried look. "Are you saying he gave us bad information?"

"I'm saying he gave the Americans a document and gave you only a verbal accounting of it. Why not simply make a second copy for you, too?"

"Information is information," Tabrizi shrugged.

"But detail is another matter."

"I saw Russian transports already moving into Azerbaijan," Tabrizi offered in an attempt to change the subject. "And from what they were carrying, I would say they were preparing to move large numbers of troops into the country, and do it soon."

"What was on the trucks?"

"Tents, portable latrines, boxes of supplies."

"Any munitions?"

"None that I saw, but they don't transport it that way." He didn't know how the Russians routinely transported munitions, but he was certain Shokof didn't either.

"I am sure this is only another Russian exercise," Shokof took the bait on the diversion.

"Then this is a very large exercise," Tabrizi replied.

"Perhaps." Shokof looked away in a dismissive gesture. "But even so, that is not a concern for you."

"But why would they do that?" Tabrizi was determined to keep the conversation away from questions about how he obtained the information in his report. "Why would the Russians move a major portion of their army into Azerbaijan? Azerbaijan has no problem with internal unrest or outside aggressors, and certainly none that would require Russian assistance. And they have no quarrel with us, or we with them."

"That is why we think it is a military exercise."

"But that—"

"As I told you already," Shokof cut him off brusquely, "this is none of your concern. We have analysts to determine what the information means."

"But I think—"

"I am not interested in what you think," Shokof snapped angrily. "I am only interested in what you saw and what you heard." He paused to collect himself. "Tell me the name of the source who supplied you with this information."

Tabrizi bristled at the suggestion. "That is highly irregular."

"Excuse me?" Shokof was indignant. "I am the director of VEVAK!" he shouted. "Now tell me the name of your source!"

"Murtuza Nagiyev," Tabrizi offered reluctantly.

"And why did you deem him reliable?"

"He is an assistant in the office of Jalil Qurbani."

"I understand he is dead."

"Yes," Tabrizi replied with disgust. "Apparently the Americans found out he was working with us also, behind their backs, and they killed him."

"I am sure you will find another source," Shokof snarled. "That is what you're paid to do."

"I am paid to do many things," Tabrizi leaned back from the table. "Is this going to take much longer? I've been detained for the past three days."

"No," Shokof sighed. "That is all."

Tabrizi rose from his seat at the table, crossed the room to the door, and stepped into the hall.

Following his meeting with Tabrizi, Shokof drove across the city to Sa'dabad Palace, Kermani's official residence. Located on the slopes of the Alborz Mountains, in the Shemiran section of Tehran, the palace offered a view of both the city skyline and the surrounding mountain wilderness. Shokof's car brought him to the side entrance where a servant ushered him to Kermani's private study. Someone brought them tea and cakes, and when they were alone, Shokof turned to the matter at hand.

"Our operative has returned from Baku."

"I heard," Kermani replied. "You have talked to him?"

"Yes. Just now. As we suspected from the rumors, Shahat gave the Russians access to our border. The first of their troops are already inside Azerbaijan. I told you this would never work."

"And what of Nagiyev?"

"He is dead."

"How did he die?"

"Painfully, I am sure."

"Your team took care of it?"

"Their official report blames the death on the Americans, but I am certain Tabrizi did it himself."

"He told you?"

"No. Not in so many words."

"Good," Kermani nodded. "That is as it should be. You have informed Qurbani that we dispatched his traitor?"

"Yes."

"Was he appropriately grateful?"

"Yes. But I do not think he is strong enough to dislodge Shahat from office."

"You worry too much. We do not need to see Shahat removed. The important thing is that we now own Qurbani, and when he is president of Azerbaijan, we will own the whole country."

"You are forgetting the Russians."

"The Russians are merely posturing," Kermani said with a wave of his hand. "As they have always done."

"That was the Russia of the Soviet era," Shokof countered. "This is the new Russia. They are amassing their army on our northern border. And we are hearing rumors that Chinese troops are gathering on the border with Afghanistan."

"Rumors?" Kermani looked interested. "From whom?"

"From our contacts with the Taliban and from members in the Haqqani network."

"You discussed this with your operative, too?"

"No. He knows nothing of the situation with China."

"Our contacts in Russia and China can verify these reports with hard intelligence. You should have asked them earlier, as I suggested. The Russians would have been glad to tell us about the Chinese, and the Chinese about the Russians. That is how we have always done it."

"We have asked," Shokof replied, "but neither of them will tell us anything."

"They would not tell you what they know of this?"

"No."

"That is interesting," Kermani mused.

"This is going to be a problem for us," Shokof said with a downcast voice.

"What is going to be a problem?"

"This situation. With the Russians to our north and the Chinese to our east."

"What are you saying?" Kermani frowned. "That they are coming for *us*?"

"What other explanation could there be?"

"That the Russians have a problem with the Azerbaijanis, and the Chinese with the Afghanis."

"I do not think that is the case."

"So what are you suggesting we should do about it?"

"We should leave now," Shokof answered emphatically.

"And go where?"

"Montenegro, Andorra, Togo, Benin."

"Benin?" Kermani smiled. "Where is Benin?"

"Africa."

"I would never go to Africa."

"Well, we should get out of here now, regardless of where we go. There are places we could go and simply disappear."

"You should relax," Kermani insisted. "The money is deposited in a safe place. No one will find it."

"I am not worried about the money."

"Then what are you worried about?"

"Us. We are not safe here."

"How is it we are not safe?" Kermani asked, gesturing to the surroundings. "No one can reach us here. And besides, I do not think they will ever suspect a thing."

"You must at least call a meeting of the council. You have a duty to inform them of this latest intelligence."

"I suppose," Kermani reluctantly agreed. "But I do not enjoy dealing with them."

57

TEHRAN, IRAN

INSTEAD OF CONVENING A MEETING of the entire Supreme National Security Council, Kermani gathered a much smaller group of carefully selected Council members that included Abadeh Ardakan, the foreign minister; General Mehran Bizhani, commander of the Iranian air force; General Reza Modiri, commander of the Iranian army; Admiral Emud Kianian, commander of the Iranian navy; and Maziyar Shokof. They met that evening around the table in the main dining room at Sa'dabad Palace.

When they were seated, Shokof explained the latest news from Baku. "As we suspected," he began, "the Russian agreement with Azerbaijan is not as benign as they would like everyone to believe. We have learned that while they were negotiating the renewal of their trade agreement, they also reached a separate agreement that allows Russia to position military units in southern Azerbaijan. Operatives in the region report that Russia is moving a large portion of its army into the region even now."

Modiri spoke up. "You know this for—"

"Please, allow me to finish," Shokof held up his hand for silence. "In addition to the situation with Russia, we have heard rumors that the Chinese army is gathering on the border with Afghanistan. Analysts believe these two developments are related and they are concerned this may be the first indication that both armies intend to invade the region."

"Is this a coordinated effort?" Bizhani asked.

"We do not know."

"I do not think so." Modiri's face was twisted in a skeptical expression. "When have Russia and China ever worked together on anything? I think the bigger question is, Why would Russia invade Azerbaijan?"

"They aren't invading Azerbaijan," Shokof explained. "The Azerbaijanis are allowing them to be there."

"Is there any difference?" Modiri chuckled. "If I park a tank in front of your house and ask for your wife, is that any different from me kicking down the door and taking her?"

"The coercion issue aside," Bizhani spoke up, "why would the Azerbaijanis agree to such an arrangement?"

"Money," someone suggested. "If they reached the military agreement while they were negotiating the trade agreement, the one paid for the other. I'm sure if we examined the trade agreement we would find it was far more than generous."

"Yes," Shokof nodded. "That is precisely what they did. They bought military access with the trade agreement."

"I think," Admiral Kianian injected calmly, "we are assuming this aggression is really directed toward us."

"Can we afford to assume otherwise?" Ardakan asked.

"But why would they show this kind of aggression toward us? Assuming that's what this is."

"Oil," Ardakan replied.

"Oil?"

"We are not honoring our contracts with China."

"And you think the Chinese will attempt to invade us merely because we are now brokering our oil through Germany, rather than selling directly to Chinese companies?"

"We didn't merely agree to broker our oil through Germany," Ardakan countered. "We made a deal to sell them our oil. They control it now, not us. In a true brokerage arrangement, we would still hold control of the sale, which we could withdraw at any time."

"But we are a country free to do as we please," Modiri almost shouted. "We could sell that oil to whomever we desire."

"Yes," Ardakan agreed. "Which is what we did when we reached an earlier agreement with China. Now we have chosen another path and our decision has provoked the Chinese."

"How do you know this?" Modiri asked.

"Neither of these countries was gathering their troops along the border before the agreement. This is something that happened after we signed with the Germans."

"But let's be real about this," Bizhani had a wry smile. "To invade us, China would have to invade Afghanistan and come by land all the way across to our border. The Americans would never let that happen. China would not be so arrogant as to attempt such a thing."

"The Americans are too weak to prevent it," Modiri sneered.

Admiral Kianian caught Shokof's attention. "If the Chinese were really going to invade, as you suggest, they would come overland to reach us. How would they do it? What would it look like?"

Shokof glanced in General Modiri's direction. "Perhaps you would like to show us the probable routes."

Modiri stood. "With an invasion of Afghanistan, the Chinese would face two defining criteria—getting their troops through the mountains without encroaching on Pakistan-controlled territory, and without directly confronting the American troops stationed there. There are two avenues for invading Afghanistan from China. One is through the Wakhan Corridor. The other is through a smaller pass to the northeast of that location. Those are the only two places from which they could enter Afghanistan without also crossing through Pakistan and its autonomous regions."

"And is that area patrolled by the Americans?"

"I am sure they are there, but this is the most remote area of Afghanistan and there is very little Taliban presence there. So I do not think the Americans would be an issue until the Chinese reached Kabul."

"And what about Azerbaijan?" Kianian asked. "How would the Russians invade from there?"

"Again, there are only two options, which are well-known. Overland from Parsabad, assuming they could find a way across the river, then through the pass at Germi. Or down the coast and through the passes near Rostamabad."

"This discussion is ridiculous," Bizhani scoffed. "We should not even waste our time on such useless speculation."

Ardakan spoke up. "Why not just sell the Chinese the oil we were previously obligated to sell them?"

Shokof and Kermani exchanged looks, then Kermani answered, "That is no longer an option. We have agreements in place with the Europeans. They have obligated themselves to us and us to them."

"Then we should demand the Europeans come forward and protect us."

"We shall, but in the meantime, we should ascertain the true nature of the threat we face."

"What are you suggesting we do?" Bizhani asked.

"I think we should direct Shokof to send VEVAK agents to the border with Azerbaijan and to the Afghan border with China, and let them see firsthand what is happening in those regions."

"I agree," General Modiri concurred. "As long as operatives from the army go as well."

"Very well. Does anyone object?" When no one spoke up, Kermani looked over at Shokof. "Then you shall undertake this mission with all due haste, and report back to us as quickly as possible."

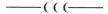

While Kermani met with members of the Security Council, Ruhollah Tabrizi dined alone at a restaurant in Chaleh Meydan, Teheran's oldest neighborhood. When he finished, he left the restaurant and walked up the street. After half a block, he was met by two men who ushered him toward a waiting car. Tabrizi's first instinct was to run. Automobiles were deathtraps from which few in his line of work escaped, but the men who approached him were unarmed and appeared to pose no threat. So he walked with them to a gray Mercedes parked at the curb.

When they reached it, one of the men opened the rear door, and Tabrizi saw Adnan Karroubi inside. Karroubi smiled and patted the seat with his hand. "Come," he invited quietly. "Join me for a ride."

Tabrizi knew Karroubi only by reputation, but even so, he was a man of enormous influence and someone whose request no one dared refuse. With a cautious eye on the driver, Tabrizi crawled into the car and took a seat. One of the men who met him on the street closed the door behind him and the car started slowly forward. Karroubi looked over at him. "You know who I am?"

"Yes," Tabrizi nodded.

"Good. Then there is no need for me to explain my interest in what we are about to discuss. I understand you were recently in Baku."

"I am not supposed to talk about that."

"It is okay," Karroubi reassured him. "I am cleared at the highest levels."

That was not how security clearances worked, but Tabrizi still was angry at the way Shokof had dismissed his concerns. "Yes," he sighed. "I was recently in Baku."

"They tell me you were debriefed by Shokof personally when you returned."

"I talked to many people when I returned," Tabrizi replied. "He was one of them."

"I understand that meeting did not go as well as you would have liked."

Tabrizi arched an eyebrow. "How do you know about my meeting with Shokof?"

"Surely you must understand," Karroubi smiled. "I know many things. Tell me about your meeting with Shokof."

"There is not much to tell," Tabrizi shrugged. "He would not listen."

"You had things to tell him but he did not wish to hear?"

"Yes."

"Tell me those things." Karroubi spoke in a disarming tone, the words rolling smoothly from his lips. "The things you wanted to say but no one would listen. Tell me what those things were about."

"The Russians," Tabrizi groaned. "I wanted to talk about the Russians."

"Ah," Karroubi nodded. "A most important topic and one to which we give very little notice. I would be glad to hear all that you have to say about the Russians."

Tabrizi saw himself as a master of espionage, but he had little patience for the nuanced social interaction necessary to build a network of relationships that would allow him to practice the craft of spying in a nonintrusive manner. Instead, he relied on force, snatching and grabbing key players, then beating them into submission and killing them when he was through. The sense of power that gave him, and the success he obtained by those methods, fueled an ever-growing ego.

Karroubi, on the other hand, was a master at finding the soft spots in human personalities and exploiting them with little more than a smile. By the time their conversation reached the topic of the Russians, Tabrizi was as pliable as putty and for the next thirty minutes he talked about the Russian trucks he saw on the streets of Baku and the cargo they carried, and about the troops moving through Azerbaijan to the border with Iran.

"You told these things to Shokof?" Karroubi asked.

"I tried to tell him, but he would not listen. I saw Russians in trucks, always with someone from the Azerbaijani government, but they were military trucks carrying military equipment and no one wanted me to talk about what I saw."

"And why do you think the Russians are gathering on our northern border?"

"They are coming for us." Tabrizi glanced at Karroubi, his eyes opened wide. "I know it sounds crazy, but I am certain the Russians intend to invade us."

Karroubi nodded. "I think you are correct."

"But why? Why would the Russians want to invade us? We pose no threat to them."

"There are many things that you and I can talk about, and many things we cannot." Karroubi smiled at Tabrizi once again. "But there are others in positions of influence who are as concerned as you about the situation developing to our north. Would you like to join with us in an effort to prevent these things from happening?"

"Prevent the Russians from invading us?"

"Yes."

"I would like that very much."

"Good," Karroubi nodded. "I knew we could count on you."

"What would you like me to do?"

"It is important that you continue reporting through VEVAK as usual, so no one suspects a thing. Just make sure you tell me everything you report to them, and be ready to act when I call. Will you do that?"

"Yes," Tabrizi nodded. "I will."

Karroubi handed Tabrizi a plain white card. On it were written a series of numbers taken from Dirbaz's phone. "This can be your first assignment. Find out who belongs to these numbers."

"That should not take long," Tabrizi replied.

Karroubi turned away and looked out the window. "The sooner the better," he said quietly.

58

MOSSAD OPERATIONS CENTER ASHDOD, ISRAEL

THE FOLLOWING MORNING, Hofi was seated at the desk in his office, still sorting through details gleaned from his investigation into General Khoury's attempt to commandeer the missile command center. A knock at the office door interrupted him and, as the door slowly opened, his assistant, Mara Moss, appeared. "They need you in the operations center," she announced.

Hofi closed the file and stood. "You know, you can use the phone to buzz me. You don't have to come in here every time you have a message."

"It is only two steps from my desk to your door," she replied. "I do not mind delivering the message in person."

Hofi slipped on his jacket. "But wouldn't it be more efficient just to call me on the phone?"

"By the time I press the button to ring you, I can be here in person," she smiled. "And besides, it takes only a few seconds to tell you in person, if you don't stop me with these questions."

"As you wish," Hofi chuckled. He moved around the desk and started toward the door. "Call them and tell them I'm on my way."

When he reached the operations center, Tzipi Levanon waved him over to her workstation. "We received these a few minutes ago from the National Reconnaissance Office," she pointed to the monitor on her desk.

"From the Americans?"

"Yes."

"What is it?"

"The latest satellite images from the Afghani-Chinese border."

"Why would they send those to us?" Hofi moved behind her chair and pointed to the monitor. "That looks like troops."

"It is," Levanon agreed. "Several hundred thousand by my estimate."

"That's not a military exercise."

"No. It's a mobilization." She moved to a second image. "And look at this."

Hofi leaned over her shoulder. "Trucks and tanks," he whispered.

"There's more." A third image appeared on the monitor showing a long line of trucks snaking down a highway toward the border.

Hofi studied the picture a moment, then stepped back. "Why would the Chinese gather their army on the Afghan border?"

"It looks like an invasion."

"But for what purpose? The Afghanis haven't bothered them. They've had no incidents of cross-border conflict. No armed incursions by the Taliban against Chinese citizens." Hofi gestured to the screens on the wall. "Put those up so everyone can see them." When the images were in place he turned to those in the room. "Okay, now listen. We have a situation developing on the Chinese border. These images on the screen are only a few hours old. They show a Chinese force of several hundred thousand troops with heavy equipment gathered at the Wakhan Corridor. We need to know why."

Someone called from across the room, "Chatter from Beijing says it's only an exercise."

"Anyone in here believe that?" When no one answered, Hofi continued. "I didn't think so. Do we have anyone in the region who can tell us about this?"

Naomi Tayeb spoke up. "We have one person."

"A name," Hofi insisted. "Give me a name."

"Natan Yavin."

"Good. Contact him and tell him to send a report on Chinese

activity. We need it immediately." Then he turned to the operator at the console in the center of the room. "Get these images downstairs and tell them we need every detail they find, and we need it fast. Then call the prime minister's office and tell them I need to brief him."

59

TEHRAN, IRAN

HIS DISCUSSION WITH TABRIZI left Karroubi genuinely worried. The Russians were an odd people but they were not given to relocating large portions of their army merely on a whim. If they were moving into southern Azerbaijan, they were doing so for a reason and Karroubi was certain it did not bode well for his country. Images flooded his mind of the last time he'd witnessed a Russian invasion. As a young man, he'd seen it firsthand in 1979, when the Soviets arrived to "liberate" Kabul. Memories from those days still haunted him and they replayed over and over in his mind as he thought of what lay ahead. Someone had to do something to avert a disaster.

As a member of the Assembly of Experts, he could obtain an audience with Kermani and explain in detail his worries and concerns. But Karroubi had little regard for Kermani and found him inept in all but the art of getting himself elected to office. Instead, he placed a phone call to Abadeh Ardakan, the Iranian foreign minister, and asked for a meeting. The two were old friends and had weathered many political battles together as allies. Moreover, Ardakan's brother had served with the Mujahideen in Afghanistan, where he died in 1980 at the hands of the Russians. Of all the officials in Kermani's administration, Karroubi was certain Ardakan would have a sympathetic ear for his concerns. And, even more importantly, he was confident that what they said to each other would go no further.

Ardakan took Karroubi's call, but he was reluctant to meet in his office. Instead, he suggested the Great Adorian Fire Temple, a Zoroastrian religious center located in Vanak, a neighborhood on the north side of the city. They met in an anteroom just off the Atashgah near the central room of the temple.

"I am sorry to bring you to such a location," Ardakan said when they were alone. "It is awkward coming here and I do not like it, but this is one place our Arab brothers will not come to eavesdrop on us."

Karroubi had a twinkle in his eye. "Perhaps our ancestors are listening."

"No, Adnan," Ardakan cautioned with a wag of his index finger. "Do not make light of the past. We do not need more trouble now."

"Are you becoming superstitious? Now? After all these years?"

"I just don't want trouble," Ardakan countered. "This is a day to be careful."

"Then I will get right to the point." The playfulness left Karroubi's voice, and the look on his face turned serious. "Why are the Russians preparing to invade our country?"

Ardakan's eyes darted away. "I...know of no such plan."

Karroubi pressed the point. "Surely you are aware of the agreement they have reached with Shahat that gives them the freedom to occupy fully one-third of Azerbaijan. VEVAK's agent just returned from Baku. Have they not briefed you on his report?"

"Yes," Ardakan groaned. "They briefed us."

"I understand from that agreement," Karroubi continued, "the Russians will gather their forces right on our border."

"It is nothing more than an exercise." Ardakan said the words, but his heart was not in them. "That's all. Just a military exercise."

"Nothing more than an exercise?" Karroubi's voice grew loud. "Abadeh," he cried, "they are amassing troops in Azerbaijan even now. At the rate they are going, it would be the largest military exercise in the history of the world."

"Shh," Ardakan said, gesturing for silence. "I'll tell you why they are coming. I'll tell you. Just lower your voice and don't shout." He glanced around nervously, checking to see who might have heard. Then he took a deep breath and continued. "They are coming because of our oil."

Karroubi had a puzzled look. "They want our oil?"

"No," Ardakan shook his head. "They have oil. Lots of oil. And they have ports that are open year-round. Their reasons have nothing to do with any of that or the thousand other reasons some say they will eventually invade us anyway."

"Then attacking us makes no sense," Karroubi argued, his voice growing loud again and more forceful. "An attack on us would interrupt the supply of oil to China. China would see such an attack as a threat to their economy. Their very existence. They are our single largest customer. If the Russians attacked us, the Chinese would be forced to counter that attack in order to secure access to the oil their economy desperately needs. Russian analysts can see this at least as clearly as I. It's a key element of our regional security. Everyone knows the Chinese stand behind us the way the United States stands behind Israel. Which brings me back to my original question. Knowing all that, as they most certainly do, why would Russia suddenly decide to attack us?"

"That's just it," Ardakan explained. "We don't sell oil to the Chinese anymore."

A frown wrinkled Karroubi's brow. "Since when?"

"Since Kermani struck a deal to sell our entire production to the Germans."

Karroubi's jaw dropped. "He did *what*?"

"He reached an agreement with the Germans to sell them our entire production. They have explained it as a brokerage arrangement, but that is not what it is. We sell, they buy. I'm surprised you did not know this already."

"This is the first I have heard of it. When did this happen?"

"Months ago."

"And the Germans take it all?"

"Yes," Ardakan nodded. "Every drop."

"How much is Kermani making from this arrangement?"

"I don't know."

"But you know he's getting a share."

"Not for a fact, but I'm sure he is."

"That still does not explain why the Russian army stands on our border," Karroubi observed. He waited for a response but when

Ardakan remained silent, he pressed the point. "Abadeh, what are you not telling me?"

"We are hearing rumors," Ardakan answered slowly.

"What kind of rumors?"

"That the Chinese army is assembling along the border with Afghanistan."

Karroubi frowned once more. "Why?"

Ardakan gave him a knowing look. "Why do you think?"

Karroubi's eyes opened wide in a look of realization. "They are coming for the oil we should be selling them."

"Exactly."

"And the Russians are planning to preempt that move," Karroubi spoke quickly now. "Have we confirmed that they are really doing this?"

"Normally, we would ask the Russians or the Chinese for satellite images, but neither one of them is willing to share that type of information with us now."

Karroubi's mouth gaped open again. "The Russians won't tell us about the Chinese?" Ardakan shook his head. "And the Chinese won't tell us about the Russians?" Ardakan shook his head once more. "This is not good. What are we doing about it?"

"We have dispatched agents to both regions to find out."

"That will take days."

"There was little else we could do. We still have time. Not much of it," Ardakan shrugged, "but a little. The Russians do not have enough troops in Azerbaijan to mount an offensive."

"How do you know this?"

"I have my sources."

"Other than VEVAK?"

Ardakan took a sarcastic tone. "No one but Kermani relies on VEVAK. We all have our own sources."

"And what are they telling you?"

"Just as you said. That the Chinese are preparing to invade through Afghanistan, to seize our oil. And that the Russians are preparing to invade through Azerbaijan to prevent the Chinese from being successful."

"So, the Russians will come first?"

"I suspect they will move as soon as they think the Chinese are ready."

"Weeks, months, years? How long do we have?"

"Weeks," Ardakan sighed. "We have only weeks, my friend."

60

JERUSALEM

AFTER A BRIEFING FROM HOFI on the developing situation with China, David Oren gathered the National Security Cabinet for a special meeting. A concentrated group of government leaders, the Cabinet functioned as an executive committee of the Knesset, streamlined to make quick decisions on matters posing a threat to the country's security. They gathered in a conference room across the hall from the prime minister's office and were seated around a table.

Oren called the meeting to order, then turned proceedings over to Hofi for an overview of the latest developments. When he finished the presentation, Oren glanced around the room. "Does anyone have any questions for Hofi?"

General Grossman, Chief of General Staff for the Israel Defense Forces, spoke up. "While I agree that the appearance of such a large Chinese force along the Afghan border is troubling, I have to ask, is this really a problem for us?"

"It does not appear to be," Hofi replied, "at least from a strategic point of view."

"There is no reason for them to move against us," Foreign Minister Simon Epstein added. "We pose no threat and have nothing they need."

"I should think the Americans might be concerned," Grossman continued. "You said they were your source for the satellite images?"

"Yes," Hofi responded.

"And I imagine they are concerned. They are in a vulnerable position right now. A disruption in the world's oil markets could be expected to have a significant impact on their situation."

"And upon ours as well," Epstein added. "High costs for energy affect us all."

"Yes, that is true," Grossman agreed. "But while a doubling of prices would hurt us, it might spell the end of the American economy. At least for the foreseeable future."

Yorman Herzliya, the minister of defense, was seated to the left. "So, why are they amassing on Afghanistan's border? Do we know?"

"We don't know for certain," Hofi replied. "As I mentioned earlier, we have operatives working in the region already and are in the process of contacting them to see if they can help determine why the Chinese are doing this."

"Any chance it is merely a military exercise?" Everyone chuckled. Herzliya looked embarrassed. "You never know," he shrugged. "It might actually *be* an exercise."

"The size of forces involved would tend to rule out an exercise. This is a huge force numbering in the hundreds of thousands and growing every day. A force like that would be virtually useless for an exercise."

"Unless," Herzliya added defensively, "the exercise was an exercise in the deployment of large forces."

"Yes," Hofi conceded, "I suppose so."

Epstein spoke up, moving on to a different but related topic. "We have heard rumors regarding a similar Russian move along the Iran-Azerbaijan border. Have you picked up any of that?"

"Yes," Hofi nodded. "There has been chatter about that. But we've not been able to confirm any of it or obtain hard information about anything like that."

"What does chatter mean?" Epstein asked.

"General discussion. Nonspecific. No one mentions a date or time or location. But many people mention 'they heard' something was about to happen. That sort of thing."

"You will let us know what you find from your sources?" Herzliya asked.

"Certainly."

"So," Oren cut off further discussion, "I think we have reached a consensus that this situation poses no immediate threat to us and requires no action on our part at this time."

"Other than for Hofi to report back to us regarding what he learns from our operatives in the area," Epstein reminded.

"Yes," Oren nodded. "Of course."

"And I would like to be added to the routine updates on this situation," Epstein turned to Hofi. "Just copy me on whatever you provide in your routine reports to Defense."

"We will."

"In the meantime," Oren cleared his throat for emphasis, "we will maintain our current state of defense readiness and monitor the situation closely." He pushed back from the table and stood. "And with that, we are dismissed."

As the others filed from the room, Oren took Hofi aside. "Keep on top of this. We have no idea what the Chinese are up to, but if the Russians are preparing for something as well, this could get really big, really fast."

"Certainly, Mr. Prime Minister. We should know more in a day or two."

Oren lowered his voice. "Did you talk to General Khoury?"

"Yes."

"What did he say?"

Hofi wasn't ready to answer that question. Not just yet. "After I met with him, I took the liberty of speaking with some of the others involved at the launch center. I'm still working through those interviews. I'll have a report for you soon."

Oren had a puzzled look. "Khoury didn't tell you anything?"

"He told me plenty, but I don't want to give it to you like this. I'll prepare a formal report and then we can talk."

Oren was not pleased but he didn't push the matter. "I'll look forward to it."

61

BERLIN, GERMANY

JOSEF MUELLER SAT AT HIS DESK, eyes glued to a television set on a shelf across the room. On the screen, news footage showed German troops arriving in the streets of Madrid. They looked sharp and distinguished as they marched in formation through the center of the city. Then the images changed and footage from riots appeared. Cars were overturned and on fire. Demonstrators carried handmade signs that read, "Nazis go home," and they shouted and screamed at the German troops who fought to restore order. In image after image, the presence of the German soldiers seemed to only make matters worse, with the crowds even more aggressive than before.

Video from Barcelona showed the large crowds assembled there, with the Barcelona Cathedral in the background. Soldiers formed a line across the street and moved forward, dressed in full riot gear, holding shields before them to ward off the bottles and bricks hurled in their direction. Then the shooting started. Later inquiries were unable to determine who started it, but the reaction of the troops was swift and lethal. Those at the front of the crowd dropped in quick succession, ten, twenty, as many as forty killed in the span of just a few seconds as the army unleashed its weapons on them. Wild-eyed and terrified, the crowd stampeded in the opposite direction and in the ensuing melee, a truck roared past the demonstrators and collided with the soldiers.

Before it crashed to a stop, four soldiers were dead. Another eight were seriously injured.

Mueller winced at the sight of it as he watched from his chair behind the desk. "I can't believe this is happening," he mumbled to himself. "This is almost full-scale war."

The office door opened and Karl Murnau, one of Mueller's many assistants, appeared with a file. He laid it on the corner of the desk and turned to leave, but Mueller called after him. "Did you see this?" he asked, pointing to the screen.

"Yes, sir," Murnau answered. "We were watching it on the monitor out front."

"Call Brody and Hölderlin and tell them I need to see them."

"Certainly, sir. When do you want them?"

"Now," Mueller growled impatiently.

A few minutes later, Konrad Hölderlin, head of the German Foreign Intelligence Agency, and General Erhard, Mueller's military adviser, arrived at the office. Mueller replayed the news video for them. "Are we making any progress?"

"Brody tells us we are," Hölderlin replied. "I'm not so sure."

"Where is Brody?" Mueller asked. "He was supposed to be here."

"I haven't seen him in several days."

Mueller pressed a button on the phone and in a moment the office door opened. Murnau appeared again. "Yes, sir?"

"Did you tell Brody we were meeting?"

"He said he couldn't come right now. Said his sister was visiting from out of town and you would understand."

"Thank you." Mueller waited until Murnau was gone, then turned to the others. "That's our code to say that he can't be here because there's a crisis at his office."

"He's head of Bundesbank," Hölderlin offered. "If he has a crisis, don't we all?"

"Not really. They're just swamped with this work in Spain." Mueller shifted positions in the chair. "So, tell me," he changed subjects, "what should we do? Several of our own people have died. We can't just ignore it."

"We should eliminate the protest leadership," Erhard suggested. "Find them, snatch them, get them off the streets."

"You mean rendition," Mueller observed. "Like the Americans did after the 9/11 attacks."

"I mean, fight the enemy on his own terms," Erhard was emphatic. "Fight them in a way they understand and do it with an eye toward ending the trouble rather than merely containing it."

Mueller glanced at Hölderlin. "What do you think?"

"I agree, as long as it is done quietly and discreetly."

"Right," Mueller nodded. "We cannot disrupt markets any further and still effect a recovery."

"I was thinking more of the safety of our own people," Hölderlin replied. "We want them openly attacked as little as possible, and rounding up herds of protesters would be a disaster. But grabbing key leaders would be another matter. That might actually work."

"All right. Let's do it." Mueller glanced at Erhard. "Do I give the order to you?"

"Yes."

"Very well, then. Seize the local protest leaders and detain them."

"Yes, Chancellor. Shall we use the Spanish judicial system or ours?"

"Neither," Mueller intoned flatly.

"Neither?"

"Hold them without judicial process." Mueller's face was emotionless. "When word gets around, they will be loath to act so boldly."

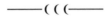

Three nights later, Manuel Carrillo sat in a darkened corner of the basement beneath his Madrid apartment building. For weeks he and the others from the neighborhood had worked to organize protests, first against the austerity measures imposed by the government, then against the use of German troops to impose order. Their goal had been simple: topple the government of Juan Gomez Bayona and force early elections for a new president. Two weeks ago they were on the verge of success, with Bayona teetering on the edge of resignation. Then the bankers prevailed, forcing Bayona to seek help from their

European neighbors. Shortly after that, the German soldiers arrived. Now Carrillo and the others faced regular, disciplined troops in the streets. Almost three hundred of his fellow protesters had died in the resulting clashes.

From above him came the heavy thudding echo of booted feet as they climbed the stairs to the third floor and moved down the hallway. He listened intently, calculating their position as the sound of their steps reverberated through the building. They moved past the apartment by the stairwell, then past Judit Perez's door across the hall, finally coming to a stop outside the door to his own apartment. A muffled sound of angry voices was followed by shouting and the sound of breaking glass. A baby cried and a woman shrieked.

Carrillo leaped to his feet. "I cannot sit here and wait while they pillage my home and terrorize my family." He charged across the basement to the door and ran up the stairs. At the top he threw open the door to the hall and stepped out to the first floor. And there they were, half a dozen German soldiers dressed in their gray uniforms and shiny black jackboots, waiting for him.

"I knew you were hiding," a lieutenant grinned. "And I knew you could not resist."

Maria appeared at the bottom of the stairway, led by a soldier with a firm grasp of her arm. "I'm sorry, Manuel." The soldier grabbed a handful of her thick, dark hair. Grinning from ear to ear, he pulled her head back, tipping up her chin, and used it to steer her across the hall. "They came for the children, Manuel," she said in a frightened voice. "They came for the children. I could not let them go." The soldier pressed her against the wall and held her in place with his forearm against her back.

"It's okay," Manuel reassured her. "As long as they are safe. It's okay."

"Yes," she nodded. "They are safe."

"For now," the lieutenant warned. "Fortunately for you, we are not yet interested in taking your family. But we know where they are and we'll be back to get them if you give us any trouble. Understand?" He glared at Carrillo as if waiting for an answer.

"You'll pay for this," Carrillo snarled. "One way or another, you'll pay for this."

The lieutenant turned to the soldiers beside him. "Get this scum out of here."

Two soldiers stepped forward and grabbed Carrillo by the arms. Then they hustled him down the hall to the front door and out to a van that was parked at the curb. The side door was open and they shoved him toward it. As he stepped inside, he glanced over his shoulder to see Maria standing at the steps, staring down at him. Then the door slammed closed and the van started forward.

All across Madrid, in Barcelona, and throughout all the major cities of Spain, German soldiers tracked down leaders of the street protests and took them into custody. In a single night, they rounded up every known leader and anyone openly associated with them. Without warrants, without judicial authority, and without the knowledge or consent of the Spanish government, they gathered dissidents of every stripe—doctors, lawyers, teachers, professors, and laborers—and hauled them all to the one place all Spaniards dreaded: Carabanchel.

Constructed on the outskirts of Madrid during the Spanish Civil War, Carabanchel Prison had once been home to Spain's most notorious terrorists and revolutionaries. It was closed in the early 1990s and abandoned long before Carrillo and the others arrived, but its reputation lived on as legend in the minds of all who sought to change the government by force. That night, as the van came to a stop and the door opened, Carrillo looked up at the foreboding structure, dark and eerie against the night sky, and saw not a single light inside.

"You are putting me in here?" he asked.

"With your friends," someone replied.

Headlights appeared as a van approached. Then behind it a line of vans and buses emerged from the night and rolled up the road toward them.

"This place has been empty for years," Carrillo protested. "Surely you can't be serious about keeping us here."

"I'm sure you can clean it up and make a nice place out of it."

Carrillo's eyes opened wide. "You've done nothing to prepare it?"

"We checked to make sure the locks still work," a guard chuckled. Other soldiers stepped forward and together they shoved him toward the entrance. "Have a nice stay." Then they pushed him inside and slammed the door closed.

———(((———

The following week, Hölderlin and Erhard met with Mueller to report on the results of their increased efforts in Spain. Eduard Bloch, recently appointed head of the Federal Police, and Georg Scheel, the foreign minister, were present for the meeting.

"We have captured and detained everyone on the list of known organizers," Erhard announced.

"How many in total?"

"As best we can determine, a little over fifteen hundred."

"Ach!" Mueller exclaimed. "That's more than I thought."

"We began with about a thousand and added a few more as we went. When we made the arrests we picked up a few more who tried to prevent us from doing our job."

"And did this produce the desired result?"

"Yes," Hölderlin answered. "Protests on the street have virtually ceased to exist."

"Well, Georg," Mueller turned to Scheel, "What about the Americans? Surely news of this has reached their journalists. Has Hedges kept his word? Or has he given in to popular sentiment and spoken out against what we are doing?"

"Not at all," Scheel replied. "In fact, President Hedges was asked about it today at a press conference. He said he was glad to see us taking action to shore up the safety and security of Spain and of Europe."

"Good," Mueller beamed. "Then we shall press forward in doing just that and use whatever force necessary to maintain order in Spain and solidify our control of the situation. And," he said with a mischievous look, "we shall prepare our next move."

"Which is?" Hölderlin asked.

"Offering our complete cooperation with the Americans."

"Cooperation?" Scheel looked skeptical. "What kind of cooperation?"

"Economic."

"I thought we wanted them rendered an economic footnote."

"Yes," Mueller nodded. "We do. And the best way to eliminate them is to make them truly our friend."

"I thought they *were* our friend."

"They think so, too," Mueller explained. "But now we must involve them further in our plot. That way, they will be prevented from ever opposing us again, on any subject. No matter what the stakes."

"And how do we do that?" Erhard wondered.

"We offer them much-needed assistance for their recovery. And when they take it, the door will be open to us. And just like the Chinese, we will burrow our way into their economy, fragile as it is right now, and gobble it up from the inside." He gave them a sly look. "Before they realize what is happening, we will own America."

62

NORTHERN IRAN

KIA OMIDYAR TRAVELED NORTH by car from Tehran as far as Basmenj. On the east side of town he came to a café and steered the car to a parking lot in back. A blue Volvo flatbed truck was parked there and he brought the car to a stop alongside it. In the cab of the truck he found work clothes and boots. He changed into them, then took a cap from behind the visor and plopped it on his head. The engine cranked on the first try and he let it warm a moment, then drove from the parking lot and headed north.

Near Ahar he purchased kebab and bread from a roadside vendor and ate it while continuing north toward the border. Finally, late in the afternoon, he reached the junction with Highway E-12 and turned right, driving along the Aras River that formed the border with Azerbaijan.

At Parsabad, he turned from the highway to a dusty street and followed it down to the river's floodplain. A dirt road meandered across the boggy expanse and came within a few meters of the riverbank. He guided the truck in that direction and finally brought it to a stop within sight of the water.

Using binoculars, he scanned the bank on the opposite side, checking carefully for the slightest hint of activity. When he saw none, he climbed from the cab of the truck and picked his way through dense undergrowth to the river's edge. After a quick search along the bank he found a small flat-bottom boat covered with branches. A paddle lay in it.

"One day," he grumbled, "they will give me a boat with a motor."

By then it was almost dark. He waited while nighttime descended, then pushed the boat into the water and started across to the other side. He paddled hard to make headway against the current but in spite of his best efforts he drifted east with every stroke of the paddle. When he finally reached the opposite bank, he was tired and his muscles ached. Hiking through the marsh at night on the Azerbaijani side was unthinkable so he beached the boat at the shore and lay down in it to rest. Before long, he was fast asleep.

The warmth of the sun on his face awakened him the next morning. He climbed from the boat and made his way up from the river to a highway. Though he'd crossed the border into Azerbaijan, he met no one who challenged his right to be there and he appeared at the road as one of the many rural farmhands.

In a little while, a truck slowed and the driver offered him a ride. Omidyar climbed into the cab and rode all the way to Bahramtepe. At the junction with Highway R-11, the driver brought the truck to a stop. "This is where I must turn," he said. "You wish to go on?"

To the right was a bridge across the Aras River, but by then the border had turned south and no longer followed the stream. There, Omidyar caught his first glimpse of the Russian army. A detail of a dozen men stood guard at either end of the bridge. "What are they doing?" he asked, pointing toward the soldiers.

"Russians," the driver groused. "They're everywhere now."

Omidyar did his best to act surprised. "But that is the first I have seen all morning."

"That is because we have been traveling on the highway. Turn down one of the roads just north of here and you will see them. They are camped in all the fields. Fields that should be planted now are all covered up with their tents and trucks and tanks." He gave a gesture of disgust with his hand. "They are worse than swine." He put the truck in gear. "I have to get going. Are you coming with me?"

"No," Omidyar replied. "I'll get out here."

"Suit yourself."

Omidyar pushed open the door and climbed from the cab. He

waited while the truck started forward, then stepped behind it as it moved past. As the truck drove away, he walked in the opposite direction.

Before long he came to a road that turned north. A farm truck turned in that same direction. It slowed to a stop and the driver waved for him. Omidyar climbed in the back and the truck started forward. Not long after that, they rounded a bend in the road and he saw what the driver had been talking about earlier. In every direction along both sides of the road, the fields were lined with rows and rows of tents.

At the top of a low hill, the truck slowed to make a turn. As it did, Omidyar slipped from the bed of the truck and continued up the road on foot. On the opposite side of the hill, he saw a sight that brought him up short. Beyond the rows of tents were lines and lines of trucks, tanks, and artillery pieces. And to the left he saw track-driven vehicles loaded with steel deck panels for portable bridges. *This isn't an exercise. They intend to cross the river.*

63

LANGLEY, VIRGINIA

LATE IN THE EVENING, Jenny left CIA headquarters in Langley and drove a short distance to a house off Georgetown Pike that she and Hoag rented as a temporary housing solution. It wasn't as cozy as the townhouse he'd leased in Georgetown, and the neighborhood was much too suburban for her tastes, but it was close to the office, which seemed important in light of the amount of time they spent there each day.

She turned into the driveway and brought the car to a stop in front of the garage. As she stepped out from behind the steering wheel, a familiar voice spoke to her. "Hello, Jenny." She looked up to see Debby Kinlaw standing to the right. They exchanged a hug but it was an awkward moment for both of them.

"I was going to call you," Jenny excused lamely. "It's just that we've been so busy, there just was never a good time."

"I know. It's like that sometimes."

"We've been going nonstop since we arrived. David's back at the office now. I just finally had to leave for a break."

"Dennis told me you guys were working great together."

"Well, it's not like we didn't know what we were getting into. We were both married to what we do long before we married each other."

"I think that comes with the territory." Debby glanced down a moment. "Listen, I'm really worried about Dennis." She looked Jenny in the eye. "I haven't heard from him in a long time."

Jenny shook her head. "You know I can't talk about that."

"I know, but since he left there's been nothing but silence. And it's been weeks. Can he still be alive?"

"I can't really say anything." Jenny pushed the car door closed and activated the locks. "You shouldn't even ask me."

"It's the not knowing that's the worst." Debby began to cry. "I think of him out there, by himself. All the times before, it was him and David together. But this one, he's all alone."

"I can neither confirm nor—"

"No!" Debby shouted. "I'm not taking that agency line from you. We've known each other too long for that. No one at the office will even take my calls and if they did I would expect that answer from them, but not you."

"I'm sorry." Jenny stepped away from the car and started toward the door. "I really shouldn't even be talking to you this much."

"I haven't heard a word from him since the morning he left for the office," Debby pleaded. "I have no idea where he is or what he's doing, and I don't care about that. All I want to know is whether he's alive or dead!"

Jenny slipped the house key in the lock. "I can't talk about it."

"Look, I know that, okay?" Debby snapped. "I know the agency line. They neither confirm nor deny anything. They just don't talk. But I'm not asking the agency. I'm asking you. Please, we've known each other a long time. Is he alive, or is he dead?"

Jenny looked at her a moment, wanting to tell her everything, and knowing she had to say nothing. Finally, she nodded toward the door. "Come inside. We'll have some tea."

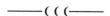

A few hours later, Hoag arrived at the house, exhausted and weary. Jenny greeted him with a kiss and as they came through the kitchen he noticed two teacups sitting on the table. "You had a visitor?"

"Debby stopped by," Jenny replied. "Actually, she was waiting for me in the driveway."

"How is she?"

"Stressed."

"I can imagine." By then they'd reached the living room. Hoag dropped onto the sofa and pulled her down beside him. "Did she want something in particular?"

"Just to know if Dennis was alive…mostly." She glanced away, avoiding his gaze.

"Is that all you told her?" he asked with a smile.

"Why do you assume I told her anything?"

"I know you said something," he grinned.

"I tried not to at first," Jenny admitted finally. "I gave her the standard 'I can't discuss that' line, but we've known them a long time and if the roles were reversed I'd expect her to tell me more than that."

Hoag had a wry smile and his voice took a sarcastic tone. "I hope he at least told her good-bye before he left."

"I'm sure he did. She knew he was going to be gone for a while." A puzzled frown wrinkled Jenny's forehead. "What's going on? Why did you talk about him in that tone?"

"He didn't say a word to me before he left." There was a hint of sadness in Hoag's voice. "Just volunteered to go and that was it. I didn't even know he was gone until after he'd already left."

"You knew he was leaving. You were standing right there when he agreed. If there was more to be said about it, you could have said it."

"I know," he sighed.

"You two act like a married couple."

"You've said that before."

"I'm serious."

"I just don't know what's going on with him anymore," Hoag lamented. "He doesn't seem like the same old Dennis."

"Well, from talking with Debby, I'd say he was hurt that you went off to Omaha and left him behind."

"I didn't have a choice. You were there. You saw what happened. Winston told me I was going. He didn't ask me. He didn't ask you, either. Just told us we were both going out there and then he sent us to catch the plane."

"I know. And I think he realized it was a good opportunity for you. But then you got promoted and he didn't and when we came back, you two were in separate worlds."

"Still …"

"Stop complaining. You two have been friends too long to act like that." She nudged him on the shoulder. "Did you say good-bye to *him* before *you* left?"

"I think so. I can't remember."

"Neither can I. We were there in the building, and Winston said go, and after that it was mostly a blur until we landed out there."

"I'm so tired right now," Hoag moaned, "I can hardly remember my own name."

"This has been a tough stretch for us."

"Yeah." He looked over at her. "Not exactly the storybook first year of marriage so far, is it?"

"I'm not looking for the storybook version," she replied.

"Good. Because that isn't how it's turning out. What were you looking for?"

"The version that has you in it."

He leaned against her and closed his eyes. "I'm not sure how much good I am to anyone right now. I feel empty." He glanced up at her and added quickly, "Not about you. Just inside."

"I know," she snuggled beside him. "We haven't been to church in months."

"No time. There's so much to do."

"We should make time."

"Yeah," he answered without enthusiasm. "I guess so." Conversation lagged between them and in a few minutes he felt the easy rhythmic motion of her breathing as she slipped off to sleep.

Sitting there in the quietness of the moment, he glanced to the end of the sofa and saw his Bible lying on a table beneath the window. A thin film of dust coated the cover. It had been so long since he opened it that he had forgotten putting it on the table. Moving carefully, he held Jenny's head up with one hand and leaned toward the table, reaching the other hand until his fingertips touched the Bible. He worked it carefully to the edge, then grabbed it just before it fell to the floor and laid it beside him on the sofa. A sofa pillow lay against the armrest. He placed it against his thigh and slowly lowered Jenny's head to rest on it. Then he placed the Bible in his lap and turned back the cover.

With no real purpose in mind he began flipping through the pages in the front of the book until he reached the Table of Contents. He scanned down the list of writings until he came to *Revelation* at the end. As he turned to it, he remembered how months earlier, when they first began searching for the container ships, Kinlaw had tried to convince him of the similarities between events foretold in prophecy and the events then occurring in the world. Descriptions of the two never quite matched up perfectly, at least not in a mathematical sense, and he had been able to easily defuse Dennis' arguments. But then the missile exploded over Washington and suddenly his view of the world changed. That seemed like a long time ago, much longer than it had actually been, but as he began to read, the words found a place in his mind and the connection between the prophecy given to John more than two thousand years ago and the events happening right then, even that very day, seemed not at all vague or disconnected.

64

NEAR ISHKASHIM, AFGHANISTAN

ON A FLAT SPIT OF LAND near the banks of the Wakhan River, two dozen steel cargo containers were arranged in a circle around eight wood and canvas huts that provided shelter and workspace for a detachment of US Marines. Inside one of the huts, Trevor Cotner sat at a workstation, busily tapping away on a laptop. "You sure we're supposed to do this?" he called over his shoulder.

David Pierce, a lieutenant, stood nearby. "Yes," he ordered. "Do it now." Pierce, a recent graduate of VMI and the third generation from his family to serve in the Corps, was on his first deployment to Afghanistan. When he was a senior in high school, his father had lamented that the war would be over before he could get to it. Now, just when he was getting in the thick of things, the brass in Kabul ordered him to evacuate.

"Once I hit the button," Cotner warned, "that virus will zap the software and wipe out the working memory. It'll be cleaner than the day it was made."

"Do it," Pierce replied.

"Everything on here will be gone."

"Do it."

"It'll be wiped cleaner than a—"

"Do it!" Pierce shouted, no longer worried about hiding the tension in his voice. "Press the button. Release the virus. We have to go."

"Once I do, we can't get it back," Cotner warned. "They tried it at Microsoft. Even Apple couldn't find it."

Pierce reached over Cotner's shoulder and jabbed a button on the keyboard with his finger. A tiny hourglass appeared in the center of the screen, showing the top emptying and the bottom filling up. "We don't have time for this," Pierce snarled. "As soon as that thing dings, sink an axe in it and make sure it's unusable."

"Yes, sir," Cotner replied, "but I—"

The computer dinged and the screen went black. Cotner dropped the laptop on the floor, picked up a hatchet from the table beside him, and chopped into the keyboard until the blade went all the way through the case on the other side.

"Do you have your gear ready?" Pierce asked.

"Backpack and a duffel. Got a parachute bag with some more stuff and I was—"

"No," Pierce snapped, cutting him off. "Backpack only."

Cotner threw his hands in the air. "But all my stuff won't fit in a backpack."

"Pack your standard-issue equipment first, fit in any personal gear you can accommodate after that. Keep it to a single pack and get moving. The chopper will be here in thirty minutes."

"Chopper? They're only sending one?"

"Just be glad we don't have to hike out of here."

"But I can't get my—"

"Look, Cotner, space is tight. There's only room for one backpack per man."

"But I—"

"We're two hundred miles from the nearest town. You can't possibly have a duffel bag full of personal belongings."

"It's stuff they sent me from home."

"Deep-six anything identifiable and leave the rest."

"But I—"

"Cotner, that's an order!" Pierce barked. "Men, backpacks, on the chopper. Everything else gets left behind."

Cotner's eyes opened wide. "Even the weapons?"

"Even the weapons."

"No way," Cotner replied, shaking his head from side to side. "I'm bringing my rifle," he said defiantly, "and my sidearm."

"Look," Pierce said, his eyes ablaze with anger, "we don't have room for them. This isn't a withdrawal. This isn't a retreat. This is an evacuation."

"And you listen to me," Cotner retorted. "I am a United States Marine!" He reached over the desk and picked up a rifle that leaned against the corner. "This is my rifle. I look after it. It looks after me. If I'm leaving, it's going with me." He made a broad, sweeping gesture with his arm. "And everybody else in this place feels the same way."

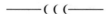

High up a mountain to the east of the river, Lo Gai Zong crawled onto a ledge and looked down at the Marine Corps encampment. After a moment, he gestured over his shoulder to the three men crouched a few meters away. They came to him and lay on the ledge, one man to his left, two to his right.

Below, on the flat near the bank of the river, the Marines scurried about, moving from hut to hut with quick, nervous steps. "They are in a hurry," Zong whispered.

"Frantic," someone observed.

"Do they know we are here?"

"Impossible."

"Perhaps they fear an attack."

"But we've been on patrol all day. There is no one out here except us."

In the distance, the familiar thumping sound of an approaching helicopter caught their attention. Zong tapped the first man to his right on the shoulder and scooted back from the ledge. "Come with me," he said in a loud whisper. "All of you. They will see you if you remain there."

All four men crawled back from the ledge and crouched behind the rocks, pressing their bodies into nooks and crevices in an attempt to avoid detection. Moments later, a Chinook helicopter appeared directly overhead. It banked to the right and swung around to the left, then slowly descended to the river bottom below.

As it settled onto the ground, Zong gestured for the others to stay put, then crawled back to the ledge for a look. Down below, the helicopter sat between the makeshift compound and the river, its twin rotors turning quietly as it waited. While Zong watched, Marines emerged from behind the cargo containers and hurried toward it. He counted them as they went, thirty-two in all. Each of them dressed in battle fatigues and carrying a fully-loaded backpack with their rifles slung over their shoulders. Only one man was unarmed. "That officer has no weapon," he whispered to himself.

The sound of the helicopter's engines changed and they began to whine. Then the rotors turned faster, kicking up a cloud of dust and dried leaves in a circle around it. Zong scooted back to the rocks and ducked his head, hoping to blend in with the terrain. Slowly the helicopter lifted off the ground, rose in the air, and banked away from the mountains. Safely clear of obstruction, it accelerated forward and flew west, in the opposite direction from which it came.

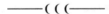

On a ridge to the right, Kamshad Kazemi, an Iranian operative, peered over the back of a burrow. Wearing a shalwar and kamzee—the pants and dress familiar to all Afghanis—with a pakul on his head, he looked like any of the Afghanis who made their home in the mountains. But in reality, he was an Iranian operative from VEVAK, sent by Maziyar Shokof to see firsthand whether there was any truth to the rumors of a Chinese military buildup on the Afghan border.

Kazemi stared down at the river bottom and watched as the Marines boarded the helicopter. He, too, noticed they were all armed except one and, by his count, the compound was now completely empty of men. "They have evacuated," he said to himself. He took binoculars from a small rucksack and used them to scan the compound. Then, slowly, he panned up the mountain to the left and caught sight of four men crouched in the rocks near a ledge about two hundred meters away. He focused the glasses and saw they were Chinese. One of them wore the green pants of the People's Liberation Army. As the helicopter rose in the air and banked away from the mountains, the men to Kazemi's left turned away and started up the trail that led to the ridge above.

Moving quietly, Kazemi worked his way up the mountain to a parallel ridge above where he'd been standing. There he caught sight of the four Chinese men, moving along a ridge to his left. He paced them, walking parallel to their path, then descended the opposite slope and converged on the trail behind them, following after them at a safe distance as they made their way east toward the border.

In a while, they descended onto a broad, flat plain about a kilometer in length and almost as wide. Kazemi lingered behind them and hid in the rocks, watching until they reached the far end and started up a low hill that lay on the opposite side. When they were over the crest and out of sight, he came from hiding and made his way after them. Half an hour later, he crested the hill at the end of the plain and stumbled to a halt.

Below him, as far as he could see in every direction, were tents, trucks, men, and all the equipment of war. "The rumors," he whispered, "are true."

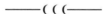

While Kazemi watched the Chinese, who were observing the Americans abandon their post, Natan Yavin stood on the opposite side of the river, watching them all through the lens of his binoculars. Contacted by the operations center in Ashdod with a request for reconnaissance, he traveled from Tajikistan to see if Hofi's analysis of the satellite images was correct. He'd heard rumors for weeks about the Chinese army gathering there and was curious for himself, too. Now, seeing four Chinese soldiers on the ridge opposite his position, he was certain trouble was brewing.

As they moved up the mountain, Yavin caught sight of a fifth man, standing on a ledge to the right. Using his binoculars he focused on the lone figure, and studied his features carefully.

When the helicopter was gone, he started up the river valley, moving at a deliberate pace. The Chinese soldiers disappeared over the ridge, as did the fifth man, who led a burro. Instead of trying to keep up with them and risk tipping them to his presence, Yavin chose a different approach. If an invasion was planned, as Hofi and others in Ashdod suspected, there was only one route through the region and that route led straight down the Wakhan Valley. If the Chinese army was gathering on the Afghan border, they would do so near the head of the valley. All he had to do was go there and see. He needn't bother with following the others. If they really were planning something big, he would find out soon enough.

That four Chinese men, all of them apparently soldiers, were watching a US military encampment struck Yavin as appropriate and expected. After all, the Chinese border wasn't far off. China and Afghanistan were neighbors and enjoyed a longstanding relationship of mutual respect, but the Wakhan area was a long way from anywhere. The Chinese might rightfully feel they needed to keep tabs on activity in the region and take liberties with national boundaries that might not apply in other areas. That much was understandable. The presence of the fifth man, however, was puzzling.

Though dressed in typical Afghan garb, his physical features were different from most of those who lived in the area. His eyes were darker, his skin less bronzed, and his hair thick and black. Yavin was sure the man he saw was from somewhere else. From Iran or Iraq, perhaps, but not Afghanistan or any of the surrounding countries.

Five kilometers east, the valley flattened into a broad, barren plain. In the distance, the four Chinese soldiers were strung out in a line as they plodded forward. Yavin moved to the left and proceeded in the same general direction, making his way through the rocks at the base of a mountain ridge that skirted the plain and doing his best to keep out of sight. He maintained a steady, deliberate pace but always with an eye toward the plain as the soldiers continued on to the opposite side where a hill lay in the distance. As they moved out of sight over the crest, the man he'd seen before appeared once more, following the path of the Chinese. The man crossed the plain and started up the hill, then disappeared over the crest.

In a little while, the sun began to set. As the sky darkened, Yavin came from the shelter of the ridge, made his way around the edge of the plain by a more direct route, and climbed to the top of the same hill the others had crested. Though standing a little to the north of where they crossed, he had a commanding view of the swale on the opposite side. And what he saw there made him stop and stare.

As far as he could see in either direction, there were rows and rows of tents. Behind them were rows of trucks and tanks. And farther in the distance, missiles rested on their mobile launchers. It was the largest assembly of military personnel and hardware he'd ever seen.

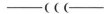

When Lo Gai Zong reached camp, he reported to Luo Li-Jen, who was waiting in the command center tent. "You had no trouble?" Li-Jen asked.

"None, sir."

"And what of the Americans today?"

"From all appearances, they have left."

"They are out on patrol?"

"No sir," Zong was emphatic. "A helicopter came for them and they left."

A puzzled look clouded Li-Jen's face. "Where did they go?"

"Sir, I believe they have abandoned their post."

The puzzlement on Li-Jen's face turned to an amused look. "What makes you think this?"

"They left with full packs."

"They have never done this before?" Li-Jen asked with a sardonic note.

"When they patrol, they do so with light packs," Zong explained. "Sometimes they take no pack at all. Yet always they leave with weapons, and almost every time with more than their personal arms. Today, that is all they carried. Each man had a rifle, no more. And the officer who led them bore no arms at all."

"And they boarded a helicopter?"

"Yes. All of them."

"The entire unit?"

"Yes. Their encampment is completely empty. They left no one behind."

"You counted?"

"Yes, sir," Zong nodded. "I counted."

"Most unusual," Li-Jen said with a thoughtful look. "You should go back there tomorrow."

"Yes, sir. But should we not file a report with our commanders?"

"You have given me your report." Li-Jen turned away in a dismissive gesture. "That is your sole duty in the matter."

65

MOSCOW, RUSSIA

VASILY KERENSKY, the Foreign Intelligence Service chief, sat at his desk reviewing budget and personnel reports when the door to his office opened. He did not bother to look up. "I told you not to disturb me."

"I am sorry for the disruption," an unfamiliar voice said, "but I was told you wanted to review these personally."

Kerensky looked up to see a courier standing in the doorway. He held a briefcase with his left hand, which was secured to his wrist by a digital handcuff. Behind him was an office assistant. "I tried to tell him he couldn't come in," she lamented. "But he wouldn't listen."

"General Sviridov said you wanted to review these personally," the courier explained.

The mention of that name caught Kerensky's attention. Sviridov was head of the Space Intelligence Center, the agency responsible for maintaining Russia's satellite system. It was also the Ministry of Defense's initial source for imagery analysis. "Very well," Kerensky gestured for the courier to come closer.

The courier crossed the room and set the case on the desktop, then waited while Kerensky entered a numeric code that unlocked the cuff. When it was loose, the courier removed the cuff and turned toward the door to leave. The assistant followed him from the room and closed the door behind them. When he was alone, Kerensky opened the briefcase.

Inside were three photographs and a two-page written report.

He read the report, his heart rate quickening with every word. According to analysis of the latest satellite images, the Chinese army was indeed gathering along the Afghan border. Troop and equipment concentrations were located at two primary points— one at the head of the Wakhan Corridor, the other a little farther to the east. Kerensky reviewed the report quickly, then scanned the photographs. Even without specialized equipment he could see the rows of tents, trucks, tanks, and associated vehicles. "This is not good," he muttered. "Not good at all. There are too many. Way too many."

He picked up the phone and called Vostok's office. "I must see the president at once," he directed when Vostok's assistant answered.

"He's in a meeting," she replied. "Shall I ask him to call you back?"

"This is a matter of national security." Kerensky's voice was louder than usual. "Tell him I am on my way." He slammed down the receiver. "I do not know why he appointed me to this position if he doesn't want to hear my advice." He took the photographs and report from the desktop and placed them in a leather satchel, then grabbed his jacket and hurried from the office.

Twenty minutes later, Kerensky arrived at the Kremlin. He exited the car, bounded up the steps, and hurried down the hall to Vostok's office. Vostok's assistant was seated at her desk. She looked up as he approached.

"As I told you before, he's in a meeting," she informed dryly. "If you have something for him, I would be glad to give it to him."

Kerensky ignored her and pushed open the office door. Inside he found Vostok alone and seated at his desk. "They told me you were on your way," he smiled.

"They told me you were in a meeting," Kerensky said, doing nothing to hide the sarcasm in his voice.

"You know how these things are," Vostok shrugged.

"Yes," Kerensky sighed. "I'm afraid I do. And I would like to discuss the way you treat me, but we have no time for that now." He opened the satchel and took out the photographs and report. "Chinese troop strength is greater than we expected." He laid the photographs on the desktop. "They have many times more men and equipment than we have seen before."

"How many troops would you say they have?"

"We estimate at least five hundred thousand. But they also have thousands of tanks, trucks, and other equipment there as well." Kerensky laid the report on the desk beside the photographs. "The analysis is brief and succinct."

"I can read the report later," Vostok replied dismissively. "What does all this mean?" he asked, gesturing to the photographs.

"It means they will attack soon," Kerensky said grimly.

"And how do you know this?"

"Because of the numbers. They can't keep that many troops in one place for very long."

"Logistics," Vostok nodded. "We discussed that before."

"Yes. It is both a problem and a predictor."

"And what of the Americans? Are they aware of this buildup?"

"The United States has evacuated its bases in Afghanistan."

"They know something is up."

"Yes," Kerensky agreed. "They most certainly do. We have reports that they took only the personnel and their effects. Our operatives report seeing them simply walk away from equipment and even stockpiles of munitions."

"Then they must think the threat of action is imminent."

"That would be our conclusion. If we are to preempt the Chinese in Iran, we must consider that the time for our own action has arrived."

"Very well," Vostok nodded. "We will convene the planning group and review the status of our readiness."

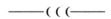

In Tehran, Shokof found Kermani in the garden behind Sa'dabad Palace. They talked while they strolled among the flowers. "The agents we sent to the border with Azerbaijan and to Afghanistan have reported."

"That was quick."

"The one who went to Azerbaijan had but a short distance to travel. The one in Afghanistan reported by text message."

"The wonders of modern technology."

"Too bad their report is not more wonderful."

"What did they see?"

"The Russians are gathering a large force in southern Azerbaijan. Tanks, trucks, missiles, and men. The Chinese are doing likewise along the border with Afghanistan, only their force is considerably larger than the Russians."

"How much larger?"

"The Russians have approximately two hundred thousand men. The Chinese, over half a million and rising."

"And what do they intend to do with these forces?"

"They are coming for us, sir. Coming for our oil. China because they think we owe them, and Russia because they do not want the Chinese located this close to their border."

"They share a border already."

"But only far to the east, where it does not matter so much. Here, they would occupy the central portion of the Middle East and control vast deposits of oil."

"What do you suggest we do?"

"We should leave, Mr. President."

"Leave?"

"Yes. Nothing good can come from staying."

"But if the Russians and the Chinese are set to attack us, might we not be better served by staying?"

"Perhaps, if one seeks the glory of choosing one's demise."

"You are too funny," Kermani laughed. "Choosing one's demise. I like that."

"We have the money. We can simply disappear. Regardless of who wins, in a struggle between the Chinese and the Russians, we will be destroyed."

"The world will never let that happen." Kermani dismissed Shokof's concern. "The Americans will not let it happen." He burst into laughter. "Can you picture it? The Americans stepping between us and our adversaries, defending Iran, the one country they love to hate?"

"I do not think they will rescue us."

"I think they all must yield to Allah's plans." Kermani paused to take a deep breath. "We will be fine. But we should make plans in case we need to assist in our own defense."

"What do you mean?"

"I mean we really don't want Russia to prevail. If that happened, our people would become slaves. They would be treated even worse. So if the Chinese attack from the east, and the Russians from the north," Kermani explained, "we should position ourselves to assist in Russia's greatest historic failure."

Later that day, Kermani reconvened the advisory panel derived from carefully selected members of the Supreme National Security Council. They met around the conference table in a secure room at the Ministry of Intelligence and National Security.

When they were seated, Shokof rose to address them. "The Russians are gathering a large force in southern Azerbaijan." He nodded to an assistant who circled the table, passing a manila folder to each of them. "The packets you are receiving contain photographs taken just north of our border. As you can see, they have positioned tanks, trucks, missiles, and men in large numbers." He paused while the assistant picked up a second stack of folders. "The Chinese are doing likewise along the border with Afghanistan, only their force is considerably larger than the Russians'." Again the assistant circled the table distributing folders to each of those in attendance. "Pictures in this second packet are of the Chinese." He paused while the assistant finished and left the room. When she was gone, he continued. "The Russians have approximately two hundred thousand men, with more arriving each day. The Chinese have over half a million and are increasing their numbers as well."

"Is there any indication of what they intend to do with these forces?"

"One might assume that with such a large ground force, the object would be something or someone in close proximity to their location. In these instances, Afghanistan and us."

"The Russians are convinced the Chinese intend to cross Afghanistan and invade us as well."

"Is this a coordinated effort?"

"I have seen no indication of that."

"If they are preparing to attack Iran, what can we do to stop them?"

General Mehran Bizhani, commander of the Iranian air force, spoke up. "The only way to thwart such an attack is to close the passes—the two we have discussed along the Azerbaijani border and the two into Afghanistan."

"That would still leave open the area to the west of Parsabad," General Modiri offered, "but the river forms our border there and we have no river crossings. A strike against the passes would make that area much more manageable. Reduce the Russians to attacking only at that location."

"So is that your suggestion?" Ardakan asked. "Deploy the army along that area and close the passes to their east?"

"Yes," Modiri nodded. "That would be my suggestion, if we are to make an armed response. But it would take a nuclear strike to do that."

"That would bring an international army against us." Ardakan shook his head. "It would be terrible."

"The passes to our north would be within our own territory," Bizhani countered. "Only the strikes to close the passes in Afghanistan would be outside our own country."

"Yes," Ardakan lamented, "an attack against our neighbor. The Americans would surely use it as an excuse to invade us."

"The Americans have gone home," Shokof advised.

Ardakan was caught by surprise. "They have gone home?"

"Our operative took pictures of them leaving," Shokof continued. "They abandoned their bases, left all their equipment, and flew away."

"That is difficult to believe."

Shokof turned to a folder that lay on the table. He opened it and took out a series of photographs. "See for yourself." He slid the pictures down the table in Ardakan's direction.

Ardakan looked them over. "This is incredible," he mumbled.

Admiral Emud Kianian, commander of the Iranian navy, spoke up. "There is another option."

"Please," Kermani replied, "by all means, tell us."

"It is risky—perhaps the riskiest of all—but also the one strategy that could bring us victory at their expense." Kianian glanced around the table as if waiting for a response.

"I think we would entertain any suggestion you might have to offer," Kermani added. "Go ahead."

"Let us assume," Kianian began slowly, "that the Russians are planning their action as a response to the Chinese, rather than in concert with them in a coordinated attack against us. They know the Chinese are coming but don't want them to occupy the entire region. "So as soon as they see the Chinese advance into Afghanistan, they will make their move from Azerbaijan against us, and attempt to sweep across us as quickly as possible in order to grab as much of our territory as they can before the Chinese get here. If we can draw both forces into conflict against each other, one army will neutralize the other, without our need to fight either."

"Preposterous," someone sighed.

"It has the advantage of avoiding a two-front war," Modiri added, "which is something we cannot sustain."

"If we combine it with the earlier suggestion to close the passes," Bizhani added, "we could cut off the route of retreat for both armies. They would be trapped and forced to fight."

"But what of the devastation to our own people?" Ardakan asked. "These two superpowers would be fighting right here, on top of us."

"Perhaps it would have been better if the Americans had remained in the region," Modiri opined. "They would be far better for us than the Russians or the Chinese."

"If we use our nuclear weapons against either location," Ardakan argued, "we would have to divert them from their primary target, Israel."

"We must survive to do anything," Modiri countered.

"Or strike Israel at the same time," Bizhani suggested.

"That would surely be our undoing," Ardakan grumbled.

"If we can survive this threat from Russian and China," Modiri continued, "we can deal with Israel later. In any event, we must be prepared to act quickly."

"Wait," Ardakan interrupted the conversation. "Didn't we say before that the Germans were obligated to defend us as part of the deal for the oil?"

"They are obligated to assist us," Kermani corrected. "It was not a mutual defense pact."

"But I thought you said they would come and defend us if we requested."

"They would assist us," Kermani reiterated. "I am requesting today that they grant us access to satellite imagery of the region. They have access to US satellites through their NATO relationship."

Ardakan slid back in his chair. "That is not what we said earlier."

"I am sorry if you misunderstood. They will help us, but not with troops."

The discussion continued to range far and wide with suggestions that were either profoundly practical or wildly imaginative. Finally, Kermani drew their deliberation to a conclusion. "So, regardless of how this plays out, we should deploy our ground forces to the area west of Parsabad, and reprogram as many of our existing missiles as necessary for effective strikes against the four entry points we've discussed—two passes in Afghanistan and the two on our border with Azerbaijan." He glanced around the room as heads nodded in agreement. "Good! Then it is so ordered."

66

TEHRAN, IRAN

WHEN THE MEETING WITH KERMANI and the other council members ended, Ardakan left the Intelligence and National Security building and rode across town to find Karroubi. They met in the study at Golestan Palace. Karroubi glanced up as Ardakan appeared in the doorway. "Are you sure you should be here?"

"After today," Ardakan sighed angrily, "I no longer care about appearances." He crossed the room to a chair near the desk and took a seat.

"What happened?" Karroubi asked.

"A few days ago," Ardakan explained, "we directed Shokof to send operatives to the border with Azerbaijan and to the China-Afghanistan border to see if there is any truth in the rumors about troop buildups."

Karroubi leaned back in the chair. "And what was their report?"

"It is worse than expected," Ardakan spoke with a heavy voice. "Much worse, in fact, and none of them realizes the danger."

"Oh." Karroubi rested his hands on his lap. "Tell me what we face."

"The Russians have hundreds of thousands of troops positioned south of Kabul." Ardakan studied Karroubi's face, watching to see his reaction, but there was not even the slightest hint of emotion in his eyes. "They are heavily armed and they are preparing to cross the border. The Chinese have even more on the Afghan border, at least equally armed." Still, he saw no reaction in Karroubi's expression.

"And what response has the Council decided to give?" Karroubi asked.

"Kermani has steered them into re-targeting missiles away from Israel, for use in multiple strikes at the invasion routes."

This time, a flash of anger flitted through Karroubi's eyes. "Invasion routes? They would come from multiple directions."

"Yes," Ardakan answered. "The Russians would most likely use two passes east of where the river turns from the border. There are two more in Afghanistan, which the Chinese would use to enter Afghanistan. Nuclear strikes against them would effectively eliminate retreat as an option for either." He slumped back in the chair. "The prevailing idea is that we should draw the Chinese and the Russians into battling each other, thus eliminating both armies."

"And we know for a fact these armies are prepared to advance against us?"

"No one knows anything for certain, except that if one of them makes a move, we will launch a nuclear strike to block them."

"Do they realize this fight to the end would occur right here, on top of us?"

"Some of them do, but even they don't seem to realize the extent of the misery they are inviting."

"Why not just sell the Chinese the oil we're already obligated to sell them?"

"I and others suggested that earlier," Ardakan nodded, "but they said it was no longer an option."

Karroubi leaned forward and rested his elbows on the desktop. "Kermani has not yet issued instructions for demanding that the Germans come to our defense?"

"He now says that was not the agreement." Ardakan had a tight, thin-lipped smile. "He insists that the German offer was merely to assist us and that he is requesting their assistance in giving us access to NATO satellite imagery of the region. But I know what he told us before and he said, in no uncertain terms, that the Germans would come and defend us in the event the Chinese chose to attack us."

"Why did he make the deal in the first place?"

Ardakan's eyes darted away. "I do not know."

"Yes you do," Karroubi insisted.

"What could possibly be the reason?"

"Money," Karroubi said flatly. "He did it for money."

"You are probably right," Ardakan agreed.

"And I'm not sure that's all there is to this," Karroubi added. "I think there is much more to this than we understand."

"You are probably right about that, too."

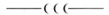

When their conversation was over, Karroubi remained in the study, seated at his desk. He picked up a pen and twirled it while he listened as the sound of Ardakan's footsteps moved down the hall toward the door. Kermani was shrewd and resourceful, but he was a fool to think Iran could use the Russian army to counter an attack by China and still remain a sovereign country. And he was even more a fool to think he could use the riches of Allah for his own benefit, and do so with impunity. "Riches from the land are a gift from Allah. Selling Iran's oil to Germany, and taking the proceeds for himself, is a sacrilege which must be avenged."

When Ardakan's car left the palace, Karroubi picked up the cell phone and sent a text message to Tabrizi requesting a meeting. A few minutes later, Tabrizi responded, "Outside Café Viuna. Ten minutes."

Karroubi called for a car and driver, which took him to Derakhti Boulevard. Tabrizi was waiting at the corner on the far side of the café. They came alongside him and stopped while he climbed inside. When he was seated in back, Karroubi caught the driver's eye in the rearview mirror and nodded. The car started forward. Karroubi looked over at Tabrizi. "I have a job for you."

"Will this require travel? I have something else coming up."

"I want you to investigate someone's bank accounts," Karroubi replied, ignoring Tabrizi's question. "You can do that? You have the resources for such an endeavor?"

"Yes," Tabrizi nodded. "I can do that. Who is it?"

Karroubi leaned close. "Kermani," he whispered.

Tabrizi's eyes opened wide. "*President* Kermani?"

"Yes," Karroubi nodded. "You can do that? Or should I find another?"

"We are allowed to investigate someone like that?"

"You are instructed to do so by me," Karroubi declared sternly. "I want you to get busy on this at once and report back to me with what you find." He tapped the back of the driver's seat, and the car came to a stop at the curb. Then he looked over at Tabrizi "You will help me with this?"

"Yes," Tabrizi nodded. "But if anyone finds out, we'll both be executed."

Karroubi gave him the tiniest hint of a smile. "Then make certain no one finds out."

Tabrizi turned to open the door, then paused and reached into his pocket. "This is the information for the phone numbers you gave me earlier." He handed Karroubi a slip of paper. "When we were in the car the night you picked me up."

"Ah, the phone numbers," Karroubi feigned surprise. "What did you find out about them?"

"They are cell phone numbers in America. Registered to an address in Virginia. No name on the account." He pointed to the paper. "That's the address." Then he opened the door and stepped from the car.

When the door closed, Karroubi tapped on the driver's seat once more, and the car started forward. As he rode to the palace, he stared at the information on the paper and thought about what it meant. The phone numbers he'd asked Tabrizi to investigate were from Dirbaz's phone and if those numbers were registered to an address in the United States, it could mean only one thing. Dirbaz was an informant.

67

WASHINGTON, D.C.

HOAG'S EVENING WITH JENNY a few nights earlier, sitting on the sofa remembering the kinds of things he and Kinlaw explored in their earlier attempts to locate the container ships, rekindled his interest in ancient prophecy. Over the next two days, he found himself turning again and again to the book of *Revelation* and thinking about how those words from the past might relate to the growing threat of war in the Middle East.

Back when they first began searching for the ships, Kinlaw had tried to convince him that apocalyptic prophecy in Scripture foretold some of what they faced. He'd initially discounted the notion, but as events continued to unfold with the cargo ships, he finally agreed to go with Kinlaw to see Vic Hamilton, one of their colleagues on the faculty at Georgetown University. Hamilton taught courses in Near Eastern History and Archaeology and was a recognized expert in apocalyptic literature. What they learned from him during that visit helped focus their attention on crucial details about the case that they might otherwise have overlooked.

That visit was almost a year ago, and Hamilton now was retired from the classroom. He kept a full schedule with research and writing but agreed to see Hoag the following morning. Hoag arrived at his home about nine and was greeted at the door by Hamilton's wife, Shirley. She led him to the sunroom, where he found Hamilton seated at a table, sipping from a cup of hot tea. He glanced up as Hoag entered.

"I hear you received a promotion."

"Yes," Hoag replied, dropping onto a chair across the table from him. "Not sure how long they'll keep me around, but for now I'm a deputy director."

"Well," Hamilton smiled, "enjoy it while it lasts." He took another sip of tea and gestured with his cup. "Where's your friend Dennis? Haven't seen him in a while."

"Oh, he's around," Hoag offered, hoping Hamilton wouldn't press the issue. "We keep him busy so he'll stay out of trouble."

"Shirley uses the same technique on me." Hamilton lifted his teacup again. "Care for some tea?"

"I'd love some," Hoag smiled.

Shirley brought a cup to the table and filled it with tea from a porcelain teapot. Conversation at the table turned to friends and colleagues while she brought out a box of doughnuts and a plate of coffee cake. When everything was set, she retreated from the room, leaving them alone to talk.

"So," Hamilton began when she was gone, "you said on the phone you wanted to talk some more about *Revelation*."

"Yes," Hoag nodded. "A lot has happened since we talked before, but I was wondering if we could pick up where we left off."

"You think the things that are happening now have some relationship to that?"

"I think that the connections you suggested before between *Revelation* and events in history were too intriguing to ignore, though I admit I haven't made much time for studying it since then."

"You've had a lot to handle."

"I suppose. But I wanted to get back to that topic."

"You realize we're talking about apocalyptic literature. This isn't a technical manual."

"I understand."

Hamilton took a bite of doughnut. "Where would you like to begin?"

"You were talking about how people who try to address end-time prophecies usually don't take a large enough view."

"Right," Hamilton nodded. "They concentrate too much on the

details and try to assign meaning and significance to each little thing the writer mentions. The details are there to paint a picture, for the most part."

Hoag looked puzzled. "For the most part?"

"Like I said, it's not an exact science. Prophecy is a mystery. All of Scripture is mysterious, but the prophets particularly so. I'm not suggesting what they said was fiction, but it helps if you think of it from a mystery writer's point of view."

Hoag picked up his cup to take a sip. "I'm not sure I've ever been invited to think of it that way."

"Well, look at it like this. Both writers—the prophet and the novelist—are trying to describe something they see that does not exist in the material world. A mystery writer imagines events in his mind. The prophet sees them in a vision. Then they turn to language to describe for us what they saw. So when you read it you have to let the words wash over you, rather than stopping to pick each one apart."

"The big picture."

"Right. Prophecy is strategic, not tactical."

"Okay," Hoag said, trying to keep the conversation moving forward, "you were saying when we talked about this before that the first three chapters of *Revelation* contain letters to seven churches in the Roman province of Asia, which is now Turkey, and that none of those churches exists today."

"Right." Hamilton reached to a ledge behind him and picked up a Bible, which he set on the table.

"So, you could think of those chapters as prophecy fulfilled."

"As to that much," Hamilton nodded. "Yes. That much of it I think you could say has been fulfilled. When you read it, you see those letters to the churches are really more like a pronouncement of judgment that is then suspended, pending their continued obedience. When he said, 'Do what I say, or I'll take away your lamp' he was saying, 'Do what I say or else I'll wipe you out.' And none of those churches exist anymore. They're all gone. In fact, today hardly any Christians remain in Turkey."

"They left."

"They were deported from Turkey following World War I with the Treaty of Lausanne."

"So," Hoag continued, "when the Turks signed that treaty, human history moved beyond the third chapter of *Revelation*."

"Right." Hamilton opened the Bible and turned to *Revelation*. "And then the scene in *Revelation* shifts to heaven and you see the four horsemen."

"Which you told us before are actually nations."

"I'm certain of that," Hamilton pointed to the page. "They're described here in chapter six. The first one is a rider with a bow on a white horse. A conqueror bent on conquest. Then a rider on a red horse, with a very large sword. He has the power to take away peace and to make men slay each other. Followed by a black horse with a rider who carries a set of scales and announces an exorbitant price for wheat and barley."

"And that's not describing a famine?"

"No," Hamilton replied, shaking his head. "It doesn't say there is no wheat; just that it costs a very high price." He pointed again to the text. "And then the last horse is the pale one. The rider's name is Death and he kills by sword, famine, plague, and wild beasts."

"Then if we passed beyond chapter three at the end of World War I, where are we now? In terms of *Revelation*."

"Okay, if you look ahead at chapter seven, and this may be more involved than you wanted to talk about—"

"No," Hoag assured, "this is exactly what I wanted to talk about."

"Well, if you look there in chapter seven you'll see a reference to angels holding back the winds from the four corners of the earth, protecting the earth. And then in chapter nine it talks about how the four angels that were bound at the Euphrates are to be released. I think those references—the wind held at the four corners of the earth and the angels bound at the Euphrates—are references to the four horsemen."

"The four nations."

"Right."

"Why were they held up?"

"For the sealing of the 144,000," Hamilton explained, "which occurs between the point where the four winds are held back and the angels at the Euphrates are released."

Hoag enjoyed listening to Hamilton talk about this topic, but the words were beginning to buzz around his head and he felt bewildered. "What does that mean, though?" he asked, hoping to slow things down so he could clear his mind. "The sealing of the 144,000. It sounds like we're getting lost in the details. Does that number have some particular meaning?"

Hamilton grinned. "If you don't work with this stuff every day, it can get rather confusing." He paused and took a sip from his cup. "You want some more tea?"

"Sure," Hoag replied, and slid his cup closer to the teapot.

"The numbers don't really matter that much except as imagery," Hamilton continued while he filled Hoag's cup. "That number is there to describe a group of people. You find out when you read that section that the people he's describing are twelve groups of twelve thousand, each from the twelve tribes of Israel."

"Oh." Hoag's eyes opened wider. "The 144,000 are Jews."

"Israelis, to be specific," Hamilton smiled. "I think this is a reference to the founding of Israel."

"So, if you're trying to correlate this with the events of human history, World War II would already be over by the end of chapter seven."

"Right," Hamilton nodded. "If we're past chapter three already in human history—if that's actually where we are now—then we're also past chapter seven, too. And that means the four nations—the horsemen—have already been identified. They've made their initial appearance."

"But they're being restrained?"

"Yes. By the model we've been discussing, they emerged at the end of World War I and have been restrained from pursuing their ultimate end."

A frown wrinkled Hoag's brow. "By the model we're discussing?"

"*Revelation* is a glimpse into the future. You have to hold what you think you know about it in tension with the part you don't understand."

"So then, what is the ultimate end for the four horsemen?"

"*Revelation* reads like judgment, and it *is* a judgment, but the judgment arises out of decisions mankind makes. In a theological sense, it arises from the effects of sin in the heart of Man, as it works out in the decisions Man makes, and that can get very dark, as we've seen glimpses of in the past. In restraining the four horsemen—the four nations—God has held them back from giving free rein to that propensity for evil."

"Setting off a nuclear bomb seems evil enough."

"But it could have been much worse. And that isn't the sort of thing that gets mankind into trouble in the end. It's his devotion to money, idolatry, and sex that does him in, not his propensity for war."

"So, if the four nations have already been identified, who are they?"

"At the end of World War I we had several clusters of nations that were more or less working together. World War II clarified those relationships. And by the end of that war the primary powers were Russia, England, China, and the United States. So, I think if you looked at this in sweeping generalities—and if this approach we're taking is correct—you could say that the four major powers—the four horsemen—are Russia, England in the form of the European Union, China, and America."

Hoag was skeptical. "The EU isn't really a military power, though."

"In one sense, that's correct. But in another, NATO is the EU's army."

"But we control NATO."

"For now, but it is rapidly coming under genuine European authority."

Hoag took a piece of coffee cake from the plate on the table. "What happens after those four nations are released? After the restraint is removed. What happens then?"

"That takes us to chapter eight." Hamilton paused while he turned a page in his Bible. "Which is where you see the destruction of a third of the freshwater, a third of the sea, and a third of the stars. We talked about this before, I think, and how it has already happened. One-third of the world is in a drought right now. One-third of the sea life is gone. One-third of the freshwater is polluted beyond use."

"But what about the part where it says one-third of the stars and the moon are gone?" Hoag asked. "They aren't gone, even though it says they will be. And you can't extinguish the moon anyway. It's just giving reflected light."

"Pollution," Hamilton offered. "All of it manmade—easily blocks one-third of the heavenly bodies from our sight."

"Interesting," Hoag mused. "Then what?"

Hamilton pointed again to a place on the page. "In between the time the horsemen are identified and the time they are released, the Abyss is opened and locusts come out to attack humans, then the four horsemen are released and a third of mankind perishes in a war."

"Rather frightening imagery."

"Not so much when you look closer," Hamilton suggested. "The Abyss is actually a reference to the underworld. Hell, hades, the abode of the dead, a place where godless beings are kept in order to protect the rest of the world from them. This again is a return to the theme of God loosing restraints previously placed against evil. But always doing it incrementally, hoping mankind will repent and giving them the maximum opportunity to do it."

"You ever think about how none of the things that have happened— the attack on the Trade Center, the explosion over Washington—were as bad as they could have been?"

"Exactly," Hamilton nodded. "I think about it all the time. They were bad, but they could have been much worse." Then he pointed to the page. "But let's keep going. I have an appointment later this morning. The Abyss is opened and evil comes out."

"And then the horsemen are released and evil begins to take full effect."

"Yes," Hamilton nodded. "But you're jumping ahead. That part comes a little later. Right here, the beings that come from the Abyss are described as locusts. These are desert locusts. Normally they eat vegetation, yet here they attack humans, only they can't actually devour them. They just make them wish they were dead, but they have no power to destroy anyone. Destruction doesn't come until the four horsemen are released. Then there's a huge war, apparently in the Middle East, which involves two hundred million soldiers."

"Literally?"

"I don't know," Hamilton shrugged. "It could be a poetic way of saying the war is really big and awful."

"So, where are we now? In terms of history. Lining up the things in *Revelation* with the events of human history, where are we?"

Hamilton leaned back in his chair. "This is always the tricky part of this subject to discuss. I don't want to be quoted in a briefing paper."

"This discussion is just for me," Hoag assured. "That's all."

"Okay," Hamilton continued. "If this analysis is correct, then we're in chapter nine. We've had the attack of the desert locusts—since the 1970s, terrorists from the desert, the Middle East, have been loosed to attack in various places around the world, including their recent attack on us. It fried the electrical grid but didn't harm a single person or building. Didn't hurt anyone, just made life miserable. All of that has happened already and the next thing that occurs is the battle described at the end of the chapter."

"So, if we're in chapter nine, and there's a battle coming, who's fighting?"

"Scripture doesn't say. Only that these four nations are released and they kill one-third of mankind with fire, smoke, and sulfur. Wouldn't have to be a war in the Middle East, necessarily. And it wouldn't have to involve all four. But it's a war that's really big and many people die."

"And no clue as to why they're fighting."

"That would be a great way to cut to the chase on all this, but I'm afraid I can't help you with that part. Remember, prophecy is strategic, not tactical. The prophets saw the big picture, not always the minute details. The bigger answer as to why they're fighting is simply that Man has forsaken God, but that doesn't give you the tactical precision you need."

"I'm not sure it would matter if I knew," Hoag said with a sigh. "I think one of the messages in *Revelation* is that this kind of thing is going to happen. Maybe not exactly because God decreed it to happen, but it's going to occur, and even after that no one sees it as arising from our need for God."

"And that's what John is saying in *Revelation* when he says that all these things occurred and still no one repented. That's an indication, too, of the depth of deception that plagues mankind. He doesn't even realize that what's happening has anything to do with his relationship with God. But the war in chapter nine isn't the war that ends all wars. It's just the war that turns us toward an even worse end."

68

TEHRAN, IRAN

AS KARROUBI RODE AWAY IN THE CAR, Tabrizi walked up the street lost in thought about what he'd been asked to do. Investigating the president's bank accounts—there wasn't much else he could do that would expose him to greater risk. Or offer such a tempting challenge.

Tabrizi was certain VEVAK had no information about Kermani's personal finances, and if it did, he wouldn't be able to access it without drawing the attention of multiple officials at several levels. That meant there was no shortcut to the information they wanted. If this investigation was going to work, he would have to develop his own sources and apply his own methods. But first, he had to figure out where to begin.

Kermani, though an important political figure, was only one individual. His financial transactions entered the same global banking system as everyone else's, which meant both the money and the account from which it came disappeared in a sea of electronic exchanges. At first, the prospect of sorting through that to find one or two particular accounts seemed overwhelming and virtually impossible. But the more Tabrizi thought about it, the more his mind turned from the vastness of the modern financial system to the human limitations of one individual.

Obviously, Karroubi thought the president was engaged in an

illicit if not illegal financial arrangement. If that was true, the probability was low that records of those exchanges would be kept at Kermani's office. In spite of State Security, too many people had access to that location. "And it's probably not on a government computer," he mused aloud, "where it would be accessible to a technician in systems administration." Probably not even on a computer at all. This was the kind of thing kept in one's head, or in a separate handwritten file, or cryptic notes with only enough detail to jog the memory. As he continued up the street toward his apartment, Tabrizi became convinced that records for Kermani's personal accounts would most likely be kept at his home, in Sa'dabad Palace. And that raised the stakes even higher.

The history of Sa'dabad Palace was well-known to most Iranians. First constructed in the 1800s, then renovated in the 1920s for Reza Shah, and again in the 1970s for the Shah's son, Pahlavi, it included an enormous main residence with a dozen outlying buildings. After the Islamic Revolution removed Pahlavi from power in 1979, those outlying buildings and most of the campus became part of a state-owned museum. The primary residence, however, fell into disuse. Then, in the 1990s, the rise of the Islamic Republic's international stature brought the need for an official presidential residence where guests could be entertained in a style befitting a leader in world politics. Sa'dabad Palace was once again renovated and expanded with improvements that included additional security features. Tabrizi knew this much, but for the kind of information Karroubi wanted, he'd have to get inside the palace, to Kermani's private study, and get out without getting caught. For that, he needed the kind of detailed information about the president's home that was as closely guarded as the residence itself. To complete Karroubi's assignment, he'd have to find a way to penetrate those defensive measures.

The following morning, Tabrizi took the bus to the National Library and began his search in the Archives section. A quick review of the library's catalog revealed three books that detailed the original construction of Sa'dabad Palace. Most of the work even in the 1800s was documented with photographs, which found their way to publication in the 1960s. He spent an hour studying pictures in the books, letting his eyes focus on every detail. When he'd exhausted that source, he turned to books about the Shah and about Pahlavi. That helped him understand the layout of the building and provided the location of the study, but in order to break into the building, he still needed information about the security system.

A second search of the library catalog showed documents from the construction and earlier renovations were held in collections that were archived in the basement. In order to access that section of the library, patrons were required to provide a copy of their identification card. Tabrizi carried a false identification card, but he didn't want that identity or his face associated with the files he sought to read.

Near the back corner of the first floor he found a door to a basement stairwell that was secured by a lock with a numeric code. It looked forbidding but he knew from experience that it was easily hacked with a few calculated guesses. He glanced around, checking to see that no one was watching, then entered a series of numbers on the touch pad. After the fourth try, the lock clicked and he opened the door.

A few minutes later, he was wandering through the basement searching rows and rows of shelves for the palace blueprints. He located boxes that held plans and drawings for almost every building in Tehran, but nothing on the palace until he came to a cardboard box on a shelf in the corner. Scrawled across the end of the container were the words *White Palace*, which was the former name of the building. He moved it from the shelf to a nearby table and lifted off the top.

Inside he found drawings from the 1800s and a few from a renovation that took place in 1920. There was nothing on the more recent work and certainly nothing on the building security system. But the plans for the 1920 improvements showed details for the placement of electrical fuse panels and the installation of the building's first telephone lines. Wires for all of those systems were routed through a network of tubes that ran from between the floors and had originally been used as a crude sort of intercom. With it, a person on the top floor could speak to a butler in the pantry merely by stepping to the hall, flipping aside the cover on the opening of a tube from that floor, and speaking into it in a normal voice.

That system worked well for the first several years of the building's life, but when phones came into widespread use, the palace was equipped with the latest telecommunications technology, albeit crude by today's standards. The talking tubes provided an obvious course for routing the new lines through the house. Tabrizi was certain it was the same location chosen by workers used for routing upgrades in technology installed in subsequent years too, including the addition of electronic security systems, which the building surely had. If his hunch was correct, the main panels for those systems would be located in a closet off the old pantry, next to the main kitchen near the rear of the house on the first floor.

The following day, Tabrizi dressed as a Bedouin and purchased a ticket for a midmorning private tour of the city. The highlight of that tour was a stop outside Sa'dabad Palace where passengers were allowed to disembark from the bus and take pictures from the street. Posing as a tourist, this would give him an opportunity to view the location without arousing anyone's suspicions. He joined a group from Qatar outside the Escan Hotel and climbed aboard a large van for the morning trip.

The first few hours of the tour took them to the usual tourist stops—museums, mosques, and the Tehran bazaar—then shortly after noon, the van turned onto Darband Street and wound its way uphill toward the palace grounds. Tabrizi took a small camera from beneath his robe, pointed it out the window, and snapped pictures as they rode past.

At the corner of the property, they came to a traffic circle and after rounding it arrived at the entrance to a long driveway that led toward the center of the palace campus. The driver slowed the van to an idle and as they rolled quietly beneath the overhanging branches of towering cypress trees, the tour guide described the stages of palace development.

A few minutes later, they arrived at a security checkpoint. Steel gates barred entry but beyond them the palace was clearly visible about a hundred meters away. As advertised, participants on the tour were ushered from the bus and allowed to mingle near the gates to snap pictures. Tabrizi took the opportunity to photograph the building, surrounding grounds, and the guardhouses that stood on either side of the driveway.

After ten minutes at the gate, the tour guide ushered them back to the van. Tabrizi stood on the far side of the driveway, beyond the guard building, and as he turned to leave, he pretended to stumble. In a reflexive action, he thrust out his hand to catch himself against the fence that ran the perimeter of the property. Tabrizi lingered there a moment, as if collecting himself, and the guide came to help him. A guard watched too, nervously glancing about as if expecting trouble. And in that same moment, a man appeared atop the palace roof. He held a pair of binoculars. He put them to his eyes and gazed in Tabrizi's direction. And Tabrizi knew there was only one reason for his sudden appearance. Sensors in the ground or along the fence told him someone was in a forbidden area.

Later that afternoon, Tabrizi returned to his apartment and downloaded pictures from the camera to a laptop. He spent the remainder of the day studying them for a point of weakness in the system. From what he could determine, the perimeter fence was ten feet high in most places. Coupled with motion sensors embedded in the ground, he would need weeks to determine where and how to circumvent it.

As he studied the pictures taken near the front driveway, he caught a glimpse of something blue in the background. Using a program on the laptop, he enlarged the image and removed some of the foliage in the foreground to reveal a delivery truck arriving from the west side of the property. A smile spread across his face. The fence might indeed be formidable. "But there are always other gates," he said to himself. "And other ways to get past them."

Using Internet access at a coffee shop down the street from his apartment, Tabrizi determined the blue delivery truck he saw at Sa'dabad Palace was from Barbari Bakery. The next morning Tabrizi arrived at the bakery early and slipped into the building through a door near a loading dock in back.

Near the kitchen, he located an office. A desk sat beneath a window on the wall opposite the door. In a basket on the left corner he found a stack of invoices from the previous day's deliveries. The delivery to the palace was made by a driver named Javad Farahani, using truck number five. On the opposite side of the desk were invoices prepared for deliveries to be made during the current day. Tabrizi flipped through them and saw that Farahani was scheduled to make another delivery to Sa'dabad Palace that morning.

Outside the office was a rack and on it hung freshly laundered uniform shirts. Tabrizi found one that appeared to be the correct size and lifted it from the rack. Just then, the front door opened and he heard someone come inside. He stuffed the shirt beneath his jacket and made his way quietly back to the door near the loading dock. Behind him, the sound of footsteps came from the hall. As they drew near, he opened the door, stepped outside the building, and walked up the street.

At the next corner, he turned and walked to an alley in the middle of the block. There, he turned again and doubled back to a building that was opposite the bakery. Out of sight in the shadows, he watched as the morning crew loaded the trucks. An hour later, workmen closed the door on truck number five, then retreated inside the building. This was the moment Tabrizi had been waiting for. He came from his hiding place, darted across the road, and climbed inside the cab of the truck.

A doorway led from the cab to the compartment in back where the baked goods were stacked on rolling racks. He concealed himself there and in a few minutes the driver climbed in behind the steering wheel. Moments later, he started the engine and steered the truck from the loading dock to the street.

Half an hour later, the truck approached the hillside where the palace was located. A traffic light turned red and the truck was forced to stop. Tabrizi came from hiding, struck the driver in the head and drug him from the seat. Unconscious and unable to resist, Tabrizi quickly tied his arms behind his back using the man's belt. He took a sock from his foot and stuffed it in the driver's mouth, then jumped into the driver's seat and started forward.

A few minutes later, he turned onto the street on the far side of the palace grounds, then entered a drive that led to the west side of the building. At the gate, a guard checked the invoices for the day's delivery, opened the rear door to glance inside, and waved Tabrizi through the gate. Two minutes later, he was inside the palace and quickly found his way to Kermani's private study.

With no time to spare, he went straight to the desk and opened the top drawer. In it he found pens, papers, and a datebook. He flipped through the pages of the book but saw nothing other than entries for appointments. He was about to give up when he spotted a notebook lying near the back corner of the drawer beneath a brown envelope. He moved the envelope aside, took out the notebook, and opened it. The first page was blank but on the second was a series of numbers along with the phrase *"God is One"* written in Arabic. Tabrizi repeated the numbers in his mind three times, visualizing them in sequence each time, then closed the notebook and returned it to the drawer.

Back at the kitchen, he unloaded the baked goods from the truck and found a chef to sign for the delivery. Then he stepped into the cab and drove from the building. The guards waved to him as he passed through the gate on his way to the street.

69

MOSCOW, RUSSIA

PRESIDENT VOSTOK SAT AT ONE END of the conference table and looked down the length of the room to General Garasimov, the secretary of defense, who occupied the chair at the opposite end. Garasimov, he knew, held deep reservations about the plan to occupy Iran, but he intended to use those doubts, which others shared, as leverage to ensure both Garasimov and the others stayed onboard with the effort.

Gathered with them that day were the members of Vostok's planning group for the proposed incursion into Iran. In addition to Garasimov, that included Kerensky, the Foreign Intelligence Service chief, and Mirsky, the foreign affairs minister. They were joined now by Admiral Anton Brusilov, commander of the Russian navy, and General Andrei Govorov, commander of the Russian air force, both of whom had taken strategic roles as the operation moved from planning and preparation into full-scale mobilization and deployment. Vostok's chief of staff, Anatolyn Luzhkov, sat in a chair along the wall to the left.

When everyone was in place, Vostok began. "As all of you are aware, in the past few months we have grown increasingly concerned with developments between China and Iran over the Iranian decision to broker their oil through Germany, to the exclusion of their prior commitments to China. You are also aware that one of our diplomats in Beijing has been working with sources there to secure information about a suspected buildup of the Chinese army along the border with

Afghanistan. That source delivered much useful information, which proved to be highly accurate. However, while on his way to a meeting with our diplomat, that source was murdered by operatives from China's Ministry of State Security. Our satellites have since confirmed what we already suspected and what that source told us—that China has indeed repositioned a significant portion of its army to the Afghan border. The size of that force is much larger than we originally anticipated. And judging from the lengths to which they have gone to protect that buildup from detection, one can only assume they mean to use it. They have no quarrel with Afghanistan, and no reason to wish a confrontation with the Americans who have been stationed in Afghanistan for some time, which leaves only the matter with Iran as the potential source for their current efforts. We have developed our plans to this point around that assumption." It was a long soliloquy, but he wanted to say it. Years of practice in Russian politics had taught him that when groups like this were involved in decision-making, the better choice was to forestall any possibility that participants could later claim ignorance of the underlying basis for the decisions reached. He paused and looked over at Kerensky. "Is that a fair summary of where we are?"

"Yes," Kerensky nodded. "And I would add, it would be impossible to overemphasize the size of this buildup."

"Why don't you give them the latest information," Vostok suggested.

"Certainly." Kerensky pushed back from the table and stood. "We estimate at least five hundred thousand Chinese troops are gathered along the Afghan border." Those at the table murmured in response. Kerensky continued. "In addition, they have positioned thousands of tanks, trucks, and other equipment there." He stooped to retrieve a leather satchel that sat on the floor beside his chair. He placed it on the table, opened the flap, and took out three photographs. "These are some of the most recent images from our satellites." He gestured to them. "You may see for yourselves what I am talking about." Admiral Brusilov picked up one of the photos to study it.

General Govorov leaned forward, resting his forearms on the table. His eyes darted from person to person around the table. "You realize, do you not, that a force of this size cannot be maintained at a state of combat readiness for an indefinite period of time?" He said it as a question, but the inflection of his voice made it purely rhetorical. The others acknowledged him with a nod. "Deployments of this nature generate their own momentum. The Chinese will either use this force or disband it, but they will do so within a matter of weeks, if not sooner."

"Logistics alone will compel them to act," Garasimov added, by way of explanation.

Brusilov spoke up. "And what do the Americans say about these developments? Are they aware of the Chinese force and its size?"

"They have made no comment on this matter whatsoever," Mirsky replied. "But they have acted."

"In what way?"

"They have evacuated their bases in Afghanistan."

Brusilov looked back to Kerensky. "So they know something is up?"

"Yes," Kerensky nodded. "They most certainly do."

"When did this withdrawal take place? I have heard nothing of it."

"It wasn't a withdrawal," Kerensky corrected. "It was an evacuation. They took only personnel and their effects. Our operatives reported seeing them simply walk away from equipment and even stockpiles of munitions."

"They not only think something is going to happen," Brusilov mused, "they think it will happen soon."

"That was our conclusion as well," Kerensky offered.

Vostok looked at Garasimov. "What is the state of our readiness in Azerbaijan?"

"We have two hundred thousand troops in place, with supporting equipment."

"And our plan of attack?" Vostok gestured with his right hand. "Perhaps you could explain it briefly."

Kerensky took a seat as Garasimov stood. "We would begin with a two-pronged attack, sending a portion of our troops down the coast through the pass at Rostamabad while a second force moves simultaneously across the border at Parsabad. We originally thought to bring them through the mountains at Germi, but we now think the bulk of our force would move more quickly by traveling just to the west of that location. This will permit our units to cross the Aras River at multiple points inside Azerbaijan. When that force is fully engaged, drawing the principle Iranian response in that direction, we will send a third group—the largest number of troops—on a swing much farther to the west, crossing the river at multiple points using portable bridges. Once across the river, that force will sweep into Iran over much more hospitable terrain. If all goes well, they will reach Tehran in approximately four days, long before the Chinese can reach our border through Afghanistan."

Brusilov spoke up once more. "Have the Iranians made any military moves that would indicate they know what we are about to do?"

"No," Kerensky answered. "So far as we can determine, their forces remain in place at the bases to which they are typically assigned. None of them has been repositioned."

"I've reviewed the force depletion report," Vostok continued, his attention focused on Garasimov. "We seem to be assuming the Iranians will offer no resistance."

"It appears that is so," Garasimov nodded. "They have no forces in the area. At least none of any consequence."

"You are comfortable with these estimates?"

"Yes, Mr. President," Garasimov replied. "Very much so."

"If I may," General Govorov interrupted and turned to Vostok. "Our alternative plans would anticipate the extensive use of air cover to eliminate any substantial resistance that might materialize. Are we prepared for the diplomatic and political consequences of that action?"

Vostok smiled at the question. He had assumed Govorov would welcome the opportunity to show how well his air force could perform, but he did not know until then that the general was reluctant to act. "We are fully aware of the problems such action could precipitate," Vostok responded. "If your airmen perform as well as your efficiency reports suggest, we should have little diplomatic difficulty."

"I ask," Govorov replied defensively, "only because this could get messy very quickly. We can eliminate most of the military targets inside Iran with a single air strike. And we could do it now, before we cross the border. Perhaps in a way that would blame it on someone else."

"You mean the Jews."

"Yes, Mr. President. To be frank. We could bomb targets in Iran and make it appear, at least for the moment, that the planes came from Israel."

"I will keep that in mind," Vostok's tone was dismissive. Then he turned to the others at the table. "Gentlemen, I believe it is now time to act."

A troubled frown wrinkled Mirsky's forehead. "Without waiting for the Chinese to move first?"

"If we wait," Vostok warned, "we will be forced to fight both the Iranians and the Chinese at the same time. By going first, before the Chinese cross their own border, they will know that if they attempt to invade Iran they will be unable to avoid a confrontation with us. We do not have sufficient troop strength for a conventional war of attrition with them. Our best hope for success, and the only way to avoid using our nuclear weapons, is to act first. To move preemptively into Iran as quickly as possible and seize as much territory as possible."

To the left, Govorov glanced down at the tabletop, and Vostok knew in an instant that he had underestimated his generals. All along, it was only Govorov who opposed the action.

At the far end of the table, a confident grin broke across Garasimov's face. He pushed back his chair and stood, then squared his shoulders and said in a loud voice, "Mr. President, this will be the day that the world learns there were always two superpowers. And that ours is the superior of the two."

"Let us hope you are correct," Vostok replied. He paused a moment, then glanced around the table. "We cross the border in seven days." And as if on command, those seated in the room stood to their feet and applauded.

70

LANGLEY, VIRGINIA

HOAG'S CONVERSATION WITH VIC HAMILTON left him both intrigued and worried. Russia and China were moving toward war and if the intelligence he'd seen was accurate, they would meet in Iran, probably sometime in the next few months, perhaps earlier. But the battle would begin before the two forces actually clashed, when China invaded Afghanistan. US troops were moving out of the way, most were already gone from the country, but Afghanistan possessed a solid, albeit small, military force. They would fight, as would the tribal warlords. Many would die, including civilians, before the Chinese army reached Iran's border. By then the Russians would be well into Iran and dug in. When the two forces finally met, Hoag was certain they would cover the desert with bodies.

Yet for all the carnage he saw coming, the thing that worried Hoag most was the fate of his friend Dennis Kinlaw. When last they heard from him he had located the warehouse in Tunis where the cargo containers from the ship were being held. Presumably, the missile from the *Santiago* was still inside. Then his phone dropped off the grid and weeks had passed since anyone had heard from him. Hoag wasn't concerned at first and even after several weeks went by he was only mildly apprehensive. Now he was worried. If an apocalyptic war was looming in the Middle East, it could easily involve everyone in the region. Tunisia was thousands of miles to the east of Iran, but with the kind of war biblical prophecy foretold and he imagined, that distance might not be enough to ensure Kinlaw's safety.

He told Jenny the things he'd learned from his conversation with Vic Hamilton—how human history had already moved beyond the third chapter of *Revelation*, and even past the seventh chapter, and now we were in the ninth when all restraints were off and the four nations made war. But talking about it only made him more apprehensive about the future.

Late one afternoon, he came downstairs to Jenny's office and took a seat across from her desk. She glanced over at him. "You don't look so good."

"I haven't been sleeping well."

"I noticed. You were tossing and turning all night." She closed the file on her desk and leaned back in her chair. "Still thinking about your conversation with Vic Hamilton?"

"I'm sure Vic is absolutely correct. We are about to witness the biggest war in the history of the world. Russia and China are going to meet in Iran and this will be the beginning of the end."

"And there's nothing we can do to stop it," she muttered matter-of-factly.

"I know," Hoag sighed. His eyes darted away. "I know."

Jenny turned to face him. She knew that the real reason he was worried had nothing to do with the end of the age or the war that appeared inevitable. She took his hands in hers. "Listen to me." She looked him in the eye. "Dennis is in Tunisia. That's about three thousand miles away from Iran. And even if the Russian and Chinese armies started advancing toward each other today it would take several weeks for them to get within fighting distance of each other."

"Right," he nodded.

"So, that gives us plenty of time to work this out." She stood and gestured for him to follow. "Come on."

He stood beside her. "Where are we going?"

"Home. I'm not spending another night here and neither are you. Someone else can cover things until morning. We're going home, having dinner, and getting to bed early."

Hoag walked with her to the elevator and they rode in silence to the first floor, his mind lost in thought. When the doors opened, they crossed the lobby to the parking deck entrance. As they stepped outside to the deck, Hoag looked over at her. "Think we could find a church that's open this time of day?"

She had a puzzled expression. "Why do you want a church?"

"We need to pray. There isn't much we can do about what's going to happen, but God can. And we can pray."

Her look of puzzlement turned to a wry smile. "You want to find one now?"

"You said we needed to," he grinned. "The other night. You said we needed to get back to church."

"Okay," she said slowly. "Why do you want to go to church now?"

"We need to pray. For us. For the world...for Dennis."

"Well, Potomac Church isn't far from here. We can stop by there."

"Good. I like that church."

"You've only been there twice in your life, and you weren't a Christian either time."

"Well," he shrugged. "I liked it just the same."

Fifteen minutes later, they arrived at Potomac Church to find the lights were on inside and cars were parked in the lot out front. Jenny brought the car to a stop in a space near the entrance and waited as Hoag came around to open the door for her. Then hand in hand they walked up the steps and into the vestibule, where they were met by Mark Ale, the pastor.

"Are you having a service?" Jenny whispered.

"No," Mark replied. "Just prayer."

"But is it something special?" Hoag asked. "We don't want to interrupt."

"It's been like this since the power grid went down," Mark explained. "We opened the doors the first evening, thinking with all that had happened people might like to come and pray. They've been coming here every night since." He gestured toward the sanctuary door. "Please. Stay as long as you need to."

"Okay," Hoag smiled. "We will." He shook hands with Mark, then pushed open the door to the sanctuary and waited while Jenny stepped past.

Ceiling lights over the pews were dimmed, but the glow from candles burning on the altar table near the front of the church lit up the sanctuary. As he and Jenny took a seat on the back pew, Hoag let his eyes scan the room. Scattered across the sanctuary were several dozen congregants. Some of them seated in the pews, others knelt at the altar down front. They sat there quietly for a moment, then Hoag slid to his knees and began to pray.

71

TEHRAN, IRAN

ADNAN KARROUBI WAS ONCE AGAIN SEATED at his desk in the study at Golestan Palace, engrossed in the effort to authenticate the recently discovered copy of *Life of God's Messenger*, when an alarm on his cell phone chimed indicating a new text message had arrived. He picked up the phone and glanced at the screen to see the message was from Tabrizi. "Museum of Contemporary Art. Twenty minutes."

Karroubi laid aside the book he'd been working on and called for his car and driver. Fifteen minutes later, he was seated on a bench in a private gallery off the main hall of the museum. He'd been there five minutes when a man entered through the doorway to his right. He was dressed in the robe of a Bedouin with a leather belt around his waist and sandals on his feet. He crossed the room from the door and took a seat on the bench beside Karroubi.

"You have news for me?" Karroubi asked, not at all confused by Tabrizi's appearance.

"Kermani keeps a notebook in the top drawer of the desk in his private study. Numbers from that notebook correspond to a bank account in Singapore. The account for those numbers is registered in the name of a Singapore corporation."

"You know this for a fact?"

"I have the documents to prove it," Tabrizi replied. "The account in Singapore regularly receives large deposits. They arrive in the account by a circuitous route, always passing through different accounts but always arriving in Singapore on the same day of the month."

"Taking a circuitous route to conceal their point of origin?"

"Yes," Tabrizi nodded. "They are not entirely untraceable transactions, but it would take some time to run them all the way back to the place where they began."

"Can it be done?"

"I have someone working on it now."

"Good. That information may be necessary. Any indication what happened to the money after it reached Singapore?"

"As I said, the account has received multiple deposits, but so far there has been only one transfer out of it, which was wired to a bank account in Andorra."

"And the name on that account?"

"Kermani," Tabrizi said in a sorrowful voice.

"As we suspected," Karroubi sighed. "You can give me the documents and information to support all of this?"

"Yes. I can provide a full report." Tabrizi took a slip of paper from behind his waist belt and handed it to Karroubi. "This is the name of the bank and the account number in Andorra."

Karroubi took it from him, glanced at it, then placed it in his pocket. "I will need records."

"I can get copies, but nothing official."

"Copies will be fine." As he withdrew his hand from his pocket, he produced an envelope, which he handed to Tabrizi. "This is for your trouble," he said softly, then stood and turned toward the door. "Wait here five minutes before you leave."

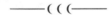

From the museum, Karroubi rode across town to Ardakan's office. He arrived without appointment and was met by an assistant in the outer room. "I have to ask the nature of your visit," he bowed respectfully.

"I need to speak with him regarding an ancient text we are both studying," Karroubi explained. "It won't take long."

The assistant disappeared inside Ardakan's office. Voices drifted through the walls, then the door opened and the assistant ushered Karroubi inside. Ardakan was seated at his desk as Karroubi entered. Both men waited in silence as the assistant left the room.

When they were alone, Ardakan leaned back in his chair. "Now I must say to you," he grumbled, "is it really a good idea for us to be seen together?"

"This time," Karroubi replied with a smile, "it was unavoidable."

"I seem to remember that line. What has happened?"

"Much has happened, but you don't want to know about it."

"I suspect that is wise," Ardakan nodded slowly.

Karroubi took a seat on a chair across from the desk. "I need information about our sales of oil to Germany under this new agreement." He spoke quietly but did not whisper. "And I need records for the corresponding payments supposedly received for it."

"You ask too much," Ardkan shook his head from side to side. "That is not possible."

"You are the foreign minister," Karroubi argued. "You have those records at your disposal, and if not, you can readily obtain them without suspicion."

"I am afraid nothing is without suspicion now," Ardakan sighed.

Karroubi looked him in the eye. "I need those records."

"I can request the records, but if Shokof finds out, he will know it is you who really wants them."

"Is he that suspicious of us?"

"Shokof is an idiot, but I fear he has already marked me as an enemy." Ardakan took a deep breath and looked over at Karroubi. "What have you found?"

"Do you really want to know?"

"No," Ardakan admitted. "But I feel compelled to ask and equally compelled to wait for an answer."

"Very well," Karroubi said in a resolute tone. "We found bank accounts." He paused a moment for effect before continuing. "Foreign accounts, in Kermani's name."

Ardakan heaved a heavy sigh, "I will see what I can do for you."

"Good," Karroubi smiled. "And now, so that neither of us has to lie, I will tell you, I am making good progress on authenticating the copy of *Life of God's Messenger*."

Ardakan's sat up straight and his face brightened. "Is it a genuine copy?"

"I think it is. Come by and I will show you what I have discovered in the pages."

"I think it is better that we not be seen together again," Ardakan cautioned. "Certainly not at Golestan Palace."

"Then pick a place and I will bring it to you so you can see."

"Perhaps later, after the current situation resolves itself."

"The current situation will never resolve itself. We must do that. And we must do it soon, before we all perish."

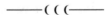

Early in the morning, three days later, Karroubi came downstairs at Golestan Palace to find Ardakan waiting in the study. Karroubi was surprised to see him. "I thought you wanted to distance yourself from me," he said with a hint of sarcasm.

"As we both have said before," Ardakan replied dryly, "this time it's important."

"It must be," Karroubi chuckled, "to bring you out this early."

"I checked on the information you wanted," Ardakan ignored Karroubi's last comment. "Thus far, there have been ten payments from Germany for our oil." He handed a sheaf of documents to Karroubi. "These are the records for the payments."

Karroubi moved to the chair behind the desk and took a seat. He opened a drawer and took out summaries of the banking information Tabrizi gave him earlier and laid them on the desktop. A quick comparison of the transaction amounts told him what he already knew. He waved Ardakan over and pointed to the figures on the pages. "These are records from the accounts we found, showing deposits that were transferred into the account in Andorra. The deposits match perfectly with the oil sales transactions. Sales dates, deposit dates. They all line up. And he made it easy for us," Karroubi added, pointing to the figures. "The amounts are all dollar-denominated."

Ardakan slumped against the corner of the desk. "Dollar-denominated deposits from Germany to a foreign account held in the name of our president."

"From the looks of it," Karroubi continued, "he received one dollar per barrel for each barrel of oil sold and delivered."

"No wonder he doesn't want to sell it to China," Ardakan said with a wry lilt. "He's getting rich."

"And he's about to destroy our country in the process."

"Yes. He very well may." Ardakan stood up straight and smoothed out his jacket. "Which reminds me. The Assembly of Experts will be briefed tomorrow on the situation we face."

"Which situation is that?"

"The Russian army gathering on our northern border and the Chinese amassing to the east."

"Will they discuss the oil sales to Germany?"

"No. And make certain you do not give away the fact that you already know everything they will tell you."

"Your confidence is safe with me."

"If you have to talk," Ardakan added, "tell them you were in Sochi and saw much of it for yourself. Just don't tell them it came from me." Then he turned toward the door and disappeared down the hall.

When Ardakan was gone, Karroubi picked up the cell phone from his desk and typed a message. "Monitor those accounts." Then he pressed a button and sent it to Tabrizi.

72

TEHRAN, IRAN

AS ARDAKAN HAD SUGGESTED, the following day Shokof briefed the Assembly of Experts on the latest information regarding both the Russian presence on Iran's northern border and the Chinese buildup on the border with Afghanistan. Following that presentation, Karroubi requested an appointment with President Kermani to discuss the matter. They met in a private parlor down the hall from Kermani's ceremonial office.

"So," Kermani began, "what do you think of our situation?"

"I think we are about to be invaded. The only question is, by whom?"

"You make it sound so dire."

"It is dire."

"Perhaps," Kermani shrugged. "But we will come out on top, either way."

"Oh?" Karroubi was puzzled by the response. "How is that so?"

"Either the Russians will invade us to preempt the Chinese, or the Chinese will invade to obtain the oil they claim is theirs. One would come to prevent us from selling it to anyone else, in which case we have our deal with Germany and profit by it. The other comes to compel us to sell it to them, in which case we have our previous arrangement with China and we profit by that. Either way," he grinned, "we profit."

Karroubi found the lunacy of such a statement staggering. How could a follower of Allah fall under such a spell of deception? And what could he, a mere mortal, say that would roll back the scales from Kermani's eyes? They lived in two different worlds—he in reality, Kermani in a fairytale. Karroubi felt his heart pounding against his chest. Veins in his neck throbbed as he struggled to maintain his composure and form a response.

"If the Chinese invade us," he began, struggling to keep his emotions in check, "they will not come merely to force us to sell them our oil. They will not come as benevolent protectors. They will sweep across Afghanistan, Iran, and Iraq, occupying everything from the Chinese border to Jordan. Whatever oil this region holds will be subject to their control." His voice grew louder. "They will not come to buy our oil. They will come to take it!"

Kermani seemed unmoved. "In any event, the Russians are preparing to cut them off," he added smugly. "They will never reach us."

"Have you not heard the reports from Azerbaijan?"

"Yes. Of course I have heard them." Kermani took an indignant tone. "I heard the same information you heard in the briefing just now. And much more in many briefings long before you were made aware of the situation. Of course I have heard the reports."

"Then you know the Russians are not merely preparing to traverse our country in order to cut off the Chinese advance. The Russians are about to invade our country to occupy it for themselves. Our oil will become theirs."

"Attack. Counterattack," Kermani shrugged. "Mere semantics."

"Semantics?" Karroubi's emotions spilled over. "We face an invasion! The Russians are gathering their army on our border to invade our country and take control of our oil in order to prevent the Chinese from getting it first. This is no benevolent act by the Russians. This is a shrewd power play. The Chinese are racing to prepare their attack in the hope of launching it before the Russians reach full strength. Two of the most powerful nations in the world are in a race and we are the prize!"

"Perhaps you are correct," Kermani showed not the slightest hint of emotion. "But I do not think so."

"You know I'm correct," Karroubi blurted. "How close are the Chinese to taking action?"

"You heard what they said," Kermani replied, parrying the question. "You were in the briefing."

"They would not commit to specific times."

"That is because they do not know," Kermani expressed disdain, finally showing his emotion. "No one knows. I don't know."

"Is it days? Is it weeks?" Karroubi implored. "Surely someone has an estimate?"

"Weeks," Kermani grudgingly conceded. "Perhaps days. Certainly not months."

"Then sometime in the next two weeks, the Russians will cross our border."

"You think the Chinese are coming that soon?"

"I think the Russians will not wait for them. They will assemble their forces on their own timetable and do everything possible to attack before the Chinese cross into Afghanistan."

"But what would provoke such a thing from the Russians?"

"They are not awaiting provocation. They have already been provoked."

"How so?"

"By that deal you made with the Germans. Russia and Germany are ancient enemies. They have occasionally enjoyed periods of peace between them, but historically have always been adamantly opposed and highly suspicious of each other. The deal you made with them changed the balance of power in Europe. If it continues, Germany will eclipse both China and the United States. Russia will not allow it."

"And that is provocation enough for them to invade us? Even if the Chinese do not?"

"The Chinese have already shown their hand. They are coming. Right now the Russians hold a strategic advantage because of their close proximity to our border. If they wait, they will lose that advantage. They will act now, while we are defenseless and the Chinese are still in their barracks." Karroubi paused and both men stared at each other in silence. Then Karroubi asked quietly, "Why did you make that deal with the Germans in the first place?"

"We had no choice."

"There is always a choice."

"Not this time. The Germans presented us with the opportunity of a lifetime. We could not pass it up."

"Opportunity?"

"If we sell only to the Chinese, we are at the mercy of the Chinese. If we sell through Germany, the Chinese can obtain their oil through them and we have access to a much broader market. And, most importantly, we will have fractured the NATO alliance."

"Fractured the alliance?"

"With a strong Germany, growing wealthy from our oil, they will become the strongest nation in the west. The Americans will never again be able to impose sanctions against us. Germany would oppose it. With access to our oil, Europe will become as addicted to plentiful energy as the Americans. They will no longer be able to ignore our best interests. Then if China opposes us, Europe must oppose China. If Europe threatens us, China must oppose Europe."

Once again, the absurdity of what Kermani suggested left Karroubi struggling to form an answer. On its face, the plan sounded brilliant—play one enemy off against the other to neutralize an even more powerful third player—but the reasoning had a single fatal flaw. In order to succeed, Russia and China must each see the other as the source of the problem. If either of them saw Iranian policy as the threat, the gambit would fall apart and Karroubi was certain both countries viewed Iran as the source of their trouble. *Only a madman could think his plan would work.*

"But the Germans are not protecting us," Karroubi said finally. "The Chinese are gathering to annihilate us, and the Germans are nowhere to be found."

"I did not say the Germans would defend us," Kermani corrected. "I said Europe would do so. And Europe, in the form of the Russian army, is gathering a force now along our northern border in response to the Chinese threat. Even though they have only begun to take the first sips of our oil." He had a self-satisfied smile. "Just as I explained to you earlier and as I foresaw when the Germans first approached us with the deal."

Karroubi felt the veins throbbing in his neck once more. Of all the things that were offensive to Allah, arrogance was the most infuriating and Kermani was the height of arrogance. Karroubi wanted to slap him. At the same time, he was angry with himself. The Assembly of Experts approved Kermani's rise to the office of president. They should have seen through his confident manner long ago and denied him the position from the outset. But instead of giving free rein to his emotions, Karroubi stuffed them down again and asked quietly, "How much are they paying you?"

"Paying me?" Kermani shouted. "How dare you make such an accusation against me!"

Karroubi refused to be moved by the outburst and, instead, stared straight at Kermani. Through clinched teeth he hissed, "How dare you take us to the brink of obliteration on such an ill-conceived scheme!"

73

MOSSAD OPERATIONS CENTER
ASHDOD, ISRAEL

HOFI WAS SEATED NEAR THE OPERATOR'S CONSOLE when a text arrived from Natan Yavin, one of the agents sent into the Wakhan Corridor. The message read simply, "They are evacuating the area in face of an overwhelming force building to the east." Then pictures arrived showing US troops leaving their camps and bases. Photos from inside the complex near Ishkashim showed the room littered with disabled and destroyed computer equipment. A trashcan filled with ashes stood nearby.

"Either they're leaving," Hofi speculated as he viewed the images on the operator's monitor, "or they're doing their best to convince someone they are."

In a few minutes, they received pictures of the Chinese army gathered on the border. Hofi studied them a moment, then stepped back from the operator's workstation. "Put all of these on the screens."

At the press of a button, images appeared on two screens that hung along the wall, one to the left, the other to the right. Hofi called out to those in the room, "Please pay attention!" He pointed over his shoulder, "We've put up the latest images from our agents working in the Wakhan Corridor. They'll give you an idea of current conditions there. For any of you who can't figure out what these are, the Americans are on the screen to the left. The Chinese on the screen to the right."

"There it is," someone called out. "They're abandoning their posts."

"Not abandoning," Tzipi Levanon corrected. "Look at the screen on the right."

"Yes," Leon Zukerman added. "That would get anyone moving in a hurry."

"The Americans have nothing to gain by getting in the way of the Chinese."

"They tried that in Korea and Vietnam."

"And that was sixty years ago."

While they reviewed the photographs, video arrived from other operatives working the same region. A comparison with live images from NSA reinforced what they already knew: the Americans were withdrawing their forces from Afghanistan. But Hofi had dealt with the United States for many years and he had learned never to assume anything. Before he could brief David Oren and the National Security Cabinet, he needed confirmation of his hunch, but without going through official channels, that would only give him the approved policy position. What he needed was the Americans' real strategy, apart from all the posturing and spin. He knew of only one person who might give him that kind of frank assessment.

As the others continued to banter back and forth over details of the pictures, Hofi took his cell phone from his pocket and typed in a message. "Let's talk." Then he scrolled down the contacts list until the name Wilson Blundell appeared. Moments later came the reply, "King David. Two hours."

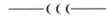

Two hours later, Hofi was in Jerusalem, seated at the bar in the King David Hotel. He'd been there about ten minutes when someone tapped him on the shoulder. He turned to see Blundell standing behind him.

Unlike most of Hofi's embassy contacts, Blundell was a career foreign services officer who worked in consular affairs, processing visas and solving problems for US citizens traveling abroad. He had no official ties to any intelligence organization, but he knew everyone and often functioned as an intermediary in challenging situations. Embassy staff referred to him as a generalist. Those who knew his true talents thought of him as a "fixer," the go-to guy in times of trouble. Hofi had met him while helping a relative obtain a visa to attend school in California. They had met several times since then, usually when circumstances demanded the unvarnished truth.

Blundell took a seat on a stool at the bar. Hofi gave him a smile. "Hope my text message didn't interrupt your schedule too much."

"Not at all," Blundell replied. He motioned for the bartender and ordered a drink. "Glad to get out of the office." When his drink arrived, he glanced around, checking. "Is there someplace a little more private?"

"I have a table where we can talk." Hofi slid from the barstool and started toward the door. Drink in hand, Blundell followed as they made their way to a private room off the back hallway.

Inside the room, a sofa sat along the wall to the left. Three leather chairs sat to the right. There was a table near the back wall. Hofi pulled a chair from the table and sat down. Blundell took a seat across from him. "I assume you want to talk about the situation with Iran."

"Yes." Hofi leaned forward with his elbows on the table and spoke in a low voice, "We have agents working in the Wakhan Corridor."

"I know," Blundell nodded.

Hofi feigned a look of surprise. "You know?"

"Some of our troops saw them. People in Washington wanted me to talk to you. I was going to call you later today."

"So," Hofi shrugged, "what did Washington want you to say?"

"I'm sure your guy told you about the Chinese buildup on the border."

"As did the satellite images."

"We're facing a major change in the region."

"Power has shifted once already, when Iran made their deal with Germany. Now it is about to shift again."

"China is coming for their oil."

"It is not their oil," Hofi countered. "I would not want to be seen as supporting Iran in any way, but the oil beneath their ground belongs to them."

"Try telling that to the Chinese." Blundell paused to take a sip from his drink. "Oil is vital to their economic interests. Iran had a standing obligation to sell it to them, then reneged and sold to the Germans. The Chinese are coming and I don't think anyone can stop them, though the Russians are preparing to try."

"What do you know about Russian movements along the border with Azerbaijan?"

Blundell reached into the pocket of his jacket and withdrew an envelope. He slid it across the table. Hofi opened it and saw the same photographs Winston Smith's analysts used. "These are some of the latest images we have," Blundell explained. "Have you seen them?"

"Yes."

"Our people tell me you are supposed to be receiving live feeds of this stuff from CIA and NSA but no one knows if that's actually happening."

"We are receiving them," Hofi acknowledged.

Blundell pointed to the pictures. "These are from inside Russia, showing Russian troops moving south. Apparently they are drawing from every base in the country. Our guys at Langley think this will be the largest realignment of forces inside Russia since the Revolution."

"But the Russians have no quarrel with Azerbaijan. Everyone knows this. Surely others will recognize it for the ploy that it is. We cannot be the only ones who see this. Your allies in Europe have access to these same images."

"I'm not sure the Russians care anymore about who knows," Blundell said flatly. "There comes a time when you have to act, regardless of the reaction you might get. From what we can see, the Russians are more worried about preventing the Chinese from gaining control of Iran than they are about public opinion of their actions."

"The Russians have never worried much about the opinions of others," Hofi scoffed. "How many men do you estimate the Chinese have on the border?"

"Their conscription-age population is easily three hundred million. By the time they reach Iran, they'll have deployed millions. Not three hundred million, but millions just the same."

Hofi leaned back in his chair. "Apparently, your troops are leaving Afghanistan." Blundell nodded in response. Hofi continued. "Is that really happening? Are you withdrawing?"

"We're getting out and staying out," Blundell answered.

"Is that actually what's happening, or is that just the spin they want you to put on it?"

"They tell me that is actually our position. We've withdrawn everyone from Afghanistan. I know that for a fact. I checked to confirm it myself. The training staff left Iraq last week. We still have CIA teams in the field, but our organized presence in the region is zero."

"Even your navy?"

"They'll be out of the Indian Ocean basin shortly."

"The Security Cabinet has already reached a similar decision for us. From our assessment, we have no reason to engage our forces in this matter or take preemptive measures."

"Good," Blundell nodded once more. "I think that is wise."

Hofi smiled at him. "We should keep the channel open between us. You and me."

"I agree. There is no way to know what might happen next and being able to see each other face-to-face will help. Maybe we should meet on a regular basis."

"I would be glad to do that," Hofi nodded. "But we must answer each other honestly and if we are not in a position to respond, we must say so. No secrets."

"Right." Blundell glanced down at his glass. "I agree."

74

TEHRAN, IRAN

AT A VEVAK FACILITY ACROSS TOWN from the presidential office suite, Tabrizi monitored Kermani's cell phone. At the same time, he scanned the primary trunk lines for Internet traffic from Kermani's laptop and email accounts. He didn't have to wait long to find activity on both devices.

Shortly after Karroubi left his meeting, Kermani placed a phone call to the bank in Andorra. Tabrizi recorded the conversation. Minutes later, a wire transfer arrived in that account from Singapore. Almost immediately, Kermani logged on to the bank's website using his laptop and sent instructions to transfer the money from the account. By the end of the day, both the account in Singapore and the one in Andorra were empty. Tabrizi worked through the night tracking the movement of money through various institutions until he was certain it had reached its final destination in a previously unknown account at a bank in Montenegro.

Early the next morning, Tabrizi prepared copies of the transaction details and placed them in an envelope, then drove across town to Golestan Palace, where Karroubi was waiting. They huddled together over Karroubi's desk as Tabrizi took him through the documents, pointing out critical details.

"You are certain of this?" Karroubi asked when Tabrizi was through.

"Yes," Tabrizi replied confidently. "I am certain of it."

"I only ask because Kermani is president. Chosen by the Supreme Leader and approved by the Assembly of Experts long before he was submitted to the people as a candidate for election. If we raise questions about his integrity that are later proved to be unfounded, we could forfeit our lives."

"I am aware of that."

Karroubi reviewed the documents a moment longer, then dismissed Tabrizi and sat alone in his study. For the next three hours he read and reread each of them, making note of the details and methodically diagramming the paper trail for each transaction. At the same time, he prepared in his mind the things he intended to say to explain the situation in simple, easily understood terms. Finally, account information in hand, he rose from his desk and called for his car and driver. Twenty minutes later, he arrived at Bagh-e Ferdows Palace, home of Abdullah bin Mahoob bin Suhail Iskafi, the Grand Ayatollah and Supreme Leader of Iran.

Elected by the Assembly of Experts, Iskafi was the ultimate authority on all things pertaining to Iran, both as to government policy and Sharia law. He came to public office after a lifetime spent in service to the army and Islamic scholarship. At eighty-four he was the oldest Ayatollah to hold the office of Supreme Leader, and by far the most beloved. Ruling from a benevolent disposition, he favored development of a secular society with a market economy, so long as it could be made compatible with the principles of Sharia law. He'd been educated as a young man in England and was more than tolerant of capitalism, but he demanded absolute devotion to Allah and was known to deal severely with those who insisted on disregarding the restrictions of a truly Islamic lifestyle.

They sat together in a first-floor parlor, which Iskafi used for audiences with dignitaries and ministerial officials. There, for almost half an hour, Karroubi carefully and meticulously laid out the evidence they had uncovered against Kermani—accounts in his name at various locations, the corresponding sales of oil to Germany with payments from European banks, the simultaneous transfers from those same banks into Kermani's accounts, and the circuitous route the transfers took to obscure their origin and destiny.

When Karroubi was finished, Iskafi shook his head. "This is most troubling. Have you discussed these matters with him?"

"Not in this great detail," Karroubi replied. "I have confronted him about the arrangement with Germany, how it directly contravenes our prior commitments to sell to China, and the serious consequences threatened against us all by that decision, but I wanted to come to you with the details first before presenting them to him. I have been concerned that if I told him first, he would have time to move the money once more and erase any hope of recovering it." He saw Iskafi's lips move to speak, but he continued. "And more importantly, we might lose any hope of recovering President Kermani. If these things are as they seem, he would be in serious breach of Sharia, and his soul would be in grave peril."

"Yes," Iskafi smiled. "I am pleased to hear you say that because that is my chief concern at the moment. His soul and the affront to Allah that these actions bring." His eyes focused on Karroubi. "You are a wise man, Adnan."

"Not as wise as you."

"They briefed you on the situation we face?"

"Yes."

"That is troubling as well." Iskafi propped his elbows on the armrest of the chair and struck a contemplative pose. "Why would Russia gather its army on our borders in such a hostile manner?"

"They are preparing to oppose the Chinese."

"But we have not offended the Russians. Nor have we asked for their help."

"That is true," Karroubi replied. "And it is not true, partly."

"A paradox."

"Yes. A very disturbing paradox." Karroubi shifted positions in his chair. "The deal Kermani struck with Germany did more than merely determine the outlet for our oil. It shifted the balance of power in the world."

A frown wrinkled Iskafi's forehead. "The world?"

"By controlling our oil," Karroubi explained, "the Germans gain control of the income from its sale and the wealth that it provides. The distribution network they build to market and deliver it will become a powerful economic weapon. With that wealth they gain the capacity to fund a well-trained army. They gain strategic economic power as well. The power we once had to boycott the market is now in their hands. Russia knows this and will not permit the Germans to gain such power."

Iskafi made a back-and-forth motion with his hands. "One goes up while the others come down."

"That is precisely what has happened. The Chinese, however, need our oil in order to fuel their economy. That overriding issue has resulted in conflict which will play out right here." Karroubi tapped the armrest of his chair with his finger. "In Iran."

"I am uncertain why they would choose to invade, instead of simply asking for clarification of our intent to sell them oil."

"We are obligated to sell it to them by our prior agreement. In turning our back on that agreement, we have taken a stance of such finality that it precludes further negotiations."

"I was told it was ours to sell to whom we wished."

"It was until we agreed to sell it to someone. That someone was China. After that, we had a commitment we were obligated to honor."

"They told me they could get out of it."

"If they did, they were not correct."

"So the Chinese are coming to take our oil?"

"Yes. But in order to take Iran, they must travel by land, which means taking control of Afghanistan. Once they seize Afghanistan and Iran, I think they will occupy most of Iraq. Certainly the southern half in order to control all major Shia population centers. They will effectively control the entire region and then the power that tipped to Germany will tip decisively in favor of China."

"Russia will never allow that to happen," Iskafi shook his head. "I can see that now."

"They will not," Karroubi agreed. "And that is why they are gathered on our northern border."

"They did not explain this to me so clearly." Iskafi reached over and patted Karroubi on the knee. "You have served me well today."

"That is my one desire," Karroubi replied. "To serve you well and in so doing to serve Allah most of all."

Iskafi looked across the room toward a mirror that hung on the wall. With barely a move of his head and the slightest gesture with his hand, a door opened and an aide appeared. He came to Iskafi's side and leaned near, listening intently as Iskafi whispered to him. Then he nodded, backed away, and disappeared from the room. When they were once again alone, Iskafi turned to Karroubi. "I have sent for Kermani. We will see what he has to say."

An hour later, Kermani arrived. He was ushered into Iskafi's presence and sat in a chair a few feet away. He was not glad to see Karroubi but before he could speak, Iskafi interjected, "We have certain questions we would like to ask you. Adnan will handle the matter for us." He nodded to Karroubi, folded his hands in his lap, and waited.

Karroubi rose from his chair and once again presented the details they had uncovered about accounts that were held in Kermani's name, providing documents, dates, and amounts for each of the transactions. He matched those transactions to each of the oil sales to Germany and showed how the totals differed in an amount precisely equal to one dollar per barrel, which was then siphoned into Kermani's bank accounts.

When he concluded, Kermani turned to Iskafi. "This is simply not true. Those accounts bear my name, we can clearly see that, but it was not me. I did not do it."

Iskafi gave him a kind smile. "You have some documents to prove what you say?"

"No," Kermani shook his head. "Of course not. One can never prove the nonexistence of a thing. But Karroubi cannot prove it was me, either. He has only shown that it looks like I did it." Then he turned to Karroubi. "In all of those documents and papers you have in your hands, is there even one single item that bears my signature?"

"No," Karroubi did his best to appear uneasy. "There is not."

"See," Kermani said, smiling back at Iskafi. "They have nothing with my signature because I signed nothing. And I signed nothing because these are not my bank accounts."

Karroubi pressed the issue. "Then how do you explain the difference between the sales price and the amount we received?"

"We should take that up with our German counterparts." Kermani leaned back in his chair and folded his arms across his chest. "And I don't appreciate you coming to Ayatollah Iskafi about this without coming to me first. These are accusations that impugn my integrity. I have a right to hear them before anyone else is told."

Karroubi ignored Kermani's indignant attitude and pressed forward, gesturing with the documents in his hand. "You are saying that none of these accounts are yours?"

"None of them," Kermani replied. "Not one of them."

"The account in Andorra is not yours?"

"No." Kermani shook his head vigorously.

"And the account in Montenegro is not yours?"

"No."

"And the account in Singapore?"

"No. It is not mine." Kermani turned again to Iskafi. "I know this looks bad, but someone has used my name to commit this fraud and I intend to find out who it is." He cut his eyes at Karroubi. "And then perhaps we will ask you some questions."

"We will not get that far," Karroubi replied bluntly, and he took a small digital tape recorder from beneath his robe.

Kermani's eyes opened wide. "What is that? You have been recording me?"

"Not today."

"Then what?" Kermani pointed. "What is on that?"

"This," Karroubi said, turning to Iskafi, "is a recording of Kermani instructing the bank in Andorra to wire-transfer the money to an account in Montenegro." He pressed the button and the recording began to play.

Kermani's face turned pale as the sound of his voice filled the room. Only a sentence or two into the recording, he slumped against the chair and closed his eyes. Karroubi and Iskafi listened as they heard Kermani giving detailed instructions about where to send the money and informing the bank official on the other end of the call that he would receive additional transfers into the account later that day, all of which were to be forwarded as well.

When the recording ended, the door opened and six armed guards entered. Two of them came to Kermani's side and took hold of him under the arms, lifting him from the chair. He was silent as they carried him from the room. Then Iskafi turned to Karroubi. "You must go with them as my witness, and return to me just as soon as they are done."

Reluctantly, Karroubi rose from his chair and bowed, then turned for the door to follow the others. He didn't have to ask what would happen next.

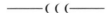

From the palace, the guards led the way as they walked with Kermani across the grounds in back to a garden a hundred meters away. There they came to a bench and dropped Kermani onto it. He sat there, head bowed and eyes closed, and began to pray, *"Inna lillahi wa inna ilaihi Raji'un."* (Verily we belong to Allah, and to Allah we return.) Over and over again he said the words quietly while one of the men came with a hood and fitted it over his head, taking care to tuck it in place beneath his chin.

Then the guards stepped aside and another man appeared. He was dressed in a black shalwar with a black kamzee tucked into it at the waist and on his head he wore a black hood that left only his eyes visible. He gripped the handle of a long, curved sword, which he carried in a confident, accomplished manner. He positioned himself squarely in line with Kermani, shifted his feet slightly apart, then grasped the handle with both hands. Slowly, he raised the blade over his right shoulder and brought it around with lightning speed.

Kermani was still praying as the blade sliced through his neck. Separated from his body, his head dropped to his lap, then tumbled to the ground. One of the guards picked it up by the open end of the hood and closed it tight.

Karroubi stood there a moment in silence while attendants gathered the body and the head and removed them from the garden. Then one of the guards nudged him on the shoulder and gestured with a nod for him to follow. Karroubi lingered a moment longer, then turned aside and walked toward the palace.

Iskafi was waiting when he returned to the first-floor parlor. "What do you propose we do now?"

"We must contact the Chinese immediately," Karroubi replied, "and reinstate oil shipments to them at once, under the terms of our previous agreement."

Iskafi nodded. "And perhaps offer them more favorable terms as well."

"If it seems necessary."

"And what of the Russians?"

"If the Chinese are no longer a threat, then there is no need for the Russians to act. They would no longer have any justifiable reason for invading. I think they would recognize that fact and the situation would be diffused."

Iskafi thought for a moment. "Very well. I appoint you the interim president of Iran. You shall serve until elections can be arranged."

Karroubi's eyes opened wide in a look of surprise. "The Assembly will approve this?"

"Yes," Iskafi nodded. "They will approve it if I make the appointment." He smiled. "And I have just made the appointment. They will agree as will the Consultative Assembly. Now go," he urged with a wave of his hand. "You must move quickly if we are to undo all that Kermani has done."

75

TEHRAN, IRAN

WHEN KARROUBI RETURNED to Golestan Palace he went straight to the study. Dirbaz, his assistant, bowed when he entered the room. "Mr. President."

"Stand up," Karroubi replied. "We have work to do."

"Certainly, sir. What would you like me to do?"

"I need you to call Abadeh Ardakan and—"

Just then, Ardakan appeared in the doorway. Karroubi looked up at him. "You have heard?"

"Yes, Mr. President. They called to inform me only minutes ago. I came as soon as I could."

Karroubi nodded to Dirbaz, who retreated from the room. When he was gone, Karroubi continued. "I'm sure word is spreading by now."

"Yes, Mr. President. News of your appointment is spreading rapidly."

"And what has been the reaction so far?"

"So far, the appointment is being well-received."

"Let us hope they remain supportive," Karroubi smiled.

"What do we do now?"

The smile quickly vanished from Karroubi's face. "You will continue to serve as foreign minister." He made it clear he was not asking. "If we are going to avoid war, I'll need your help."

"Certainly," Ardakan nodded. "I will provide you with a list of appointments shortly."

Karroubi looked puzzled. "Appointments?"

"The heads of our ministry departments are appointed by me," Ardakan explained, "but the list must be approved by you first."

"Are there changes you wish to make?"

"A few," Ardakan shrugged. "But none of them are critical."

"We will work on that when you return."

"Return?" Ardakan looked confused. "Where am I going?"

"How quickly can you meet with representatives of the Chinese government?"

"Here?"

"No. In China."

"It would take a few days to arrange such a meeting. But you could summon their ambassador here now and speak with him immediately."

"I do not want to speak to an ambassador," Karroubi replied. "The difficulty we face cannot be resolved at the ministerial level."

"Very well." The look on Ardakan's face indicated he knew what Karroubi meant. "I shall require an intermediary. Someone who will make the proper introductions that can get our request beyond the initial negative response. Perhaps an official from Pakistan."

"Use whomever you like, but time is short."

"Yes," Ardakan nodded. "That is apparent."

"You must convince them not to attack us."

"I will do my best."

"No, Abadeh," Karroubi wagged his finger. "I do not want your best. I want you to succeed. Our lives, the lives of all Iranians, and the future of our nation depend upon it."

"Very well." Ardakan took a deep breath. "What shall I tell them?"

"Tell them that the Supreme Leader has caused a change in presidents. Kermani is no longer in office. I will serve until the Assembly and the Guardian Council organize elections. Tell them we are no longer selling oil exclusively to Germany and we will fulfill all our obligations to them under our prior agreement."

"Most certainly," Ardakan acquiesced. "I will be glad to deliver such a message."

"We need more than merely the delivery of a message," Karroubi insisted. "We need your powers of persuasion. And if they still resist, tell them we will renegotiate the rate, trade every other ship of oil for an equal shipment of rice, whatever they need to hear to keep them from invading."

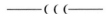

With Ardakan dispatched to deal with the Chinese, Karroubi turned his attention to the Germans and his assistant, Dirbaz. Both of them were traitors—Germany for placing the Iranian people at the mercy of two warring superpowers, and Dirbaz for sharing state secrets with the CIA—and both of them must pay dearly for their choices. He turned to the phone on the credenza behind his desk and called General Bizhani, commander of the Iranian air force.

When the general came on the line, Karroubi dispensed with greetings and got right to the point. "We need an airplane, configured to carry cargo. How quickly can you prepare one?"

"I think we usually have at least something available most anytime," Bizhani replied. "I would have to check to make certain."

"Have one fueled and ready."

"Where is it going?"

"I will send someone with instructions."

"This afternoon?"

"Yes. They're leaving for the airport now." Karroubi ended the call without waiting for a response, then called out in a loud voice for Dirbaz. Seconds later, Dirbaz appeared at his desk. The sight of him standing so close made Karroubi uneasy but he did his best to show no emotion, certainly not the anger he felt inside. "I have a special assignment for you." He had a solemn expression on his face. "The future of our nation depends upon your success." Those words were far too near a blessing to suit him, but he wanted to do nothing to make Dirbaz suspicious of what lay ahead.

"Certainly, Mr. President," Dirbaz replied. "What shall I do?"

"An airplane is waiting at the airport." Karroubi took a sheet of paper from his desk drawer and scribbled a message while he spoke. "You are to travel with it to Libya. When the plane lands, it will taxi to a hangar where you will be met by men. They will know what to do and give you further instructions." He finished the note, placed it in an envelope, and applied a stamp of the presidential seal to close the back flap. "Give this to the plane's captain." He handed the envelope to Dirbaz. "Tell him to read it at once."

With the note in hand, Dirbaz turned away from the desk and walked toward the door. Karroubi watched as he left the study, knowing it was the last time he would see him and for a moment, a twinge of sadness washed over him at the thought of what might have been, then just as quickly he remembered the numbers in the phone for calls placed to Langley, Virginia, in the United States, and his eyes narrowed with rage. Dirbaz was a traitor and he would die a treacherous death.

When Dirbaz was gone, he summoned Tabrizi, who arrived at the office within minutes. "You are familiar with computers?"

"Somewhat."

"I need you to gain access to the scheduling system at World Express Delivery Service. You can do that?"

"Probably. What do you want me to do?"

"I need you to insert a flight." Karroubi opened the desk drawer and once again took out a sheet of paper on which he began to scribble information. "It must appear as though it is a routine flight. And if they should grow suspicious, they must never be able to trace the changes to us." He handed the paper to Tabrizi. "And I need it in their system before tomorrow."

Tabrizi glanced at the paper, then smiled at Karroubi. "I will take care of it, Mr. President."

Dirbaz came from the study at Golestan Palace and stopped at his desk just long enough to call for a car and driver and grab an overnight bag from the cabinet in the corner. He'd done this before. Bag in hand he walked down the central hallway to the main entrance. He waited a moment for his car to arrive, then climbed in back for the ride to the airport.

Thirty minutes later, the car turned onto a road that led to the far side of the airport. Dirbaz watched out the window as planes took off and landed in the late-afternoon sky. He'd seen it many times before and never grew tired of watching as they raced down the runway, then leapt into the sky.

Near the end of the runway on the side opposite the commercial terminal they came to a hangar used by members of the Assembly of Experts and other top ministerial officials. Dirbaz watched as they continued past it to the hangar reserved solely for use by the Supreme Leader of Iran and the president.

Parked in front of the hangar was a Boeing 747 painted in the gray and blue colors of the Iranian air force. The fuselage door was open just forward of the wing, and a stairway led down to the tarmac below. The car came to a stop at the bottom of the steps and Dirbaz climbed out, eager to see what the flight would bring.

Without hesitation, he climbed quickly up the steps. He was met at the door by a man dressed in a dark blue uniform. "You have our instructions?" From the stripes on his sleeve, Dirbaz assumed he was the captain and handed him the note from Karroubi.

While the captain read it Dirbaz glanced around. Just to the right of the door were two seats bolted to a bulkhead. Little more than metal frames with a cushion on the bottom and back, they looked more like a grotesque form of punishment than a seat for a flight. Behind them, containers shaped to fit the curve of the fuselage were locked in place on a floor designed with rollers to make sliding the containers easier.

When the captain finished reading the note he glanced down at Dirbaz. "You're riding with us?"

"Yes," Dirbaz replied.

"Stow your bag in the locker and take a seat. We'll be leaving in a few minutes."

Dirbaz found a place for his bag and took a seat next to the wall. He'd flown like this before and knew the value of having a place to prop his head. He also knew the value of a flight jacket and lifted one from a locker near the door. By the time he was strapped into the seat, the engines were running and the crew retrieved the door.

Twelve hours later, the plane arrived in Tripoli, Libya, and taxied to a stop outside a hangar at the far end of the runway. Dirbaz came from the seat to the door and started down the steps. At the bottom he was met by Ahmad Hannaneh. "They told me you were coming," he smiled. "I am so glad to receive you as the first emissary of the new Iranian president."

"And I am glad to be here," Dirbaz replied, "though I'm not sure why I came."

Hannaneh gestured toward the tail of the plane and Dirbaz turned to see workmen unloading the cargo containers. "That is why you came," Hannaneh motioned proudly. "Supplies for our doctors and hospitals. What a brilliant gesture from your president."

"Yes," Dirbaz nodded, still unsure what was happening. "He is a brilliant man."

Hannaneh picked up Dirbaz's overnight bag. "Come." An SUV was parked nearby and he gestured toward it with his hand. "We will take you to the airport."

"We?"

"I have a driver. We are ready to assist you in making your stay here as comfortable as possible."

"I'm not sure how long I am supposed to be here. Normally I return with the aircraft."

"And so you shall on this trip. But they must rest first and we have other things to attend to." He grinned. "Relax. I know what we are doing. You won't miss your ride home."

Dirbaz followed Hannaneh to the SUV and climbed into the second row of seats. He sat there quietly while the driver put the car in gear and they started forward. As they rolled away from the hangar, Hannaneh turned sideways in his seat. "We have you in a great hotel," he noted proudly, "not far from the beach and surrounded by all the best restaurants. But don't worry. We will take care of everything."

Fifteen minutes later they arrived at the Rixos Al Nasr Hotel, a five-star facility. They were met on the driveway by a bellman who insisted on carrying Dirbaz's bag. They were whisked past the counter to an elevator where he rode to the fourth floor. When the door opened he stepped out to a private floor. The bellman led the way down the hall to the right and opened the door. "This is your room," he held the door for Dirbaz to enter. "Welcome to Tripoli." Hannaneh tipped him and waited while he left, then leaned close to Dirbaz. "Do you want us to arrange for some company for the night?"

"No," Dirbaz replied. "That will not be necessary."

"But it would be fun."

"No," Dirbaz repeated. "Not on this trip."

"Suit yourself. But if you change your mind, just let me know." Hannaneh started toward the door. "We will leave you now to rest, but we will return in a few hours and then we will show you a wonderful time."

From the hotel, Hannaneh returned to the hangar where he found the plane parked inside with the hangar doors closed. Workmen knelt on the floor over a huge sheet of vinyl wrap decals in the familiar red, white, and blue World Express colors. He made his way past them to a man standing beneath the wing near one of the plane's wheels.

"You washed it?" Hannaneh asked.

"Yes."

"The adhesive on the wrap won't stick if it isn't clean."

"It's clean," the man replied. "And besides, we only need the colors to hold until the plane takes off."

"Not exactly."

"What do you mean?"

"The plane must reach its destination. We don't want a piece of your wrap coming loose in flight and lodging in the engine."

"Relax," the man grinned. "It will hold."

Hannaneh glanced up at the plane. "Make sure it's dry, too. Before you start. Water will prevent it from adhering to the metal."

"It will be dry enough to begin in a few hours."

"Think you can get it finished on time?"

"Look, I'll take care of getting the plane ready. You just worry about finding a pilot to fly it."

Around ten the next morning, Omid Sattar arrived at the Rixos Al Nasr Hotel. He rode the elevator up to the fourth floor and knocked on the door of Dirbaz's room. A moment later, the door opened partway and Dirbaz looked out.

"Hannaneh sent me to find you," Sattar explained. "He is delayed on pressing business. We will have lunch and I will show you a few of the sights."

Dirbaz was hesitant. "He said that he would come himself."

"He meant to, but these things happen," Sattar shrugged. "It's okay. He knows where we are going and if he gets free in time he will join us."

"Okay. That sounds good."

From the hotel they drove to the 02 Café, a small shop on the beach within a few meters of the water. They sat on a covered deck in back and ate while watching the birds play in the surf. Dirbaz enjoyed the food but seemed to pay little attention to the women that passed by.

An hour later, they returned to the car and drove up into the hills. "We'll get a good view of the city from here," Sattar suggested. "You can see just how beautiful it is before we visit the other sites."

"Are you certain I have time for this? I don't want to the plane to return without me."

"You have plenty of time," Sattar assured. "You will not miss the plane."

They wound their way past house after house until they reached a secluded area at the end of the road. An SUV was parked there and they came to a stop alongside it. As the car came to a halt, the doors of the SUV opened and four men stepped out.

Dirbaz appeared apprehensive. "Who is this?" he asked.

"Just some friends," Sattar replied. "They wanted to meet you."

"I don't know. Looks rather secluded to me. And I can't see the city from here."

"Come on." Sattar had a broad smile and he gestured with a sweep of his arm. "You should meet them. Then I will show you the city."

Dirbaz opened the door and placed his right foot outside the car. As his sandal touched the ground, someone rushed him from the side, reached through the open doorway, and grabbed him under the arm. A second man reached over the door and grasped his hair. "What are you doing?" he shouted, but the men ignored him and together they pulled him from the car.

The first man lifted Dirbaz off the ground and, with his feet dangling in the air, carried him to the front of the car and propped him against the hood. Then Sattar stepped forward. Dirbaz scowled at him. "What are you doing? You have no—"

Without warning, Sattar struck him with a fist to the stomach. Dirbaz clutched his abdomen with both hands and doubled over, his face twisted in a look of pain. "Why are you doing this?" he groaned.

"This is how we deal with traitors," Sattar replied.

"I am no traitor," Dirbaz protested. "I am aide to the president of Iran."

Sattar drew back his fist and struck him on the chin. "And where are your friends from the CIA now?" he mocked. "Will they help you now?" He landed another fist alongside Dirbaz's head and sent him to his knees.

The others watched as Sattar continued to pound away on Dirbaz, raining down on him with blows and kicks to the stomach and chin. Finally, when Dirbaz was sprawled on the pavement, looking dazed and barely conscious, Sattar leaned over him and said, "This is not the end for you. This is only the beginning of the end."

One of the men grabbed Dirbaz by the hair and lifted him from the ground. A second man stepped forward with a rag, which he stuffed into Dirbaz's mouth. Then a third man wrapped Duct Tape around his head to hold the rag in place. When he finished, he pulled Dirbaz's hands behind his back and taped them together at the wrist. Then they laid him on the hood of the car and Sattar stepped forward once again, this time with a knife in his hand.

76

ISLAMABAD, PAKISTAN

WHEN HE RETURNED FROM MEETING WITH KARROUBI, Ardakan went to work formulating a plan to reach the Chinese. He could do as he suggested earlier and simply contact the Chinese embassy, but that would only add one more level of participation to the process. *Besides,* he thought, *they might see it only as an attempt to delay the inevitable in an effort to gain more time for our own preparations.* To be effective, his approach needed to be direct and straightforward. And, above all, it had to be calculated to produce success. He might get only one opportunity. What he needed was the help of someone on excellent terms with the Chinese. Someone in whom they had confidence and to whom they would listen. The only person Ardakan knew like that was Malik Zardari, Pakistan's foreign minister.

With time short and the need for action paramount, Ardakan traveled to Islamabad and arrived unannounced. Zardari was surprised to see him.

"I understand you have experienced a change in leadership."

"Adnan Karroubi is now president, which is why I am here."

"Oh?"

"We need your help."

"Yes," Zardari nodded. "I suppose you do."

"You have seen the troops building on the border with Afghanistan?"

"They contacted us about that several weeks ago and assured us they meant no harm to us."

"And you did not call?"

"Frankly, with Kermani as your president, I was relieved that they were preparing to act."

"You prefer the Chinese to us?"

"No. I prefer order to chaos. Kermani would have led us all to war. In fact," he had a wry smile, "we are almost there."

"That is what we must talk about."

"We cannot side with you against the Chinese. You must know that."

"We do not want your military help. We need to contact the Chinese and tell them we are prepared to resume oil sales under the prior agreement."

"I am not sure that will satisfy them."

"Why not? I thought this was about obtaining the oil they desperately need."

"It is. But they have their dignity, too."

"We can come to terms. We are willing to renegotiate. But we can renegotiate while delivery continues. Will you help arrange a meeting with Ming Shao?"

"Between you and Ming Shao?"

"Yes."

"Certainly. When would you like to meet him?"

"As soon as possible. I am prepared to continue my journey from here and could be there for a meeting tomorrow."

"Very well," Zardari nodded. "I will pass a note to them and see what can be arranged."

"Will our overture to them be enough to delay their advance?"

"If they are not too far along." Zardari's eyes bore in on Ardakan. "But if that is all this is, an attempt to delay for your own advantage, then I will send you home now."

"No," Ardakan insisted. "This is our position. We are ready to load their ships now. They can take delivery while we talk. We just don't want war."

"Good," Zardari smiled. "Let us see what we can arrange."

Ming Shao sat alone in the sauna enjoying the hot, steamy air. Sweat trickled down his arms and rolled down his chest, but he paid it no attention. Since taking office as president of China and chairman of the party, he had come to see the sauna as his sanctuary and his time there as the one uninterruptable moment in an otherwise —

Just then, the door opened and Yong Shu, his assistant appeared. "I am sorry to interrupt."

Ming glowered at him. "Have I not told you that I am not to be disturbed now?"

"Yes, but this seemed—"

"I don't care what you thought of it. I am not—"

"But this is most urgent."

"What could be so urgent that you would interrupt me while I am in here, and interrupt me while I am speaking? I am the president of China and—"

"The Pakistani foreign minister has delivered a message from Iran. They want to talk."

"Merely a delaying tactic. Surely even you can—"

"He does not think so."

"I will deal with him later."

"He is waiting in your office."

Ming sighed and shook his head. "Very well, I shall be there in a few minutes."

In a little while, Ming stepped out of the sauna and made his way over to his office. He arrived to find Zardari seated there, waiting for him. Rather than send a message through normal diplomatic channels, Zardari had boarded a plane and flown to Beijing to discuss Ardakan's request with Ming in person.

Ming and Zardari were old friends and understood each other well. Even so, he was reluctant to agree to a meeting. "I have seen this before. They use this sort of tactic to gain time, while their opponents lose the advantage."

"I do not think that is the case here," Zardari countered. "He is in Islamabad now, fully ready to travel here at a moment's notice.

Meeting with him does not mean you agree to a delay. He is not asking for a delay. Only for a meeting."

Still, Ming would not agree without first seeking the guidance from the Military Commission. According to commission protocol, a decision by the full commission was necessary for a binding recommendation, but gathering them for a meeting would take additional time. Besides, Ming did not want them to make the decision; he only wanted their advice. So instead of summoning them all, he sent a request to key members, people who carried great weight among their peers and who were predisposed to grant Ming his wishes.

A few hours later, with Zardari out of the way at one of the Zhongnanhai Compound's several guest quarters, Ming's hand-picked group of commission members gathered around the conference table. "As many of you are aware," Ming began, "Iran has experienced a change in presidential leadership. Adnan Karroubi is now interim president. As a result, we have received a request from the Iranian foreign minister to discuss resumption of oil sales. The request was brought to us in person by Malik Zardari. He believes it to be genuine."

"I do not." Quan Ji shook his head. "This is merely a delaying tactic to give them time while they reposition their forces."

"They have not asked for a delay in our schedule," Ming explained. "Merely an opportunity to be heard. They have set no preconditions."

"They have insulted the people of China," Quan argued. "Why should we talk to them now?"

"Why not?" Li Chengfei asked. "If it would prevent war, and they are not asking us to delay our preparation, why should we not talk to them?"

Hu Chang spoke up. "Mr. Chairman, I must advise you that our period of preparation is rapidly drawing to a close. Soon we will reach that most critical phase where going forward becomes easier than standing down. You should consider the troops in your decision."

"I agree," Admiral Xian Linyao added. "From what I understand of preparations, we are ready to initiate the first phase. I think, regardless of the reason we chose this course of action, the region could use our presence."

"Absolutely," Quan chimed in. "Afghanistan will fall apart without the Americans. They need our presence for their own security."

"The Iraqis are in disarray also," Hu added. "We could solve many problems by going forward with the invasion, regardless of the Iranian position."

They continued to discuss the matter, with the participants evenly divided—half in favor of talks and the other half against it. But as they discussed the matter, Ming began to see that a decision not to meet with Ardakan bore all the risk. If he refused to at least talk, the world would say that he had passed up an opportunity for peace merely to use military might to extend the reach of Chinese hegemony. Talking with Ardakan, however fruitless it might ultimately prove to be, bore no risk. He could talk, consider Ardakan's proposal, and still refuse to agree. But if he refused to talk, he had no option but war.

"I think Li Chengfei is correct," Ming agreed finally. "I should meet with him and hear what he has to say. We might learn some bit of information that will help us. And we might avert war altogether." He glanced around the room. "This is my decision. Make certain you take no action toward the border until I specifically authorize it."

Back in Islamabad, Ardakan sat on the sofa at an apartment not far from the Foreign Ministry office. Using an iPhone, he was able to keep up with the latest developments in Tehran and respond to pressing emails, but he found it difficult to concentrate on anything other than the situation with China.

Late in the afternoon, following a day of worry, there was a knock at the door. He opened it to find Zardari's aide with a note that read, "Ming Shao will see you. Come at once to Beijing." Ardakan left for the airport within the hour and arrived in Beijing the following morning in time to see Ming before lunch. They met at the guesthouse in Zhongnanhai Compound, where Zardari was staying.

"I consented to see you," Ming offered after they were introduced, "because Malik says you are an honorable man and because your president is held in esteem around the world as a man of respect."

"Thank you, Mr. Chairman. I appreciate your gracious consideration and hope that I will prove worthy of your effort in arranging this meeting. Over the past several weeks we have become aware that Russian troops are gathering in Azerbaijan, along our northern border. At the same time, we have observed Chinese troops gathering near the border with Afghanistan."

Ming had a quizzical look. "This leaves Iran feeling threatened?"

"It leaves us …" Ardakan hesitated. "Yes," he replied in an attempt at honesty. "In as much as Iran is the logical object of these military deployments, it leaves us uneasy."

"And why would you suppose China wished to attack Iran?"

"Former president Kermani's deal to sell our oil through Germany, even though we had a standing agreement to sell to China."

"You are right to conclude that Iran's avoidance of its obligations to us was an affront to us. But what makes you think we mean to use force to compel you to act?"

"You were offended, yet you did not seek redress through diplomatic channels."

"A nation that will not honor its commitments is not a nation with whom we would ever attempt to negotiate."

"We do not wish to negotiate," Ardakan replied. "We wish to return to the previous status between our two nations. With Iran selling oil to China in accord with the terms of our earlier agreement. We would, however, ask for your assurance that you will take no military action against us in the future because of this situation."

"I am not certain our troops are of a size that would permit the sort of action you fear."

Ardakan reached into his briefcase and took out three photographs. He handed them to Ming. "These pictures show hundreds of thousands of troops in their camps. All of them within fifty kilometers of the border."

Ming glanced at the photos. "Perhaps it is an exercise," he suggested with a smile.

"We both know that is not the case."

Ming laid aside the pictures. "Our prior agreement included a favorable price. When we were unable to obtain the oil from you as promised, we had to enter the open market to cover our demands. Those purchases were made at considerable added expense to us. Are you proposing to repay us the difference?"

"Iran is not in a position to cover China's cost in cash. However," Ardakan added quickly, "we would be willing to discount the price per barrel to a level that would allow China to recoup that loss over a reasonable time."

"I see." Ming glanced away. "That would potentially help our situation much more quickly than other...solutions."

"And," Ardakan continued in a solicitous tone, "we would offer our humble apology for the inconvenience our actions have caused."

A broad smile spread over Ming's face. "That would be greatly appreciated."

77

TUNIS, TUNISIA

KINLAW HAD BEEN INSIDE THE WAREHOUSE A LONG TIME, surviving on local water from a tap, an occasional foray outside the building to search for food, and not much else. Already trim and athletic when the ordeal began, surviving on meager rations caused him to lose even more weight. His pants sagged at the waist and his shirt hung limply from his shoulders, both of them appearing multiple sizes too big.

Through the entire time he saw no one in the building except him and the sickly man he'd seen on the ship and knew only by the name of Babak, a name used to address him by the ship's captain. Babak arrived with the container when the truck brought it from the dock and he had remained there alone, surviving on food from a cabinet in an office near the bay where the truck was parked. All the while, though, his physical condition continued to deteriorate. His cheeks took on a hollow appearance and his eyes, already dark and sunken into the sockets, now were dull and listless. He shuffled about when he walked and spent most days lying on the floor, staring up at the ceiling. Kinlaw was certain the man was dying from radiation exposure and he wondered how much he'd absorbed as well.

Then early one morning, Kinlaw was awakened to the sound of the main door rolling up and the click of footsteps on the concrete floor. He crawled to a spot from which he could see into the bay where the truck was parked and watched as Babak walked around to the passenger side of the cab and climbed inside. A moment later, the engine cranked and a driver slowly backed the rig from the building onto the road. As it did, Kinlaw climbed from his hiding spot, walked quietly but quickly to the far side of the building, and slipped outside.

From the warehouse he hurried back to where he left the car and found it still there. He pulled open the passenger door, dropped into the seat behind the steering wheel, and placed the key in the ignition. The engine turned over slowly at first, then caught and roared to life. Out the driver's window he saw the truck go by one block over. He put the car in gear and started in that direction.

Following at a safe distance, he trailed the truck back to the center of the city, then out to the airport. Just past the entrance to the commercial terminal, they turned onto a road that led around the perimeter of the facility and in a few minutes arrived at a hangar on the far side of the main runway. Kinlaw slowed his car, dropping farther behind. Up ahead, the truck turned from the road, rolled alongside the hangar, and out to the tarmac.

When he was certain no one would notice, he sped up and drove past the hangar to a building a short distance down the road. He parked the car in back behind a Dumpster and walked out to a spot near the corner of the building. From there he had a view down the taxiway at an angle that let him see through the open door of the hangar where the truck stopped.

A huge cargo plane was parked inside the building with its rear door open. Markings on the fuselage and tail indicated it was a World Express airplane. While Kinlaw watched, workmen used a forklift to hoist the cargo container from the truck chassis. Then, carefully at first, they moved it toward the airplane. The container was large and was a tight fit through the door, narrowly clearing the frame. Then partway inside, the corners snagged on trim pieces along the wall where a bulkhead had been removed. The forklift operator withdrew the container a few meters, then accelerated quickly, shoving the container past the trim and ripping it from the wall but pushing the container far enough inside to clear the door.

Babak came with a hammer and dislodged the pins that held the container doors in place. He let them fall to the floor and the tow motor dragged them from the plane. With the doors gone, the missile was clearly visible sitting inside the open container, resting on a launcher trailer. Then as the rear doors of the plane swung closed, Babak crawled inside the container.

With the container loaded and the doors closed, a tractor pushed the plane from the hangar and the engines came to life. Kinlaw took the cell phone from his pocket and pressed a button to turn it on. His fingers trembled as he waited for the operating software to load and for the first time that day he realized just how long he'd been without solid food. When the message box appeared, he typed a note that read, "Missile aboard World Express plane. Leaving Tunis. Unknown destination."

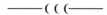

Hoag was in his office upstairs at CIA headquarters in Langley, reviewing reports from Tehran about the change in leadership, when his cell phone chimed with a text message alert. He glanced at the screen and his heart skipped a beat when he saw Kinlaw's number. With a flick of his thumb he opened the message and read it, then raced to the elevator and rode downstairs to the basement.

When the doors opened he bolted from the elevator car and ran as fast as his legs would carry him toward Jenny's cubicle at the end of the hall. She looked up, startled by his sudden appearance as he burst through the doorway. "Dennis sent a message," he blurted out.

"What did he say? Is he all right?"

Hoag came to her desk and held the screen for her to see. She read the message quickly and stood. "We have to find Winston," she pushed him toward the hall. "Go. Get moving."

They hurried down the hall and found Winston Smith at a workstation in the operations center. "Dennis sent a message," Hoag announced.

Smith took the phone from him and glanced at the message, then stood and called out to the analysts in the room. "Okay. We have a situation. This is a level-one priority. Stop whatever you're doing and listen up." He paused a moment to make certain he had their attention, then continued. "We have an aircraft with World Express markings. Airborne from Tunis. Not sure where it's going but it's carrying a missile with a nuclear warhead. Find it and find it now." He turned to Hoag and handed him the phone. "At least we know he's alive."

"Yeah," Hoag replied, still grinning from ear to ear. "He actually stayed with it."

"You thought he wouldn't?"

"I knew he wanted to. I just wasn't sure he could do it and live."

"He's a lot tougher than most people give him credit for."

"You're right about that." Hoag paused to take a deep breath, then returned to the issue at hand. "Think we can find the airplane?"

"I think we better," Smith said. "No telling where—"

"Got it," Mike Attaway called from across the room. "This is the plane."

Smith turned in his direction. "Give it to me," he snapped.

"A 747 freighter squawking World Express transponder codes," Attaway continued. "Outbound from Tunisia, headed north across the Mediterranean."

Smith turned to the operator in the center of the room. "Get me someone at World Express. And plot the plane's path on a map."

"I'm in their system already," Les Barker called. "They're showing the flight on their schedule. Destination listed as Berlin, Germany."

The operator looked up at Smith. He gestured with an impatient wave of his hand. "Call them anyway. Find someone I can talk to about it. See if it's really theirs."

"But it's right here in their system," Barker insisted.

"We may have to shoot it down," Smith snapped. "We oughta talk to World Express first." A map appeared on the screen to the left with a red line indicating the plane's path. Smith studied it a moment, then glanced over at Hoag. "None of this looks good," he said, pointing. "Extend the line of that flight path north and you get really close to Berlin."

"Not leaving us much choice, are they?"

"No, they're not."

Jenny spoke up. "Think that's really where it's headed?"

Smith glanced in her direction. "You got a better suggestion?"

"What reason would a terrorist from Tunisia have in striking Berlin, Germany, with *anything*?"

"What if he's not from Tunisia?" Attaway asked.

Hoag raised an eyebrow. "He's right. The missile is from Iran."

"World Express is on the line," the operator called out, interrupting them.

Smith returned to the workstation where he'd been before and picked up the phone. After a shouting match with the World Express call center staff, he succeeded in finding someone who would talk to him about the situation. He put the conversation on speakerphone so everyone could hear. "Is this your flight?" he asked.

"It's in our system. That much I can confirm."

"You don't sound convinced."

"It doesn't look right. Our European hub is in Paris. The African hub is in South Africa. Packages from Tunisia normally would travel there first. We have no regular flights from Tunis to any part of Europe."

Smith turned back to Hoag. "You have to alert Moore."

"Yeah, I think you're right."

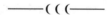

Hoag came from the operations center and walked quickly toward the elevator. Jenny followed after him. "What's going to happen, David?"

"This is it." He reached for the elevator button. "This is it."

"What's *it*?"

"This. This scenario. This thing that's happening. It's setting up just the way Vic Hamilton described it."

"What do you mean?" Her forehead wrinkled in a frown. "The four horsemen?"

"Yes."

"But there aren't four. There's only two—China and Russia."

"Not all four nations are warring nations. Only three."

"Okay," she conceded. "But I still don't see how this airplane changes things."

"China attacks from the east. Russia from the north." The elevator doors opened and they stepped inside. He held the door with one hand while he continued to talk. "They'll meet right there in Iran. Easily a million troops on the battlefield."

"But that's only two," she insisted, the frustration rising in her voice.

"This plane flying to Berlin with a bomb. It explodes and the entire city is wiped out. That gets NATO involved. Everyone knows the bomb and missile came from Iran. And if they don't know right now, they will pretty soon. So NATO gets involved, only we're in no position to participate. They go anyway and now all three of the horsemen described in warring terms are loose in the Middle East. Iran, to be specific. China, Russia, NATO." He stepped back from the door. "I gotta go."

"But what about us?"

He grabbed the door before it closed. "Us?"

"America?"

"Agriculture. We don't fight. We're the horseman with a rider who carries the scales and calls out the price of wheat and barley. We make money off everyone's fear and misery. I read to the end of the book. It gets really ugly from here." He leaned forward and kissed her. "But I gotta go upstairs. See you in a little while. We can talk more about it later." Then he stepped back once more and the doors closed.

Hoag arrived at Moore's office and paused at his assistant's desk. She waved him past without a word. Moore was seated at his desk. "We have a problem," Hoag said as he came into the room.

Moore responded without looking up. "What is it this time? More ships?"

"We tracked the cargo container from the *Santiago* to a warehouse in Tunis."

"Right. And Dennis Kinlaw has been watching it ever since."

"He sent a message just now telling us they've moved the container." Moore looked concerned. "To where?"

"It's onboard a 747 marked with World Express logos. According to the World Express scheduling system, the plane is headed to Berlin. We need to alert the White House."

"So," Moore began slowly, "let me get this straight." The look of concern turned to one of amusement. "There's a container you think holds a missile with a nuclear warhead. And first you thought it was on a ship that used to be called the *Santiago* but then became something else. We sent the navy out to stop it, and when they looked they found instead a container filled with tractor parts but no missile. Now you say that wasn't the real container. The real one is on a World Express plane headed for Berlin, Germany."

"It *looks* like a World Express plane," Hoag corrected, ignoring the real point of Moore's comment. "We're not convinced it's actually their plane."

Moore sighed and shook his head. "Your track record on this isn't very good, you know."

"I'm pretty sure we have it this time," Hoag insisted.

"Has anyone checked with World Express?"

"Yes. They say the flight is in their system, but they don't regularly fly that route."

"And you think we should go to the White House with this information?"

"Sir, if we're right, there's an airplane carrying a nuclear weapon headed for Europe. Our best guess is that it's flying to Berlin. That's the route on the schedule. That's the direction the plane is traveling. I don't know if they're taking it there to detonate it, or if this is just one more leg of a journey somewhere else, or if it's a planeload of tractor parts. But we have an indication from our agent on the ground that this is a bomb. I think we have no choice but to tell the president."

"I think you're—"

Just then, the phone at the corner of Moore's desk gave a continuous ring. He snatched up the receiver, and even though standing across the desk Hoag heard a voice say, "This is the White House situation room. We have a problem."

"We're on our way," Moore replied.

78

THE WHITE HOUSE
WASHINGTON, D.C.

BY THE TIME MOORE AND HOAG ARRIVED at the situation room, President Hedges was already seated in his chair at the head of the conference table. Admiral Marshall stood at the far end of the room near the screens that covered the wall. Carl Coulliette and Lauren Lehman sat to Hedges' right. Braxton Kittrell, Russ Williams, and Harry Giles sat to his left.

"Hoyt," Hedges said as they entered the room. "Good of you to join us."

"Yes, Mr. President," Moore replied. "We came as soon as we got the call." Hoag followed him down the table and took a seat in a chair along the wall behind him.

When they were in place, Hedges looked at Marshall. "Admiral, tell us why we're here."

"Mr. President, a few minutes ago sensors aboard an unmanned aerial vehicle loitering off the coast of North Africa detected radioactive particles consistent with the presence of a nuclear device."

Hedges glanced in Giles' direction. "Harry, you know anything about this?"

"Just that the UAV was operating above twenty thousand feet," Giles explained, "and the particles did not indicate a detonation, which precludes a ground source for the emissions. We have no indication of a missile launch anywhere in the region and have scanned the area looking for other possible sources."

Marshall nodded to an assistant, and a map appeared on the screen behind him showing Europe and the Mediterranean basin. A red dot blinked on a spot south of Sardinia. "Mr. President, from what we can determine, the only likely source is a 747 aircraft traveling north from Tunis." He tapped the dot on the map. "Right there. Headed north at approximately four hundred miles per hour."

"Is that all we know?" Hedges asked.

"That's all we have so far," Marshall replied.

Moore caught Hedges' eye. "Mr. President, we have a little more information on that."

"By all means, Hoyt. Tells us what you know."

Moore gestured to Hoag. "I'll let David fill you in on the details."

A collective sigh went up from the room as Hoag stood. Giles tossed his pen on the table and leaned back. Others at the table looked skeptical. "For the past several weeks," Hoag began, "one of our operatives has been tracking the cargo container that was removed from the *Santiago* at the port of Tunis."

"Ah yes," Coulliette quipped. "The so-called missing missile."

"Exactly," Hoag responded without missing a beat. "The container was removed from the *Santiago* and transported to a warehouse outside the city. Our operative has been watching it there since then. Today he informed us—"

"Wait," Lehman interrupted. "We've known about the location of a potential nuclear device, and we didn't do anything about it?"

Hedges shot Moore a knowing look, then turned to Lehman. "I was briefed on the issue and reviewed it with Carl. In order to send a team there we'd have to inform Tunisian authorities. We concluded that posed too high a risk that those holding the missile would learn of our pending strike and move the container before we could get to it."

"Rather high-stakes poker, don't you think?"

"It was my call, Lauren," Hedges replied. He looked over at Hoag. "Please continue."

"Our operative has informed us that the container was removed from the warehouse and loaded aboard a Boeing 747." Hoag pointed to the screen. "That one right there."

Russ Williams spoke up. "Whose plane is it?"

"The transponder indicates it's a World Express flight. And World Express has confirmed the flight is in their system. But the hub for African packages is in South Africa. They don't fly any planes directly from Tunisia to Berlin, or anywhere else in Europe."

"So why don't we simply shoot it down?"

"I have a better question," Hedges suggested. "Why is it our problem to solve?"

A frown wrinkled Coulliette's forehead. "What do you mean?"

"The plane isn't traveling toward the United States. It's going to Germany, or Spain, or France, or somewhere else in Europe."

"But we know about it," Lehman argued. "And it's carrying a nuclear device. We can't just ignore it."

Hedges looked at her. "I believe you are familiar with the fact that the Germans knew about the missile that struck us, long before it was fired off the coast of New York. They had it on the dock in Bremerhaven and let it go."

"Yes, Mr. President," she replied. "But—"

"They knew about it but did nothing."

"I understand that, sir," Lehman continued. "But the Germans are not Americans, sir. And we, thankfully, are not Germans."

Hedges' shoulders sagged and he stared down at the table, as if deep in thought. "No, I suppose you're right." The room fell silent as he toyed with a pen, spinning it between his fingers. Finally, he looked back at Lehman. "Warn them. Warn them all. Whoever we think might be in the path of this flight, but make certain they understand that it's their call on how to respond." He pushed back his chair from the table and stood. "Call me if anything else happens." Then he left the room and started upstairs. When he was gone, Moore, Lehman, and Coulliette reached for the phones to contact officials in Germany.

79

BERLIN, GERMANY

IN THE ROOM BEHIND THE LOCKED DOOR, Mueller stood at the altar table and looked across at Gregor von Bettinger, who was clothed in a hooded black robe. Near the end of the table a candle burned in a golden holder. On the wall beyond it, a single flame flickered from a sconce. They stood there, silent and unmoving, until Bettinger began the litany they used each time they gathered at the table. "Spring rises from the dead of winter."

"And brings forth the bloom of summer," Mueller replied.

"The cold darkness of death gives forth light."

"And out of the light comes power and strength."

"The earth embraces strength and victory."

"But devours the weak and cowardly."

"Indeed," Bettinger continued, "the weak inherit the dirt on which—" He stopped midsentence, his eyes open wide, his ears attuned to a world few cared to see. After a moment he looked over at Mueller. "Someone is coming for you."

Mueller had a satisfied smile. "Ostara may take me where she wills."

"No," Bettinger shook his head. "Someone is coming for you. Now." He pointed toward the door. "In the hall. Someone who is frantic and worried. You, however, must remain calm. The consequences of a rash decision at a moment like this will be tragic." Bettinger reached across the table and grasped Mueller's hand. "Ostara of spring will bring you power to lead your people in strength and might. All who oppose you will be crushed beneath your feet. With your right hand you will slay our enemies and with your left you will tame the beast on which you ride." He stood there a moment, eyes closed, Mueller's hand in his grasp, as an awkward silence filled the space between them, then he said quietly, "You must go now."

Mueller emerged from the room and found his assistant, Karl Murnau, waiting in the hall. "Georg Scheel is in your office. He said it's urgent."

Mueller had a look of disdain. "So urgent you had to come find me?"

"He said it was a matter of gravest concern."

Gravest concern. Urgent. Mueller smiled at the thought of it and remembered the prayer Bettinger had just offered for him. "Still, for a diplomat like Scheel, those words were not mere words but terms for a national threat of the highest order. Mueller quickened his pace and hurried to his office.

When he arrived he found Scheel standing near the window. "They said you wanted to see me." Mueller was aggravated that Scheel was so near his desk. He brushed past him and quickly scanned the desktop, checking to see that everything was in its place.

"We have an emergency. The Americans have informed us that an airplane is headed toward Berlin, carrying a nuclear warhead."

Mueller jerked his head around to look at Scheel. "One of their planes?"

"No," Scheel replied. "This is a 747 that took off from Tunis about an hour ago. It bears the colors of World Express, but neither the Americans nor the company thinks it's theirs."

"How do you suggest we respond?"

"That is a matter for the national security team. They are waiting for us in the situation room."

Mueller's eyes flashed with anger. "You arranged a meeting of the national security team? On your own? Without my authorization?"

"I informed staff in the room of what I learned from the Americans," Scheel replied defensively. "They gathered the team. I came to inform you first, so you would not be caught off guard when you arrived there."

"Yes. Well," Mueller said as he came from behind his desk, "thank you for at least thinking of that."

They walked together from the office and hurried across to the basement of the Chancellery. Members of the national security team were already there when they arrived. Mueller took a seat at the head of the conference table and glanced around. "What do we have, gentlemen?"

Konrad Hölderlin, head of German Foreign Intelligence, rose from his chair. "About an hour ago, a Boeing 747 took off from Tunis, headed north across the Mediterranean. The plane bore markings similar to those on aircraft operated by the World Express cargo delivery company. It is believed to be carrying a Shahab-3 Iranian missile with a nuclear warhead attached."

Mueller looked skeptical. "And how do we know this?"

"An American CIA operative in Tunis at the time observed the missile being loaded onto the plane."

In an instant Mueller's skepticism turned to anger. "They knew it was there and did not inform us until now?"

"Apparently they were concerned that if they mounted an action to obtain the weapon, or even to neutralize it, Tunisian authorities would learn of it and might inform those holding the missile, who would then move it to some unknown location."

"And where does the CIA think this missile came from?"

"It is believed to have been onboard a ship that recently docked in Tunis. The alleged third cargo ship destined originally for the western US coast. The missile's warhead supposedly would have been detonated over Los Angeles as part of the attack that struck Washington last year."

"I see," Mueller nodded. He was certain the Americans knew that he had allowed the missile to pass through Bremerhaven and were now exacting revenge. He took a deep breath and forced himself to remain calm. "Have we confirmed the identity of the aircraft?"

"Yes," Hölderlin replied. "We spoke with representatives from World Express. They told us the same thing they told the Americans. The flight is listed in their scheduling system, but they have no idea why. Their regular operations work through a hub in South Africa, and they normally have no flights scheduled directly from Tunis to any location in Europe. The World Express system, however, indicates this plane is bound for Berlin."

"When do you expect it to arrive?"

"Tunis is approximately twenty-eight hundred kilometers away. The plane is traveling at approximately eight hundred kilometers per hour and would take—"

"I don't need a math lesson," Mueller snarled. "Tell me when it will arrive!"

"Total flying time is five hours," Hölderlin said curtly. "Touchdown would come in approximately four."

General Erhard, commander of the German air force, spoke up. "I say we force it to land, or shoot it down."

Eduard Bloch, head of the Federal Police, shook his head in disgust. "With a nuclear warhead onboard?" He stared at Erhard as if waiting for a response. "Where?" he continued. "Where would you do that?"

Erhard's jaw flexed. "While it is over the water, preferably. But if not there, anywhere but here." His eyes were focused on Bloch and he spoke without hint of remorse as he reached for a phone. Receiver in hand, he glanced down the table at Mueller. "Shall I give the order?"

While they talked, Mueller remembered again Bettinger's words to him just a few minutes earlier and as he did, a sense of peace and calm washed over him. Tension drained from his body and for a moment he was filled with an overwhelming, inexplicable sense of optimism. "No," he answered calmly. "We should wait. Seize the craft when it lands. Inspect the cargo. Detain the crew." Then he pushed back from the table and walked out the door, leaving the others at the table in stunned silence.

In the basement hallway he took his cell phone from his pocket and placed a call to Murnau. "Have the helicopter ready," he barked.

Then he walked quickly from the basement and over to the residence. His wife was there, lounging on a sofa in the parlor. He leaned over from one end and kissed her on the cheek. "I have a meeting at the house in Bavaria. Would you care to join me?"

"No," she answered in a loathsome voice. "You know I detest that place. I wish you would sell it and buy something on the coast."

"And you know I will never do that."

"I know," she smiled. "Have fun."

"Okay," he called as he walked from the room. "I won't be back until tomorrow."

From the parlor, he walked down the hall to the rear entrance and stepped outside. A helipad was located a hundred meters away and the helicopter was there, engine running, doors open, ready for him to board. He walked briskly to it, climbed up the steps, and disappeared inside.

80

THE WHITE HOUSE WASHINGTON, D.C.

AFTER CONTACTING OFFICIALS IN GERMANY, Lehman, Coulliette, and Moore worked the phones getting news of the airplane and its potential cargo to the leaders of every other European country. While they did that, Hoag kept an eye on the main screen at the end of the room, which displayed a map showing the airplane's flight path, continually updated with an ever-extending red line. At the same time, smaller screens arranged down the side of the larger screen showed video captured from security cameras and traffic cams located around Berlin, images of people going about their normal daily activities with no idea of the danger lurking in the airways above.

A few hours later, the picture on the large screen changed and Admiral Marshall rose from his chair. "Okay, folks. Better get everyone in their places. The aircraft has entered Germany airspace."

Kittrell called upstairs for the president. He arrived a few minutes later and looked down the table at Marshall. "Is it time?"

"Yes, Mr. President," Marshall nodded. "The plane is in German airspace."

Hedges took a seat at the head of the table. "Any indication the missile is actually onboard?"

"The airborne sniffer detected radiation above twenty thousand feet and our man saw it being loaded," Giles chimed in. "That's about as good as it gets in this business."

"I know," Hedges frowned, "but isn't our man in Tunis the one who supposedly saw the missile on the ship earlier?"

Hoag bristled at the comment about Dennis. Hedges might be president but he had no appreciation for the work of those who made his job possible, and certainly no respect for the work of a field agent. He forced himself to keep quiet and stared down at the floor to avoid being singled out for a response.

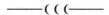

High above the German countryside, the airplane's engines slowed and Babak's eyes opened. The nose of the plane seemed to drop slightly and he glanced out the window beside the seat. Patches of the ground appeared far below between puffy white clouds. Then Ahmad Hannaneh's voice came from a speaker near the front bulkhead. "Approaching Berlin now. Breaking twenty thousand feet."

Babak unfastened the seat belt and made his way back to the cargo bay, where the cargo container sat crammed into the fuselage. There was just enough space along the side, where the wall of the plane curved out, to permit him to crawl past. He stripped off the flight jacket he'd been wearing for warmth, squeezed into the narrow space beside the container, and squirmed his way toward the opposite end.

At the back of the airplane he stepped inside the cargo container and slid down the side of the missile to an access panel located a few meters below the tip of the cone. With a small screwdriver, he unfastened the panel and set it aside. Inside the opening, he found a port into which he plugged a USB cable. A laptop rested on the frame of the launch trailer. He raised the top on it, exposing the screen and causing it to load the operating software. He attached the opposite end of the USB cable to the computer and waited while the system recognized the missile's onboard software.

From the front of the cargo bay he once again heard the sound of Hannaneh's voice over the plane's intercom. "Allah Akbar. We are breaking below ten thousand feet. Let us show the world that they will pay a heavy price for disgracing the followers of Allah." Then the adhan began to play, the nose of the plane dipped lower, and the rate of their descent increased.

Babak felt his heart pounding against his chest as he thought of what lay ahead for him. In less than a minute, he would taste the pain of death, however brief it might be, and then he would enter eternity and the reward that surely came to all of Allah's faithful. His fingers trembled and his hands shook as he moved the cursor on the laptop screen to open the launch program. A text box appeared and he keyed in the user name and access code. Seconds later another box appeared, asking for the time delay until launch. He entered ten seconds, the least amount of time the system would accept, and pressed a key to begin the sequence. Numbers on the screen ran down beginning with nine, eight, seven, six …

As the final act of his life, he knelt facing the back of the plane. By design, they were coming in from the east, traveling west, descending over the city. There, on the floor of the plane, he clasped his hands together and began to pray. "Allah, there is no god but you—the Living, the Self-subsisting, Eternal. Sleep cannot seize you. Slumber does not overtake you. All things in heaven and earth are yours. No one can intercede in your presence except as you permit and I ask you now to hear me as I—"

Suddenly, flames burst from the side of the missile, sending a chunk of metal the size of Babak's fist slicing through his neck. For an instant, searing-hot pain shot through his body, then in less than a second the air around him turned orange and his body was instantly reduced to ash.

At the White House, the national security team sat in stunned silence as images from the Berlin airport appeared. On the large screen in the situation room they watched a view off the end of the runway in Berlin as a column of smoke and ash rose in the air, then billowed into the familiar mushroom cloud of a nuclear explosion. For Hoag it was a surreal moment, seeing the ultimate symbol of death and destruction stark against a clear blue afternoon sky. Then the camera began to shake and wave after wave of dust, driven by a violent wind, roared across the airport. Seconds later, the screen went blank.

"We lost it, sir," Marshall's assistant reported.

"Find another camera."

Russ Williams spoke up. "What happened to it?"

"Heat," Marshall replied.

The assistant pointed to the screen. "Here we go, sir." Images of a barren, smoking landscape appeared on the screen

"What's this we're seeing?" Lehman asked.

Admiral Marshall turned to the assistant. "Where's that camera located?"

"This is the view from a camera atop one of the buildings at Charlottenburg Palace."

Groans echoed around the room as they realized they were seeing images from the center of Berlin. Marshall leaned over the assistant's shoulder in a whispering conversation, then turned back to face the room. "This is the view to the south, across Spandauer Boulevard."

"On a normal day," Giles added, "you would see Brohan Museum sitting across the street."

"It would be right there," Marshall tapped the screen to indicate the location.

"The center of the city is to the west," Hedges observed. "Any way to swing that camera around?"

"I don't think so, Mr. President," Marshall replied.

"I'm surprised it's even working," Lehman added.

"That must mean some of the buildings survived," Coulliette observed. "The palace is standing."

A phone rang, interrupting the conversation. Marshall turned aside to answer it. Moments later, he looked down the table at Hedges. "Mr. President, the National Reconnaissance station in Las Cruces, New Mexico, says one of their satellites has detected Russian troops moving across the Iranian border." Marshall pointed to the screen, and the view from Berlin shrank to the corner. In its place was the satellite photograph. "This is the latest," Marshall continued. "Initial estimates indicate as much as half the Russian army is within striking distance of the Iranian border. What would you like to do, Mr. President?"

Hedges seemed not at all surprised by the news and leaned back in his chair. "Do the Russians realize the Chinese army is deployed on the border with Afghanistan?"

"I don't see how they could have missed it."

"Doesn't a first move by the Russians make it more likely that the Chinese will counter it with an advance of their own?"

"That would seem likely at first glance," Marshall replied. "But these things don't exactly go like that."

"They don't?"

"No sir, Mr. President. It's more like a chess match." Marshall pointed to the screen. "This was a bold move by the Russians. They realized what most military strategists would know. They had the advantage of proximity to the enemy. They were much closer to the target than the Chinese. If the Russians move first, they have five days, perhaps a week, to advance into Iran before the Chinese can reach them. And even then the window of opportunity won't close immediately. We are talking about large forces here and it'll take a while for follow-on troops to reach the front even after the initial Chinese force reaches Iran. The Chinese would be wise to take a second look at their strategy."

Hedges glanced around the room, "It seems to me that we are in no position to do anything about it regardless of who goes first, or second, or not at all."

"I disagree," Lehman countered. "The world is plunging into chaos." Her voice was loud and her face angry. "We can't just stand here and do nothing."

"You'll be known as the president who lost the Middle East," Coulliette argued.

"Oil prices will go through the roof," Lehman continued. "This will put the entire world into a recession."

"I would remind you," Hedges responded calmly, "that we have restricted US energy companies from selling US resources abroad. World prices may rise as high as they want. Our prices are set locally and we have plenty of energy available. I would also point out that over the past year imports have dropped to their lowest levels in modern history, almost to zero, while at the same time exports of agricultural products have soared. Others can price their oil at any level they wish, but they can't eat it. For that, they must come to us."

"This is unheard of!" Lehman shouted angrily. "No strategy like this has—"

Marshall interrupted, once again pointing to the screen, "We have something else, Mr. President." The satellite photo disappeared and an image of Chinese Chairman Ming Shao appeared in its place. He was standing at a podium with Abadeh Ardakan, the Iranian foreign minister, next to him. Beijing newsmen were gathered before them with the clatter of cameras in the background as they rapidly snapped pictures. Ming's words, delivered in Chinese, were piped into the situation room from a translator.

"As many of you are no doubt aware, within the past hour Russian troops, previously assembled inside Azerbaijan, crossed the border into Iran in a hostile action against that country. Iran is our economic partner, a nation with whom China has enjoyed a long and productive relationship. Iranian Foreign Minister Abadeh Ardakan has presented us with a request from acting president Karroubi for assistance in defending the Republic of Iran in this time of crisis. After consultation with the Military Commission, we have agreed to grant their request and provide the much-needed military support. Over the coming weeks we will deploy our forces as needed to repel this Russian aggression and reestablish the security of Iran's borders. Many of the military assets necessary to accomplish that goal can be transported by air and sea, and we have set in motion those efforts even as we speak. However, in order to respond in a timely and efficient manner, the largest portion of our troops must travel by land routes that will take them across Afghanistan. That process, too, has already begun and we call on all Afghan people to cooperate fully so as to bring this operation to a successful conclusion as quickly as possible."

When he concluded the remarks, Ming stepped to one side of the podium and posed for pictures with Ardakan, the two of them alternately shaking hands and clasping each other by the shoulders in a friendly hug.

"Whoa," Lehman exclaimed. "What a turn of the tables!"

Williams cut his eyes in her direction. "Did anyone see that coming?"

"That was too convenient," Coulliette added. "It's like they set the whole thing up from the beginning."

"They have no idea what awaits them," Moore grimaced. "Russia will never allow the Chinese to defeat their army."

"And the Chinese will never allow the Russians to defeat theirs," Williams added.

"I only hope they keep the nuclear option in the box," Coulliette injected.

"I think that's already out of the bag," Williams suggested. "From what we've seen already today, this could go nuclear in an instant."

Lehman propped her chin on her hand. "Are we really going to simply watch this unfold and do nothing in response?"

"We've been over this before," Moore reminded. "We have no choice but to watch. We can't put enough troops on the ground between the two armies to change the situation. All we would do with our conventional forces is increase the body count. Our only hope for a successful intervention would require the use of nuclear weapons and that would defeat the whole purpose of a supposed intervention. Besides, by the time they are through with each other, they'll both be destroyed."

"And we will be fully recovered economically," Hedges added smugly.

"And once again the world's lone superpower," Moore continued.

"But one of *them* would control the Middle East," Lehman argued.

"And what will be left when they're through?" Hedges asked. "A radioactive wasteland? And then what will they eat?"

Lehman's jaw dropped. "Excuse me? You would use food as a weapon?"

"It's a simple matter of economics, Lauren. We'll sell to anyone, but with Russian production decimated by war, and China's economy diminished from lack of US demand, perhaps starved for oil in a few months too, the central question they will face is, what will they eat?" Hedges paused as if waiting for a response, and when none came, he continued. "I'll tell you what they'll eat. They'll eat grain from the United States, chicken from the United States, beef from the United States—if they can afford it."

"But what do we do in the meantime?" Lehman asked.

"We do nothing," Hedges replied. "They'll come to us when they get hungry."

81

NEAR ISFAHAN, IRAN

THREE DAYS LATER, Adnan Karroubi sat in an operations center at a secret air force base located halfway between Tehran and the coast. He evacuated there with General Modiri, commander of the army, and General Bizhani, commander of the air force, as Russian troops poured into Iran from the north. Since then, the operations center had been converted into a temporary headquarters for Karroubi's administration.

Similar to centers on American and European military bases, the room was filled with workstations arranged in rows across the room. A large flat screen hung on the wall at the end of the room. A map appeared on it showing the latest reported positions of Russian and Chinese troops. Smaller screens on the walls to the left and right showed images from other locations around Iran, primarily from cameras at port facilities in Bandar Abbas and Bushehr. Symbols on the map indicated the Russians controlled the west as far as Basmenj and were advancing toward Zanjan, three hundred fifty kilometers west of Tehran. The Chinese army, advancing from the east, had already traversed Afghanistan. Leading units had crossed into Iran and were reportedly racing west through the southern provinces near the coastline.

Unlike western operations centers, however, this one received no live satellite feeds, as Iran had no military satellites and only limited video conferencing capability with other centers around the country. Information was relayed to the room by email, phone, and messenger.

Even so, it was the most modern facility of its kind in Iran.

Karroubi studied the latest positions for both armies on the map, then turned aside to watch images from Berlin on one of the small screens. Few in the room, even fewer in the world, knew the details of what happened and even less understood the significance of the strike against the heart of Europe. For those who suspected the hit came from Iran, it was an act of terrorism and an indication that madmen were in control of both the government and the military. To the Chinese, it was an act of contrition, a clear indication that Iran had turned its allegiance to them, and a key factor in their determination to fight with zeal. Karroubi saw it in less grandiose terms. To him, the attack meant Iran had nuclear weapons and leadership with the wisdom and courage to use them. Islamic faithful took it as an unmistakable indication that Allah was on their side.

As Karroubi stood there, reveling in the images of destruction in Berlin, a messenger arrived, fresh from the front. "The Russians have surrounded Tehran," he announced. "And they have advanced much farther south than first reported." He handed a report to one of the aides in the room. Karroubi overheard them and moved alongside the aide, leaning over his shoulder to read the report. Then he looked to the messenger. "You saw these units at this location?"

"Yes, Mr. President."

"With your own eyes you saw them?"

"Yes, Mr. President. I saw them."

General Modiri was standing nearby and Karroubi glanced over at him. "Their forward units have reached Khorammabad."

With a worried look on his face, Modiri took the report from the aide and read it quickly. "They split their force. One part turned toward Tehran, the other continued south. No doubt driving toward the coast."

"Are the Chinese aware of this?"

"I'm sure they are. They have a battlefield management system that rivals the United States'."

"Where are they now?" Karroubi asked. "Do we have a new position for them?"

"The latest information shows them in Kerman and the outskirts of Bandar Abbas. But those reports are several hours old."

"Are we supplying them with everything they need?"

"As far as I know."

"I don't want them to stop."

"No. That would not be good."

"We need an update on their position."

Karroubi was nervous about the advancing armies. He had always assumed the Russians would move quickly and had expected they would gain control of the northern one-third of the country, but if information from the messenger was correct, the Russians were far ahead of that schedule. And apparently they were meeting very little resistance. From all that appeared on the screen, Modiri and his generals had not deployed units along the river at the border, west of Parsabad, as they had told him they planned to do. Now he wondered if Modiri was actually working against him, hoping that defeat would bring a swift end to his administration.

He was also worried about Iran's missile bases. Hidden in the mountains near the Iraqi border, they lay to the east of the Russian positions reported by the messenger. They had remained untouched from Russian air attacks, but now appeared to be at risk of falling into the hands of ground troops. Bizhani had been itching to use them, and Karroubi was certain this latest information would renew his calls for a launch.

While Modiri continued to review the report, plotting and planning a counterattack, Karroubi retreated to the back of the room and took a seat at a workstation. As he expected, Bizhani found him there. "Mr. President, with all due respect—"

Karroubi held up his hand to stop him. "I know what you're going to say."

"Sir, respectfully, it is time to use those missiles."

"Against the Russians?"

"To close the northern passes, as we have already planned."

"Show me the targets."

Bizhani led the way to the large screen with the map and pointed. "We would strike here, south of Parsabad near Germi. Over here, north of Ardabil. And along the coast at Naukale, where the road turns to go over the pass."

"And what about over here?" Karroubi asked, pointing farther to the west. "On the road from the border down to Ahar. Have you considered that, too?"

"The targets to the east are preprogrammed into the launch system. They are ready to launch at your command. A strike near Ahar could be added."

"Where are the Chinese?"

"They are continuing west along the coast. I think their intention is to seal off the ports and prevent Russia from resupplying through the south. Force them to maintain only one front."

"Once we act, the Russians will retaliate. If the Chinese are not close enough to engage them, we will be devastated."

"Mr. President, we have no choice. The Russians are about to overrun us. If we don't launch now, we may lose the missiles and never have an opportunity to defend ourselves."

"Very well," Karroubi sighed. "You may proceed. But add the road to Ahar to the list."

"Certainly," Bizhani replied. He turned away and took a cell phone from his pocket. Seconds later, Karroubi heard him say, "We have the order."

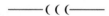

For two days, Alexander Nevsky had been crammed into the back of an army truck, squeezed between stacks of tent flooring and canvas tops. From Derbent, where they last camped, near the Russian border with Azerbaijan, they drove south in a convoy toward Baku. The highway was filled with trucks and tanks traveling in each direction. Negotiating the congestion made the going slow. Reaching the city took most of a day but they didn't stop long enough to make camp and instead slept atop the stacks in the back of the truck.

The second day they passed through Baku and continued down the coast as far as the town of Alat. They paused there for a few hours and got out to walk around some. A galley truck brought them a hot meal, and several of the drivers took naps on the ground while mechanics tended to the trucks.

Nevsky found a spot on the shore with a magnificent view of the Caspian Sea and took advantage of the moment alone to smell of Milla's scarf and gaze at Elizaveta's picture. Holding them in his hands filled his mind with thoughts of home and it made him sad, but he could not tear himself away from them. Most days he kept the items safely in his backpack throughout the day, bringing them out only at night or in the all-too-brief moments when he was alone.

After an hour or two by the sea, the mechanics finished their work and everyone climbed back into the trucks. The following day they reached Astara on the border with Iran. The trucks stopped again and Nevsky was transferred to one that carried only soldiers. Captain Sorokin sat on the floor near the tailgate. Across from him was Yury Turgenev, Nevsky's tent mate. Nevsky squeezed in beside Turgenev and braced his back against the side of the truck. He looked over at Sorokin. "Where are we going, Captain?"

"You don't want to know," Sorokin grumbled.

"Better leave him alone," Turgenev warned. "He's been like this the whole trip and if you push him he gets really nasty."

"Shut up, Turgenev," Sorokin barked.

"See what I mean?" Turgenev chuckled.

An hour later, they came to Naukale. From there, the road turned from the coast and wound through a mountain pass.

Turgenev looked over at Sorokin. "Captain, if we passed Astara, traveling south, aren't we in Iran now?"

"Turgenev," Sorokin grumbled, "you think too much."

"Iran?" Nevsky leaned through the opening above the tailgate and looked out, then just as quickly slumped back to the floor. "We're in Iran," he mumbled. His eyes were wide with a look of realization. This was no exercise. This was no friendly trip. "What are we doing here?" he asked, but he knew the answer already.

"You will find out soon enough," Sorokin answered in a surly tone. "And don't think it's going to be—" A deafening roar overhead cut short his sentence, and those near the rear of the truck leaned out to see what was happening.

A contrail traced across the sky above and then a brilliant flash lit up the foreground. Brighter than the sun, they gasped and covered their faces. Seconds later a boiling black cloud rolled toward them and behind it a dark column rose straight up into the air. Suddenly a wave of white-hot heat, more intense than anyone could withstand, engulfed them. Nevsky watched in horror as the truck melted beneath his feet, his clothes turned to smoke, and the flesh slid from his body.

82

MOSCOW, RUSSIA

PRESIDENT VOSTOK SAT AT A CONFERENCE TABLE in the Kremlin situation room, five basement floors beneath his office. He'd been there every day since the invasion started, observing, calculating, assessing, taking a break from the room only for a few hours rest when the troops periodically halted their advance.

Gathered with him were General Garasimov, the secretary of defense, along with Vasily Kerensky, the foreign intelligence service chief, Mikhail Mirsky, the foreign minister, and Anatolyn Luzhkov, Vostok's chief of staff.

"What are our latest positions?" Vostok demanded.

Garasimov stepped to a screen on the wall and nodded to an aide seated nearby. A map appeared on the screen with icons that marked positions for the major army groups. "As we reported earlier, we crossed here and here over the river on the western end of the Azerbaijan-Iran border. Smaller units came across through Parsabad, farther to the east, proceeding down through the mountains. At the same time, a battle group proceeded south along the coast through Astara. Part of that group turned west at Naukale, another portion turned west at Punel, and the remainder continued south to Rasht before making the turn. The first two crossings occurred early in the invasion. You know about them. This latest, along the coast, is a recent development."

"You divided this group along the coast three times?"

"Yes."

"Why?"

"We were unsure how much resistance we would encounter at the border, both at the coast in Astara and at the points farther to the west where we crossed the river. Those crossings were made with mobile bridges and would have been strategic places for the Iranians to attack. And so we wanted to be able to offer them support and reinforcements from the east. And," he pointed again to the map, "we wanted to clear this area from the border south to Tehran. We wanted to control all of it."

"And still there is no resistance?"

"None, Mr. President."

"Interesting."

"The two elements of the coastal brigade that we sent west now occupy the region and we are steadily sending reinforcements down these same routes. The final unit in the coastal brigade crossed the mountains at Rasht and is now within striking distance of Tehran."

"This has gone much more rapidly than I expected."

"Yes, it has."

"So, how are we to the west?"

"We control everything down to Kermanshah."

"But not all the way to the Persian Gulf?" the president wondered.

"No, sir. Not yet."

"And in Tehran, what is your plan?"

"We intend to surround it for now. Isolate it. Await the outcome of the fighting elsewhere."

"Why not take it by force?"

"We were hoping not to destroy it, if possible."

"Take it," Vostok said tersely. "We'll lose a hundred thousand men laying siege to it."

Garasimov shook his head. "I'm not sure we should devote—"

The aide called out from across the room, "We have a ballistic missile launch."

Garasimov turned in her direction. "Where?"

"Tracking stations in Perm are showing it originating from inside Iran." She pointed to the map on the screen near the table. "I'm giving the location to you now. Two missiles fired from a site in Iran west of

Hamadan. Both of them armed with nuclear warheads."

"What is the target?" Garasimov asked.

"Trajectory software says one will hit west of Naukale. The other will strike a location west of Punel."

"The highways," Garasimov muttered.

"Yes, sir," the aide replied. "That's exactly what they'll hit."

Garasimov looked over at Vostok. "They are cutting off our access points," he noted grimly. "And our retreat route."

Vostok looked stricken. "This whole thing is a trap."

Images on the screen switched to cameras mounted atop equipment near both locations in time to catch a brilliant flash, then the screen went blank.

"What happened to the cameras?" Garasimov demanded.

"That was impact," the aide called out.

"Get me a casualty report!" Garasimov shouted.

Vostok rose from his chair and stood at his side. "Where are the Chinese?"

"I don't know," Garasimov answered in frustration. "I think—"

"General!" Vostok snapped. "Where are the Chinese?"

Garasimov turned back to the screen with the map and pointed. "Their first units crossed Afghanistan in only two days. Crossed into southern Iran here and here," he said, tapping the screen with his index finger. "They continued west and now control the southern half of the country, and more are arriving by the hour."

"Have they seized the entire coast?"

"No. As nearly as we can determine they are only as far west as Jam. Not as far as Bushehr yet. But they are moving quickly and bringing up additional troops by the hour. They could be traveling faster but they've been slowed by a lack of trucks."

"I still think this whole thing is a trap," Vostok repeated. "We're outnumbered now three to one. Soon it could be ten to one. Can we evacuate west into Iraq?"

"Not from here," Garasimov pointed to the map. "There are mountains to our west. The better route would be to simply turn around and head back the way we came. We still have time. This would also be the best section of Iran for us to fight in."

"How so?"

"Closest to our own supply chain. Lots of space to maneuver and plenty of opportunity to use our air cover."

"They set us up from the beginning," Vostok recounted. "This is why there were no troops opposing us on the border. They were deliberately drawing us in deeper and deeper. All the while they knew they would cut us off and the Chinese would hit us hard." Vostok looked over at Garasimov. "What do you propose?"

"Mr. President, I think we should stand and fight. We are prepared to strike the site where the missiles were launched, to reduce their ability to attack us again. At the same time, we propose a strike on Tehran which would not only disrupt Iran economically and militarily, it will also create a hot zone between us and the advancing Chinese army."

"Hot zone?" Vostok frowned. "You are suggesting we use nuclear weapons?"

"I don't think we have a choice."

"Then why not just hit the Chinese army and end it now?"

"So far, we have been attacked only by the Iranians. If we strike the Chinese with nuclear arms, they will retaliate. Moscow would not be safe."

"Neither would Beijing."

"I think they know that, which is why they haven't used strategic weapons. And why we should keep this fight on the battlefield."

"Very well," Vostok nodded. "Hit the launch site and create the hot zone. You realize there will be massive civilian casualties?"

"Yes, but right now, I'm thinking about the huge chunk of our army we could lose if we don't act quickly."

"Make the strikes."

83

CIA HEADQUARTERS LANGLEY, VIRGINIA

HOAG WAS UPSTAIRS IN HIS OFFICE reviewing budget projections for the coming year when the phone rang with a call from Winston Smith telling him about Iran's missile launches. He put aside the file on his desk and ran to the elevator. By the time he got downstairs, the missiles had already hit their targets. He stood with Smith in front of the operations center's video screens and stared at satellite images of the result.

"Wiped out about ten thousand Russian troops in the pass near Naukale," Smith pointed to a map on the screen to the left. "More than that at Punel."

Hoag had a look of disbelief. "What were they doing? What were they thinking?"

"Closing the passes through the mountains," Smith replied. "I suspect we'll see a couple more hits before they're finished."

"Where?"

"Several key passes south of Parsabad." Smith pointed to the map again. "West of there, the border follows the Aras River. Not any permanent bridges across it. The Russians have only a couple of locations where they can place their mobile bridges. Might see a couple of missile strikes against those sites, too."

"You think Iran even knows where those crossings are located?"

"I'm sure they do," Smith nodded. "It's no big secret. Locals cross there, too."

The door opened and Jenny appeared. "I just heard," she blurted out, coming to Hoag's side.

He took her hand in his. "You okay?"

"Yeah. Anyone hear from Dennis yet? It's been two days since he left Tunis."

"We know he got as far as Rabat," Smith replied. "Haven't heard from him since then."

Jenny pointed to the pictures on the screen. "This is horrible. I can't believe they did it."

"I can," a familiar voice sounded from behind them. They turned to see Dennis Kinlaw standing in the doorway.

Hoag's mouth dropped open in a startled look. "What are you doing here?" A wide grin burst over his face and he gave Kinlaw a bear hug. "When did you get in?"

"Just now."

Jenny gave him a hug, too. "Have you seen Debby?"

"I haven't seen anyone. I literally walked in the door five minutes ago."

"Well, you picked a good time to do it," Smith added, shaking his hand. "Good to have you back."

"Good to be back." Kinlaw pointed to the images on the screen. "What's happening?"

"Iran launched a couple of missiles," Smith explained. "Nuclear warheads. It's getting interesting."

"Against the Russians?"

"Sort of. They hit a couple of choke points in the invasion route." Smith pointed them out on the map.

"That's also their retreat route," Kinlaw indicated. "Hitting them at those locations eliminates most of the eastern routes in and out of the country. If the Russians want out, they have to go through Parsabad or find a way across the river. I think we'll see another strike against the bridges east of Parsabad."

Hoag smiled. "We were just talking about that. Now, tell us how Russia will react."

"They won't react," Kinlaw answered. "They'll respond. And when they do, it'll be strategic, not an angry retaliation. If it was me, I would hit—"

"Sir," the operator called, interrupting them, "NORAD's reporting two missiles incoming from their base at Dvina, Russia."

"Here we go," Hoag said, and he reached down to take Jenny's hand.

"What's the target?" Smith asked.

"Two sites in Iran. First one is Tehran. Second missile will strike in the mountains west of Hamadan. That's the site where Iran launched those missiles."

"Time to impact?"

"Eleven minutes. These are Russian SS-18 missiles carrying multiple nuclear warheads."

Hoag looked over at Kinlaw. "Want to rethink that 'no retaliation' idea?"

"I don't know," Kinlaw sighed. "Where are the Chinese?"

"They crossed the border two days ago and have been traveling west along the south."

"That cuts off any Russian resupply from the south. Prevents this from being a two-front war."

"But why hit Tehran?"

"Takes out the largest city in the country," Kinlaw observed. "Disrupts everything. The Russians are outnumbered at least two to one on the battlefield. They have to do something. They can't go head-to-head with Chinese conventional forces."

"Well, let's hope they keep the nukes away from the Chinese," Smith added. "One nuclear strike against their troops, anywhere, and this will go global really quickly."

"Tehran will be obliterated," Jenny noted with sadness. "Millions will die and there's nothing we can do but watch."

Kinlaw turned away. "Well, not me. I've seen enough for one day. I'm going home." He stepped toward the door. "I haven't seen Debby in weeks."

"Wait up," Hoag offered. "I'll walk with you to the elevator." He grabbed the doorknob and held it while Kinlaw moved past, then followed him from the room. As they started up the hallway, Hoag looked over at him. "We need to talk."

"Yeah," Kinlaw sighed. "About that...I know I sounded pretty bad before I left, but the truth is, I don't like this stuff anymore. I want out."

"You don't like *this*," Hoag asked, gesturing to the building around them, "or you don't like the intelligence world?"

"What's the difference?"

They reached the elevator and Hoag pressed the call button. "What if we went back to Georgetown—like it was before?"

The expression on Kinlaw's face brightened. "Teaching and only helping Winston once in a while?"

"Yeah," Hoag nodded. "Back in our old offices, with a secretary who doesn't really know what we do, and Post-it Notes on the wall."

"Books stacked everywhere and nobody to bother us?"

"Just like that," Hoag nodded.

The elevator bell rang and the door opened. "You'd do that?" Kinlaw asked with a quizzical smile. "Give up the office and the title for that?"

"In a heartbeat."

Kinlaw stepped into the elevator and held the door open. "What does Jenny think about it?"

"She's good." Hoag shoved his hands into his pockets and gave a sheepish smile. "Actually, I've already talked to Moore about it, too."

"Think the school will take us back?"

"I think they'd love to have us," Hoag replied. "And I already have our first project."

"What's that?"

"You remember that conversation we had with Vic Hamilton?" Hoag asked.

"About *Revelation* and prophecy and the end?"

"Yeah."

"I think we should begin with that," Hoag suggested.

"Good," Kinlaw nodded as he let go of the door. "I have some new ideas about that."

"So do I," Hoag grinned.

ACKNOWLEDGEMENT

My deepest gratitude and sincere thanks to my writing partner, Joe Hilley, and to my executive assistant, Lanelle Shaw-Young, both of whom work diligently to turn my story ideas into great books. And to Arlen Young, Peter Gloege, and Janna Nysewander for making the finished product look and read its best. And always, to my wife Carolyn, whose presence makes everything better.

BOOKS BY: MIKE EVANS

Israel: America's Key to Survival

Save Jerusalem

The Return

Jerusalem D.C.

Purity and Peace of Mind

Who Cries for the Hurting?

Living Fear Free

I Shall Not Want

Let My People Go

Jerusalem Betrayed

Seven Years of Shaking: A Vision

The Nuclear Bomb of Islam

Jerusalem Prophecies

Pray For Peace of Jerusalem

America's War: The Beginning of the End

The Jerusalem Scroll

The Prayer of David

The Unanswered Prayers of Jesus

God Wrestling

Why Christians Should Support Israel

The American Prophecies

Beyond Iraq: The Next Move

The Final Move beyond Iraq

Showdown with Nuclear Iran

Jimmy Carter: The Liberal Left and World Chaos

Atomic Iran

Cursed

Betrayed

The Light

Corrie's Reflections and Meditations (Booklet)

GAMECHANGER SERIES:
GameChanger
The Samson Option
The Four Horsemen

THE PROTOCOLS SERIES:
The Protocols
The Candidate

The Revolution

The Final Generation

Seven Days

The Locket

Living in the F.O.G.

COMING IN 2013:

The History of Christian Zionism

Born Again: Israel's Rebirth

Jerusalem

Ten Boom

**TO PURCHASE, CONTACT: ORDERS@TIMEWORTHYBOOKS.COM
P. O. BOX 30000, PHOENIX, AZ 85046**